Praise for *Candlewood*

"In this mesmerizing debut, Casey unveils a luminous portrait of devotion tested against the boundaries of human longing in 1970s rural America. With remarkable finesse, she crafts an unflinching examination of a soul caught between religious commitment and the whispers of impossible dreams."
— Ann Garvin, USA Today bestselling author of
I Thought You Said This Would Work

"Casey has brought storytelling back to its roots, with characters who know who they are and what they want, wrestling with the intersections of faith, fate, and fear."
— Susanna Daniel, award winning author of *Stiltsville* and *Sea Creatures*

"Casey debuts with a not-so-ordinary romance set in the 1970s... She approaches it with welcome seriousness about love, faith, temptation, and the role of women in the church. "Candlewood" is a romance at its heart, with the protagonist navigating heartbreak and the self-discovery that follows... Underlying the romance, however, is a smart, compelling critique of the shady practices that often contaminate religious institutions and their pervasive patriarchy."
—Publishers Weekly BookLife Review

"Evelyn Ann Casey's writing is thoughtful, wry, and detailed; a pleasure to read."
— Daniel M. Lavery, author of *Women's Hotel*

"Casey charts the winding roads through violation and heartbreak with a readable style and a generous amount of empathy... Her skill at crafting characters is finely tuned, and even the book's minor characters feel fully realized. Meg's struggles with the dictates of the Church will resonate with a great many of Casey's readers; the author's refusal to settle for easy novelistic solutions to complicated issues is refreshing. A heartfelt and well-orchestrated story of disillusioned faith and elusive hope."
—Kirkus Reviews

"Candlewood" by Evelyn Ann Casey is a gorgeously written story... It's impossible not to cheer for this captivating heroine whose story takes the reader through triumph and heartbreak in her search for love and inner peace. Meg will stay with the reader long after finishing the book."
—Gregory Lee Renz, author of *Beneath the Flames*
and *Beyond the Flames*

"Candlewood" by Evelyn Ann Casey is a tender, suspenseful, and well-written story of love and its many facets—including forbidden love for a young priest. Set mostly in the St. Croix Valley, but with significant time in New York City, the story shows the challenges for a young person trying to find her footing in life beyond

matters of the heart. This is a first novel for the author but let's hope for many more. The book contains excellent research notes and questions for book clubs. Highly recommended."

—Christine DeSmet, bestselling mystery author and
director of the nationally recognized Write by the Lake retreat

"Every once in a while a debut novel presents a quiet yet powerful new voice that commands the reader's full attention. Narrator Meg tells her story with honesty, authenticity, and fearless bravery. This love story offers valuable insight into the religious culture and feminine restraints and values that were prominent during the 1970s. The pace of the plot heightens with every chapter. The reader won't be disappointed."

—Laurie Scheer, Writing Mentor/mediagoddess

"Casey's bittersweet novel emotionally grips the reader. A stunning debut."

—Kristin A. Oakley, award-winning author
of The Devil Particle Series

CANDLEWOOD

ଖ ଔ

CANDLEWOOD

⊗ ⊘

Evelyn Ann Casey

Three Towers Press
Milwaukee, Wisconsin

Scripture passages are primarily from the North American Bible
Revised Edition (NABRE)

This book is a work of fiction. Places, events, and situations
in this book are purely fictional and any resemblance to actual
persons, living or dead, is coincidental.

Published by Three Towers Press
An imprint of HenschelHAUS Publishing, Inc.
www.henschelHAUSbooks.com
Milwaukee, Wisconsin

ISBN: 979-8-9908203-2-6
E-Book: 979-8-9908203-8-8
LCCN: 2024940781

Cover art by Ann Thomas, https://AnnThomasIllustration.com

Printed in the United States of America.

He will not break off a bent reed,
nor put out a flickering lamp.
—Matthew 12:20

CHAPTER 1

FLICKER

RAIN GLANCED OFF MY SHOES like spilled secrets. A June downpour in Minnesota's St. Croix Valley left the street a blur of wet shadows. For the first time since graduating last year, I stepped off the curb in front of old St. Gabriel's arched wooden doors and crossed over to attend prayer group at the Campus Ministry Center.

Students clustered in the back of the chapel near the faux marble Madonna while faculty sorted themselves out in pecking order. On the altar, the ever-present beeswax candle flickered inside a tall hurricane glass, like Morse code from a ship's signal lamp: *God is here.* I settled into an empty pew and rubbed the bare spot at the base of the fourth finger on my left hand. Only six months ago, the promise of marriage and family sparkled. I watched the flame pulse.

At the last "Amen," I roused to check my watch. If I hurried, I could meet friends at the coffeehouse for Rocky Mountain High Night. When I looked up, Father Darren's intense dark eyes were trained on me—one of the reasons I stopped going to prayer group senior year.

"A treat to see you again, Meg. Heard you're visiting the sick for St. Gabe's now."

I nodded a quick acknowledgement and stood to leave.

Faculty women circled the rookie priest who looked like he spent more time in the gym than on his knees. They gushed over his homily on evil. As I passed, his hand slithered around my waist. I flinched, and he dropped his arm. His ploys for attention rivaled a barfly's. But he wore the collar—I told myself he was harmless. Mrs. Gregg eyed the maneuver, then looked away. She might have been the object of his attentions thirty years ago. Without missing a beat, Father Darren delivered the punchline to a joke. Something about a banana and Eve's apple. I went to the coatrack to get my trench. Father Darren caught up with me. "Stay a few minutes? Want to show you something."

Born and bred Catholic, one does not say no to a priest. "Sure, what's up?"

"Let's take the shortcut." He motioned for me to follow.

We left the gleaming limestone walls of the chapel and entered a dimly lit corridor. Father Darren said the passage led to the fellowship hall. A stippled length of sallow paint between all that was sacred and everything else. My eyes took a minute to adjust.

I hurried to keep up. Halfway down the hall, he stopped short, and I stumbled into him. He missed my lips but nicked a kiss on the cheek. A move any two-bit blind date might make— not a priest.

My neck went taut. I stepped out of range.

He slicked back his coarse jet hair. "Only a kiss. No big deal. Relax."

His furtive dodge left me clammy. "What was it you wanted to show me?"

He moved ahead and pulled a pack of Winchesters from his pocket. Must have thought they were still cool. Nobody I knew smoked the little cigars anymore. He lit one and offered it to me like the man in their ads. When I refused, he blew a smoke ring.

I let a safe number of steps fall between us. If I bolted back to the chapel, everyone from prayer group would be gone by now. And if he pursued me? Though no taller than myself, his thick build could fell me like a sapling. Was I overreacting? An exit sign flashed at the end of the corridor—the fellowship hall on the other side. Only a few more yards.

He stopped at a recessed doorway and turned the knob. "Here we are."

The fading light of day cast shadows on low objects in the room. A storeroom? When he flipped the light switch, we were steps from the foot of a mattress on the floor.

I arched my back against the door to keep it open.

Stay calm, I told myself. Don't yell. Pretend to go along— then run like hell. When Dad forced himself on Mom and she yelled, terrible things happened. He hit her.

Father Darren didn't grab me. He pointed to a large painting hanging above the bed.

I stared at bold strokes of paint. Fierce reds, lime, purple. Abstract, but no Picasso.

He began to say words, but it was as if he was speaking underwater. The echo-like belches of syllables slowly took on meaning: "I want to give it away, but she won't let me."

Who was he talking about? Who was *she*?

He turned to stand squarely in front of me. "Well? Isn't it mine now?"

Gauze seemed to cover my mouth.

He lowered his brow toward me, demanding an answer. "Can't I do what I want with it?"

My tongue felt dry as cotton balls.

"You'll have to ask her about it." Whoever she was. "I have to go now."

He lurched to one side. "Go."

My sweater snagged as I peeled away. I ripped the thread loose and rushed past the exit sign. A roomful of laughing couples sat in the fellowship hall—the weekly Cana marriage prep class.

God, I ask you for love and you give me a snake?

Once outside, I threw on my trench and ran through drizzle to St. Gabe's parking lot. Searched my purse for car keys and sank into the roar of the engine.

⁊ ⅋

Home. I cranked the double cylinder lock on my door. Safe. My breath came in drifts as I steadied myself at the kitchen table. Solid cherrywood. A four-seater from a fire sale, only a few scorch marks. I looped through the apartment until dropping into an easy chair. The old Cogswell my brother reupholstered for me. When Eddie's hands weren't wrapped around a bottle of vodka, he worked for one of the best furniture shops in St. Paul.

A shiver of cold pinpricks crawled down my spine, exactly like when Eddie and I huddled in the hallway woken by our parents' fights. I wished my brother were here. I dialed his number. Hank answered. Good. He gave the phone to Eddie.

I relayed the evening's events. The part about a priest coming onto me and leading me to some sort of bedroom. Not the part about a painting. A woman. More than I could explain.

"I never understood your church thing, Meg. I cut that cord a long time ago."

When our parents divorced, Sunday Mass became my private oasis before court-ordered visitations with Dad. Church was the beautiful, quiet place where I could dream of someday making a happy family, a good marriage, a respectable life.

"Like it's my fault for being in church in the first place?"

"Okay, so the guy's a little off. Priests aren't all holy, you know."

I knew that much. At my fiancé's frat parties, the chaplain sat in a remote corner—soused. My history prof amassed toy Crusader armies. Foibles and quirks. Most of the Clems, as we called the Order of Clement priests who ran the college, seemed good men, caring teachers.

"But why me?"

"I suppose he can't go after students, and faculty are dicey. You're fair game. A grad."

"Fair game?"

"Probably figures any woman in her twenties is on the Pill these days. Plus, you're not bad to look at, Kitten. No Raquel Welch, but cute. Like Sally Field."

"Gee, thanks. Should I tell the pastor a miscreant priest wants a go at the girl next door?"

"Oh sure, tell the pastor—or the bishop. It's not like they wouldn't know the guy's a jerk. Clergy are more than acquainted with each other. Probably glad it's women he goes after and not the other way. Hang out with me and Hank sometime. You'd be surprised who cruises the joint."

I twisted the telephone cord. "So, wise man of the world, what should I do?"

"For sure, don't go back there."

I'd lost a month's pay when the teacher strike hit. Churches don't strike. The job at St. Gabe's guaranteed security.

I sat up after our call, rocking in Grandma's well-worn spindleback. It wasn't fair that I had to cower while Father Darren swaggered across campus. But Eddie had a point. If I tried to tell anyone, they wouldn't believe me. I'd heard all the jokes about women throwing themselves at hapless priests. I would be a joke.

As the house cooled down for the night, I got a sweatshirt from my closet. The rosary Mom gave me at graduation lay on the dresser. *Mary, mother of God, give me strength.*

I boiled water for tea and debated quitting. But where would I go?

I had known St. Gabe's since I was 10 years old. After the divorce, Mom moved us from Minneapolis to Shady Bluff to be closer to her sister's family. A friendly town in a scenic river valley—and a cheaper cost of living. The steeple rose like a beacon for parents wanting to send their kids to college. The Order of Clement built the church and Incarnatus University on donated land back when lumber mills thrived. They never turned down a promising student. That's how I got there—and loans.

How did Father Darren ever get to be a Clem? He wore his alb like a pure white teabag, hiding the dark bits inside. I dumped my hot water and turned off the lights. I needed a good night's sleep. Tomorrow, I would stay on my side of the street.

℘ ℧

When Eileen insisted I go out with the gang on the weekend, I didn't object. Maybe it would dispel the lingering stench of my encounter with Father Darren and his little cigar.

Just like in college, my former roommate organized the social scene. "You'll love Irish ceili dancing, Meg. You missed a lot of fun last time." We drove together to Kelly's Pub.

I tripped on my first dance step. The lead guitar player saluted me from the stage. I must have looked ridiculous. Or was he saluting my ballet top that showed a bit of skin unlike the puff-sleeved polyester blouses on either side of me? I chose the open-neck top to stay cool in the crowded pub—also to deter any thought I might be headed for the convent. A decade earlier, working for the Church had meant a fast track to the nunnery.

When the band closed out their set of jigs and reels, the guitarist took center stage. "Let's change the pace and give some respect to our local boy made good." He strummed into Bob Dylan's "Shelter from the Storm," cueing patrons for the refrain. He had a fine voice, and the crowd begged for more, but he unplugged after a couple of verses.

During the break, he came over to chat up our lively group of newcomers. Eileen and Sheila vied for his attention with fawning quips. His uncombed tufts of dark curly hair seemed out of place with the clean wedge of his body. He projected his weight toward me like a swimmer leaning into the starting block for a dive.

"You're a natural on your toes," he said. "By the way, the name's Sean."

"Meg. Thanks, but you're a bad liar."

"No," he chuckled. "I wouldn't lie about anything so serious."

"Your band. Is this what you do for a living?"

"The band is for fun. I work at the *Herald*—sports reporter. And do you dance for a living?"

Sean's grin was all mischief. He asked the usual questions, and I told him my tale about the strike sapping all joy from my first year of teaching. Sean said the city editor foresaw a hot summer for teachers followed by "a late start" to school in the fall. I spilled the beans about my backup plan, visiting St. Gabe's sick and elderly parishioners.

Sean eyed my half-finished beer and asked if I wanted a refill. I suspected the trip to the bar gave him an excuse to flee from "an almost-nun."

"Leave it to Meg the Magnet," teased Eileen. "Sheila and I tried to catch Sean's eye last week." Sheila threw imaginary darts at me from the other side of the table.

A beefy hand nudged my shoulder. "Here's your cold one." Sean sat down. His tone changed from idle gab to quiet conversation. "St. Gabe's, huh? I studied journalism at Incarnatus University." We clunked beer mugs in tribute to our alma mater.

"You could do worse. True confession—I spent time in the Peace Corps, Honduras, to beat the Vietnam draft."

I smiled, full of relief. I could work for the parish and still date a nice guy who sought an altruistic escape—like me.

Sean and I made a date to see *Star Wars*.

℘ ଔ

Eileen grilled me on the way home. "About time you found someone to take your mind off Jake. It's been, what, six months?"

"Six and a half."

Eileen bit her lip. She'd never hidden her distaste for Jake. A smart, straight-up guy, hardworking, a good future ahead of him—but all Eileen saw was his stalling, which ended for good the last time he pushed back the wedding date, and I threw his ring on the ground. Whatever magic I felt with him—and I admit it wasn't much, not even when it was good—had faded under the weight of his father's disapproval of my wrong-side-of-the-tracks family.

"There's a much better match for you, I know it," she said, not for the first time.

"Okay, the truth—I don't know if I loved him. They say you'll know when it's *the one*. But the magic wasn't there."

"Oh, Meg, that's sad." I was grateful Eileen didn't say I told you so, like my mother had.

℘ ଔ

In the two weeks since taking the job at St. Gabe's, I'd visited Adele three times. The pastor recommended extra attention considering her illness—and her expected bequest. Today I found Adele out on her lawn, peering up at a big old maple.

"My kitty's stuck in that tree," she rasped. "Daisy never did anything like this before."

I took a deep breath. Father Mack had said nothing about rescuing cats.

Adele let me wrap a terry towel over a broom to coax the cat down. As I searched tree limbs for the tabby, the late afternoon sun nearly blinded me. When the cat let out a wail like a banshee, I spotted her. While I poked nearby branches, Adele paced the scrawny lawn, clutching a thick brown sweater around her stooped shoulders. Though a balmy day, she shivered.

"Why don't you go inside, Adele? You'll catch cold out here."

"I'll die of the cancer first, Missy Meg. But Daisy, what'll become of her?"

Adele kept watch from the porch while I continued my efforts. It wasn't long before I noticed someone parking in front of my VW Bug. A sky blue '77 Chevy Caprice. Swank car for the neighborhood. A rugged looking man ambled into our predicament.

"Nice day to climb a tree."

"Daisy-the-cat thought so."

The man laughed. "If I saw that broomstick contraption coming at me, I might run too."

"You have a better idea?" Geez.

He rolled up his shirtsleeves. "Can I be of assistance?" Mystery man looked directly at my face, not halfway down my blouse like men on the make at the disco.

Adele limped over to us in fuzzy slippers. "Welcome to the party."

The tabby hunkered her stripes around a thick limb.

I carefully angled the broom toward her again, as if I knew what I was doing. "This method worked for my cousin's cat, but Daisy's not taking the bait."

"Bet she's scared." He surveyed the situation. "You have the right notion, letting her paws catch on a towel. Too bad the tree doesn't have more of a pitch. She'd probably come down on her own." His attention shifted to Adele. "Do you have a ladder—more towels—twine?"

Adele's face brightened. "I see, make a ramp for her. Clever. My son keeps an extension ladder in the garage." She told me where to find towels and twine in the house. Her trembling hand grasped my arm for support getting up the porch steps. "I'll wait here. Got a headache." She settled into a wicker chair.

"We'll get her down. Don't you worry," I said.

The man carried the ladder across the lawn like a pro. Summer tanned. Easy stride. A thatch of hair fell on his forehead like late-season dune grass on the river bluffs I loved to hike.

We worked across from each other, wrapping towels rung to rung and securing them with twine. He came over and knelt beside me. "Let me tighten that for you." He tugged the twine and knotted it like a seasoned sailor. His thigh brushed against my khaki skirt. "Beg pardon." He caught my eye, a broad smile spreading across his face. Deep dimples framed his grin.

I hadn't felt a tussle of sparks in a while. Sean? Nice, very nice, but …

I ran my fingers through the Farrah Fawcett curls I'd taken time to style that morning. Lucky chance I hadn't twisted my mahogany mop into its usual neat knot.

Once we got the ladder-ramp leaned against the tree, we sat on the porch steps and waited for Daisy to figure things out. Adele snoozed on the broad porch.

"You're a good neighbor," I said, "but you don't have to stay. Daisy'll make it down."

"I'm more like a sometimes Samaritan. Driving back from the clinic, saw what looked like trouble. Have to see this thing through now."

He looked rather healthy to be going to the clinic, though older than my ex-fiancé, who grabbed meds for every sneeze. Ah, I thought, the good Samaritan must be a doctor. Of course.

"See anybody from *M*A*S*H** at the clinic?"

His eyes scrunched into a twinkle. "Not today."

He propped his elbows on the step, as relaxed as if sitting on sleek Naugahyde. "Does your cat do this often?"

"Daisy's not mine. I came to visit Adele and found her out here in a fit." Tucked my hair behind my ear, neglecting to tell him I worked for the parish. Would probably think I was a nun.

"Is Adele your aunt? Grandma?"

A sudden meow saved me from answering. Daisy bounced into Adele's lap. The sleepy woman jarred from her nap and stroked the cat until it purred contentedly.

The man stood, hooking his thumbs into his belt. "A good day's work."

Adele looked up from nuzzling her furry friend. "How can I thank you, young man?"

He put one foot on the step and held out his hand to shake hers. "I should introduce myself. Andy Vogel. Most people call me Father Andy."

Father Andy? A priest?

He offered his hand to me. A warm, firm handshake.

I covered a cough. My cheeks felt flush.

"I don't know what we would have done if you hadn't come along, Father," said Adele.

"The young lady had things well underway. Glad to help."

I undid the twine and folded the towels. "Let's get things put back to rights."

Father Andy bounded over to help me put away the ladder. Two strong hands laced over mine from the other side. A waft of sandalwood soap. When he hoisted the ladder onto its garage hooks, I tried not to notice the breadth of his back. I picked up a dusty yellow flowerpot in the corner. For sure, Adele would like a "Daisy" plant. I tucked it under my arm to take home.

Lost for small talk, I asked Father Andy what parish he lived in—so I could avoid it.

"I'm staying at Incarnatus University between assignments. Got back from the Algerian refugee mission a couple months ago. Waiting for my next gig. What about you?"

Incarnatus? The university spawned by St. Gabriel the Archangel Parish? That meant he was a Clem. Missions—hard work for a priest.

What about me? "I started working at St. Gabe's a few weeks ago." I glanced up to measure the effect of my news.

Father Andy thumped the rusted-out Rambler taking up space in the garage. An old chamois cloth lay on the hood. He took a few swipes at the car before twisting the chamois into a pretzel.

"Seems all roads lead to St. Gabe's in this town. What do you do there?"

"Hand me that rag." I wiped grime from the flowerpot. "I work with Ruth Jordeen in the Eldercare program. Ruth takes care of the practical needs, and I bring Communion to shut-ins, visit the sick—and occasionally rescue cats."

Father Andy kicked a tire. "Likely we'll cross paths again. Ruth sends me on runs for senior citizens' doctor appointments. Returning from one now. Where were you before, Sister …?"

So much for curling my hair.

"Margaret Joyce. *Most people call me Meg.* I'm not a Sister."

Father Andy stepped back. "Sorry. I naturally assumed. Not many laypeople work in parishes, or bring Communion, or …" His words fell flat on the cement floor.

This wasn't my first choice. My plan for college-marriage-kids? Up a tree.

"Can't regular people visit the sick? It's a corporal work of mercy, last time I heard."

My breath wheezed short. I wanted to do meaningful work, but also marry and have children—with the kind of guy who might help coax a cat out of a tree. Not this one though.

A tide tossed in his deep-set eyes. "Forgive my clumsiness?"

"Guess the feline adventure put me on edge."

He adjusted the ladder, making sure it held solid. "I should say good-bye to Adele and get Father Mack's Caprice back before he thinks I made off with it."

I managed half a smile as he waved and drove off. A capricious spin of the wheel. Father Andy would return to the missions, hopefully sooner than later. I would never see him again. Never have to put a lid on impious thoughts. Never have to hear his voice, calm on the surface but with a thousand rushing rivers beneath.

CHAPTER 2

CROSSHAIRS

ON THE WAY HOME FROM OUR *Star Wars* date, Sean attempted lowering his tenor voice to mimic Darth Vader's deep baritone. I hoped I was more successful with my fantasy of banishing Father Darren to a galaxy far, far away. Surely other priests noticed pretty girls, but they didn't accost them. Father Andy flirted a little, a cocky smile like Han Solo with Leia, but no more. When Sean dropped me off, we spontaneously said *"May the force be with you"* instead of goodnight.

On my next visit to Adele, I mused whether R2-D2 was modeled on a cat. Adele wasn't home that day, and there was no sign of Daisy. Doctor appointment, I assumed. Not to worry—Father Cronin, the somber priest with the craggiest eyebrows this side of Connemara, would see her on First Friday. He brought Communion to shut-ins once a month so they could go to Confession if they wished. I unwrapped my gift of the daisy-filled flowerpot, folded up the box's pink netting, and left the Daisy namesake on the step to surprise Adele.

Back in my dim office at the Parish Center, I unzipped my lunch tote on the timeworn trestle desk. At least the air-conditioning provided a respite after visiting frail homebound parishioners in rickety houses and stifling apartment buildings. The shut-ins were made of tougher stuff than me. I was as wilted as the lettuce on my cheese sandwich. The sun trickled through the lone casement window in the room, washing over three walnut-framed Jonathan Livingston Seagull posters that

Eileen and I made at the U-Frame-It shop downtown. Much improved the faded parchment walls. Father Mack wanted me to replace them with saints until I told him the seagull story represented the resurrection. Not sure he bought it.

When I heard Father Cronin in the entryway, I intercepted him to note Adele's absence in case the doctor visit meant a worsening in her condition.

He stopped mid-stride in black clerical suit and starched collar. "Don't you know, girl, that I offered the *Missa pro defunctis* for poor Adele yesterday morn? She suffered a stroke Saturday. Fortunate her son was there."

My hands went cold. "She died?" Tears welled up. "Why didn't anyone tell me?"

Father Cronin turned his back and headed to the dining room. "I suggest you start reading the obituaries if you want to do this kind of work, Margaret."

I froze in place, cringing like a chastised child. Soon, I heard a ruckus in the mezzanine-level dining room. I could see Father Cronin standing ramrod straight, facing someone at the dining table. "What do you think you're doing in here? This is the *community's* dining room."

When he moved, I saw a salt-and-pepper-haired woman. Ruth, the Eldercare director. She crumpled her brown lunch bag. I thought she was going to throw it at him.

Josie the cook emerged from the kitchen, arms akimbo. "There will be no shouting in this room." She threw down her potholder as if it were a gauntlet.

Father Cronin turned on his heel and headed up the next flight of steps to the priests' residence. Ruth barreled toward me like a thundercloud.

I followed her from the Oriental-carpeted main floor to the lower level and through the black-and-white vinyl tiled activity room. Her office was three times the size of my cubbyhole—

but not air-conditioned. I picked up a church bulletin from the desk and fanned myself. "No wonder you found a cooler place for lunch."

The usually businesslike Ruth Jordeen schlumped her chin on her hands. "What have we gotten ourselves into? Don't know about you, but I expected a little more respect."

"Father Cronin," I said, "seems to respect only one woman—Mary, the mother of God." I half-covered my mouth as if revealing a secret. "We can't claim that."

Ruth laughed. "They should have hired you sooner. I need a comrade in arms."

"What brought you to St. Gabe's anyway?" I asked.

Ruth tossed her lunch bag in the wastebasket. "Worked fifteen years for the state's foster care program. After one too many heartbreaking cases, I needed a change. When I heard St. Gabriel's pastor wanted a social worker to recruit other parishes in the St. Croix Valley for the Eldercare program, I applied. Seems he hoped to build a niche beyond the student focus. So far, I've gotten two other parishes to combine forces with us, and a nibble from the Lutherans. Not bad for three months in." She shook her paperclip holder. "What roll of the dice brought you here, Meg?"

I sensed this might be a good time to let my hair down.

"Father Mack knew me from volunteering at fish fry. Said he needed someone to visit shut-ins after Sister Louisa moved back to the motherhouse. Since the Vatican was pushing for lay involvement, voilà. Seemed like manna from heaven for me— strike proof."

"But I thought the district settled," said Ruth.

"Both sides agreed to a truce so students could finish the year, but no one promised anything for September. Did you know Hortonville, in Wisconsin, fired their striking teachers?"

"That's terrible." Ruth offered me a jar of jellybeans and I took a handful.

"I couldn't chance being thrown out on my ear—though I agreed with the cause. My family's not the kind to fall back on." I didn't tell her how close to the bone I lived to get a toehold on the type of life my family couldn't afford. I'd assumed teaching was a sure bet. Saddled with student loans, car payments and rent, I needed a monthly paycheck.

"Will you go back when strike fever cools?"

"Took this job as a refuge for a year or two, not a career change. I already miss my special ed kids." I wished someone would find a better word than "special ed" for students with developmental delays. They were all just kids to me. "I'm volunteering Saturday mornings at summer camp to keep a hand in."

"Good for you. We'll get through this minefield—despite Father Cronin's tantrums. Heard you met Father Andy—in the line of duty, so to speak. He's a bright spot. Can always call on him when one of my senior citizens needs a ride to the doctor. Also helps with boring mailings."

I fumbled with a licorice Jelly-Belly. "Sadly, the woman whose cat we rescued passed away. Maybe I should let him know. He lives at the faculty residence, right?"

"Sorry you lost one of your people so soon. But no need to go out of your way to find Father Andy. He's here often. Seems like a cowboy looking for his horse."

Ruth noticed the clock. "Card game for seniors coming up. Hate to cut this short."

"I should get back to visits anyway. Why don't you come over for potluck this Sunday?"

Ruth offered to bring hotdish and Hamm's, and I decided to enlist the help of my camp kids to figure out what to make for our two-person potluck.

On Saturday morning, the kids stood at wiggly attention waiting for my signal to start the day. "Okay everybody, let's take a ride on our magic carpet." A hive of little faces landed on the braided rug. "Put on your thinking caps. I need your help planning dinner for company." Hands shot up from all sides. "Make hot dogs! Hamburgers! Baloney sandwiches!"

Tony blurted, "Make Shake-and-Bake."

Brilliant. I went to the grocery store on my way home for a box of Shake-and-Bake and a package of chicken. Also, makings for red, white, and blue shortcake.

ⅈ⅓

Sean drew the assignment to cover the Chaska Town Ball game on Monday, the Fourth of July. He arrived at my apartment in a hurry to get to the ballpark. I quickly tied my hair back in last year's Stars and Stripes bicentennial scarf, and away we went— only to be marooned with his buddies while he scribbled baseballese for the *Herald*.

The guys shared peanuts and Crackerjack and gave me the once over. Must have passed inspection—they soon vied for most outrageous warnings about their friend. I learned that he joined the band on a dare, and once drove a date to Iowa just to go to a corn fest. And got lost.

Sean retrieved me after the game, and we headed to Minneapolis. After listening to warm-up bands a few hours, we staked out a cozy place to watch the fireworks display. Under a blaze of pyrotechnics, Sean kissed me feverishly. The sky exploded into a thousand fluorescent daisy petals. He loves me … he loves me not. He …

Daisy petals—Daisy! Whatever had become of Adele's cat?

CANDLEWOOD

❦

With the boom of fireworks still in my head, I swung by Adele's house after work the next day to retrieve the Gerbera daisy plant in its yellow flowerpot from her porch. I decided to keep it—to remember those who died on my watch. As I picked up the bedraggled flowers, a whine came from behind the wicker chair.

I sat down on the step to tease her out. "Daisy, you still here?"

The cat craned her neck. Her tail swayed slowly back and forth.

"It's okay. Remember me?"

Daisy meowed again, nimbled over, and rubbed her face against my leg. She seemed to determine any lap was better than none and climbed in. Her purrs settled into vibrations.

"Wish I could take you home, sweetie, but my apartment doesn't allow friends like you." I gently pet the top of her head between her ears. She let me cradle her as I looked inside the house. The curtains were gone, and boxes sat stacked amidst what was left of the furniture. Her son had lost no time getting the house ready for sale. "But he left the best part, didn't he? Adele said you never climbed up a tree before. Tell me, Daisy, were you leading Adele home to heaven?" She purred.

I considered giving the cat to Sean, but he went wherever the teams played. What about Father Andy? He was good with cats. No, he'd be off to the missions soon. Eileen lived in an apartment like me, so probably not. Sheila only concerned herself with Sheila. Mom liked dogs, but not cats. Eddie? The last time I met my brother and Hank for brunch, a cat had pawed the window of an empty car. They ranted about people not taking care of their pets. Bingo.

"Time to put on your charms, Daisy."

The box I used for Adele's flowerpot lay in the back seat of my car. I gingerly picked up the fuzzball and introduced her to the makeshift cat carrier. When Daisy moaned and scratched at her cardboard confinement, I rummaged in my insulated Tupperware lunch tote for leftover tuna salad. She chomped hungrily. I took the St. Paul turnoff to Eddie's apartment. Pulled over on a side street to re-festoon the box in its pink netting.

My brother greeted me with surprised, glassy eyes. His denim work shirt was unbuttoned, and he held a drink in one hand. Well on the way to Margaritaville. "I was expecting Hank." His voice crackled like the ice rocks in his glass.

Meows emanated from the box I carried.

"Is that what I think it is?"

"Her name's Daisy." I untied the netting and laid the box on its side. The cat sat wide-eyed on the edge between box and carpet. I told Eddie the story.

"All right," he said. "She can stay." When he offered her a pour of milk, Daisy slurped it like earnest money.

"You're saving me a phone call, Sis. I need to talk to you." He set down his tumbler. "Hank got a promotion at the art gallery."

"Give him my congrats."

"And he wants to look for a house. With me. To live together."

"Cheaper than paying two rents."

He started pacing. "What if it doesn't work out?"

Daisy pranced to his side and rubbed her cheek on his shin.

Over the years, my big brother perfected showing neither fear nor loneliness. Always the life of the party, nothing seemed to faze him. He rarely opened up to me. I worried about the demons lurking in his vodkas. I knew he cared about Hank. But I also knew about getting hurt.

"You guys practically live together already," I said. "But yeah, it's a big step, a risk." I busied myself rolling up the box's pink netting.

Eddie grabbed his drink gone watery. "How do I tell Mom?"

The summer of Eddie's high school graduation, he dropped the bomb about liking guys. Felt like a bomb. Another taboo—like divorce and bankruptcy weren't enough for one family. Mom cried every night. When she asked me where she went wrong, I had no answer. I didn't understand it myself. No one ever talked about things like that. It was a shock at first.

"Mom's come a long way, Eddie." I pointed to my heart and mouthed *me too*. "Do you remember when our aunt said she didn't want any 'twink' coming to holiday dinners? Mom turned into a mother bear—a force of nature. Bottom line—she loved you. She bought a big turkey and told you to invite all your 'twink' friends. In her little apartment, there was more love that year than all the years with our so-called family."

I hugged my brother and noogied his blond sideburns until he made me stop.

On the way out, I yelled back, "But if Hank objects to Daisy, call it off."

ℴ ℵ

Father Mack swung by my office as I dabbed ointment on a sunburned nose. By mid-July, ballpark weekends with Sean had turned my fair Irish skin into cooked lobster.

"You'll fit right in with Josie's shrimp scampi," he said. "She's making lunch for us tomorrow. I want *everyone* there."

At the infamous dining table? After the incident with Ruth and Father Cronin? The last place I wanted to set foot. Before I could object, Father Mack vanished.

I confided my trepidation to Father Leo, the kindly but fidgety priest Father Mack assigned to oversee my work and ensure I understood the spiritual side of visiting shut-ins.

"Father Cronin is old school," he said. "Our Hibernian is having a hard time tripping over women in the Parish Center. And don't get him going on changing the Latin Mass to English.

We hope he'll get on board, but 'til then, let's enjoy Josie's lunch. She's a terrific cook."

Bolstered by Father Leo, and obedient to Father Mack, I went to the lunch. The rustic refectory table was transformed with a crisp white tablecloth, bone China and silver flatware. Lemon slices floated on pitchers of iced tea.

Father Leo scurried toward me. "We should meet soon. Father Mack reminded me this morning that he wants us to recruit students to volunteer at the nursing home near campus."

"Father Mack is a spin of ideas, isn't he? Friday's good." We agreed to one o'clock.

As I turned to find a seat, Ruth came around the corner. With Father Andy. I caught my breath. "What are you doing here?" I asked him.

"Good to see you too." He smiled the same broad smile as the first time we met. I held out my hand, professionally, in greeting.

"I invited him," said Ruth, "with Father Mack's approval, of course." I admired her hutzpah finding a neutral party to flank her entry into enemy territory.

Father Andy pulled out a chair for Ruth, and Father Leo took the hint to do the same for me. As I unfolded my linen napkin, it grazed Father Andy's bronzed arm. "It *is* nice to see you." I relayed the news about Adele.

"Dang. She had that look. The cat knew."

"Pets are like my kids," I said. "They get squirmy when something's off. Sixth sense."

Father Andy's eyes opened wide. "You have kids?"

"I taught third graders, kids with developmental delays. Ended up here because of the strike."

He grew quiet and poured me a glass of iced tea. His eyes met mine. "I had a little brother like that. When my folks brought him home from the hospital, they asked all seven of us if we were up to caring for him. I was the oldest. We helped as much as we could, but the little guy didn't make it past his second birthday."

As I offered the breadbasket to him, I let what he said sink in. "Sounds like your family gave the boy seven helpings of love. Maybe that's all he needed."

A glimmer came over Father Andy. "Thanks. Hope you get back to your kids soon."

I assured him that was the plan. "What's next for you?"

"Looks like I'm shipping out soon."

Cold droplets of condensation from iced tea trickled through my fingers. "Just like that?"

"Little place in the country, St. Isadore's. The pastor is leading a tour to Lourdes, then staying on for a short sabbatical. The higher-ups saw me twiddling my thumbs, so off I go."

"Good luck," I said.

"I'll need it. 'Lone Ranger' duty—I'm not used to that."

Father Mack rose to give the blessing. "Thank you, Lord, for Josie who feeds us so well, and Hilda who keeps the altar linens—and our priests—cleaned and pressed." The pastor gave time for chuckles to die down before continuing the lilting tone that did justice to his full name of Mackelvaney.

"Thank God for Sue, who keeps track of us on her In & Out board. And our soloist, Beth. Her singing lifts us to the angels. Last but not least, we give thanks for Ruth and Meg, generous laywomen who join us in your vineyard caring for St. Gabriel's older parishioners."

Father Cronin, sitting across from Ruth and me, glowered. His folded hands clenched into a tight fist. "There was a time when women busied themselves taking care of husbands and children instead of parishioners." Nervous forks on china plates ran the length of the table.

Ruth set down her fork and laid her knife next to it.

I didn't know whether to laugh or cry. Held up in esteem one minute, shot down like clay pigeons the next. I wanted to raise a brood, but also live in the wider world.

Yet here I was—sitting in the crosshairs between someone who might have been a fine marriage prospect and across the street from a troubled priest on the prowl. In the line of sight of Father Cronin and his itchy trigger finger.

Blinking like a frog in a hailstorm, Father Leo tapped his glass for attention. "Then it's settled. The next person hired will be a matchmaker." Everyone cracked up.

Father Andy tipped his glass toward me. But I did not take a sip of iced tea.

ဆ ၁၄

When I returned to the Parish Center after Friday morning visits, I checked my mail slot as usual—only to find that Father Leo left a note to meet him for noon Mass at the Campus Ministry chapel: *We can talk to students afterward about nursing home visits.*

Thought we were meeting here, at 1:00 p.m., not at Father Darren's inner sanctum. Geez.

Father Mack's secretary came into the mailroom balancing an overstuffed folder and her ever-present coffee mug. "You look terrible, Meg. Are your eyes bloodshot?" I always laughed at Sue's bluntness—about other people. Her butterfly wing glasses slid down her nose.

"I'm fine. Gotta run."

I wouldn't have time for lunch. Hoped Father Leo was saying the Campus Ministry Mass—anyone but Father Darren. I steadied myself and crossed the street.

As I entered the Campus Ministry building, Father Darren moseyed across the lobby, still wearing his vestments after Mass. My stomach tightened.

He waved nonchalantly. "Father Leo is in the chapel with some students I scared up for the cause. Said you'd be coming, so I decided to wait."

I made a concerted effort to breathe. "Hello, Father Darren."

"Since you're on staff now, Meg, call me by my first name like everyone else."

In his green chasuble, he could have posed for holy pictures. I nearly gagged as he walked me to the chapel, where Father Leo chatted with a few students scattered in pews.

"About the night of prayer group … when, you know … I shouldn't have dragged you to my hidey-hole like that." His eyes fixed on mine. "Don't say anything. I let you go, right?"

I bore into his chameleon-like stare. Was he was ordering me, or begging me?

"You weren't at your best." This is what Mom said to Dad when he came home with a jewelry box after a row.

Darren scratched his nose. "Thanks for understanding."

My skin crawled. "I didn't say I understood." I escaped into the chapel.

Father Leo hailed me to join him at the lectern. While he described nursing home visits, I watched Darren through the clear panels of glass along the back wall. When a group of young women passed, he preened like Don Juan. The crowd thinned, and he grabbed a co-ed's shoulder. The pit of my stomach heaved. Hair the color of cherry coke, shy smile, soft curves. I recognized her as if looking in a mirror.

I missed Father Leo's cue to talk. He quietly said I looked pale and suggested I go home.

On the way back to St. Gabe's to pack up my things, I saw Nurse Lafferty coming from the opposite direction. It was the faculty nurse's day to check senior citizens' blood pressure—

another of Ruth's innovations. Nurse Lafferty favored full dress code: white cap, white stockings, white shoes, and the navy-blue cape from forever ago that set off her old-fashioned crown braid.

A nurse. A woman. Someone who would understand if I told her about Father Darren.

We reached the entrance to the Parish Center at the same time. I asked if she had a moment. "There's something I've noticed," I said, "that could become a problem."

She sneezed and took out a Kleenex. "Allergies."

"It's about Father Darren."

"Oh, the young priest at Campus Ministry. Extremely friendly, isn't he? And ambitious! I hear he started a Trivia Night. Very popular with the students."

Here we go. His charm offensive blinded everyone. Including me, for a while. "I need to tell you something." I hesitated and cleared my throat. "It's about the way he, well, for a priest, may be too friendly, extremely as you say, with young co-eds."

"Oh, dear me," she said. A blithe smile crossed her lips. "You do know that when young men and young women get together, let's just say they enjoy each other's company."

She was treating me like I had just fallen off the turnip truck. I knew all too well about attraction—healthy, natural attraction. Jake. Sean. My high school steady. Men I worked with at Sears in the camping department. Men I taught with. Father Andy—he lit up whenever he saw me, but we contained our attraction. He was a priest and I wanted to honor that. He didn't corral me into tight spaces. Ordinary attraction observes ordinary boundaries. I wanted to punch Nurse Lafferty. But I respected ordinary boundaries.

"I know the difference between 'enjoying each other's company' and—"

"Don't make a mountain out of a molehill, Meg."

She did not ask how I knew the difference.

Dear God, please let every instinct in my bones be wrong.

⁎ ⁎

A throbbing ache radiated from the back of my head and into my shoulders after talking to Nurse Lafferty. I took Father Leo's suggestion and left work early.

At home, a delivery notice was taped to my mailbox: See Apartment Manager.

I rang the doorbell for Apartment #1. My landlady's voice cackled over the intercom. "Got some mighty pretty flowers here for you. Come on up." When I got to the door, she handed me a florist vase of calla lilies and ferns. "Snagged a good one, Miss Joyce." She gave me a wink and wagged a scolding finger. "But no hanky-panky on the premises."

I read the card on the way up to my apartment: *Until next week.* Sean was out of town for a series of road games. Yes, a good one—with an unexpected romantic streak. Wished he wasn't away so much.

I set the flowers on my kitchen table. If Eileen were around, we could go to the mall. But she was trying her luck with somebody's nephew. Stay busy, I told myself. Took two aspirin and cleaned out my closet. After staring blankly at a bag of old tees and corduroys for an hour, I escaped the four walls of my apartment by heading out to the neighborhood diner.

In the rearview mirror, one last ray of sunset washed a lilac glaze on the underbelly of clouds. Matched my eyeshadow. I turned on the radio. ABBA's "Dancing Queen." I shut it off.

I couldn't get the questions out of my head: *Why did Father Darren glom onto me? Did he act this way with other women?* I hadn't put out the goods—not that I didn't know how.

Up ahead, the diner marquee lit up the block. Jake and I used to eat there. Simple dates. A lot of dates before going all the way. I'd wanted our first time to be special. Despite *Cosmo*'s advice on the pleasures of casual sex, I hoped making love would make the magic happen.

I parked in the diner's lot. Everything looked the same, yet different. I had been honest with Eileen about not being sure of Jake. Out in the cool evening air, being more honest with myself than I liked, I longed for someone to desire me, want me. Passionately. Maybe I longed for that too much. Maybe that's what Father Darren sensed.

The waitress stopped by my table to push the special: fish and chips. Okay.

I wished waitresses lived on every corner pushing easy options in life—who to marry and where to find him—places to work that didn't go on strike—which corridors to avoid.

I shook ketchup onto soggy fries. It landed like a dollop of paint. Modern art.

Like Darren's painting.

Who was the "she" of his painting? If he wanted to give it away, why did he need her permission—much less mine? I felt like a hostage to his anger.

If someone like Nurse Lafferty wasn't willing to take my dilemma seriously, no one would. I thought about telling Ruth, but she had her own issues, courtesy of Father Cronin.

I dipped my beer-battered perch into a ramekin of tartar sauce, crunchy fingers in creamy holy water. Prayed for the "she" of the painting. Prayed for myself. I wanted to move on, past other people's ghosts. I sipped my Dew and whispered the Jewish toast that Eddie's partner, Hank, often said: *L'chaim*—To life.

CHAPTER 3

DRAGONS

RUTH PUT OUT AN SOS WHEN her regular volunteers begged off for the monthly newsletter mailing ritual, so I went downstairs to lend a hand. She pointed to a tall, printed stack bearing the masthead of Gabriel the Archangel lifting his trumpet, calling the zip codes to order.

Father Leo, the lone worker at a long folding table, winced at a fresh paper cut.

"You're just in time, Meg. Haven't done this before, and I'm all thumbs."

Laughter came from the entryway.

Father Leo grimaced. "Look who the cat dragged in."

Father Andy filled the doorway.

Ruth motioned him into the room. "Finally, somebody who knows the ropes."

He elbowed Father Leo. "Let me show you how it's done." His smile fell on me. "Great to find you here, Meg." Bravado gave way to the mellow timbre of his voice.

I met his outstretched hand. "Thought you'd be off by now, Andy. I mean, Father Andy."

"Hey, 'Andy' sounds fine." He clasped my sweaty palm. "I leave tomorrow."

"We don't have time for chit-chat," said Father Leo. "I'll miss psalm service. By the way, it's okay to drop the 'Father' for me too, as long as we're getting chummy down here."

Leo's hurry reminded me that I needed to get home soon to freshen up before dinner with Sean. He was taking me to Giatta's, my favorite restaurant.

Andy rolled up his sleeves. "There's a method to this." He made a show of tidying stacks and stationing us like workers on an assembly line.

We laughed and sorted until Josie appeared with freshly baked snickerdoodles. "Any fools working late on a Friday deserve a reward." She deposited the tray and left.

Ruth ran after her, saying something about needing snacks for next week's card party.

Cookie crumbs dotted Andy's shirt. He mock-begged Leo, "Okay to chat now?"

Leo nodded his blessing.

Andy leaned forward in his chair. "Can I ask what Josie's lunch was really about last week? I came for a hot meal—not a hot collar. Father Mack didn't want to talk about it later."

Leo eyed Ruth's office. "Cronin has declared war on women invading our male enclave. Rubbed salt in the wound, letting it be known at staff meeting Ruth made less than the janitor."

When Father Cronin had shared that tidbit, it set me to wondering how the priests valued their own labors. Our "women's work" caring for people resembled their work much more closely than the "manly work" of keeping buildings and grounds clean and groomed. If they shortchanged our work, what did that mean about theirs? Or did anything done by a priest's holy hands automatically increase its value?

Andy shifted his weight. "I've heard that Mack is making valiant efforts to bring laypeople into parish work—beyond organizing bazaars and washing altar cloths." He grinned— "As important as those are." He locked eyes with Leo. "You know the saying: 'The Church always gets where it's going—a century late and out of breath.' Sorry to break it to you, Meg, but hierarchy moves slowly. Old ways die hard."

My spine stiffened. "That's no excuse for Father Cronin's rudeness to Ruth ... and me. There are limits to what people can put up with."

The teacher strike was about recognition via better paychecks. The Church proved no better haven after all. I weighed the fact that Father Cronin engaged in open warfare, not ambushes in dark corridors like Darren. On balance, I might prefer being Ruth.

Andy cupped the back of his neck and searched the heavens—ceiling tile by ceiling tile. Returning to earth, a pair of brooding eyes focused on me. "Only God is true light—like the sun. The Church is a pale reflection, very pale some days."

I studied Andy's earnest face. "Pale like the moon," I murmured, "and cratered."

Andy laid his hands flat on the long table. "I sure know how to pour fuel on a fire."

I flicked my fingers as if striking a match.

"I'm leaving tomorrow," he said. "But I hate ducking out with you all in a mope. What do you say we go for ice cream at the Brown Cow when we're finished here?"

Leo shrugged. "I can't be late again for psalms. Got a chewing out from Mack last week. The guys are throwing you a going away party later. I'll give you a proper sendoff then."

Andy turned to me. "Meg?"

I couldn't deny wanting to spend more time with a kindred spirit. His sad eyes told me I wasn't the only dented idealist. "As it is, I've got a date."

Andy's face reddened. "Sure, of course. Friday night. What was I thinking?"

Done with newsletters, I scuttled to my office. My coffee mug sat on the desk with a lipstick smudge on the rim. The signature of a woman. I hadn't stopped to consider the radical fact Ruth and I were the first lay women to work side by side with the priests—on staff—in a Church untouched for more than a thousand years by women like us—neither housekeepers nor secretaries, not volunteers or nuns. Having grown up Catholic, I thought I knew everything about a parish. But whatever I knew came from the outside, not the inside.

℘ ℭ

Sean arrived to pick me up for dinner with the news his folks had driven down from Duluth for the weekend. "Mind if we join them? We can do Giatta's next time."

"Why didn't you call?" I wasn't expecting inspection so soon.

He grabbed a Coke from the fridge. "They're visiting colleges with my little brother."

More nervous than mad at him, I wanted to make a good impression. Jake and I did fine until his dad met the girl with the less-than-desirable family.

"Where are we meeting them?"

"Angler's Inn."

Supper club. I exchanged my peasant blouse and jeans for a peach skirt and matching knit top. Brushed my hair so it swept under, tame. Dabbed on lipgloss. "Ready."

Sean wolf-whistled me and opened the car door. "Toby's set on the University of Wisconsin, but my folks want him to consider a Catholic campus like Incarnatus. They got their way with me and my sister. This is their last-ditch effort with Toby. Best if we avoid the spat."

"I won't rock the boat." About college. The rest depended on his parents.

At the restaurant, the hostess led us through a maze of tables crowded with captain chairs. I spotted a blonde woman waving to us—perfectly coifed Clairol "does she ... or doesn't she" hair. Sean's mom greeted him with a chatterbox of news from Duluth before abruptly asking him to introduce me. His dad stood until I sat down. A paunch protruded under his tucked-in polo shirt. Probably a golfer. The Gradys looked like the kind of couple who sat in the front row at church with the Knights of Columbus and Ladies Auxiliary members. My stomach churned.

Toby appeared a shorter, skinnier version of Sean, though he wasted no time scarfing down three deviled eggs from the Lazy Susan. "Beat you to 'em, big brother."

Sean crunched a pickle from the relish tray. His mom scolded her sons' manners.

When it came time to order dinner, Mr. Grady recommended the surf and turf, but I followed Mrs. Grady's lead and ordered the broiled whitefish.

The parents didn't seem to know much about me. Sean's mom turned to him. "You didn't tell us Meg worked for St. Gabriel's." He stayed busy comparing RBIs with his brother.

Mr. Grady quipped, "If you can put up with our son, more power to you."

"I heard that." Sean gave me a quick squeeze.

His parents also asked about my parents. I extracted a pin bone from the flesh of my fish.

"They divorced when I was 10. Dad's drinking got to be more than Mom could handle." Tip of the iceberg, but enough of a test for now.

Sean's mom caught his dad's eye. He gave her the nod. She said, "Sean's aunt and uncle went through the same thing, honey. Sad, but it happens."

Mr. Grady swished his Brandy Old Fashioned. "Here's to your parents' lovely daughter."

Sean continued talking baseball with his brother—as if the Titanic hadn't just avoided a glacier.

&O CB

Eileen and the gang met Sean and me at the beach the next day. His strong arms whipped through waves with precision. Indeed "swoon-worthy"—Eileen and Sheila's description. My toes sank in wet sand while sun etched a red line between my turquoise maillot and exposed skin.

My Adonis scooped me out of the water and slathered me with Coppertone in hot pursuit of ticklish spots. "Why didn't you tell me about your dad?"

"I did tell you. About the divorce, anyway. You didn't ask why."

"No need to go stingray on me." Sean capped the bottle of Coppertone. He pointed to the little girl with her frisky dog in the logo and mugged a pout. "Darlin' Meg, if you'd wear a bikini, I could tug at your bottoms." He nibbled my earlobe.

"Don't be a scuzz."

"You're fond of the elderly and smitten with kids. What about somebody in between?"

"I like you just fine, Sean."

To friends, I was the luckiest girl on the beach to have landed a catch like Sean. I agreed. But was I foolish to wish for something more than "lucky?" The wish itched worse than sunburn.

When we stretched out on our beach towels, I reached for his hand gritty with sand and rubbed his palm. "The kids are having a party for camp closing next Saturday. It'll be fun. Wanna come?"

Sean stared at me a minute. "That isn't what I thought you were going to ask." He flipped onto his back. "Saturday, huh?

No can do. I'll be covering another town ball game. Wish they'd send me out with the Twins more often."

❦

After spending the summer in Sean's company, I could call hits, balls, and errors with fortitude if not certainty. Also, strikes. Every night in September, the local news led with updates on the teacher strike now in full swing. A daily dose of guilt about ditching my colleagues.

"It's fortunate you got out when you did," said Sean. "Don't look back."

When the strike ended mid-October, the always-sequin-sweatered school librarian Sylvia called me to celebrate. I asked if everybody despised me for bailing, but she assured me they understood. Over drinks, they teased "Sister Meg" about how I would look in a veil. I rattled on about Sean. "Soon as I can, I'll be back to teaching. I miss the kids. And all of you."

Sean and I drove out to a country fair the weekend before Halloween. A steeple graced the hilltop just before the fair-grounds.

"Is that St. Isadore's? Father Andy is filling in for the pastor there."

"The priest you used to talk about all the time? Doubt it. We're going to St. Henry's Glen."

When we arrived at the fair, Sean slung his guitar over his back. We wandered through carny stalls where Sean showed off his prowess tossing bean bags through corn holes and popping Ole and Lena's Balloon. Won a Snippen Elf for me.

Late afternoon, we found a shaded bench. Sean pulled his guitar to his hip and adjusted the pegs. As he strummed "Puff, the Magic Dragon," a bunch of kids surrounded us. Sean kept them in giggles, cueing the rhyming lines: "... lived by the sea, in a land called Honahlee."

On the drive home, I strummed his arm. "That was nice, the way you sang with the kids."

"Thanks, Meg. The dime-a-dozen girls just want me to play to their fawning eyes."

Peeks behind Sean's enigmatic soul were few and far between. But a day filled with funnel cake and elves, kids, and music left me longing for more visits to Honahlee.

⅚ ⅝

I arrived early for Mass on Thanksgiving. God and I had much to talk about. Everybody liked Sean, even Mom. I liked Sean. He was easy with kids. And his parents approved of me.

Lord, how do you know when it's the right guy? When do you know? Is there such a thing as falling in love, or do people muddle through like everything else in life?

A familiar figure walked toward the altar as the entrance hymn marked the beginning of Mass. Father Andy. He saw me and flashed a smile my way.

Flutters. I shouldn't be this happy to see some priest.

After Mass, he stood on the church steps wishing everyone a Happy Thanksgiving. I hung back at the end of the line. "Didn't expect to see you again."

He rubbed his chin. "Guess I'm a bad penny, the way I keep turning up."

"Seriously, what's the plan?"

"Waiting for new marching orders. Should hear soon."

I smoothed my gloves. "How'd things go at St. Isadore's?"

"Small place," he said. "Enjoyed the two dogs and a cat."

I wrinkled my nose. "Were they good Catholics?"

He whistled into the air. "The dogs, yes. The cat, no." Andy let out a belly laugh that sounded like it came from a deep part of the ocean I didn't know existed.

CANDLEWOOD

I had missed the sound of his voice, his laugh, his crinkly smile. When I turned to go, an autumn wind tossed painted leaves at us like handfuls of confetti.

℥ Ω

It came as something of a surprise when Mom suggested we go to Midnight Mass on Christmas Eve. She may have thought she should since her daughter was working at the parish. More likely, she hoped Baby Jesus would inspire me to light a fire under Sean and start a family.

Mom and I hadn't gone to the nighttime festivities in a long while. As a kid, Midnight Mass was mysterious as Santa Claus. No matter how cold the evening, Eddie and I bundled into Dad's Buick. He whisked us to the warm church in the dead of night where the boy choir barely skimmed the notes of "Adeste Fideles." I felt the vibration of the organ in my little body.

Mom could still carry a tune, and when she lifted her voice to "O Little Town of Bethlehem," a lump came to my throat remembering her lullabies. I wished Eddie had joined us, but he begged off. Mom's hair was graying now, and she always wore dark colors to camouflage a few extra pounds. A burgundy trapeze dress, not holiday red. Her eyes moistened as the song ended. When I handed her a tissue, she said, "I wish things had worked out with your dad."

Dad wasn't always drunk. He played hide-and-seek with Eddie and me, took us swimming, taught us how to ride a bike. Mom dressed up in her satiny dress, and they'd go out on the town. She had loved him once. The all-in kind of way. *Would I ever love someone that way?*

"Oh, Mom, I wish things had worked out too."

Father Mack spotted us after Mass. "Ah, Meg, and this must be Mrs. Joyce. You two wouldn't want to be going back into the cold just yet, would you? We're having a bit of a party."

"It's late," said Mom.

"It was late a few hours ago," I said, laughing. Intrigued and curious about how the priests partied, I hoped Mom didn't kibosh this opportunity.

"Oh, come up for a short while," he said.

A squadron of black uniformed priests milled about at ease in a living room that reflected the domain of men—boxy 1960s couches and nary a knick-knack. A stereo played "Little Drummer Boy" from the *Andy Williams Christmas Album*.

Leo greeted us with cranberry punch. "Have you heard the news?"

The scent of sandalwood drifted by. Someone touched my elbow lightly. I turned. Andy.

"Leo, you might give Meg a chance to introduce me to …"

His voice sent sparks tumbling. "Mom, this is Father Andy Vogel. He's a missionary priest."

"Nice to meet you," she said. "Where's your mission?"

Andy glanced at me before answering. "Leo's news is that I've been assigned to St. Gabriel's."

I nearly dropped my punch. "But we're not a mission."

Andy lowered his head. "We go where we're sent."

The news rebounded off the drum of my neatly contained feelings for him: Andy's a nice guy—*Pa rum pum pum pum*—That's ALL he is—*Pa rum pum pum pum*.

"We should be getting home, Mom."

⅚ ⅛

When Andy made no appearance at the Parish Center the week after Christmas, curiosity led me to Father Mack's secretary.

Sue's knitting needles clattered. "Booties for the new grand-child?"

"Trying to get them done at last—after the Christmas hoopla and before the baby's born."

I noticed Andy's name on the In & Out board. "Another priest to keep track of, huh?"

"Not until next week. Father Andy's spending time with family in Minneapolis."

I fingered the letters of his name. "I wonder why he's not going back to the missions."

Sue put down her knitting. "I probably shouldn't tell you this, but Father Mack asked that he be assigned here. Seems nice, doesn't he?"

I recalled my first impressions. The way he lit up when our eyes met. The fun of saving Adele's cat. His warm handshake.

The discovery he was a priest.

I avoided eye contact with Sue. "Yes. Seems nice."

"We'll finally have a full roster again," she said.

There was another name on the board when I first started, but Leo told me the invisible man was on a long retreat and study term. "What happened to Father Bob?"

Sue looked both ways and drew her yarn close before telling me in a hushed tone, "He wanted to get married, so he had to leave the priesthood."

"Married? No one said a word."

"These things aren't spoken of, Meg. You'll learn."

I knew many priests left—but hearing Andy's name in the same conversation about this fact knocked me like a snowball in the back.

I pressed my knuckles into Sue's desk. "Thanks for the warning."

On New Year's Eve, Sean took me to his friend's party. We entered the house to Yamaha speakers blaring tunes *From the Mars Hotel.* A circle of Deadheads called me "Scarlet Begonia" for my red wrap dress. A platinum blonde in a snug glittery sweater gave Sean the eye. One of the guys I met at the ballpark last Fourth of July offered us a joint, but we boogied over to the beer and spirits.

Toward midnight, Sean led me to a nook in the pantry. "Wanted to find a quiet spot."

I held my breath. Maybe a claddagh ring? A traditional Irish step toward commitment. A respectable direction for my life seemed within grasp. Settled. No more questions. No more untidy feelings for an unavailable priest.

Sean crossed his arms. "We get on together, Meg, so it's hard for me to say this, but … I gotta be honest with you. I'll just come out and say it—I started seeing someone. You're the marrying kind, and I'm not ready to settle down. Maybe it's better if we part ways."

I scanned the pantry shelves behind this man who had occupied my every weekend, holiday, and spare day since summer. The shelf held all the staples of settled life—flour, sugar, coffee. Soup cans—tomato, chicken and noodles, chicken and stars. Mushy Fourth of July stars.

Sean's dark, wavy hair swept across watery Seagram and Seven eyes.

A tsunami crested in me and gained force. I deluged Sean with cans and jars and stars.

I tore out of the kitchen, past a weed-induced love-in, raked through piles of fake fur and leather on the bed to find my tweed jacket. Nabbed a flute of Cold Duck on my way out.

Midnight. Sean found me shivering outside and fighting back tears. I raised a toast for auld lang syne. "Thanks for not wasting any more of my time."

When Eileen squeezed me the next day for an update on Sean, I told her the bitter tale.

"If you guys can't make it, what hope is there for the rest of us?"

"I'm swearing off men."

"Good luck. You work with a raft of them."

I reminded her they were supposed to be neutered so they didn't count. "Right?"

CHAPTER 4

RAW EDGE

I RESCHEDULED VISITS WITH SHUT-INS from twice a month to once a week. Less time at the parish meant less time with church politics and church men, especially Andy.

Halfway between Mrs. Olsen's house and Mt. Tabor Hospital, my stomach growled. Too late to meet Ruth for lunch at the Parish Center, but only a short detour to my apartment. A quick bite and a change into warmer clothes seemed wise on this freezing Friday in January.

As I approached the front entrance to my six-unit building, a scraggly teenager busted through the door and jumped into an idling car in the parking lot. Whoosh. I went up the stairs to the second floor and pulled out my key, but the door stood ajar. Odd. I always locked it from the outside. Had I forgotten? As I opened the door fully, a million pinpricks riddled my back. Furniture helter-skelter. Overturned drawers. Belongings strewn. Like a scene from a bad movie.

He hadn't found my just-in-case $100 bill in the freezer, the only cash in the place.

When the police came, I described the teenager tearing out of my building—and realized he had pulled his sock hat off instead of putting it on to go outside.

The police said there'd been a rash of break-ins and hoped I could help nab the kid. I spent the rest of the afternoon looking at mug shots. A blur. By the time I finished, the police who drove me to the station were nowhere to be found. I needed a way home.

Sean had left a bunch of messages on my phone after New Year's Eve, but I didn't return them. I would rather not play "damsel in distress" today.

Eddie? No car—DUI history. I didn't know Hank's number at work.

Awfully cold for a bus.

The station wasn't far from St. Gabe's, so I used the pay phone to call Sue. As keeper of the In & Out board, she mustered available staff when folks came to the Parish Center— the regulars who wanted a Mass offered for their deceased loved one, down-and-outers seeking a tide-over, alcoholics needing to justify themselves to somebody, and poor souls not infrequently hearing voices or seeing visons. Today, a ransacked Meg needing a ride.

"I'll send someone to fetch you."

I sat down on a sooty chair in the lobby watching the comings and goings. About half an hour later, Andy came scrambling toward the door in a beat-up brown bomber jacket. He had the shoulders for it. Not a heavy build but looked like he could handle a hard day's work.

Andy entered the station and clapped his shearling gloves. "Hang out here often?"

His levity rattled me. "Only on Friday the 13th. You? Lured by sirens?"

He raised one eyebrow. "Let's get you out of here. Sue told me what happened."

I reached for my brand-new long wool coat, a splurge after the holidays despite waiting for markdowns. The one thing of value the robber might have taken except I was wearing it. The lining of my old tweed looked like a crazy quilt of mended patches. My new coat—a libation of sangria, double-breasted, warm, its lining intact.

"You okay?" Andy held out his arms to help me on with my coat. He probed my eyes.

My vain attempt at bravery disintegrated. "I don't want to go home tonight."

The whole wingspan of Andy's arms encircled me.

"If anything happened to you … if you'd been there when whoever did this …" His voice changed from angst-filled blurts to deep waves of breath. "Meg, dear Meg." He pulled me close.

My ear pressed against his chest. I heard the sound of the ocean, like listening to a seashell washed ashore.

Andy drove me to St. Paul to stay at Eddie and Hank's house. Next day, they helped me clean up my apartment—and urged me to move to a safer neighborhood.

My landlady waived the usual month's notice so I could move sooner. I found a first-floor flat in an old bungalow with a wide porch. Bookshelves flanked the living room fireplace, and the adjoining dining room boasted a built-in breakfront. I could finally unbox and display the good tableware Mom gave me when she downsized. Big windows everywhere including the eat-in kitchen. Perfect to hang houseplants in the macrame holders I made at crafts class. The landlord agreed to lower the rent if I shoveled snow and mowed the lawn. Done.

On moving day, Eddie and Hank pulled up in a U-Haul. I was ready with donuts for them and a couple of friends they brought to help.

I wasn't ready to see Andy emerge from a blue Chevy Caprice parked at the curb. He tipped his cap's visor, and I introduced him to the crew.

Eddie nudged me and whispered in my ear. "Not Sean?"

"Long story." I didn't tell him Andy was *Father* Andy. Nice of him to want to help, but much too personal.

By 11:00 a.m., the U-Haul was crammed with boxes big and small, furniture, and a few lamps. Andy's sweaty forehead glistened. He dawdled in the kitchen while the others loaded the last small pieces. "Wish I could stay for the second half, but I have to do a wedding."

Morning sunlight filtered through tree branches outside the empty apartment. "Maybe I'll get a tabby for the new place."

Andy's trademark dimples deepened. "See you around, Meg."

When I told Eddie why Andy had to leave, his face became a question mark. "Priest?"

"No, not like that other one. Andy's a nice guy." Nice guy—my mantra. "That's all there is to it."

Eddie rolled down the U-Haul door and latched it. "Be careful, Sis."

਒ ਓ

Sometimes in winter, snowmelt gives way to patchy tumbles of grass. Hints of spring teased early March days.

"Hey, Sunshine!" Andy leaned on my office doorjamb like a robin at his daily perch. We always found something of utmost importance to talk about—how Blood, Sweat & Tears came up with their band's name, or how many inches of snow a tree limb could bear before breaking.

I started to say, "Hey, Moonshine!" But as I looked up, his eyes met mine. His look lingered. I felt as if a sheer waterfall rushed through me.

I looked away, but when I raised my eyes to him again, it was like someone had taken a crayon and etched a wide silver outline all around his being. He shone.

Without words because I had none, I moved toward him, drawn like a spark on the wind.

We faced each other, close, the raw edge of a chasm falling between us.

"*Chandelle*," he whispered, "you glow … like a candle."

Our fingers brushed each other's. His gaze roamed my face. Soon his hands trembled on my waist. He pulled me toward him, and I let him, our lips about to kiss.

He backed away. "I'd better go."

My eyes followed him as he slipped out the door. Halfway down the hall, he paused.

I waited.

He didn't turn around.

I closed the door, leaned my back on it and let the wood support the weight of my body.

CHAPTER 5

HARPS

FATHER MACK INTRODUCED DARREN at the staff meeting, saying he was there to make a pitch for campus ministry students to do more volunteer work. When Ruth said she could use some help setting up starter plants for the garden she was planning, Darren clarified that he meant help with the upcoming Holy Week liturgies. To me, it seemed he was angling for a bigger stage for himself, not satisfied with his chapel duties across the street.

Seeing Darren and Andy in the same room sent me reeling. Only yesterday, Andy and I almost kissed, tenderly. Wonderfully—if he weren't a priest. Darren only knew how to taunt with a kiss. I excused myself to leave early.

My first visit of the day was at the Veterans Hospital in Minneapolis, at least a 30-minute drive, plus parking and finding my way through the hulking facility. The receptionist directed me to Otto Byrne's room—Bed #518, 5th floor, end of the hall. A single room. Must have been brass. Almost nobody got a private room at the VA.

But the bed was empty. A catheter bag hung over the side-rail. Dangling bag of dark urine. Acrid air. Bed raised to the height of a gurney. Bleach.

An orderly paused from stripping soiled sheets. "Can I help you?" he asked.

"I came to visit Mr. Byrne. When is he returning? Did they take him for tests?"

"You family?"

"No, I'm from his parish."

The orderly stuffed bed linens into a bin. "He ain't comin' back, Miss. He done died."

I caught my breath. A tear for an unknown man trickled down my cheek.

The orderly resumed his chores. "You better get out of here. I got to clean up this mess."

I stopped in the hospital chapel and knelt to whisper the prayer for the dead: *Eternal rest grant unto him, O Lord, and let perpetual light shine upon him.* The profound stillness of the chapel brought me back to the quiet moment Andy and I shared the day before. Much as I tried to deny it, a light had shone on us.

When I got back to the Parish Center, I needed some downtime. Thought if I closed my door, I could do mindless paperwork, but Beth came bubbling into my office.

"You'll love this, Meg. Father Mack gave me the nod to get a St. Pat's party going for the senior citizens. Ruth's already on board."

Beth's enthusiasm often made more work for herself—and others. Already soloist for St. Gabe's choir, she recently took on duties as wedding planner. And now, party planner?

"What did you have in mind for entertainment? Jigs and reels aren't your specialty."

"I can sing ... and ... you could get Sean to play for us."

Beth joined Eileen and me at Kelly's Pub a few times last fall, so she knew Sean and I had dated. "I can see why you'd think of him, but we called it quits. It would be a lot to ask."

Beth bit her lower lip. "Maybe a chance to rev things up?"

Was Eileen behind this? She wanted to see us get back together. "He'll be booked solid by now."

"Let's ask him anyway. Or—I could go with Eileen and ask him myself."

He'd think I put them up to it. Was I going to hide from Sean because I didn't want to see him, at the same time I was hiding from Andy because I did? "All right. I'll go with you."

When Sean spied me at Kelly's, he bungled his chord. Angry? Happy to see me again? I hung back while Beth asked him about playing for the parish party.

"Might consider it." Sean shot me a look. "For auld lang syne." He offered March 10, the week before St. Pat's Day.

Beth, Ruth, and I presented the plan and budget at the next staff meeting. Father Cronin's concerns regarding cost quickly dissolved when we noted that music, decorations, and food were donated. However, he couldn't resist stating that the maintenance man would need overtime pay.

"Not to change the subject," said Leo, "but may I come to the party for a while?" Father Mack exhorted all the priests to lend their presence at the "jolly" party.

Andy made a show of flipping through his Pocket Planner. "I'll try, but I have a meeting. I may not be able to get away."

Andy and I hadn't spoken in the two weeks since we nearly kissed in my office. I drew a shamrock on my notepad, though whether luckier for him to attend the party or stay away remained a question. How long before we might find the courage to be friends again, just friends? I traced the trinity of heart-shaped shamrock leaves.

One for the Father,
Two for the Son,
Three to get ready,
And nowhere to go.

The day of the party, we decorated the Parish Center social hall like the land of Erin. Henrietta, ubiquitous volunteer, toddled through the door early. "I wanted to make sure everything was ready," she said, and proceeded to rearrange our carefully placed centerpieces of green plastic hats, paper honeycomb harps, and pots of gold.

Sean and the band set up on a makeshift stage. I stayed busy on the other side of the room. If the evening went well, I planned to ask Sean for a ride home. My car's oil change wasn't done when promised, so I could test if he agreed to this gig as a prelude to getting back together. Maybe ask me out for the real St. Pat's next Friday. A date would be a test for me too, though I doubted it would work out any better.

Leo soon bustled down the hallway, looking every inch the leprechaun. "I asked Hilda to dye my shirt green when she did laundry last week. Grand, yes?"

We took turns greeting and seating senior citizens.

Nearly seventy partiers left their aches and pains at the door. Father Mack put on the brogue and blessed Sean's band. The trio opened with the "Ballad of Sweet Molly Malone" *crying cockles and mussels, alive, alive, oh.* Wrinkled dowagers and sunken-cheeked men had not forgotten how to make merry. They sang along—*alive, alive, oh.*

Father Cronin appeared, casting a shadow thin enough to slide between death and taxes.

Darren must have gotten wind of the party. He dallied with the young women from Campus Ministry serving punch and cookies. When he left, minus any co-eds, I breathed easier.

No sign of Andy.

Toward the end of the evening, Sean succumbed to repeated requests for "Danny Boy" but soon lifted the song's melancholy mood by segueing into "When Irish Eyes Are Smiling." As I brought a plate of Josie's lemony mint shortbreads to the sorely neglected stragglers' table near the door, Andy walked in.

My heart ached. I wanted to smile for him but didn't. Were we going to spend the rest of our days avoiding each other? I looked up, hoping my eyes smiled if not my lips. Andy smiled back. Maybe things would be all right.

"Nice party," he said.

Lemony mint mixed with the scent of his sandalwood soap.

As the party wound down, Beth led the crowd like a choir in one last chorus of "*Too-ra-loo-ra-loo-ra ... that's an Irish lullaby.*"

Sean waved his usual farewell, "No loitering with leprechauns!"

I was about to ask him for a ride home when Henrietta set a green plastic hat filled with a heap of crunched dollar bills on the stage.

"What's this about?" asked Sean.

Henrietta piped up. Said I told her the band didn't get paid, so she took up a collection.

Sean snapped, "Meg, why didn't you stop them? I don't need old folks' bucks."

I tried telling him I had nothing to do with it.

"You knew the score." He glared.

Did I? Seemed all I ever knew with Sean were hits and misses.

Andy stepped up to the stage, between Sean's slow burn and my flushed face. "Thanks very much for coming to play. Great tunes."

Sean continued packing equipment. "My pleasure." He pushed the hat to me like a dart. "Meg, give the proceeds to the good padre." He flipped his guitar on his back and left.

Andy turned to me. "How do you know him?"

"From Kelly's Pub."

"Bit of a temper."

"Tempest in a green hat," I said.

Andy shrugged and called to Ruth. "Bet you could up the ante of Cheesy Tid-Bits for your whist and canasta parties." She hurried to her office to drop off the hat trick before escorting a stray senior to her chair.

I toasted the canny way Andy had put the money back into the hands of those who had given it. "*Sláinte.*"

A scant crew of volunteers, plus Leo and Andy, returned the room to its mundane order while a wind-driven rain pelted the windows. Beth and I were stashing the last harps and rainbows in a bag when she asked if I could give her a ride. She lived in the neighborhood and usually walked, but she'd be soaked in the storm.

"Any other time," I said, "but my car's in the shop. I'm bussing it myself."

Andy tossed used cups and plates in the trash. "What's wrong with the jalopy?"

I waved away his concern. "Nothing. She runs slick as a whistle but was due for an oil change. The shop got busy and missed my pickup time."

Andy looked toward Leo. "Sounds like our lasses need wheels."

"I've got the 6:00 a.m. Mass tomorrow," said Leo. "Sorry, I need to call it a night."

Andy picked up more paper cups. Disposed of them. Came over to where Beth and I were dismantling decorations. "Well, I have no excuse. Let's get this stuff packed and be on our way."

Beth was the shorter run, so he dropped her off first. With the lilt of her humming gone, only the metronome of windshield wipers punctuated the silence.

"Nice party," Andy said for the third time.

"Thanks, but it was Beth's idea."

"Glad the Bug only needed an oil change."

The car seemed a safe topic. I went on at length about the reliability of my neighborhood garage ... how unlike them not to have the car ready. Driveled about the convenience of a close bus stop, and how I could pick up the car any time Saturday morning.

Wet blocks passed.

"Turn here," I said. "The bungalow with double dormers. Next to last from the corner."

Andy turned into the shared driveway and parked next to the side entrance. The car's motor hushed. A light above the side door threw a foggy beam in the dissipating rain.

Andy turned toward me and put his arm across the back of the car seat. Leaned in, the way a man does when he's about to kiss a woman. I wanted to kiss him. I wanted to kiss him the day we stood hardly a breath away from each other in the glow of an early spring morning. He held me in his eyes for a moment, then looked out the car window.

"Rain's letting up a bit." His eyes returned to mine. He touched a strand of my hair and curled it in his finger, then let it go with a shy smile. "We should get in the house."

I could feel his breath, warm on my wet cheek, his face not matching his words. We couldn't take this chance. I couldn't take this chance.

I pressed my fingers to Andy's lips. "Don't ... don't be like Darren."

He pulled back. "What?" Winced. "No, I'm not like that. Please don't think I'm like that. I'm not ... he's a pig."

My brother was right. These guys knew each other well.

"Did he do something to you? Meg, be honest."

"Tried once, but no."

He removed his arm. "Let's get this stuff unloaded."

My shoulders sank. How could I think for a second that Andy was anything like Darren?

I grabbed a stuffed bag and rummaged for my key. "Can you hold this bag a minute?" Rainbows and harps and lucky charms toppled out of a too-small bag and onto watery pavement. Andy retrieved the fallen trinkets, and I opened the side door that led into the kitchen. He entered and set the bag down on the floor. In the dark, I tripped over the bag. Lost my balance and fell against the window wall. Andy switched on a light. An unclaimed pot of gold tumbled askew.

I sat up and folded my knees into my chest, my whole body trembling.

Andy sat down next to me. Drippy coats and rainy faces.

He put his arm around my shoulder. "Shh," he murmured, "shh."

I burrowed into the damp leather of his bomber jacket. Wind-whipped weeks of wanting and not wanting to want stirred a storm inside, dangerous as a hurricane.

Andy unbuttoned my coat. He steadied his hand on the curve between waist and breast, where breath moves in and out. Our breathing came together and slowed. I closed my eyes. Safe in the wide wings of his arms.

He touched my eyelids tenderly. When I opened them, Andy looked into my eyes and beyond. "You are like the dawn."

Dawn. The moment when night loses power over day.

I slid round to see his eyes. Steady, bright, liquid. True. I traced the ridge of his brow. Strewn straw on an open field. A rush of seagulls flew through me. I lifted my face to him.

We embraced, our lips touching.

Light prickle of shaved stubble. I grazed his mouth.

He caressed the bow of my upper lip with his full lower. Breath moist, warm, fresh. Our lips rippled over each other's, gliding.

CANDLEWOOD

A shudder of lightning flashed. At the crack of thunder, Andy jumped to his feet. "I should get going." He reached for my hand and pulled me up.

Under the back door awning, he brushed my cheek with his thumb. "Thank you."

I laid my hand on his chest, on his heart, then let him go.

I wish he'd stayed. Was glad he left. *Why, God, why? This is the wrong one!* Any other time, any other person—like finding a pot of gold at the end of the rainbow.

But there was no rainbow, only rain.

Monday morning, I entered the Parish Center under the watchful eye of a gargoyle on the ledge above. The stony creature's gaping mouth accused me of dragging a Catholic priest into the gutter. It knew nothing of flesh and blood.

I dreaded seeing Andy at staff meeting. When he didn't show, I loosened my clutch on the armrest. Agenda items rolled over me like a distant radio. I tapped my pen on a yellow legal pad, wanting the lines of ruled paper to hear my defense. But the case was clear cut, and not in my favor. Mother Church has rules. Rules are supposed to protect us. I believed in rules, followed rules. Rules didn't come out of thin air. People agreed on the best way of doing things after hundreds of years of experience. Who was I to question millennia? There must be a reason for the rule that priests can't fall in love, marry, have children. Andy and I had to walk away before it was too late, before we fell off the edge of the cliff, forever shunned by our Church.

My family had broken all the taboos—divorce, bankruptcy, alcoholism, homosexuality—and we paid for it. Lost our home, good name, financial security. Since my teens, I strove to restore a modicum of respectability to my family. I knew what it was like to be shunned. If I wanted a respectable life, I couldn't let myself go any further with Andy.

All week, I busied myself, stayed out of Andy's line of sight. Late Friday afternoon, I returned to the Parish Center to log the week's activities. We nearly collided in the entryway.

His face brightened in surprise. "Forgot to change my 'Out' to 'In' on Sue's board. Probably doesn't matter. She's gone home."

I stood paralyzed and tongue-tied. My head roller-coastered: Yes—No—Stop—Run.

Andy lowered his voice to a hush. "Missed you."

And I'd missed him. Missed everything. Our morning banter—his laugh—his easy saunter. Missed the brush of his stubbly cheek when he kissed me Friday.

"Want to come over later?" The words spilled like milk. No way to take them back.

Andy took a step closer. "Yes ... very much."

I swallowed hard. "Missed you too."

Once home, I flurried into dusting and vacuuming and fluffing pillows. Getting ready for exactly what I tried hard to avoid all week—to melt into his arms again. To learn every muscle and ligament of his body, to smell clean sweat and taste his mouth again.

To sin.

As I put the vacuum back in the hallway closet, the crucifix on the wall stared at me.

Thorns.

Andy was a priest.

Maybe if we didn't make love, we could stay friends, like before. We didn't have to act on our feelings. We could tell ourselves we kissed once—a foolish act on a rainy night. Nice.

Warm. Coming to naught. We could return to living between the lines. Living by the rules.

If we made love, our lives would never be the same again. Making love with Andy wouldn't be testing the waters; it would be parting the waters to a land of milk and honey.

And locusts.

Andy stood at my front door holding a small bouquet of green carnations for St. Pat's.

My resolve dissolved. I reached around his neck and hugged him. Warm sweat. His usually choppy hair neatly combed.

One of his hands landed gently, tentatively, on my shoulder blade.

"Let me put those flowers in water," I said.

"You've got this place fixed up real nice. So many plants. Did you do the macrame? Wow."

"Yes, and thanks, I like tending them."

A dimpled grin flitted across his features. "Couldn't see much the other night."

All I saw the other night was Andy. All I saw now was Andy. I motioned for him to sit down in the old Cogswell. "You carried it to the U-Haul when I moved. You should try it out."

"Isn't this the chair your brother reupholstered for you? He's a good guy."

"Eddie's a gem—when he's sober."

Andy jumped at a topic not about us. "Yeah, he passed a flask on the truck but seemed to be keeping things in check." He asked where Eddie worked, whether he was older or younger than me, and did I have any other brothers or sisters. He wanted to know where I grew up.

I knew Andy came from a big family. He knew little about me except what I saw, what I let him see. I seldom told anyone the story behind my carefully crafted mask. For the curious, I started by telling a corny story about flunking drivers ed. Folks always changed the subject.

Andy sat up, expectant, hands on his knees, waiting.

I took a deep breath and let the story unfold. Truth. Not every detail, but the outlines of my parents' bitter divorce, Dad's drinking binges, my brother growing into a chip off the old block. "We had tough times," I said. "I worry about Eddie."

Andy didn't flinch. "Families are checkerboards. Best ones worry about each other."

I tucked my legs sidesaddle on the couch. Would he be as big-hearted if he knew the rest?

"Besides," Andy said, smiling, "good to know someone who can find her way around a catastrophe or two."

I sniffed the carnations and hoped we wouldn't become another catastrophe.

"What kind of music do you like?" I flipped through albums next to the hi-fi. "Fleetwood Mac? Beatles? Dylan? Chuck Mangione?"

"Mangione is good."

I cued the title cut, "Chase the Clouds Away." Jazzy chords filled the room.

"I'm a little out of practice, but would you care to dance?" Andy asked.

Was it his hands or mine that quivered? Both. Our bodies swayed to the rhythms. Our fingers asked and answered. I softly rubbed the calloused pads of his upper palm. He pressed his other hand on my back in time to the music. Warm waves surged through me.

He led me back to the couch. I rested under his arm, breathing musky, soapy sweat. Closed my eyes, listened to music. I didn't want the moment to end, for in the next moment I would offer him my lips, unbutton my blouse, feel his breath on my breast. And we would be forever lost.

"May I kiss you, Meg?"

I looked up. He wasn't wearing a collar. Tonight. But tomorrow he would.

Tears burned. "I don't want to get hurt. And I don't want to hurt you."

His arm slid off my shoulder. "I shouldn't have come tonight."

I brushed my tears away. "I'm glad you came tonight. This is what real people do. I wish we could be real."

Andy touched my hair and hugged me close before leaving.

CHAPTER 6

SORE SOULS

EXTRA-LONG CONFESSION LINES signaled the holiest week of the year, the days leading up to Easter. Sue's In & Out board showed Andy signed up to hear Confessions every single one of the dozen or so slots that week. If his emotions were as frayed as mine, the Confessional room, "the box," made a good cover. Wish I had a box to hide in.

I wondered whether Andy confessed our kiss, and the "near occasion of sin" we indulged last week. Should I go to Confession? God wrote things in our hearts and bodies that didn't jibe with what the Church wrote on parchment.

I knew my catechism. The Church only condemned willful actions. The Church couldn't condemn us for falling in love. Andy probably confessed our kiss and was doing penance by sitting in the box for hours on end. Offering mercy to others as God had mercy on him—on his lips that kissed a woman. Nothing was sinful about my kissing a man—except that he was a priest. Geez, I didn't want to confess something like that. A good way to get thrown out on my ear. No, I couldn't go to Confession. I was living my penance by letting him go.

Lord, I need your help. I need your grace.

Leo came to my office at 3:00 p.m. for our weekly meeting about visits to shut-ins and nursing homes, hospital rounds, and volunteer training. I hadn't prepared.

"Meg, you don't seem yourself today."

My mind clanged. "I'm not a poker-face?"

He put aside his notebook. "Nice day out. Let's go for a walk."

Leo chattered about Easter bunnies and egg-coloring traditions. "Symbols of spring," he said, "and mating rituals." He blushed.

I burst into tears.

"Ah, Meg. Do I have a notion what's bothering you?"

"You wouldn't understand."

"Try me." He stopped at a bench in the woods on the edge of campus, and we sat down. "There's only one other person I know who's as glum as you. He's a six-footer, hair like straw. Can you think of anybody who fits that description?"

He knew.

"You and Andy are two of my favorite people. Talk to me."

I told Leo the whole story. He looked down, saying nothing.

I squirmed on the bench, expecting the wrath of Moses.

Leo took my hand. "If Andy weren't my brother-priest, I would encourage him to woo you properly and put a ring on your finger."

Leo's sympathy jarred me. "But he *is* a priest."

The man sitting next to me with a small square of white starched collar poking out from his Adam's apple said, "And there's the rub. You two haven't done anything terrible, nothing irreversible, but you've made it harder for yourselves. Do you want to say an Act of Contrition?"

"I can't be sorry for loving Andy. But I am sorry I made things more difficult."

Leo pointed to a sparrow in the trees. "The Lord is merciful, Meg, and will give you strength. I know you pray the rosary, so say three Hail Marys—one for yourself, one for Andy, and say one for me. It's not going to be easy watching you two navigate this road."

He said the words of absolution and we walked back to the parish in pardon and peace.

I hadn't realized my dreams were so fragile. Marriage and family seemed an attainable goal. Almost everyone finds a way. Since I was a little girl, I prayed to give my children the kind of family where a mom and dad loved each other in the no-matter-what kind of way. My children would never jitter in fright as their parents fought.

I tried to make love happen a few times, but love can't be forced or eased into place. No one can make it happen any more than a mortal person can make the sun to shine, or the grass grow. When love happens, there it is.

Andy was the first man who tapped the deep reservoir I always hoped was inside me—a place filled to the brim with joy, tenderness, passion. Andy wanted to give himself to me in the same way. Amazing. The Lord himself blessed marriage—turned water jugs into vessels filled with wine. But a huge crack marked our jug that no amount of glue could fix—a rule that said Roman Catholic priests cannot marry.

Lord, help us. I thanked God for Leo, one friend in this big barricade of a Church.

In the days before Holy Thursday, Father Mack asked Josie and every other woman staffer or volunteer in the parish to bake unleavened bread for Communion—a reminder of the original Last Supper.

Mixing dough for Communion wafers, I grew ever more conscious of the simple ingredients that would become the Bread of Life—flour, oil, water, honey. Didn't seem possible. Then again, how does anything become something else? I watched dry flour change into white mud as it absorbed the oil. Plain water lapped honey and became sweet. Yes, I thought to myself, things are always changing into something else. Flour— once wheat and before that, seed. Oil—not always oil, but crushed fruit of an olive tree grown from seed. Somewhere, a flower blossomed from seed, oozing nectar for bees. Bees released the nectar's secret—honey. Sea evaporates into air and returns as mist in a cloud.

The world hums.

And so, perhaps not strange at all that bread becomes a new creation when mottled grains hear words of consecration. Christ appears: three-parts seed to one-part mist, incarnate by the same breath of life that hovered over Mary's womb.

What words had God hummed over Andy and me to change us into something new? Though we'd entered forbidden territory, a full measure of thanks at finding each other outweighed my guilt. Fear and trembling, yes, at breaking a big rule. But deep down, though I tried to fight it, I believed the hand of God was kneading us. Into what, I did not know.

As I entered the red brick walls of St. Gabriel's church on Holy Thursday night, the stone arches framing stained glass windows looked like praying hands. Standing candelabras, ceiling lights and a multitude of altar candles reflected on the marble aisles, making them ripple like the St. Croix River. White and gold banners, altar cloths, and vestments signaled the specialness of the feast. When the choir sang the processional, the sound spilled over the intricately carved wooden loft and filled the whole church.

Darren gave a silver-tongued sermon at the Mass of the Lord's Supper. One would almost think he knew about love, the way he used the word so many times.

Andy had trained in the same seminary as Darren. How did one come away grubbing the body while speaking ecstatically about the spiritual, while the other treated both body and soul as sacred? Maybe it was easier for Darren to commit to the spiritual if he stomped on the body.

I sat in the pew, bewildered, knowing I was not the first to question the tradition of unmarried priests. I knew the tangled history. Since the 12th century, the Church required men to remain unmarried, many said to prevent its coffers emptying into the hands of women and children. Though Pope Paul VI upheld the tradition he called "a brilliant jewel" following Vatican II in the 1960s, chatter about changing the rule continued. He conceded bachelorhood was not essential to ministry. After all, Jesus called Peter and other married men.

Many men were leaving to obey the rules of their heart. And were shunned.

I wanted more. I wanted the rules to change so that Andy and I could remain on the right side of the Church, not shunned by friends and neighbors, family, and Rome. Surely with so many questioning the tradition, things would soon change. The Church wouldn't hemorrhage its priests for an arbitrary rule. If the love growing between Andy and me was true, it would last until then. For now, I prayed hard.

On Good Friday, the purple cloth of sorrow covered church statues. The altar lay bare, a slab of marble, our Paschal Lamb slaughtered. Blood separated from flesh. There would be no Communion, the sacrament that knits flesh and blood back together. It was the feast of death.

Lord, are you asking me to wear sadness like a purple cloth until the rules change? Only you know how much I wanted to break all the rules—but I don't want to break Andy.

CANDLEWOOD

At sundown on Saturday, the Vigil of Easter, a crowd gathered in front of St. Gabriel's for a candlelight procession. Father Mack held his hands over a blazing cauldron and intoned a blessing on the fire. At the "Amen," a deacon presented the three-foot tall Paschal Candle, symbol of Christ's rising. Father Mack inscribed a cross on the beeswax. He traced the letter "A" above the cross and what looked like a horseshoe below the cross. His words revealed their meaning: "Christ yesterday and today, the Beginning and the End." The first and last letters of the Greek alphabet— "A" and "Ω"—symbols for Alpha and Omega.

Startled, I saw our names, Alfons—Andy's given name— and Meg, hidden within the inscription on the candle—**Al**pha and **Omeg**a—as if carved into the trunk of a tree. Carved into the wood of the cross for all the world ... and no one ... to see. Our beginning and our ending. Two lives in the procession of life that one day would merge into the great unknown.

Four quadrants of the cross comprised the landscape of our lives. Did the horizontal and vertical lines of the cross paint an intersection or prison yards? I wasn't sure my horseshoe was a sign of good luck—it could be so many things—one of what should be a pair, Cinderella's lost slipper, or steel for the flint. The beginning was a sure thing. We were created by a power born before time began. Where we would end was not so sure a thing.

Christ, I want to trust you, but what are you asking? I'm lost.

Father Mack touched the wick to the roaring fire as he said, "May the light of Christ, rising in glory, dispel the darkness of our hearts and minds."

I repeated the words in earnest prayer as the light passed to each person's hand-held candle.

I caught sight of Andy in the candlelight procession. Though moving, he seemed motionless. I wanted to tell him we must trust in the Lord, tell him that I was scared too. But he knew that. He was trying to honor my need for dry land to cross the Red Sea, and his own need to live up to a promise he made before he knew what it meant.

I was more glad than ever that I took Beth up on the invitation to visit her family on Long Island for Easter break. A cheap flight lifted us far above incense and flames. Soon, bike rides near the beach, viewing the Manhattan skyline from Windows on the World, and eating dinner with her family soothed my sore soul.

Searching for razor clams in a back bay inlet one morning, Beth mused that Andy wasn't poking around my office as much as he used to.

I put some salt on a bubble of sand to coax out a clam. "Lent is a busy time."

"He seemed happier a few months ago," Beth said. "I wonder what happened."

Wished I could confide in her, but I didn't want to live in a fishbowl. Bad enough Leo was onto us.

"Andy has a big family. Maybe his mom or dad or one of his sisters or brothers is sick."

"You would be the first to know, Meg. You two are, what's the word? *Simpatico*."

"Andy seems closest to Leo. If it was any of our business, Leo would tell us. Let's not ask for worries we don't need."

I missed Andy yet dreaded going back to the parish at the end of the week. I called the school district and applied for a summer teaching job—the best way to escape the parish scene. Though all the positions were filled, my former supervisor offered a shred of hope for the next fall. "I'll tag your application experienced."

CANDLEWOOD

I crossed my fingers that a teaching job would open in the fall. If Andy and I could avoid each other for a few months this summer, then we could return to the lives we knew before Cupid's arrow struck. It would be okay. We'd be happy as clams—so long as we stayed in our shells.

CHAPTER 7

CALL

I WAS GETTING READY TO MEET friends at a new barbeque joint when the phone rang. Busy deciding between my new coral blouse or a more practical sweater, I let the call go to voicemail.

Leo's voice. Scratchy.

"Meg, I don't know how to tell you this ... it's about Andy. Call me."

I jogged my brain for his extension and called back. "What's wrong? What happened?"

"Ah, you're home. Andy's okay, but he was in a car accident."

My heart raced. "Is he hurt? Where is he?"

"He's not badly hurt. Really. He's here, but his sister is in the hospital. Andy was driving. He's a mess."

"I'll be there as quickly as I can."

"Maybe it would be better if you called."

I fumbled for a pen and paper and took down the number Leo gave me.

The phone rang six times before hearing Andy's voice, a muted guttural "Yeah?"

"Andy, it's me, Meg. Leo called." I gathered my breath. "He told me what happened."

"I can't ... I don't think I can talk about it."

"That's all right, Andy. I'm here if you want to talk later."

"Thanks, okay. Later." But he didn't hang up.

And I couldn't hang up either. I ached, imagining him sitting alone in the dark.

"Andy, do you want to come over?"

He paused a long minute. Breaths like gasping for air.

I waited.

He made a sound like coughing. "Are you sure?"

"Yes, Andy. Come over. Please."

I found my rosary and waited by the window, praying for the right words to say when he came. The right things to do. Leo said Andy was a mess. Surely he was whipping himself about the accident, blaming himself. Such a close family. What if his sister didn't make it? He'd never forgive himself.

Hail Mary, full of grace. The Lord is with thee.
Holy Mary, mother of God, pray for us sinners, now and at the hour of our death.

A car slowed and parked in front of the house. I pulled the drape. Steps on the porch. The doorbell buzzed. Andy drooped like a mangy dog. He let me take his hand and we walked inside. He sat down on the couch. Ashen.

I sat next to him. Quiet. Gently touched the bruise on his cheek.

"End of semester. Went to get Jenny—to bring her home from college. Nice day. She's got a boyfriend—wants the family to meet him." And then he broke down. "If anything happens ... my fault ... didn't see it. Truck jumped the median. Should've seen it. Crashed right into us. Jenny ... oh, God."

"Andy, geez, so sorry."

"I was driving. Should have been me got hit. Why wasn't it me?"

"Jenny's in the hospital?" I didn't know how badly she was injured.

"Yeah, she's pretty banged up."

"Anything broken?" I braced for the worst of it.

"Jenny's a toughie, strong. She'll have to be. Broken leg." And then his beautiful eyes went dark. "Blood ... everywhere."

I laid my hand on his arm. "What do the docs say?"

"They're letting her rest. It'll be a while. Traction."

"Sounds like she's in good hands, Andy." I traced the scratch marks on his forearm and the gash that ran from brow to earlobe, just missing his eye. "What about you?"

"Well, I found out my blood's red." A slight edge of humor. A lifeline.

I grabbed the rope, "No, you don't say!" Our laughter broke the gloom. With a leap of faith, I said, "Jenny's going to be okay." I flung my arms around this man who had come so close to oblivion. Tears welled up. He started to push me away, but then slipped his arms around my waist.

Without a word, because none was needed, we made our way to the bedroom. He caressed each pearl button on my coral blouse between his thumb and forefinger. I loosened his knit shirt and pulled it over his head. The palm of his hand imprinted on the lace of my bra until I turned so that he could reach the hook and eye.

The lights of a passing car searched our nakedness as we tumbled into each other on the unmade bed. His kisses sparked upon my skin like stardust might. My arch swept across his thigh and calf, warming the sole of my foot. The hair on his chest rubbed between my breasts like sand on a beach. His arms, strong and sure, rolled my hips beneath him. I pressed my knees into the flank muscles below his ribcage, making of us a boat riding the sea, buoyed by its depth. We set across the wide, clear, bright, unfathomable ocean, to a place we had never been. I opened to him, and he glided into me, filled me, our breath carrying us on waves.

Spent. Calm. We curled into each other.

CHAPTER 8

SEEDED GLASS

ANDY ASKED ME TO JOIN HIM visiting Jenny in the hospital. At first, she seemed dubious about her brother's companion, but he introduced me as St. Gabe's visitor to the sick and elderly. He joked to Jenny that she fit half the criteria. She laughed, and said she hoped they'd let her out of traction before she grew old and gray.

By week's end, Jenny rallied, and the doctors released her. Andy wanted me to come to a party at his family's home for her return. I hesitated, worried his family would misunderstand—or understand all too well. But Andy wanted me there, so I went.

Situated on the far side of a Minneapolis park, the house was not hard to find. A boulevard of graceful old trees separated a low-rent neighborhood like mine from the cut-stone homes where Andy grew up. I found a parking spot amidst the clutter of cars in front of the house, blotted my lipstick, and stepped out of the car. The two-story house expanded to a third floor under its multi-gabled roof. In the neatly planted front yard, a rubbed bronze post light with seeded glass shade sat ready to illuminate the slate tile pathway at night. Gingerly, I walked up the path and peered through the door's mullioned oval window. I saw Andy among twenty or so merrymakers and held my breath. Should I knock or ring the bell? I wasn't sure anyone would hear either.

Andy turned, saw me, and quickly opened the door. He greeted me warmly, though I resisted his hug. He blinked an acknowledgement of my jitters. "They don't bite," he said.

Jenny waved from the couch. A young man sat at her pillow-propped feet, her right leg in a cast.

Andy followed my eyes across the room. "The beau."

When Andy introduced me to his mother, she extended her hand formally and without a smile, but then her face softened, and she pulled me in for a hug. "Jenny tells us that you came with Andy every day to see her in the hospital. So good of you."

I had feared being seen as a stray cat, but she welcomed me like a lost kitten.

Andy offered to bring me a lemonade. As he made his way to the pitcher, he ran a gauntlet of laughter and slaps on his back. Seeing Andy surrounded by his big family explained much about his down-to-earth personality. One would need a sense of humor and feet on the ground to navigate this bunch.

Andy introduced me to a bulkier semblance of himself. "Meg—from the parish."

"So, this is your sidekick," his brother joked. "Everybody calls this guy *Father*, but what does that make his brothers?"

"Meg, meet Brother Brian."

Brian tapped his tummy like a monk. "Good one." He studied the glass of lemonade in my hand until I thought his stare would crack an ice cube. Was he sizing me up? He threw back a puckish laugh before moving on. "I wouldn't drive with this guy if I were you."

Andy winced, taking the jibe on the chin.

"I think that's his way of saying the family forgives you for the accident," I said.

"I know. I wish somebody would punch me."

Mrs. Vogel called everyone to the dining table for cake. Andy took me by the arm. Such a natural gesture, I didn't stop him, and no one reacted oddly. The crowd passed under a wide archway wall decorated with a painted mural of grapevines. I noticed small, scrolled words at each cluster and asked Andy if they were scripture passages.

"You'd think so with all the Bible verses about vineyards, but nope. When we were little, Mom wrote each of our names on the wall—'so we'd know we belonged here,' she used to say.

I scanned the mural. "Where's your name?"

He pointed to *Alfons*. "By high school, I didn't want to be Alfie anymore, so ... Andy." He pretended offense when I giggled. "Blame it on my mom's favorite uncle."

"Sorry. Truly."

Mrs. Vogel looked up from cutting cake and motioned Andy with a folded hands gesture.

"Time for me to lead a prayer." Andy went to stand next to his sister.

"Let us pray." Gabbing gave way to bowed heads. "Give thanks to the Lord, for he is good. He heals us with his love and tender mercies." Andy choked up, and Mr. Vogel put an arm around his son's shoulder. "Lord, thanks for bringing Jenny back to us."

The brothers and sisters enveloped Jenny, Andy, and their dad. Soft whispers soon erupted into laughter. Mrs. Vogel worked her way over to me.

I swallowed a morsel of cake. "Delicious, Mrs. Vogel."

"Call me Helen," she said. "How long have you been working at the parish, Meg?"

"Since last summer."

She blinked a few times and touched the fingertips on one hand as if calculating. "A few months before Andy started. How's our boy doing?"

"Everybody loves him." Wrong word, for sure. I could feel heat rising in my cheeks. "He's good with people."

"Always was." She untied her apron and folded it over her arm. "We should have known he'd become a priest." Helen looked over at her husband deep in conversation with Andy. "His father expected he would join him in the family business. We kept waiting for Andy to bring a girl home from college, but his arms were loaded with Greek texts instead."

"The study hasn't gone to waste," I hurried to say. "He surprises parishioners with what he calls the 'better translation' of the gospel. We learn a lot."

"Is the parish your first assignment?" She paused. "You're on your way to becoming a nun, right?"

"Not exactly. I was a teacher until strike fever led to my dilemma about staying in the school system." When I told her that I taught kids with developmental delays, she looked at me intently. "We had a 'special' child," she said. Her voice was tinged with sadness.

"Yes. Andy told me."

"He did?" She knit her brow and looked over at her son, then slowly back to me. "Let me show you something." Helen walked over to the mural and pointed to one of the names. "Rudy."

I touched the printing. "I had a little brother, Max, for about two months. Every Christmas, Mom reminds us that we have an angel in heaven. Maybe that's what drew me to teaching these kids."

"I hope you can get back to teaching soon." A heartbeat later, the crow's feet at the corners of her eyes crinkled. She turned to me with a wry smile. "Sometimes God closes one door only to open another." She laid her hand gently on my forearm. "It's nice to know our Andy has someone to ... talk to. It can be a lonely life."

My head swirled. She was saying she trusted me with her son—and trusted God to do the opening and closing of doors. I prayed to be worthy of her trust, and to trust God as she did.

Andy retrieved me a few minutes later. I said I needed to get going. When he walked me to the door, I hugged Helen's eldest son. She waved goodbye to me from the archway mural.

This was the kind of house where the walls seemed to magically expand to fit whoever was there. It was a home. It was the kind of home I wanted to make. Maybe with Andy.

He called a few days after the party. "So, what did you think of the Vogel horde?"

I jumped at the sound of his voice. "They're not so bad. Like you said, they don't bite."

"Brave woman. My brother said he was surprised such pretty ones worked in the parish."

Just as I thought, his brother was wondering if I was going to get his brother in trouble—or if I had. I said, "He must not have seen Ingrid Bergman in *The Bells of St. Mary's*."

"Yeah, but she was a nun."

"Okay, what about *Superstar?* Jesus didn't seem to mind having Mary Magdalene around. And I don't think she was a nun."

"Ah, Meg. Not only pretty but clever." He grew quiet. "My mom liked you a lot."

I thought of the way she rested her hand on my arm. "She's a lovely woman."

"Maybe your family could get to know me somehow?"

"You already met my brother—the U-Haul day. And you met Mom at Christmas. She comes to Mass sometimes at St. Gabe's. You might strike up a chat?"

Andy paused long enough for me to take a breath. "I'd love to see you again, Meg."

My chest tightened. Our kisses, tender as May buds, each time I left the hospital after seeing Jenny. I longed for more. But if I opened to him again, what did that mean?

"You should take your time and let those nasty scratches heal." I didn't mind his scratches; I wanted to kiss every one of them. But I was afraid I might never let him go, and I had to be sure he wanted to hold onto me forever. "I'll still be here next week."

"Whatever you say, Meg. I ... Next week, then."

⁎ ⁐

Father Mack gave Andy time off to stay with his family following the accident. I was thankful for a few days to let my feet meet the earth again. I needed to calm myself before facing the inevitable question of fully entering this relationship freighted with hurdle upon hurdle from Church, family, parishioners, everyone we knew. Or, let him go and savor the few hours no one could hold against us under the circumstances.

As I was leaving to visit my morning schedule of shut-ins, Leo flitted by in the hallway. "Went to see Andy yesterday. Don't know what you did, Meg, but he's a new man."

His words sounded like blessing and absolution at the same time.

Leo must have known, guessed, what happened in the aftermath of his call about the accident. His cryptic acknowledgement that something had changed—in a good way—told me he was willing to withhold judgment about an intimate relationship while we figured out the bigger questions.

I knew what Leo said was true. Yes, Andy was a new man, just as I was a new woman.

On Andy's first day back, my desk phone rang shortly after I arrived at the Parish Center.

"Hey, Meg! Saw you pull in. How are you?"

Andy's voice was pure delight. "Hi yourself! Beautiful day, huh?"

"It is now."

"You're a sweet goofball."

"I'll take that as a compliment." His voice grew softer. "You going to be around later?"

The question was laden with desire. I closed my eyes, breathed deep. "Yes."

"After dinner. I'll come by then."

All day, I looked forward to seeing him. When I visited Millie at the senior housing apartments, she commented on my happy demeanor. I said it must be the good weather. She cocked her head and chuckled noting that her African violets were also perking up for spring.

Andy arrived at my flat with the last rays of sunset at his back. We fell into each other's arms. I kissed the scratch on his cheek, healed from the gash it had been the night of the accident.

We walked to the bedroom hand in hand.

Andy's lips met mine. We undressed. Kisses like fireflies lighting on bare skin. He slipped into me, warm, rich. We rode and rocked long after the sun went down. Spent, our arms and legs jumbled over each other like a mound of moist violets tossed on the bed.

My fingers tapped along the curves of his silly grin as we lay stretched out and relaxed.

He rolled over and caressed the notch at the center of my neck with his thumb. "Thank you," he said. "Wish I didn't have to go."

The sound of bricks came crashing down. "You'll always have to go, won't you?"

"For now, Meg, yes. It's the best I can do."

"I wish I didn't understand."

"Do you understand it's to protect you? The guys will get suspicious if I'm out all night." Andy raised himself up on one elbow. "Relationships take time, Meg. And we've got more to work through than most. You do know I want to work things out with you, don't you?"

"Oh, Andy, I needed to hear you say that." I held him close. Bought one more minute.

⁐ ⁐

Mother Nature turned out to be our first big hurdle. When Jake and I were engaged, I had tried an IUD. After a week of excruciating cramps, I was desperate for the doctor to remove it. Jake was not thrilled. Some of my friends were on the Pill, but I rarely took an aspirin. I didn't want to overhaul my whole hormonal system for the one day a week Jake's buddy lent us his apartment. When I suggested Natural Family Planning, Jake said that's how his younger brother was born unexpectedly. I didn't convince him that NFP had come a long way since the old Rhythm Method. He wore rubbers for backup and complained, while I charted temps and checked tackiness of my cervical mucus. The beginning of the end.

Andy joked about having to follow his own rules given the Church teaching on birth control. Never mind the teaching about premarital sex—and priestly taboos. We found ways to be affectionate short of making love on the iffy days of my cycle. Walks along the marshy footpath—at dusk, so no one would recognize us. Back rubs. Watching *All in the Family*.

Some nights, we read to each other. Andy lay on his back with knees bent while I couched myself resting against his thighs. He recited verses from the *Song of Solomon*:

> *As a lily among brambles,*
> *So is my Love among other women.*

CANDLEWOOD

And I shared Khalil Gibran's poetry:

Let there be spaces in your togetherness,
And let the winds of the heavens dance between you.

The chair in my office became Andy's late afternoon landing pad. "Up for a listen to some homily ideas?" Since Andy studied the original Greek, he dove deep into the meaning behind the words of Scripture. He looked to me for ways of bringing the Word into people's everyday lives. I could see it would be hard for him to leave behind the kind of work he relished.

Only half joking, I said, "You know, if you were a Lutheran minister, I could be mending socks by the fire while you prepared your homilies."

He turned red as a beet at my challenge.

Just then, Father Mack made a surprise appearance in the hallway. "Now, Andy, don't take up too much of Meg's time," he said. "She's got work to do."

Andy quickly folded his papers and left.

I didn't know how much of our conversation the pastor heard.

After church one Sunday, Mom had said, "Father Andy seems nice. He's a lot more down to earth than your pastor, Father Mack. There's something false about that man."

My mom had a knack for reading people. We needed to be wary. ෴

Meeting at my flat gave us a modicum of privacy. Day by day, we shared our stories. I wanted to give Andy the good parts first, or at least the not-so-bad parts, provide enough cushion to absorb the rest later.

We discovered common ground with dads who worked in the food business. Andy's dad marked the third generation of sauerkraut-makers in the family. A big contract for condiments at State Fair helped put the kids through college. He told me about his crazy uncle who spilled kraut juice all over the shop floor one day. His dad heckled the klutzy man into taking a bath in the stuff to teach him a lesson.

I told Andy about summertime forays to my dad's grocery, only a block from our house. He'd let us kids spend a few minutes in the meat cooler on hot days, then lure us out with nickels for the Coke machine. The grocery lost out to supermarkets in the 1960s.

Bankruptcy followed on the heels of my parents' divorce. Less happy memories were harder to tell. Mom moved Eddie and me from Minneapolis back to her hometown of Shady Bluff, where she hoped her bookkeeper's salary would go further. Andy was aware of the drinking problem my brother inherited from Dad, but I said nothing about Eddie's harrowing coming out.

One evening in early June, I put on Fleetwood Mac's newish album, *Rumours*, and waited for Andy. I had put off asking him why he had become a priest, but the question was overdue. I needed to understand. When he arrived, I opened the fridge and poured a glass of Lancers for each of us. From the kitchen, I asked as casually as I could, "Whatever got you thinking about the priesthood?" I turned down the volume on the hi-fi and sat next to Andy on the couch.

"It wasn't much on my mind," he said, "beyond the usual way boys in Catholic school are encouraged to think about it."

I remembered the pages pasted on the inside cover of my schoolbooks: *Is God calling you to be a priest? Do you have a vocation to religious life as a sister?* I asked Andy if his school did the same.

"The question was everywhere," he said. "We were supposed to listen for God's whisper. If it was meant to be, we believed we'd get a sign."

"And did you get a sign?"

"My 8th grade teacher kept me after class one day. I'd gotten in a fight at noon with another kid. Last thing I expected Sister Mara to say was that I should think about being a priest. She said it was brave the way I stuck up for a 6th grader who was bullied by my classmate. That's what the fight was about. That's when I started thinking about priesthood."

"Sounds like she was giving you the best compliment she could. Were you taught like me that a 'calling' is a privilege? From kindergarten on, I learned that priests, and nuns, serve a higher purpose than the everyday lives of other people."

Andy laughed. "I'm not a very good example of priests being above anybody else."

"I wanted to be a nun—in 2nd grade. I had a fabulous teacher that year. Wanted to be just like her. But I got over it with my 3rd grade teacher." I rolled my eyes.

"Did your mom encourage you one way or the other?"

"I loved my dollies, so let's just say Mom never wrapped rosary beads around my waist. By the time I realized I could be a teacher—and have a family—done deal." I took a sip of wine and remembered the make-believe house I played in with a make-believe happy family.

"Thoughts about being a priest faded fast in high school. But then, my girlfriend went to Homecoming with someone else rather than waiting for me to ask her. I took it as a 'sign' from God that I should think again about being a priest."

"How long did you wait to ask her?"

Andy coughed. "I guess I could have asked sooner."

"Were you playing Russian roulette with God?"

"You know, when people start telling you that you should be a priest, you start thinking that maybe you should. How do you know for sure?"

Andy told me that his parents took their family to Christmas Day Mass at St. Gabriel's every year. They liked the Gothic grandeur and old-fashioned holiday decorations more than the austerity at their parish. "Junior year of college," he said, "the priest gave a homily about his time as a missionary—the hovels where children lived, and how he tried to help them. It sounded heroic, meaningful. Better than chopping cabbages for sauerkraut the rest of my life. I decided to give it a go. Figured it must be the right decision when the Order of Clement accepted me."

"So, it came down to a decision between God and cabbage?"

Andy didn't laugh. "More like between God the Father and my dad."

I took his hand. "You would have been good at whatever you did. And God would have blessed you." I chuckled. "Bet you would have been the best cabbage-chopper for miles around."

"Maybe." His laugh faded. "But, you see, I didn't want to chop cabbage."

≈ ∞

One June night, Andy stayed longer. The 10 o'clock news carried a story about a wedding half-way across the world. Jordan's King Hussein had married the American daughter of Pan Am's CEO. I was intrigued when bagpipers paraded with the army; Andy was riveted to see the King and his bride, Queen Noor, cut their gigantic cake with a sword.

On his way out the door, he asked me to come to his brother Pete's art show at a storefront gallery in St. Paul.

"Don't you think your family will get suspicious if you bring me around so much?"

Andy looked askance. "Just thought it'd be nice to have a few people there for him. I asked Leo yesterday."

"Will there be cake?" As if that mattered.

"Of course," Andy grinned, "and swords."

"Okay. If you're trying to rustle up a crowd for him, I could ask Eddie and Hank."

Andy's eyes twinkled. "Now who's trying to ease family into the picture?"

I demurred. "Only occurred to me because they live in St. Paul."

"Cool. Love to see them again, someplace other than the back of a U-Haul."

I showed up at Eddie and Hank's in time for brunch before heading to the art show. Daisy the cat snuck outside when Eddie opened the door. I promptly scooped her up. "Oh, no you don't. Your wandering days are over, milady."

At the restaurant, Hank side-eyed me. "Since when do priests shill for art?"

"Andy, I mean Father Andy, only wanted to drum up a crowd for his brother. Okay, and maybe rustle up some business for him."

"Don't priests leave their families behind when they go off to seminary?" asked Hank.

"Not exactly," I said. "Priests don't cut their ties or live on another planet after ordination."

"Could've fooled me," said Hank. "I thought they gave up families exactly so they could live on another planet. Rabbis and ministers have families to keep their feet on the ground, but not those Holy Romans."

I crunched a slice of bacon. "You're Jewish. I don't understand a lot of your traditions." I turned my attention to Eddie. "Didn't you go on a weekend in 8th grade to learn about the priesthood? Mom jabbered the whole time about you becoming a priest."

"No shit," said Eddie. "Mom pestered me a lot, but I doubt God would have been happy."

Hank dipped toast in the runny yolk of his poached egg. "Nobody's God is fond of fags."

"Hey, you guys believe God made you, right? And God doesn't make mistakes, right? Churchy people may not understand you, but God does."

Hank raised his mimosa to me. "Here's to Meg, a true believer. *L'chaim.*"

"Can we go now?" asked Eddie.

A black-and-white poster hung in the window of the small gallery advertising the art show, Getting Around. The room was abuzz with a lively crowd when we arrived. Only a few members of the Vogel family.

I spotted Leo inspecting an array of line drawings—retro cars, double-decker busses, a pair of bulbous clown shoes, stilettos, and other means of "getting around." He hailed me over, and I introduced Eddie and Hank. Andy soon joined us, greeting my brother and Hank like he'd known them for ages. Leo gave me a puzzled glance, but I didn't try to explain.

Andy corralled his brother, Pete, the unlikely Rembrandt in the family—looked like a Marlboro Man who'd be more at home with spurs than a fine-tip pen.

"What do you think of my brother's doodles?"

"This is good stuff," I replied. "Is he a perfectionist about everything?"

"Don't answer that," said Pete.

"Terrific drawings. Where did you learn to do this kind of art?"

"In school, of course." Needling Andy, he added, "*Some of us have talent.*"

"Hey, buddy, you can stop with the chops now. What's Meg going to think?"

Whatever Pete presumed about us, he seemed more preoccupied with the show.

Eddie took me aside as we left. "Is there anything you want to tell me, Sis? The way *'Andy, I mean Father Andy'* looks at you … if he wasn't a priest …"

I wanted to share the happy part, but I couldn't tell anyone, not even my best friend Eileen. I kept putting her off every time she begged to meet my mystery man. "I don't know what you mean, Eddie. I work with him, same as with Father Leo."

"Not the same as Father Leo. No worries there. My guess is he's like Hank and me." Eddie put his hands on my shoulders. "Listen, I wouldn't mind sharing black sheep honors with you."

"Your place is secure."

⅛ ⅜

Andy arrived earlier than expected on the dewy night of the Summer Solstice. I ran to the door, comb in hand, my hair damp from the shower. He swung me round and teased the comb from my grip. "Let me play with your hair." We sat on the gray and ivory tufted Danish rug in the living room as he alternately tugged on snarls or tickled me behind the ears. After a while, it was all long strokes. He put down the comb and nuzzled smooth strands. "Smells like a forest."

Breezes through the open window carried the sound of neighbor kids playing outside. I rubbed my back against his chest. Hairy. Must have unbuttoned his shirt.

He inched his hands down my tee, swept them underneath.

When he touched my breasts, familiar waves rushed through my body. But it was an "iffy" day. Not that it made any sense to follow Catholic rules on contraception while breaking every rule in the book about Andy's priestly vows.

"I want to make love with you, but … not today."

He sighed and released his legs from around me. Disappointed fingers crawled out from beneath my tee.

I turned full around. "What if I got pregnant?" My jaw tightened. We'd been so careful, but tonight? If we'd had a glass of wine? Been a little less careful? It would have been so easy. "Andy, I couldn't, you know … even though it's legal now."

"No, course not." He stared at the floor. "I would do the right thing."

A chill went down my spine. "Do the right thing? Big of you."

He buttoned his shirt.

"We're doing everything backwards, Andy. Maybe we should wait. Until the rules change."

He looked at me with big ox eyes. "You dream dreams, Meg. Nothing's going to change in the Church any time soon."

I didn't want to believe him. "How can things *not* change when so many priests are leaving? People have talked about changing the rule for years."

Worlds apart, though we sat mere inches from each other. The wooden window blinds slapped against the sash, cutting the silence between us.

"I can't give you a regular courtship. Wish I could. I want to spend time with you, be with you. Figure things out."

"Is there that much to figure out?" My voice was barely a whisper.

Andy lifted my chin to make me look at him. "It's not about you, Meg. Oh, *Chandelle*, my little candle. So bright. You're as true as they come. But me? I already made one commitment. If I leave, there's no turning back. I need to be sure."

Chandelle. The name he called me the first time we tread the edge of the precipice one early spring day months ago. If only my little candle could light the dark ages of tradition.

I took Andy's hand and stretched the silver links on his wristwatch. "Time ... to figure things out. Do the dance backwards." The watchband snapped. "That's what you're asking?"

He nodded and kissed my shoulder.

I should have walked away months ago. I tried. But I gave myself to this man. In the no-matter-what kind of way. We had to figure things out. If I left now, we'd never know if we might have made it. I ran my fingers through the thatch of hair that always fell on his forehead. "I want to dance with you."

CHAPTER 9

TWISTER

THOUGH A STEADY PARADE OF priests left to marry in the years after Vatican Council II ended in 1965, I only knew one in a fix like mine and Andy's. Father Jim was a family friend, one of the few adults who knew how to talk to kids as if they were people. He came to birthdays when he could, before his bishop shipped him to Rochester. Some said to help with chaplaincy services at Mayo Clinic in addition to parish duties, but others wagged about getting him away from "that woman." A floozy? Or someone like me? He remained a priest to this day. What happened? How did they handle it?

Rochester was at least a two-hour drive, but worth it to get some guidance. I called Father Jim about visiting. He was delighted to hear from me, and we set up the first Saturday in July. As I drove south, sun gave way to clouds and gathering storm gusts buffeted my VW Bug.

Father Jim, full of smiles and welcome, ushered me into the rectory. He wanted to hear all my news. Though he still sent cards for my birthday, I hadn't seen him in the six years since Mom took us to Minneapolis for the twenty-fifth anniversary of his ordination—just before he got transferred. High school and college years went fast. I wasn't sure if Mom told him about Eddie. When I hemmed and hawed about my brother, he stopped me. "It's okay, Meg. Your mom wrote me a long letter about Eddie, his drinking—and the gay thing. Is that what brought you here? I can tell something's on your mind."

Knowing me from childhood, I could never put anything past Father Jim. "It's not about Eddie. He's great. I think you'd enjoy his—I don't know what to call him—his 'friend,' Hank."

He patted my hand. "It's good to have someone to care about who cares about you."

I held back hot, stinging tears. Bad idea to come.

Father Jim did a double-take. He stood up abruptly. "I'm famished. What about you?" We went into the gray-paneled kitchen, and he pointed to where I could find plates and silverware. "Go set the table. I'll heat things up in the microwave. A generous parishioner said the rectory 'had to have one.' Neat appliance." On the radio, we heard the weatherman cut in for a tornado watch. "Must be summer," said Father Jim. He appraised the darkening clouds. "Could be a twister."

I escaped into the dining room and dabbed my eyes. The lines I practiced explaining things to him seemed awkward and stilted.

Father Jim brought meatloaf and mashed potatoes to the table. "Ouch, hot." He jabbered about Rochester, how different it was from Minneapolis. A small town with a huge hospital. He asked about my work in the parish. I regaled him with stories about the more colorful personalities among the shut-ins I visited and described Father Mack and Leo—and how Ruth and I irked old Father Cronin. It seemed easier to swap war stories … and abandon my plan to tell him about Andy.

We were doing dishes when a call came in. Father Jim dried his hands as he held the phone between cheek and shoulder. "Gotta go, Meg. Sounds like Mrs. McCaffery isn't going to make it through the night. Ach, she was telling jokes yesterday— today, Last Rites." He looked at me searchingly. "Can you stay a little longer?"

Though ready to turn tail and drive home, mission derailed, I agreed to stay.

"Good. But just in case this storm turns into something more, I don't want you to be alone." He made a quick call.

We drove to a saltbox house with a tidy garden in a residential neighborhood a few miles from the rectory. A slightly plump woman with upswept light brown hair came to the door. "Carol, this is the young woman I told you about from back home. She's come all this way. Can you keep her company for a little while? I'm off to banish the devil for Mrs. McCaffery."

"Of course, Jim. On with you now. You don't want to keep the devil waiting." She smiled warmly. "Ah, Meg. So glad to meet you. Come in."

Carol led me into a cozy kitchen with a bistro table and chairs. "Tea or coffee? Pie?"

Framed photos covered the striped wallpaper—Father Jim from earlier years, many of them with young Black children.

"Did you know Father Jim in Minneapolis?" I asked. "Our family used to see him more often before he transferred here. I was a kid when he got involved in civil rights. Mom sent him what money she could as if his Black parish was a foreign mission."

"Yes, we met in the Twin Cities. He needed a secretary, an assistant—somebody who could be a Jill of all trades to help him with the dozens of projects he started. Never met such a workaholic in my whole life. He's still like that. No wonder he had a heart attack last year."

"We didn't hear about a heart attack. Is he okay? He seems himself." Gradually, it sank in how long she'd known Father Jim. It dawned on me that this must be the rumored paramour. Hardly the hotsy-totsy people made of her.

"He's slowing down a bit, but fine. More of a spasm than a full-blown heart attack, thank God. Thought he had indigestion. The doctor advised exercise, less salt, and quiet time."

I asked her to tell me about the photos.

CANDLEWOOD

Carol brightened, bringing each one to life. "This is Callie on First Communion Day. She ran up to Jim after Mass, a ball of excitement. She told him, 'Jesus tastes like plastic, just like my brother said.' Jim roared."

We returned to the table to finish our pie. I scanned the wall of photos again. "You've been with him a long time."

Carol stirred her coffee. "Yes. I'm *that* woman."

I apologized. "Rumors, you know." I could see myself in her. She cared about Father Jim the way I cared about Andy. "Was it very hard for you?"

"At first, terrible. The feelings crept up on us before we realized what was happening. We both took it for granted that priests didn't fall in love. But there we were. He'd just gotten back from marching in Selma. Saw men beaten for the right to vote, beaten for the color of their skin. Nothing made sense anymore—except maybe loving someone."

Clouds were gathering and the wind picked up. "Why didn't you marry?"

A wan smile came over her face. "Not as easy as it sounds. Jim fought discrimination, especially redlining, for the people in his neighborhood. Parishioners, people he knew, who worked hard and saved their money got shut out of mortgages and insurance because banks charged them so much more than market rate. But when Jim accompanied them, the banks backed down. As a priest, he could do those sorts of things."

"But what about you?"

The brightness left her eyes. "The dilemma of two people seemed trivial compared to the hurt we saw around us."

Her words sounded noble, but prickles ran down my back listening to her. "Not fair."

"Maybe not, but practical. Jim was middle-aged. He'd been a priest most of his life. I had to let him figure it out. For myself, I was past prime time to start a family.

I saw the logic. "So, you compromised."

"Improvised."

A couple of hours had passed, and the wind gusts were getting stronger. Father Jim dashed into the house. "We'd better get you on your way, Meg. The radio's reporting flash floods. You don't want to get stranded."

He gave Carol a peck on the cheek, and I hopped into the car. "Thanks for letting me meet Carol," I said. "I sometimes wondered if the rumors were true."

His brow held a question. "Don't worry," I said. "I believed you when you said it's good to have someone to care about who cares about you."

"And what about you, sweetheart? Do you have someone?"

My stomach flipped. It was now or never. "Andy," I said. "His name is Andy."

"So … am I going to have to pry this out of you after you came all this way?"

We were nearly back to the rectory. "I didn't tell you about all the priests at the parish."

A flash of understanding crossed his face, and he shook his head. "Oh, Meggins. That's what your dad called you when you were little. Guess he's not much help to you these days." We turned into the driveway. "Falling in love with a priest is not a cross I would wish on anyone."

"But what about you and Carol?"

"Love is a wonderful thing." He pulled up the hand brake. "But hiding your love, no. I feel guilty every day that I can't give Carol the life she deserves. Or God what he asks of me."

"I want to shout our love to the world."

Father Jim untwisted the St. Christopher medal from the dashboard mirror. "Don't ever give up on love, whatever you do. But don't give up on your dreams either, Meg. Stay true to yourself, alone or together." He handed me the medal. "Here, this guy will lead you home."

On the way out of town, I saw a line of trees along the highway cut down in half by straight-line winds. Sheared of their leafy limbs like sheep, shorn.

৪০ ৫৪

Andy was eager to hear about my visit to Rochester. We sat in my kitchen the next day drinking lemonade. I decided not to tell him about Carol. We had to write our own story.

"Not everybody sees priests as regular guys coming from regular families," he said. "Hate the pedestal thing."

"Father Jim worked a lot with civil rights," I said. "Joined the march to Selma."

"Rough times that changed history," said Andy. "He's a good man, an *homme de bien*."

"Andy, what have you been most proud of doing so far?" He wasn't a great preacher but looked for ways to quietly help people. I respected his low-key approach.

"Once upon a time, when I worked at a *Le Pont* community for Algerian refugees in Marseille ..."

I refilled his lemonade. "And you speak French every chance you get."

"*Merci.*" He leaned his elbows on his knees, holding his glass intently. "There was this older, disheveled man, Louie. If I only pretended to be listening to the same story he told *every single day*, he would poke me in the chest and say in the best English he could manage, 'Father Andy, listen—look me—I talk you!' He was right." Andy sat up. "Louie taught me everything I know about paying attention. It's important to pay attention to the people around us, especially when we don't want to."

I unhooked the spider plant from its perch in the big kitchen window and took it to the sink for watering. "Most of the elderly women I visit say they wish their sons and daughters came by more often." I removed the plant from its macrame holder, trimmed dying leaves, and misted it. "I try to console them, but all I can offer is someone who's being paid to pay attention to them. I want to do better."

"You do great, Meg. When I cover some of the First Friday visits for Father Cronin, the gray-hairs talk about you glowingly. You care, and they feel it." He rehung the plant in the window for me.

"What did you call that place—*Le Pont?* What does it mean?"

"*Le Pont* means 'The Bridge'—we were trying to bridge the gap between our differences. Laypeople and usually a priest or sister lived in communities with several migrant families—like big extended families."

I wondered if Andy and I could make that kind of home, a bigger family. Would it be so hard to blend our own family with the larger world?

Andy told me something else that happened in Marseille—about a young woman who volunteered at *Le Pont.* "It took a while before I got that she *liked* me," he said. "I didn't know what to do about it."

I drew back. "And how did you feel about her? Did you *like* the woman?"

"I was a wreck," he said. "The Clems moved me to a high school in Canada—to teach French—ha." He paused. "I don't tell many people this, Meg, but I had to see a psychologist. It's easy not to feel things in seminary with only men around, so I believed I had 'the grace' as they called it. Then, plunk."

"You're worrying me, Andy. You didn't expect to leave sexual feelings at the door when you became a priest, did you?"

"I thought that's what we were supposed to do. They assured us in seminary God would give us the grace to overcome those kinds of feelings."

"Andy, feelings are part of being human. You wouldn't be human if you didn't feel anything. Doesn't God give us grace to understand our feelings—and what to do about them." I edged closer to him. "Isn't that what we're trying to figure out?"

Andy got up and went into the kitchen. He rinsed his glass of lemonade. "I'm telling you these things because I need you to know I'm still working on stuff. Can you deal with that?"

Andy was being bluntly honest with me. I groped for a response. "Did therapy help?"

"Yeah, it did. I had a lot to learn." He told me about the time his sister got married, and his seminary rector forbade him to stay for the reception. "Too many long-hairs." His voice boomed, "They warn you about the devil putting women in your path as a temptation." He twisted a strand of my hair.

I dried his glass. "I need to ask you, Andy—am I a flirtation … a temptation?"

"No. The woman in France may have opened my eyes, but you … it's different." He wrapped his arms around me. "You've opened my heart, Meg. You … are a ray of light."

I wanted everything to be settled, but mostly I wanted him to be sure. Deep down, I knew he needed time, despite being sure myself.

I kissed his neck and said with as much courage as I could scrape together, "Yes, Andy. I can deal with that."

My head told me Andy was sincerely searching for balance. But the queasiness in my stomach was not from the lemonade.

80 CB

I ate breakfast on the Fourth of July lamenting Andy's "priest on duty" assignment that day—meaning no fireworks for us. But as I buttered my toast, he called.

"Meg, I've got an emergency here." The rill in his voice belied a joke.

"And that would be …?"

"Two little ragamuffins need help decorating their bikes for the parade." I heard high-pitched shrieks in the background. I imagined Andy making funny faces at them.

"Where are you?"

"Bound and tied at the usual place. Can you get over here—and bring crepe paper?"

Hmm, ragamuffins—and their bikes—at the Parish Center. I made a quick stop at the dime store for red, white, and blue crepe paper. Also, streamers, flags, and balloons. When I arrived at the scene, Andy was pulling a quarter from behind a little girl's ear. He grinned and introduced me.

Betty asked, "Can you help Father Andy? He doesn't know how to decorate a bike.'"

Lars said, "Mom would've helped us, but she had to go to work." He dug streamers out of my bag. "Dad helped us last year, but he don't live with us no more."

I showed the kids how to weave crinkled crepe paper between their bike spokes. They outdid each other vying for the best place to put flags and balloons.

"Let's see how they ride," said Andy.

The kids, all smiles, showed off their creations.

"Let's get this show on the road," I said. The parade was soon to begin in front of St. Gabe's. I told Andy that Ruth, Beth, and I had volunteered to hand out ice cream and Josie's famous snickerdoodles at the parade—and to judge the bikes.

Andy whispered to me, "Be sure our ragamuffins win."

I winked. "Of course they'll win, pardner. They're the best."

When Andy and I made love a few days later, I ached with longing to have children with this man. "You'd be a good dad."

He stroked my cheek. "And you'd be the best mom." His forehead creased. "I wish the Church made it easier, Meg. Wish I could be *dad* and *Padre*."

"It's my struggle, too, Andy."

He kissed my shoulder. "If you want to jump ship, I wouldn't blame you."

I was not a gambler by nature, but I had rolled the dice. "You're a good Padre, Andy, but you'd also be a good dad. Just wanted you to know that."

After he left, I turned on the news. The local station carried footage of a massive flood in Rochester. Hundreds of people evacuated, homes devastated. I called Father Jim. He assured me he was okay but couldn't talk long. Had to find milk for hungry kids rescued from homes floating on the river. I offered to bring help, but he said the National Guard was telling folks to stay away. He and Carol and dozens of workers were turning the school into a makeshift shelter.

The dog days of summer brought plenty of storms our way, but nothing like the floods in Rochester. Andy and I enlisted a crew to send provisions for flood victims. It felt good to do something useful, more worthy of worry than the state of our relationship.

CHAPTER 10

SPITTLE AND MUD

TEACHING SEEMED LIKE A LIFETIME ago, but it was the obvious path out of the parish. I needed breathing space. The new school year was less than a month away and I champed at the bit. I had hoped to hear from my old department head by now. Although she hadn't been able to offer me a summer school position when I talked to her last spring, she sounded encouraging for fall. I wanted terra firma—known and familiar ground. I loved Andy, but not sinking with him into the quicksand of indecision. My students gave me a sense of purpose and possibility. I made the call to beg for a way back to teaching.

"Oh, Meg, why didn't you contact me sooner? As of last week, we're fully staffed."

She asked how I was, and I lied. Told her I missed the kids. That much was true.

With Shady Bluff a no-go, I applied in the Twin Cities. St. Paul needed teachers for students with physical handicaps, but I was only licensed to teach students with intellectual disabilities or developmental delays. Minneapolis offered me a substitute spot, but I needed a permanent landing pad.

My old supervisor called back a few days later. "Stay in touch, Meg," she said. "Remember Mrs. Olson? She's decided to retire, so I may need you for the second semester."

I hung onto her news like a branch in quicksand.

CANDLEWOOD

Another Vogel family gathering was coming up in August, this time at the clan's lake cottage. Andy invited me, but I put him off. He seemed blind to the stakes. Didn't he understand what it meant for a man, any man, to bring a woman around to get to know the family—for a whole weekend at their home away from home? No one did that unless he was darn serious about a relationship. Andy was still a priest—for him to bring me around tripled the ante. We had thrashed out the seriousness of our relationship between ourselves, but he kept telling me he needed more time to go public. Was the lake gathering going to be the occasion? I wish he would clue me in.

Maybe after Beth's spaghetti dinner Thursday night.

Spaghetti dinners at Shalom House had grown famous, largely due to Beth's killer tomato sauce. Not quite a sorority, the young women of Shalom House met through Campus Ministry activities and decided to set up a residence together. A few, like Beth, stayed on after graduation to save a little money. She said her roommates wanted to give their old Victorian a name and came up with "Shalom House" as a blessing for those coming and going. They often hosted Campus Ministry events. A modicum of wine and beer added to the convivial scene.

Before accepting Beth's invitation to the dinner, I checked with her about smarmy Father Darren's attendance. I didn't want to chance another run-in with him. She puzzled about my question, but the coast was clear.

Andy ducked into my office late Wednesday afternoon. "You're going to the spaghetti dinner at Shalom, right?" he asked. "Should be good. Bruce is a great storyteller."

"Wouldn't miss it." Father Bruce Jensen, an Order of Clement priest recently back from sabbatical in the Holy Land was slated to expound on New Testament miracle stories.

I looked forward to a good dinner and interesting company—and, inviting Andy over afterwards to talk about *our* story, and hope for a miracle.

Campus Ministry guests sat around the table as Father Bruce retold the biblical stories in a way I hadn't heard before. He described Jesus healing the whole person—not only their limp or sore or blindness—but also their spirit, past wounds, and present barriers. Father Bruce said that listening, visiting, saying a kind word—reaching out to the people in our lives and parishes and communities—was following the example of Jesus. He opened fresh eyes to our work.

I nudged Andy. "Like the man at *Le Pont* who bugged you to pay attention to him?"

"Bugging me always works," he said.

"I'll keep that in mind."

The last story Father Bruce told was about healing the blind man. "Jesus mixed his spittle with the dust of the earth, then spread the mud on the eyes of the blind man. When the man washed the mixture from his eyes, he could see."

Father Bruce compared the healing to the creation story. God made man from mud and breathed life into him. Jesus made a new creation, healing our broken and blind spots.

Mud. Like the flour I mixed with water on Holy Thursday to make Communion wafers. I wondered then if God might be kneading Andy and me into something new.

Lord, are we blind or is the Church blind to us? What kind of new creation are we?

Everyone milled about in the living room after dinner, and Andy found his way to my side. He slung his arm around my shoulder as if it was the most natural thing in the world. I loved the warm weight of it, but worried about the appearance. I was trying hard to be discreet on all fronts. Andy—he seemed unconcerned. He would take my arm, hang out in my office, look for me after Mass—and now resting his arm around me in plain sight. Strangely, no one seemed to notice. Or if they did, no one looked askance. Were they also trying to be discreet?

I quietly asked Andy if he wanted to come over later.

"Can't," he said. "We're having a reception for Bruce at the rectory. Maybe tomorrow."

I felt my cheeks grow hot. Perhaps it was the wine. Andy dropped his arm from around my shoulder. Tomorrow seemed a long time away.

ⅎ ⅏

I overslept Friday morning after the big dinner for Father Bruce. No time to look for Andy. I hurried to the "priest on duty" office to request the Communion wafers needed for the day's visits to homebound parishioners.

Leo laughed at my yawn. "Running a quart low this morning? Too much spaghetti?"

In no mood for pleasantries, much less probes, I pointed to my watch. "Need five today."

Leo quickly obliged, returning from the chapel with five consecrated hosts.

Lucille headed my list. An Army nurse in her day, she not-so-patiently instructed me how to support her head while she took a sip of water after Communion so that Jesus could dissolve on her tongue without choking her.

My last call of the day was Millie. Her African violets drooped in a dark corner. She asked me to move them to the windowsill to get more sunlight. When she folded her hands to let me know she was ready to receive the Lord, we prayed:

The Lord is my shepherd…
Though I walk in the valley of the shadow of death,
I will fear no evil…

ꗋ ꗞ

Since Andy didn't bother leaving a message about coming to my flat or not, Friday evening I joined Eileen and Sheila for the summer feel-good movie, *Grease*. I had just gotten home when Mom called in a panic. Her voice came in gasps. "Eddie. Hank found him. Out cold in the basement. Can you get over there?"

Why hadn't I gone out for burgers after the movie? Maybe I would have missed this call. How many times did I need to clean up after my brother?

Eddie's last partner got him into rehab years ago. Mom and I, everybody, hoped for the best. When they broke up, I contacted a couple of his friends. We rotated asking Eddie to dinner and making casual calls. "Checking up on me, huh?" he'd say.

True, but necessary.

When Eddie asked me to go with him one night to the "fag bar" as he called it, I went. I knew it was a test. Did I love my brother enough to be seen with him in this place? Did I really want to know him, or did I only want to check up on him?

At the bar, I watched as men in make-up fawned over other men in tight jeans. Pretty boys with gold chains leaned against the wall where an arrow pointed to the restroom. Reminded me of a college bar we called the "meet market," fully knowing it was a "meat market," flesh for sale. The only difference, college women smeared in lipstick.

Eddie had introduced me to his drinking buddies that night. Howdy-dos and small talk. One of them told a wildly coarse joke. When I laughed nervously, he said, "She's blushing!"

"She's led a sheltered life," said Eddie. An inside joke—we grew up under the same roof.

Eddie's world. He wanted me to see it. He wanted me to understand. To accept. To not judge, not run away. To know him—and love him anyway.

I loved him anyway. But it wasn't enough. The hard drinking had started again. Phone calls went unanswered.

Then, Eddie met Hank. Mom and I dared hope again. Eddie did get his act together, enough for them to find a house in St. Paul and live happily ever after.

Until Mom's call—Saturday night at 10:56 p.m. I sped and got there by 11:30 p.m.

Hank led me down the basement steps. Furrows creased his forehead, his voice monotone. "Thought Eddie left early this morning. Didn't see him. Worried when he didn't come home, but he's been hanging out at the bars again. Came down to the basement for a lightbulb. Oh, Meg, he was here all the time." Hank broke into sobs. "Couldn't wake him. Called your ma. Thank God you came. I'm so scared."

My brother lay in a pool of his own vomit. Pale as a ghost in a dark corner. Drunk. Drenched in sweat.

Eddie finally came-to after a few pinches and slaps. I sat propped against the basement wall, cradling his head to one side and draping his arm behind my neck so he wouldn't choke— exactly as Lucille taught me. I thanked God for Army nurses.

As much as we tried, Hank and I couldn't keep Eddie awake. His eyes kept drooping to half-mast. "Call emergency— or we're going to lose him," I said.

Hank went upstairs to call for help. He returned with an old blanket to cover Eddie's clammy skin and cloths to wipe up the puke. I kept patting Eddie's hand, trying to wake him.

The EMS team banged on the door, slid the stretcher down the basement stairwell, and bundled my big brother like he was a little boy. One of them said, "It's good you called." They took

Eddie to the ER. We followed, streetlights rolling like cold snowballs in summer.

In the hospital waiting room, Hank and I took turns trying to rest while the other drank coffee and ate Kit-Kat bars. By early morning, Eddie was in stable enough condition to nod "Yes" when the doctor offered him in-patient rehab treatment. My brother's bloodshot eyes winced, and he moved in a shaky slow-mo. The alcohol and who-knows-what-else emitted stench through his pores.

The Lord is my shepherd—though I walk through the shadow of death. ...

Lord, don't let him die.

The nurse admitted him to detox in the hospital. From there, he'd move to the program in a few days. Hank and I hugged our bedraggled Eddie and left.

When Mom called me Saturday morning, I told her Eddie was sleeping it off and not to worry—all I could manage of the truth. He had done so well for more than a year. What went wrong? I went back to bed. I needed to gather my wits.

By Sunday, I was ready to tell Andy what was going on. I needed to feel his strength and borrow some of it. But Andy wasn't at the 10:00 a.m. Mass. I'd forgotten he was going out on the circuit, pitching Le Pont communities to raise funds. I tried calling his room in case he hadn't left yet, but only got the answering machine. His recorded voice said to leave a message, but I didn't want to talk to a machine.

On Monday morning, I contacted the upholstery shop where Eddie worked to tell them he was sick and wouldn't be coming in. Mr. Feinstein, the owner, answered the phone. I met him a couple of times when I picked Eddie up after work. "Is this his sister?" he asked.

"Yes, it's Meg."

"Your brother's been missing a lot of work lately. Don't bullshit me about why. I told him he wouldn't have a job if he didn't get help."

I realized Eddie had been sinking a while. "He's worried about starting treatment," I said. "It's a month-long program." I was the one worried he'd lose his job if he took off the time.

"A month? *Oy vey.* So ... tell him he's got to do the program. He's my best stitcher, and I don't want to lose him— but I can't afford taking his crap either. Tell him that from me, hear?"

The hospital allowed me a short visit with Eddie. He was revived enough to chuckle when I told him about the conversation with Mr. Feinstein. "Gotta love the man, don't ya?"

"Eddie," I said, "you're a good guy and you've got a lot going for you. People like you a lot. Hank more than likes you. Heck, Mr. Feinstein is holding your job! Get well, will you?"

"I'll try, Kitten. I'll really try. Does Ma know what happened?"

"Mom knows you got real sick drunk, but that's all she knows."

Eddie pleaded, "Don't tell her where I am, please?"

"She'll want to see you soon." I didn't tell him she was calling me morning, noon, and night, wretched with worry over her firstborn. Like I could do anything about it. I suggested she come with me to an Al-Anon meeting like we used to, but she only wept, "What good would that do? Nothing ever helps."

Eddie bargained for time before seeing Mom. "Maybe next week."

"All right, Eddie. I'll do what I can. Concentrate on getting well." We hugged at the door where I turned in my visitor badge. A nurse came to take Eddie back. They'd move him to the rehab facility the next day, where he'd start the long-haul. I clenched and unclenched my hand on the steering wheel driving home.

℘ ℭ

When I heard Andy's voice in Sue's office Thursday afternoon, I hurried to see him.

"Whoa, Nellie," he said.

Sue's eyeglasses dropped on their chain, "Something wrong?"

I realized I was wound up tight as a spring. "No. Thanks for asking. My brother. He's ... having a hard time."

Andy walked me into the hall outside the receptionist office. He mimed drinking shots, question mark on his face.

I nodded. "Come by later?"

"I'm supposed to do dinner and give the guest talk for the Knights of Columbus later. Maybe tomorrow?"

Tomorrow. How many tomorrows before he'd have five minutes for me? "Yeah, sure. If you're not too booked." Would he have blown me off if I was anybody else?

He crossed his arms. "Tomorrow."

By the next afternoon, I was tired of waiting. As I was getting ready to leave the Parish Center, I heard his footsteps in the hallway.

"Hey, Meg, finally have a few minutes." He hung in my doorway. "How are you doing?"

Do I tell him now? Blurt it out? Let it go? We had so much to talk about. Should I start with Eddie's news or blast him for abandoning me? I turned away, looking outside.

"What's up, Meg?" He came over and peered at me with troubled eyes.

Andy knew me too well to hide anything. I had worn a mask okay with Sue the previous day, but now, tired, and alone— "Andy, there's something I need to tell you."

"Yeah, sure. Here? Now?" It wasn't a very private space.

I asked Andy to come to my flat later.

"Tough tonight. You know the community eats dinner together on Fridays."

My stomach roiled. "Tough? Tonight? Unbelievable. How many times, how many ways are you going to put me off?"

Andy crept inside my office and closed the door. "I've got some time right now," he said.

I needed to talk to him. I needed him to hold me. I sat down in my hard-armed office chair. "I'll be fine."

"Meg, I can see you're not fine. I do want to be there for you. Listen, nobody's upstairs right now. It would be okay if you came up."

Not my first choice to enter the priests' residence, but I followed him like a starved cat. Up the mezzanine steps. Past the "community" dining room. Up another flight. No one spotted in the priests' living room. We continued rounding the corner to the next floor where doors lined each side of a hallway. Andy's name, affixed to a small brass plate, appeared on the first door.

He didn't have much of an anteroom—a littered desk and an old chair. Andy looked like he was going to sit down in the chair, but then he offered it to me. An awkward arrangement.

I didn't sit down. "This isn't a good way," I said. "I'll go."

"No, you're here now. Something's wrong. Just tell me."

My voice came in blurts. "You asked me to go to your family's lake house. I can't. How can I? We ... And now my brother's in rehab."

The story came tumbling out at once. Everything I feared saying.

"Rehab?" asked Andy. "Why didn't you tell me yesterday?"

"You didn't have time. Remember? When could I say anything? We're not supposed to be … I tried calling. I can't even leave a message—someone might hear and wonder. This is nuts!" My heart pounded against my chest. Trying to speak quietly—discreetly—when my lungs wanted to shout. I felt like someone punctured them. I burst into tears.

"Meg, my Meg. I'm so sorry. I'm an idiot."

I buried my head in his chest, sobbing big gobs of tears.

Andy led me through a short narrow passage with rods on one side and drawers on the other. Past that, we entered a room that held a bed and a bathroom.

I calmed down. This was our reality. Stolen minutes, hiding places. It wasn't like I didn't know what I was getting into.

We sat on the edge of the bed, and he put his arm around me. "What happened?"

We had much to deal with, overdue conversations. But first, I needed to tell him about this side of my life. Would he love me enough to understand?

"Eddie got falling-down drunk last weekend. I thought he was going to die." I pummeled my fist on the bed. "Oh, Andy, he's my big brother and there he was, passed out with puke all over him. Hank didn't know what to do. We ended up calling emergency. Do you know what detox is?"

Andy caught his breath and nodded. "Detox. Rough." He took me by the shoulders, holding me out at arm's length. Staring. "You saw some godawful stuff."

"Yeah. Anyway, they took him to detox and now he's in treatment." I had been talking to the wall. I turned to see Andy's face gone slack. *Oh, no, I've said too much.* No one ever wanted to hear this stuff. I lost my high school jock boyfriend the first time Eddie went down the tubes. Then, when my college fiancé's father learned about my family, he made sure I knew his son could have done better than get mixed up with me.

Andy let me go and sat upright. "Oh, my God, Meg. And you came to work this week?"

"Sometimes it helps to keep whatever bit of routine you can." I blew my nose. "Father Bruce said God can do anything. Wants us to be whole. Maybe God can heal my brother's alcoholism. Maybe this time. He's going to kill himself with the drink." The floodgates opened. "It's not his fault," I said through my tears. "He saw bad things growing up. My dad, well, he, when he drank, he got mad at my mom and, so, he hit her."

"He did what? Did you see that too? Oh, geez." Tears formed in Andy's eyes, and he reached for me, pulling me tight into his chest.

I stayed there, safe for a few minutes before raising my head. "Most of the time, my dad was like any hard-working man. But when the business started failing, he often didn't come home all night. Then, one Sunday morning, I heard the front door slam. Soon, loud yelling, screaming. Eddie ran into my room and told me to call the police. I got up and dialed the phone but could hardly speak. I was only 10 years old. Eddie ran toward the shouts. Nothing was ever the same again."

I moaned, my cheeks wet, warm saltwater dripping from my lips. Andy gave me his handkerchief. I let him stroke my hair for a long time.

After a while, he tipped my chin and asked, "Do you want to say more?"

I had never told the whole story to anyone, but it was like Andy gently turned the knob on a door I had kept locked. I explained I learned the story in pieces over the years, and that's how I would have to tell it. "Are you sure you want to hear this?"

He offered me a drink of water. The water ran a while. When he returned, his face was splashed with droplets. He pressed a cool washcloth to my forehead and cheeks. We both drank from the tumbler. "I want to hear whatever you want to share," he said. I took another sip and began.

"Sometimes my mom slept on the couch to avoid my dad when he came home at all hours. He found her there. She, well, she refused him. They started fighting. She went to the window to yell for help, and he went crazy. Andy, he tried to push her out the window." I swallowed hard. "We lived on the second floor. Eddie got there right then. He grabbed a hobnail candlestick holder from the mantle and crashed it over our dad's head. That stopped him—until he reeled toward Eddie. The police came. They handcuffed Dad." I choked back sobs. "So, like I told you before, my parents got divorced. That's when we moved to Shady Bluff."

My breath came in great heaves. "It's okay, Meg. I'm here. It's okay." Andy gently massaged my belly. "Breathe," he said. "Everything's all right now."

I felt sheltered. And somehow stronger. "I need to tell you something else."

A line appeared in his forehead and his massage turned into tickling my belly. "I think you've used up my hanky, *Chandelle*. Should I get the Kleenex box?"

I managed the slightest of smiles. "Yeah, good idea." While he rustled in the drawer for a box of tissue, I sat up, twisting straggly hairs behind my ear. I opened the window next to the bed. Muggy, hot. When he returned, we smoothed the heaps and wrinkles that had been a coverlet and propped pillows against the headboard for our backs.

Andy held my hand to his lips and kissed my fingers. "I'm ready," he said.

Words were failing me. Where to begin? "This isn't the first time Eddie's been in treatment. Or the second time either. The very first time, that first time ... The summer after he graduated high school—I still had a year to go—Eddie came home one afternoon and sat on the couch not moving a muscle for a long time. When I asked him what happened, he turned away, grimaced, and picked up the porcelain clown from the coffee table. 'You wouldn't understand,' he said. Then he threw the little clown across the room. It hit the wall and broke. I yelled, 'What's wrong with you?' Wish I could take those words back." I held my head in my hands.

Andy rolled his shoulders and pulled me up. "Let's take a stretch. I have a feeling this might take a while." He rubbed my back before I sat down against the bed pillows, then he grabbed his desk chair from the anteroom for himself. I picked at the coverlet on the bed, twisting nubs between my thumb and forefinger.

"A few weeks later, Mom called me at my part-time job. She never called me at work. She wanted me to come home quick. She told me Eddie was in the hospital, and they had to pump his stomach. When I turned to ring up my customer, I fainted dead away. My boss called a cab and sent me home." I clutched the other pillow and held it tight to my middle as if for protection. "Eddie tried to kill himself."

At first, my tears came in a trickle, but soon a torrent flowed from that place inside where I built a dam many summers past. "He couldn't tell me. He said I wouldn't understand. I wanted to understand, truly I did. Why didn't he tell me? He was so sad, too sad. Maybe I could've done something."

"Meg, don't beat yourself up." Andy got up from his chair and sat on the bed facing me.

I reached for Andy's embrace and rocked back and forth in his arms.

"What couldn't he tell you, Meg?" He searched my eyes.

"I didn't think it was so bad a thing, but everybody else did. When my aunt found out, we were banned from holiday dinners. She didn't want a 'twink' around her grandsons."

At the word *"twink,"* Andy shut his eyes tight.

How could I explain it? The Church mostly pretended the condition didn't exist—the *Baltimore Catechism* never mentioned it. In a college course on Church history, I discovered that bishops through the ages referred to homosexual acts as *crimen pessimum*—the foulest crime—something to be kept secret.

No one ever said the word out loud. After a long hesitation, I said the word—"Eddie's homosexual."

Andy opened his eyes, let me go, and leaned back on one arm. "Some people are that way." His voice was soft, kind. He was the first person I knew who hadn't gone berserk.

Just to be sure he understood, I added, "You know—queer."

Andy assured me he knew what it meant. "Meg, everybody's learning more now, including the Church. But it must have been awful for him as a teenager."

"Eddie only knew he was *different*," I said. "It was the 1960s. I didn't know what guys meant when they called other guys 'fags' or 'queers.' I only knew it was a put-down." Feeling stupid, I hit my hand to my head. "I'd never even heard the word 'homosexual' until ..." I stood up and paced the small room. Andy put his hands on his knees and watched me.

"On Family Day, Mom and I went to the mental health hospital where they kept Eddie after pumping his stomach. Anyone who attempted suicide was held for treatment in the mental ward—whether they did it by alcohol, drugs, a gun, or whatever. I guess they treated both alcoholism and homosexuality in the mental ward."

"You were in high school?" Andy rubbed his forehead with the back of his hand.

"A junior. I wanted to run screaming from the place, but I had to be strong for Mom."

Andy shook his head back and forth, not looking at me. I sipped the last swallow of water in the tumbler he'd put on the side table and sat down on the foot of the bed, not looking at him either. I wanted to get the story out as long as we'd come this far.

"The therapist, a thin woman with a notebook, sat with the families in a circle and asked us to say how we felt. I passed, numb. Mom passed, teary. Eddie went on at length. He said he knew now why he got drunk at the party and did drugs. Said it made him feel like he fit in. Said he hated being *different*.

"The therapist asked Eddie how he felt about being with guys. I wasn't sure why she asked until Eddie slowly said, 'I know I shouldn't want to, but ...' He looked down at the floor as if he was ashamed of something. The therapist asked him if he knew there was a name for what he felt. He didn't, so she said, 'It's called *homosexuality* when guys like other guys more than girls.' 'Oh,' he said."

Andy looked up, incredulous. "So, Eddie didn't really know either. Wow."

"When Eddie took a walk with Mom and me on the hospital grounds later, he said, 'So, now you know. Hate me?' Mom cried but told him she loved him. I made a ridiculous joke saying the only thing I hated was missing a bunch of pizza parties to come visit him. I told him to get well so I could get back to date nights. 'At least one of us is normal,' he said."

Andy came over to sit beside me at the foot of the bed and squeezed my hand.

It wasn't exactly true that I was dating. My jock boyfriend suddenly got too busy to see me when I told him what happened to my brother—only the drunk part and pumping his stomach. Enough for my linebacker to run the whole field from somebody whose brother was in the loony bin. I didn't talk about the homosexuality because I didn't yet fully comprehend what the word meant, much less why it made my big brother freak out.

I pushed back the lock of Andy's hair that always fell on his forehead.

"Believe it or not, I had to look up the word *homosexuality*. I got the gist but didn't understand what all the fuss was about. Mom worried about Eddie's drinking, but the therapist made a big deal about this other thing."

Andy fanned me with a holy card from his side table. "You were such an innocent."

"Curious—not entirely innocent."

Andy laughed and fanned me faster.

"When school started a couple of weeks later, I used study hall to look up the word in the library. *Ho-mo-sex-u-al-i-ty*: Men doing sexual things with men instead of women. Took me a few minutes to fathom. It meant a lot more than *liking* boys more than girls."

"Not an unusual reaction—and why folks have such a hard time accepting," said Andy.

"You won't believe my first thought."

Andy grinned. "Try me."

"Eddie wouldn't be able to have kids that way. It made me sad. But my very next thought—if Eddie could have a good relationship, a better relationship than our parents did—good on him."

"You got all that from the dictionary?" Andy tapped my nose.

"Yep. Best catechism around."

Andy broke out into one of his marvelous laughs. We stretched out across the tousled bed, our arms lightly resting on each other as we relaxed at last.

The quality of light in Andy's room had changed. At least two hours must have passed since we came up to the priests' residence for what I thought would be twenty stolen minutes. I couldn't stay through the night, as much as I wanted to. A bead of sweat trickled down the back of my neck. My hair matted against my scalp.

"I should be getting home, don't you think?"

"Huh?" He had dozed off.

I ran my fingers through his hair, nearly wringing the strands. "We're a mishmash. Would you mind if I took a shower before leaving?"

We looked at the clock and saw that it was past eight o'clock. "I'll be quick," I said.

Andy's hands skimmed me like warm gelatin. "Okey doke."

I undressed and hopped into the cramped shower stall. "Got a washcloth?"

Water cascaded over my body like a cool fountain, the sound of April rain splashing promises. Like last spring when we first made love. We had much to sort out, but someday, somehow, we'd make it. For sure.

As I washed my face, my fingers measured the hours of tears in swollen eyelids. But now, with painful memories shared, all that mattered was the wonderful knowledge that Andy had not run away. I was no longer alone. I would never be alone again. I let the water stream over me another minute. Fresh as Lourdes water.

"Andy, can I have a towel?"

He averted his eyes as he handed me a slightly threadbare towel.

An odd time to be shy. I smiled and waited until he turned toward me. I stood quiet, naked, silently saying: Look at me, Andy. I've spilled my secrets. Washed and cleansed them with water and tears. See? No one else has ever seen me like this. Am I still beautiful to you?

Andy held the shower door, washed in sweat, beautiful to me. Slowly, his eyes caressed my body. I stepped out of the shower and wrapped my hand around the back of his neck, pulled him toward me to kiss, perhaps make love. But he shook his head no and went to the window, peering outside.

I dressed, zipped my damp skirt, and slipped on sandals. "I'll see Eddie on Saturday with his friend, Hank. Probably be back by midafternoon. Come over then?"

Andy hesitated. "Can't. I'm covering Confessions for Leo."

"Too bad," I said. "What about Sunday? Oh, wait. I'm taking Mom to an Al-Anon meeting in the afternoon." I hoped she'd agree by then. "Maybe Sunday night?"

"I'll have to let you know," he said. "Let's get you out of here." Andy cautiously opened the door a crack. "Ready?"

We tiptoed as if dodging the dorm police and quickly made our way down the stairwell. Andy scoped the living room before motioning for me to come further. The dining room on the mezzanine level was dark, safe to scoot past. I would've giggled if he hadn't grown so pensive.

At the back door of the lower level, Andy held my face in his palms. He studied me a long minute, touched a tendril, and unlocked the door. "Go quickly."

The door locked behind me.

CHAPTER 11

RISING

AFTER SHEDDING MY SECRETS in Andy's arms, I slept the sleep of the dead Friday night. The morning dawned brighter than any morning ever before. My whole being felt lighter. On the other side of yesterday, I could be myself, all of myself, with Andy— not the one who had to be strong, keep secrets. I could just be Meg. Now, Andy knew me completely.

I cocooned in my bed, enjoyed the summer dawn, and pondered the fact I never let myself cry like I had with Andy. Always held my dark moments in check.

After my parents' big fight that I told him about, our downstairs neighbor had taken in Eddie and me while the police talked to Mom. I sat on the top bunk of the neighbor kids' bed. Numb. The kids played a game and my brother joined in. When a fight broke out over a toy, I covered my ears, panicked at the sound of shouting. But I didn't cry.

Later, Eddie helped Mom bolt the door and push the hallway table in front of it in case Dad came roaring back. I stared at them, dumbfounded. Hadn't they seen the police take Dad away? Were we supposed to be afraid? I hardly slept for days. But I didn't cry.

In high school, the morning Mom called me at work to tell me Eddie was in the ER getting his stomach pumped for alcohol poisoning, I fainted. But I didn't cry.

With Andy holding me, it was finally safe to let the tears fall.

I pushed back the covers and looked out the window. Along the back fence of the parking lot, a flutter of butterflies sipped coneflowers. Coneflowers, happy as a child's sun.

ᛞ ᛤ

I drove to St. Paul to meet Hank and go with him to visit Eddie.

He turned to me at the first stop light. "I want to stick with your brother through rehab. He's the sweetest guy I've ever met. But Meg—if he pulls this again, I won't be able to handle it."

I waited for the red light to turn green. "You're a good man."

Eddie met us with a big smile on his mug as if we were visiting him at a resort. "Great to see you," he said. "Let me show you around."

I surmised the medical team was giving Eddie drugs to ward off the worst of the withdrawal symptoms. I whispered to Hank, "It should get easier from here on out."

Eddie's veneer cracked when Hank leaned in to give him a hug.

I took a few steps away to give them a moment.

Eddie showed us the activity room, with its rows of folding chairs and card tables. A metal bookcase held a few puzzles, games, and books. He stopped at the slide projector. "Next week, I get to see the show about how I trashed my brain." Eddie's shoulders shook. "I'm so messed up."

Hank tossed him a nerf ball. "You're not messed up, man, you just got bagged."

"I'm so sorry. I'm gonna get it right. I'm gonna get my act together. Promise."

I never heard Eddie as determined before. "I believe you," I said. I did believe he wanted to set things right—I prayed he could.

Before we left, Eddie asked Hank to bring some old *National Geographic* magazines next time. "They don't have shit to read around here." Mom gave him a subscription for his 15th birthday after he devoured an issue in a doctor's office years ago.

"Are you ready for a visit yet from Mom?" I asked.

"Not yet."

Mom agreed to go to an Al-Anon meeting with me Sunday afternoon. She said nothing during the session, but on the way home, she unloaded.

"Meg, you know how your father was. I wanted better for your brother." She fidgeted with her hanky. "And I hoped your uncle would show Eddie how to be a man. Don't you know that's why I left, why I moved you kids to be near family?"

No, I didn't know that. "Mom, you worried about Eddie back then? He was only 12."

"Someday you'll be a mother, Meg. Mothers know their children."

"Eddie has Hank now, Mom. I went with him to see Eddie yesterday. We should've told you sooner, but Eddie's doing rehab, for real this time. Do you want to go see him next week?"

"Stop the car, young lady. Right this minute. You didn't tell me?" Before I had a chance to defend myself, she said, "Of course I want to see him. I've been praying for this." She stared at the dashboard. "I would much rather see Eddie—anywhere—than talk about him at these infernal meetings. I know too well there's nothing I can do."

Not much I could do either. I sat up late Sunday night, as I had on Saturday, expecting Andy to call. No word. Though I welcomed quiet time after the seismic weekend, I wanted to hear Andy say my name, hold me. It was a little too quiet.

ಓ ಅಂ

At Monday morning's staff meeting, Andy waited for me to say the first hello as if he read the question in my eyes. Why hadn't I heard from him?

Following a short agenda, Father Mack asked me to stop by his office.

Andy and I hung back after the others left. We stood pale as Rodin's statue of a kiss, our motion caught like a stop in film that might go on after a pause—or cut to a new frame entirely.

Leo popped back into the room, "Andy, are you coming? 'Scuse me, Meg."

Andy bent toward me as if he wanted to say something. He raised his hand and nearly touched my hair but instead let his hand fall as he turned to go. Was this the same Andy whose body had curled around mine three days ago, his warm flesh a shock absorber for my pain? His love, the balm that made the unbearable bearable.

I shuffled into Father Mack's office.

He motioned for me to sit down. "Meg, you've been looking tired lately. You can take a few days off if you need to."

Had Andy told him what was going on? The last time Father Mack called me in, he'd suggested I bring church bulletins to the shut-ins. I naively thought he wanted to keep them informed—until he mused that no one sent in donations on the heels of my visits—"You're leaving bulletins, with envelopes, aren't you?" I wished people around here would say what they meant instead of these wearisome allusions.

I decided to take Father Mack's sudden concern for my health at face value. "Thanks, but I'm fine. Busy, that's all."

A few days passed before Andy made an appearance in my office. "How's your brother?"

My shoulders dug into the back of my chair, recoiling at his late overture. "Day by day."

"And what about you?" I must have given him a Mona Lisa smile because his knuckles seemed to turn white. "I'll be gone next week," he said. "The family thing at the lake. Want to be sure you're okay."

So, definitely uninvited. Why had he ever asked me in the first place? What did it matter that he'd be gone next week at 'the family thing'? I'd hardly seen him this week. I took a deep breath before asking the question I most dreaded. "Was it so hard hearing my story?"

Andy let go of his clutch on the door and stepped toward me. "I don't know what to say."

This is something people say at funerals. He seemed to know what to say, what to do, how to be real only last Friday.

"I'll be fine." I stared at Andy as if he was a stranger new upon the scene of an accident.

"Meg ... don't be like that. Okay, yes, it was hard to hear. You put a lot out there. I'm glad you felt like you could share that deep stuff. But I don't know what to do with it." He shifted from one foot to the other, not coming any closer.

"I need to get back to work, Andy."

He opened his mouth but gulped back whatever he was going to say.

I closed the door after him, wondering if I knew him at all.

Maybe Father Mack's offer of a few days away would remedy my anxiety, but I wanted time away to be time I could enjoy. There *would* be joy again, wouldn't there? At least Andy was going somewhere else, miles away at the lake. It hurt too much seeing him unable to deal with me. Better when other men said they didn't want to hear the gory details of my life, or when they simply ran. Andy had listened, wiped my tears, lightened my load, held me. Loved me. Now I felt more naked than ever, vulnerable—and apparently, untouchable.

How had I suddenly become untouchable? It didn't make sense.

Oh, no! Had Father Cronin heard us when I opened the window? His brass-plated name hung on the room next to Andy's. Had Leo come by to ask Andy why he missed dinner when I was in the shower? What if Father Mack had seen me leaving the parking lot so late?

I wished I knew what had happened.

Or—was Andy thrown by seeing a woman unclothed in this cloistered bastion of a men's armory? This place where men guarded, purified, sharpened their swords to slay worldly dragons. I hadn't sought to trespass. He asked me there. I had not blunted his sword—I gave him a dragon to slay. His sword, sharp as any arrow in Cupid's quiver, slayed my terrors with the armament of love—the only thing that has ever slain a dragon.

He could only do that because I had given him my heart as target practice moons ago.

I prayed the whole long week Andy was away. In church, I contemplated the statue of Mary holding the child Jesus. Can you only hold life after giving bloody birth, crying your eyes out with the pain? On the opposite side of the altar, the statue of Jesus as a grown man stared back at me, his cloak pulled open to reveal a heart on fire. Between the statues, a crucifix held Christ dripping with bloody wounds above the altar where he came back to life every day.

Would Andy and I come back to life, or would we live the rest of our lives as statues?

∽ ∾

With Andy away, I attempted to act like nothing happened. I chit-chatted with Sue at the end of each day. Leaving the Parish

Center on Thursday, I noticed Beth's name still posted on Sue's "In" column. Funny, I hadn't seen her in the last hour. The oddity soon answered itself.

Through the beveled glass in the door leading outside, I saw her sitting on the wide stone steps with Flynn, the seminarian stationed at St. Gabe's for the summer. He came to meetings now and then, joined me on a few visits to homebound parishioners, and sang in the choir. He seemed like a promising priest-in-training, once you got past his unruly shock of red hair. I vaguely registered hearing him humming tunes down the hall—with Beth—often.

With a flash of déjà vu, I saw them hanging on each other's word, saw the smiles and giggles, mirrored motions, the flushed cheeks. Sparks. Rainbows. Fireworks. Lightning. Oh, my God. I didn't have to be a weatherman to see the signs of a storm a mile away. Is that how Andy and I appeared to everyone around us? Being discreet does not come naturally to those in love.

I backed away from the door. They'd have few enough moments like this if Andy's and my experience was any measure. I dared hope it might be easier for them—Flynn was in what they called the "novitiate," the year or two before committing to the Order of Clement. He and Beth made a cute couple. They could blend in among the growing numbers of laypeople involved in church work without the baggage of "leaving the priesthood." Listen to me! I had them married off and ensconced in a lay vocation that barely existed.

Sue called to me from her desk, "Back so soon?" I quickly made the excuse that I forgot something and left by the back exit.

80 C3

With so many trips to see Eddie, I had neglected regular chores like grocery shopping. I would have to stop at the store on my way home—nothing in the fridge for dinner. I wondered if

Andy was catching fish at his family's cottage—or feeling like a fish out of water.

An ordinary trip to the grocery store offered a dose of stability amidst new worries about Beth—and my own familiar ache. At the onion bin, I heard someone say, "Where have you been keeping yourself, Meg? We've missed you." Eileen. Stalwart of the Irish ceili dance group that I skipped much too often.

"Life's been a little crazy lately," I said as casually as possible.

"There's a ceili Saturday at Kelly's—with a new band. Sean's trio broke up. Can you come to dance practice tonight?"

I nearly begged off but decided to change course. I wanted my old life back.

Putting on the Irish American lilt I said, "Blimey, Eileen, if I hadn't run into you tonight, I might have been lost to you forever. Thank ye for a most gracious invitation."

Laughing at my brogue as if it was hilarious instead of patently pathetic, Eileen extended her invitation further. "Let's grab something to eat and go from there. Good plan?"

"A grand plan. The onions will keep." Cutting onions would only make me cry anyway.

I needed to let go of the dissonant fugue playing its insufferable "what-if's" in my head. I would never be able to resolve the question on my own. Relationships take two.

∛ ∞

The day Andy returned from his family's cottage, needles and pins pricked my hopes for seeing him soon. He called, but not to come over. "You know that rocky boat launch?"

Rocky. Like our relationship. "Yes, I know the place." We'd spent an hour there last month skipping stones. "The patchy stretch where we wouldn't be seen and cause scandal."

"Meg, please. I'm trying. Can you meet me there at four o'clock tomorrow?"

At least he wasn't avoiding me. "Yes, I can meet you there. I'm trying, too."

The first time we went to the boat launch, Andy taught me the fine art of skipping stones. "On a calm day," he said, "smooth stones can skip a bunch of times before sinking. On a rough water day, it's harder to get the right lift to keep them going."

Either way, sooner or later, the stones sink.

Andy was skipping stones when I arrived at the boat launch. Not getting much lift.

I didn't want to play the game anymore.

We sat on the grayed-out bench nearby, neither of us saying much. Andy broke the awkward silence. "You sure know how to cry."

Although his love had opened the spigot, my crying scared him off. I wouldn't make that mistake again. "Didn't know I had so many tears in me. Thanks for the hanky."

"Meg, I had a lot of time to think last week at the cottage."

"You mean, when your brothers weren't razzing you."

Andy flipped a stone like a coin, and it fell on the sandy ground. "Yeah, you've got their number. How's *your* brother?"

"Eddie comes home in a few days. If he sticks with the program, he's got a chance." I picked up the stone that dropped when Andy flipped it. "What about us? Do we have a chance?"

Andy stood up but stumbled on the rocky path down to the shore.

I tread carefully toward him on the uneven launch. "Listen," I said. "I've also had a lot of time to think about things. You know my background now. I didn't need another taboo in my life—but then you came along. We're good together, Andy. I'm willing to go the distance."

Ripples on the water crested into waves as the wind picked up.

"Meg, did you tell me those things last week because … well, would you have told me if I wasn't a priest?" When I didn't answer, he said, "People tell priests stuff, that's all."

I looked at his face, kissed by the sun eight days at the lake, and the shaft of dark blond hair that always fell across his forehead. His eyes were hazel, commingled flecks of green and brown. I had touched every inch of him, and he was asking me if I knew who he was. Didn't he know who he was?

"Andy, I came to you because you're you."

Was he saying he was a man when he was with me, but a priest when he was comforting a penitent or sick person—or a crying woman? When had he split himself in half? How could the same experience that knit me together split Andy down the middle? It was like asking me to pick one of the two colors in his eyes, brown or green, green or brown—man or priest, priest or man. He was all one person to me.

"I never told anyone the things I shared with you. If I wanted help, I might have gone to Leo—he would have understood, don't you think?"

Andy picked at the rough gray bench with his fingernails. "Yeah, no doubt."

"Or, I could have gone to a psychologist, right?"

"A psychologist helped me. Obviously, not enough."

"I didn't want help, Andy. I wanted someone who could love me, see past the garbage. I needed you. You. Like you needed me after the accident with Jenny."

I knew it wasn't because he was a priest that my deep rift healed during the long cry—it was because that's what lovers do for each other. After the accident with Andy's sister, Leo had sent him to me. Plenty of priests around, but none doing him much good. Andy and I would not have been able to bear each other's burdens if we hadn't fallen in love long before the accident, well before we made love. Making love only said what was already true.

Andy took my face in his hands and looked into my eyes. "I do love you, Meg. Don't you know that? It's just the marrying part I can't figure out. But I'll always love you."

The sun slid behind a cloud. A storm was rolling in. There was so much more to be said, but neither of us seemed able to broach it.

"I'll always love you too, Andy. But I can't stay in this limbo."

CHAPTER 12

PATHS

MILLIE, WHOM I FONDLY CALLED my African violet lady, showed up on the hospital roster of visits—her third stay in as many months. When I entered her room, she was sleeping peacefully, curled up like a child. Down to the weight of a child. I placed my hand on her shoulder and prayed the Lord would scoop her up in his arms, like a child.

Millie's bedside table held one of her overwatered violets and the array of photos she had kept next to her favorite chair at home. She had told me the story behind each one. Her burly husband—lost to lung cancer. Her son, the electrician, moved to the burbs with his wife and three kids. "Wish they came to see me more often," she'd say. Her daughter, a 40ish woman standing alone, wore a cross around her neck. Millie was of mixed minds whether to call her Sister Genevieve or by the name she'd grown up with—Ginny. I could tell when Ginny had spent a few days visiting—a tidied house, dusted, with good smells lingering in the kitchen.

Scanning the obituaries a few days later, I wasn't surprised to see Millie's name.

At the wake, a friendly woman in modest garb thanked me for coming. "You must be Sister Margaret. Mom talked about you. Nice that someone from St. Gabe's looked in on her."

I told her it was my privilege getting to know Millie. "You must be Sister Genevieve. Your mom liked to call you Ginny."

She acknowledged the nickname gracefully.

I told her I wasn't "Sister Margaret," just Meg.

"I'm sorry," she said, "I assumed you were a Sister working at the parish."

For the first time, the idea didn't strike me as preposterous. Anything would be easier than the path I was on. How much longer could I wait for Andy to carry me over the threshold?

"A lot of people assume I'm a Sister. Maybe I should be."

Sister Genevieve knelt with me at the casket to say a prayer.

Few people showed up for the wake. Small family, and most of Millie's friends were waiting for her "upstairs," her reference to heaven. I was glad I made the effort to attend. Father Cronin came to say a rosary and some nice things about Millie to comfort her son and daughter.

As I was leaving, Sister Genevieve caught up with me. "Here's my card," she said. "If you ever want to talk about convent life, I would be happy to meet with you."

I took the card warily, as if she was offering me a fortune cookie.

"Wait," she said, "better yet, let me write the name of our novice director on the back. She can probably answer your questions better than me."

I tucked the card in my purse. Out of the parish—and into the nunnery? Oh, Lord!

On my way to hospital visits the next week, I scratched my finger on the edge of Sister Genevieve's card when I dug for parking meter change in the bottom of my purse. I read the name she had written on the back of her card: Sister Loretta, novice director.

God, is this your way of telling me to stop hitting my head on the brick wall of marriage? But the convent? Okay, a respectable choice—and no one would have to know how dismally I failed at my simple dream of marrying a nice guy, making a home, and raising a family.

I plugged the meter. Didn't think time would run out on Andy and me so quickly.

When a patient at the hospital greeted me as "Sister," I didn't correct her.

ꕥ

A week later and three-hours from Shady Bluff, Sister Loretta met me at the front door of St. Christopher's Novitiate and Retreat House. Wisps of gray hair curled out from under her modified veil. She wore a tailored beige "Sister suit," the hybrid between long habits and modern garb. Despite her short stature, she appeared as sturdy as the woodland surrounding the spacious grounds, and placid as the stream running through it. A belltower initialed with a silver cross graced the building framing her.

Her first words startled me with their abruptness, "So, where shall we begin, Margaret?"

I laughed nervously and said, "Nice to meet you."

She led me to a parlor and offered me coffee before reiterating her question.

"I never considered becoming a nun," I said, "except of course as a child in Catholic school, but working at the parish, I do a lot of things that nuns do."

"And you're ready to consider a vocation now?"

I fiddled with the purse in my lap. "I should be honest with you, Sister. If having a vocation means giving yourself away, I thought it would be in a different way."

Sister Loretta sat back in her chair, "Go on, Margaret, I'm listening."

"Please call me Meg."

"All right. Meg, tell me what it is you want to tell me."

I expected she'd send me packing immediately, but I needed to tell her. I needed to tell someone. "I fell in love." I squirmed in the straight-back chair. "He was a priest. He is a priest. It looks like he's going to stay a priest. When Sister Genevieve suggested I call you, I wondered if it might be God's crazy way of getting me to enter the convent after all."

A bridge of sighs came from deep inside Sister Loretta. Her eyes softened. Intense blue, the color of larkspur as it readies itself to flower. "You are not the first young woman who has passed through that particular vale of tears, my dear. Many are those who talk about the Church changing its rules so that priests can marry. But I must tell you, talk is cheap. Tradition is the bedrock of this institution. If you were waiting for the Church to bless your marriage bed with this man, I dare say your bones will creak long before your mattress does."

A shudder ran through me. "I'm sorry, Sister. I was foolish to come here."

But Sister Loretta shushed me. "God often leads us by winding roads, Meg. You must be sure, though, that this is a way of life you can commit to. There are many ways to love— none of them are about escaping. Are you hoping this priest will change his mind?"

She seemed to understand, yet she also challenged me. I found the answer at the root of my coming to Christopher House. "If he doesn't know by now, I doubt he'll leave to marry me. I'm here because I need to get on with my own life, and this is the door that opened."

"Meg dear, I'm thankful you were honest with me at the outset. That will save us both a lot of time. Let me invite you through that door. Come and explore. Take time to pray."

Her directness refreshed my searching soul. "Yes, Sister. Thank you, Sister."

After dinner, Sister Loretta introduced me to two other Sisters who were planning retreats for young adults. She asked me if I might want to work with them on a couple of weekends in the fall. Retreats were a large part of the Christopher Sisters' work, so I surmised this was her way of letting me get my feet wet, as well as assess my aptitude. I agreed, though I had never gone on a retreat myself. I didn't tell her that.

Over dessert, we talked about the theme for the upcoming retreats: *Navigating Aloneness.* "How should we frame the discussion questions?" asked Sister Joanne. "All the registrants marked the box for 'single,' so they must know what it is to be alone."

Sister Barbara said, "If they thought they knew everything there was to know about 'aloneness,' I doubt they would've paid money for a retreat. What do you think, Meg?"

The word *navigation* caught my attention. Weighing both Sisters' comments, I said, "It's true a single person experiences 'aloneness.' I would be interested in hearing how others *navigate* this stage of life."

Sister Loretta interrupted, "Is 'aloneness' a stage of life?"

Like dropping a stitch in a sweater, I saw the hole in my answer. For these uncoupled women, *aloneness* was not a stage of life but a way of life. All eyes were upon me, seeing if I could rescue the knitting.

"*Aloneness* seems a natural part of being single," I said, "but compared to *loneliness*, well, that can be experienced at any stage of life. Perhaps *aloneness* also can span a lifetime."

The sisters sat back. "Now we have a place to begin," said Sister Joanne.

I hesitated to ask where that might be.

"Living in the convent," she continued, "I sometimes fear we take *aloneness* for granted. The retreat will be a time not only for the singles to embark on their journey, but also a time for us to check our bearings. Before I came to the convent, I thought much like you, Meg—that *aloneness* was the stage before getting married."

I often wondered if sisters thought about marriage or always knew they had a vocation.

Sister Barbara said, "A divorced woman came on retreat a few years ago. The circles under her eyes told me that being married to the wrong person was the loneliest lonely of all."

Thinking of my mom, I asked, "Was she happier alone?"

"Seemed resigned. Our work for the time she spent here became teasing out the difference between being alone and being lonely."

I pondered how my mom coped. She never talked about it.

"You must be getting tired," said Sister Loretta. "You've had a long day." She walked me toward my room but stopped at a side parlor. "Let's sit a minute."

I sank into an overstuffed, much-sat-in chair.

"Meg, are you lonely?"

I paused, turning the question over in my mind and heart. Was I lonely? I realized with some relief that I was not. "Not exactly lonely," I said. Though I sorely missed Andy's companionship—before he backed away. "It was wonderful sharing myself with someone. The priest I told you about. His name was Andy. Father Andy."

"You miss him. But you say you're not lonely. Tell me more about that."

I searched for an example. "There's the 'alone in a crowd' feeling," I said. "I think that's what loneliness is. When I'm with friends or when I was with Andy, it's like being part of the crowd, you know, togetherness. And yet, there's a part of me that's always 'alone'—the part that makes me who I am. But I much prefer being together/alone than alone/alone."

"I think I see what you mean." I appreciated the gentle way Sister Loretta responded to my awkward musings, but then she asked, "Where is God in your aloneness?"

When I prayed of late, I often asked God who he was, why he had created me as a woman, and where he was.

I paused and took a long deep breath.

"Maybe, Sister, the part that makes me who I am, the 'alone' part is the speck of dust or shard of rib God used to fashion me. They say God knows you before you're born. Could the 'alone' place be where God speaks to me, or tries to?"

Sister Loretta smiled an inward smile before reaching for a book of psalms on the table. She browsed through it, book-marking a page. "You might want to read this later."

In my room, I opened to Psalm 139:

> Lord, you have probed me, you know me:
> you know when I sit and when I stand;
> you understand my thoughts from afar.

I may not have come to the novitiate for the best of reasons, but I believed exploring this place would not be time wasted. If God knew me as well as the psalmist said he did, perhaps he would tell me who I might be with or without Andy. With Andy, God had opened my woman's heart. What other unknown places lay within me?

As I drove through campus Monday, nervous about asking Father Mack for time off to work with the retreat team, jaywalking students only put me more on edge.

Father Mack surprised me with his immediate support. "A retreat for young singles with the Sisters at Christopher House? Of course, we can spare you two Fridays. You say Millie

Dayton's daughter got you into this? Hmm." He came around from his desk and offered me his blessing.

I bowed my head.

&O C&

In my office, the overgrown Gerbera daisy plant on top of my file cabinet begged repotting. If I was going to salvage it before fall set in, I needed to do it soon. I put off the chore because the plant reminded me of the day Andy stopped to help me rescue Daisy the cat. Eons ago. I carried the plant to the potting shed—a project of Andy's so Ruth could store fertilizer, soil, and tools for her Eldercare gardeners.

Ruth was sorting tools.

"Okay if I work on this rangy thing?"

"It does need work. Come by for lunch when you're done." She left me to it.

As I knocked the plant out of its pot and set about separating the good roots from the rotten ones, Andy pulled into the parking lot.

He peered into the shed. "My mom had a saying when she worked in the garden: *Divide to multiply.* Never knew what that meant."

I wanted to dismiss him by telling him to go ask his mom. But I warmed to his voice.

"It means living things need room to grow." I teased out tangled root chunks. "See, they're struggling. If I repot the stronger roots, they'll be happy—and multiply."

"Like the Garden of Eden," said Andy.

"For sure." I tapped the new roots into fresh soil and doused them. "Plus, a dose of TLC."

Andy took a handful of soil and sifted it between his fingers. "Meg, do you think, I mean, maybe, that we were given to each other for a little while? Maybe we just needed a little TLC."

Tender. Loving. Care. Just a little. One way to rationalize what happened between us.

"Given? For a little while? You'll have to ask God."

I wanted to spit holy water.

&℧ ℭ&

When I heard Beth practicing new songs—incredibly out of tune—I swung by the music room.

"Learning a new song?" My greeting trailed off. She slumped over the strings, strumming them like Picasso's weary *Blue Man*. "Beth, what is it?"

"I hate Clems," she said.

I plopped into the bean-bag chair next to a musical tripod. "Want to clue me in?"

"They take a vow of poverty—that's a load of bull. They never have to worry about a roof over their head or something to eat. All they do is go from one of their rectories to the next. You'd think they were Rotarians."

"Beth, what's this about?" I wedged myself as upright as possible in the bean-bag chair.

"Flynn." She looked at me like I should know, and suddenly I did. This was about the redheaded "Clement-in-training" who warbled around Beth whenever he had the chance. Why do songbirds have to light on the most precarious of branches?

"Oh, Beth, I'm so sorry."

"Yeah, me too. He left yesterday."

I wished I didn't know the territory. "How serious was it?"

Beth blurted, "I was saving myself—for a guy who cared about the same things I did."

Andy had not been my first—unexpected solace that our lovemaking wasn't freighted with that rite of passage. Beth hadn't only lost her heart, but also her virginity. A woman's heart isn't something for priests to test their chastity chops on—why don't seminaries teach their men *that* sacred truth?

How could I reassure her she wasn't as much of a fool as she felt? Like a big sister, I didn't want to weigh her down with my saga. Instead, I told her what I was telling myself: "He did care about the same things you do, so you got that part right."

"Oh, yeah, he cares about the same things I do," said Beth. "That's why he has to be a priest. As he put it, 'I'm called to serve the marginalized.' Does he even know what that means? Fancy word for poor."

"Beth, *you* know what that means, and serving forgotten people *is* a good thing. I wish there was a way you could do that kind of work together."

She plucked a discordant chord on the guitar. "When pigs fly," she scoffed. "Don't you know? Women get in the way of men's work."

I lofted a paper airplane. "So now what?"

"I don't know. Guess I'll look for a job in retail until I finish my music therapy degree. Can't stay here. Remind me not to be so short-sighted that I overlook men in business suits."

Vaguely remembering someone from the spaghetti dinner at Shalom House who seemed to pay a lot of attention to her, I asked, "Anyone in particular?"

Beth put down her guitar. "Keith. He wanted to marry me, but all I saw in our future were country club parties. That's not the kind of life I want. Was I wrong to wait?"

With Sister Loretta's advice fresh on my mind, I said, "I don't know if you were wrong about Keith, but you weren't wrong to wait if you weren't sure." I added my hard-won insight— "You were sure about Flynn. Seems he's the one who wasn't sure, and he should have waited."

"Thanks, Meg. I'll get over this, but geez."

"You'll be all right, Beth," I said. "You were a good woman yesterday … and you are today. Don't forget that."

We had tumbled into a thicket of men who lived as if in a foreign land. They spoke a familiar language, but their words and actions had different meanings than our understandings of those words and actions. Worse, they coated their rationalizations in "spiritual-speak," like when Andy wondered out loud if we'd been "given" to each other for "a little while."

❧ ❧

I took to the retreat work with the Christopher Sisters like a duck to water. Driving home after being part of their team for two *Aloneness* weekends, I was amazed by the serenity that replaced the restlessness in my heart about Andy. How did the Sisters create this magical space where God could touch people? I felt a sense of the sacred in a new way. I had witnessed something I didn't know could be done by the simple act of hospitality and caring. I wanted to do this work. I wanted to be like these women. The possibility of becoming a Sister had become tangible. Perhaps I could make a life without Andy after all. Alone, but not lonely.

I called Sister Loretta when I got home and asked her if I could stay with them for a week to pray seriously about becoming a Christopher Sister.

Father Mack had been generous giving me two Fridays off to work with the retreat team but asking for a week to make my own retreat might not be met as enthusiastically. When I asked Sue if Father Mack had any "uninterrupted" time available—I didn't want to say why—she dithered by turning the pages in his calendar until I assured her nothing was wrong.

At the appointed hour, I knocked on the closed door: *Office of the Pastor.* Father Mack's bellowing voice granted me entry. He adjusted the blinds to vanquish an errant thread of light slicing the blotter on his desk. Satisfied, he plunked into a swivel chair. I eased into one of the two guest chairs covered in oxblood leather.

"You're looking chipper this morning, Meg."

I told him a few anecdotes about the uplifting weekends at Christopher House and thanked him for letting me take the time.

"Retreats usually portend either enlightenment or calamity, sometimes both." His eyes glazed over. "Are they giving you something for your efforts?"

"Interesting you ask. I wasn't expecting anything, but after the first weekend they handed me an envelope—the check was more than generous."

"Well, I'm glad to hear they appreciate you." Father Mack paused for a moment. "You know, when the priests take on extra activities, they turn the proceeds over to the parish."

This was a wrinkle I did not see coming. Apparently, I was supposed to accept the stipend and then "donate" it to the parish. The only trouble was that I didn't accept the check. I opened my hands, empty. "Father Mack, if I had known the expectation, I would have given it to you. I told them I couldn't accept it."

Little surprised Father Mack, but a look of shock, followed by a pinching of the eyebrows, skewed his carefully measured demeanor. "Well, what you do with the money is your own business. I was only mentioning the practice of our community."

I surveyed the Chinese vases adorning the rare empty spot in his wall full of books, his crocodile-embossed desk set and ivory-handled letter opener. He surely had no need of my stipend. But apparently, he considered me part of the "community" when convenient. Though in no position to bargain after nearly being accused of pocketing "community" money, I launched into the purpose of my appointment.

"Honestly, Father Mack. I didn't keep the stipend. You see, I'm wanting to make a retreat myself soon, so, I thought forgoing the payment would cover my room and board." Attempting to lighten the uncomfortable moment, I said, "They provide very nice rooms and good food out there in the country. They can't do it for free."

Father Mack rubbed his chin, glancing from me to the window and back again. In contrast to his displeasure only moments ago, he calmly folded his hands. "Of course, Meg. A personal retreat. With the Sisters. Yes. When were you thinking of going?"

"That's what I wanted to talk to you about." I dropped my gaze to his desk calendar.

Father Mack's eyes narrowed. "Whenever you like … as soon as possible. You can use your vacation time."

I expected he would ask for time to consider it, voice a few objections, or flatly deny me. I couldn't tell if he was eager to support a possible vocation to the Sisters—or if he truly thought I had kept the stipend and wanted to rid himself of my greedy paws. He never spoke plainly.

Although I hoped for a gratis week, I did have the vacation time. "Thank you. I'll work things out with Father Leo."

Father Mack rapped his knuckles lightly on the desk. "On with you now."

I opened the door to leave. Andy stood on the other side, about to knock. Part of me wanted to disappear, but the other part wanted to pull him to a quiet place where I could share my plans—the way we used to share everything. He gave way, and we passed, like ships in the night.

ℰꙨ ᏟᏳ

Sister Loretta was delighted to hear I could make arrangements so quickly. She suggested I arrive the next Sunday, October 1, and stay through the following Saturday.

The last week of September dragged. My enthusiasm held more than a dose of obsession. I had a plan. I was only too ready to leave the parish hothouse, where I inevitably failed to meet Father Mack's nebulous expectations. The hothouse where Andy could never meet his own vowed expectations. Mine was a realistic expectation—soon I would be entering the novitiate.

When Leo and I held our monthly meeting with the nursing home volunteers, I told them I would be away the following week. I must have said it with too much eagerness because one of them asked if I was going to see my boyfriend. My cheeks warmed, surely blushing. "Not quite. I'm going on retreat for a week."

A good laugh was had by all when Father Leo said, "Well, nuns do marry Christ." I recovered as quickly as I could, "This isn't about marrying anyone. It's just a retreat. Lots of people make retreats. I'll be back the following week."

"Okay, Meg, sorry," said Leo. He proceeded to give the final blessing.

Afterwards, I confided to him that I was going on retreat to pray about becoming a Sister.

"The guys in the house, us priests, kind of thought so when we heard you were doing retreat work. But I'm sorry if I let the cat out of the bag. By the way, did Andy tell you that he's going to Canada for a few weeks? Father Mack thought it would be a good idea for him to keep up with his French. Seems everybody's going somewhere but me."

The last time I saw Andy, at Father Mack's door, his eyes were bloodshot. If he knew he was on his way to Canada, he wasn't happy about it.

"Someone's got to hold things steady, Leo."

CHAPTER 13

FEAR NOT

AUTUMN BLAZED IN ITS brilliant colors when I arrived at Christopher House. Cool air whispered through leaves, making sounds like a wind chime, a call to prayer. I followed the banks of the meandering creek surrounding the place. Not like a river or a lake. Small, like me, and on a winding course. I ambled over the wooden slats of a bridge that spanned the creek. Was this the bridge that would lead me across my troubled water?

Andy and I had crossed a deep ocean and nearly drowned. *Lord, are you offering me an anchor at Christopher House? What are you offering Andy in Canada?* I doubted Father Mack sent him there to practice his French—Canada was where the Clems sent him the last time he didn't know what to do about a woman.

Sister Loretta met me with a hug and an offer of tea. "Isn't the news terrible?"

"What do you mean?"

"My dear, haven't you heard? The Pope died in his sleep—only a month into his reign."

I shuddered. In my preoccupation, I hadn't watched or listened to the news in days. I recalled the Angelus prayer the Pope raised when the leaders of Israel and Egypt met at Camp David trying to forge a lasting peace. He chose a psalm that described God as both a father and a mother—maybe more so a mother. Tenderness as strength. More than a few priests and bishops sputtered over his emphasis on God's "feminine" qualities, but Pope John Paul I opened my soul to what it might mean to be a woman in God's eyes. How would the next pope see women?

"We must be brave, Meg. The bible has hundreds of passages encouraging us to trust in the Lord. Let me share the one I've been praying today. It's from Isaiah 41: *For I am the* LORD, *your God, who takes hold of your right hand and says to you: Do not fear; I will help you.*

She rolled her eyes. "Glory be, if 1978 hasn't been a year to need the Lord's help—test-tube babies, mail bombs, and now losing not one but two popes in the same year. We need the Lord very badly. But it is hard to put our trust in someone we can't see. Don't you agree?"

I did.

Sister Loretta wasted no time getting down to business Monday morning. We met in the parlor nearest the chapel. "You came to pray about joining the Sisters of St. Christopher. I'm encouraged when a young woman wants to serve the Lord and surprised at the many ways he sends them to us. Yet, it is my job to tell you that he doesn't always ask them to stay."

Bees swarmed in my stomach at her abrupt reminder. I might not make the cut. "Why would God send someone to you and not want her to stay?"

"I trust he has his reasons. Our work this week, Meg, is sorting out what the Lord wants. I'll be happy as long as you're running toward something, not away from anything, whether it's here or elsewhere. Understand?"

I thought I followed God's breadcrumbs here. No more trying to "figure things out" with Andy only to have him figure out he didn't know if he could be a man and a priest at the same time. I wanted this to be a done deal.

I cleared my throat. "I want to run toward life, Sister, and I hope that's why the Lord led me here."

The next day, Sister Loretta invited me to lunch in the Sisters' refectory rather than the retreatants' cafeteria. Sisters of all ages lined two long tables. Never had I been in a roomful of make-up-less women. Their lack of camouflage neither hid their flaws nor distorted a beauty that was much more than skin-deep. I didn't exactly fit in. Reactions to my presence ranged from formal politeness to gracious curiosity as Sister Loretta introduced me around. When she eventually seated me with two young novices, knowing nods passed among them.

Since there were only two novices, I assumed they hoped for a companion. Sharon, a 30ish woman in a corduroy jumper, asked me the typical getting-to-know-you questions about where I lived and what I did, but her younger counterpart, Mindy, got right to the point. "Are you in discernment, Meg?"

"Is that what you call it? If you mean, 'Am I thinking about joining the Christophers?' then 'yes' is the answer."

"That's great," said Mindy. She fixed the barrette in her naturally curly headful of hair. "I'm still in discernment. This is my third visit. I think of myself as a novice, but it's not formal yet. Sister Loretta wants me to pray some more. What about you? Do you know yet? Have you been here before?"

I peered out the refectory's windows. Plump clouds spattered raindrops on the glass. How many nosy women would I encounter here? Maybe the way Andy and the priests kept to themselves was not an entirely bad thing.

Sharon intervened, "Don't feel like you have to tell us your life history. It's nice to see we're not the only young women odd enough to consider this kind of life. Nobody joins the convent anymore."

I laughed. "A year ago, it was the furthest thing from my mind." Heck, only a few months ago, Andy and I played Mom and Dad by helping a couple of ragamuffins decorate their bikes on the Fourth of July.

Done with our lunch of ham and beans, we deposited plates in the kitchen, where a stout Sister rewarded us with warm apple crisp drenched in sugar and nutmeg. "Let's take our dessert to the room off the kitchen," said Sharon. "It'll be a pleasant nook on this dank day."

Once we were seated in front of the small fireplace, Mindy said, "By now you know I'm awfully direct, so I'm going to come right out and ask the elephant-in-the-room question. Are you worried about not getting married?"

Worried wasn't the word I would have chosen to describe not marrying Andy. I faked a smile. "The fact of the matter is that it's no sure bet Mr. Right will come along, nor that he will marry me if he does."

"You're realistic," said Sharon, "but it's one of the most important questions."

"I know," I said. "How did you handle it?"

Mindy nudged Sharon. "Maybe you should tell her."

"I was engaged, but my fiancé got drafted." Sharon took a deep breath. "He lost his life in the Tet Offensive." Mindy and I moved closer to her. "It was five years since I lost Craig, but I hadn't moved on. One day I came here. Found the quiet I sought—and deep peace. I came to Christopher House often." Her shoulders relaxed. "Gradually, I wanted to share that peace with others. Sister Loretta made me wait a whole year after telling her, to make sure I wasn't trying to bury myself. But truly, I learned to love again, in a different way." Sharon fairly glowed.

Mindy set down her apple crisp. "The Sisters call it an 'inclusive' way of loving."

"That's a good name for it," said Sharon. "Somehow, my heart opened wide, and I wanted to reach out in love to everyone. It's hard to explain."

My heart had opened when I fell in love with Andy. Calm yet buoyant wherever I went, whoever I saw. Words of cheer or comfort came easily on every hospital visit. Kindness at the grocery checkout, gas station, or encounter with a neighbor. Forgiveness of Father Cronin despite his demeaning remarks. No space in my heart for anything but love.

"You don't have to explain," I said. "Love is like that. It just is."

Mindy chirped, "The opposite of 'inclusive' love is 'exclusive' love—that's what married love is. I try to love inclusively. I've never wanted to be tied down to a family. Maybe that made it easier for me to think about the convent."

I doubted Mindy had ever been in love. "Isn't love always inclusive?" I asked. "If couples only focus on each other, they smother to death." Andy's seminary probably warned him about inclusive versus exclusive love. After we got together, he radiated more love than ever—giving deeper homilies at Mass, forgiving the rough edges of those who came to the Parish Center asking for a favor, saying kinder words to Ruth's codgerly crowd, working with me to fill disaster relief boxes for the folks in Rochester. Our love included everyone, excluded no one.

Mindy stirred heaping spoonfuls of sugar into her coffee. "If you have a family, they must come first. But when you're a Sister, you can spend every bit of your energy serving people who come on retreat. God has to be at the center of your life—nobody else."

Her pat answers chafed. Not a very loving sentiment, but from what I had seen of the Clems, the inclusive-versus-exclusive argument seemed more a question of where one lived than who one loved. Did Father Cronin love anyone? He firmly asserted membership in "the community." Was God the center of his life, or was the priestly community?

"Mindy, I think you're scaring Meg." Sharon winked at me. "What Mindy means is that you need to give your whole heart in one way or the other, no looking back. People who have families certainly don't stop loving God."

I believed when love was at the center of your life, that's when you glimpsed God—it didn't make a difference whether married or single or a priest—or a Christopher Sister. I never saw love as a choice between God and man. I would have missed out on something if I'd never known the love of a man. I might never reach Sharon's sublime peace, but I did want to learn to love again.

On Wednesday, I left my comfortable but austere room and set out to explore the town where I would soon be living—unless God also jilted me.

Main Street hosted an array of shops where customers carried groceries to their cars, window-shopped, and chatted with neighbors. An *Our Town*.

On the walk back to Christopher House, I took a shortcut through the playground. A young mother pushed her little girl back and forth on a swing. The to-and-fro of life.

The heartbeat of life.

"Higher, Mommy, higher!" Red Keds scampered through the sky like maple leaves in autumn. When the mom whisked her little girl off the swing, she buttoned the child's sweater up to her neck. The little girl ran after a squirrel, laughing.

If I joined the convent, I would miss bundling a little lamb into her wooly sweater.

How did Andy make this decision? He was good with kids. They gravitated to him. I understood the concept of sacrifice to live this kind of life, but wasn't it as much a sacrifice to get up in the middle of the night to feed a crying baby as to answer a sick call?

It's the kind of intimacy that's different. That was the question.

I passed an old schoolhouse. Looked like the town had turned it into a library. Which school of love would teach me the lessons I needed to learn? The convent, in the company of other women, each honing intimacy with God through prayer—or—home and hearth, surrounded by family, finding God and each other in the ordinariness of life.

I never considered remaining single—likely the most difficult school of love.

Sister Loretta listened as I shared my journal jottings. She calmly folded her hands when I expressed my confusion about the "inclusive versus exclusive" conversation with Mindy and Sharon. "Love is love, Meg. Your task is to ask the Lord to show you how you love best, because that's where he will find you—and where you will find the Lord."

The next morning, Sister Loretta met me for breakfast. "Have you found your pearl of great price yet?"

"I found pearls of tapioca pudding," I joked. "Honestly, this is harder than I expected."

"It always is. But is it worth the search for you, Meg? Are you doing all right?"

I was caught off-guard by her more motherly than holy concern. "I'm not sorry I came, but I didn't expect to have so many questions. I wish the Lord would speak a little louder."

"Patience, my dear. He will speak when you're ready, and you will hear him." With no further comment, Sister Loretta flipped through the New Testament paperback she had set next to her orange juice. She stopped here and there before handing it back to me. "Read this one today." She buttered a piece of toast. "Oh, by the way, I've been meaning to ask you about your family. Do you have responsibilities?"

The mound of tapioca suddenly seemed a mountain. "What kind of responsibilities?"

"Something you need to consider is if your mother will need you as time passes. Sisters often have siblings who care for aging parents, but sometimes not. What's your situation?"

I realized I hadn't thought my decision affected anyone else's future, only mine. I told her Eddie's upholstery job paid decently. An earlier conversation had covered the territory about his homosexuality, so I felt comfortable telling her that he and Hank did practical things like take Mom to the grocery. "They treat her to dinner out each week. I think she'll be fine."

Sister Loretta seemed satisfied.

But my mind spun. What if Eddie and Hank didn't stay together? What if Eddie got back on the booze? I would need to help out at some point.

In my room, I sank into the nubby recliner to read the day's assigned passage: the story about the disciples' boat getting tossed in a storm at sea. Afraid they would drown, the disciples woke Jesus, who slept in the stern of the boat. He calmed the wind for them. My stomach rocked like a boat in a storm. *Wake up, Lord.*

I wandered down the hall to the chapel and slipped into a wooden pew as if it were a boat. I sat rather than knelt. I needed to think more than pray. Had I separated myself so completely from my family that it never occurred to me how my decision might affect them? Geez. It made sense as a youngster to build walls against the chaos in our house, especially during the fighting years before the divorce. Did it make sense now?

I was a grown woman, on the verge of making a life-changing decision. Who was I in relation to them—daughter? caretaker? chauffeur? Christopher Sister, or sister? Would I give them grandchildren, nieces, nephews—or prayers? Who were they to me? Who would I let them be? I insulated myself from them as parents and brother for the reason they so often failed me in those roles. Easier to think of them as people in proximity to me, but not in my private orbit.

Memories rose like waves—playing hide and seek with Dad; Mom braiding my hair; Eddie walking me to school. They may have failed me dozens of times, but they'd cared for me hundreds of times.

I remembered something Andy often said: "Everyone is always doing the best they can." I usually tossed it off as a worn-out platitude, but today the truth of the saying sank in.

Was there any way I could set things right with my dad? That was the tough one.

On Friday, I spent the morning hours in the large novitiate parlor where young women used to gather to read or sing together, perhaps say a rosary. A row of casement windows looked out on the convent grounds. I tread the wide floor-boards like walking the plank. Five days ago, I expected to join the Sisters—and live in holy separation from Andy the rest of my life. All I needed was a sign from the Lord blessing my decision. Day Five. No sign yet.

I put on my jacket and followed a path leading to a white picket fence. Neat, pristine. A low border, not a barrier. How many people live on the other side of the fence who never cross into this sacred place? The Sisters worked wonders with those who found their way to this quiet retreat, but what about everybody else? *Which side of the fence do you want me on, Lord?*

Leaves crinkled underfoot as I roamed through an old oak grove that spread beyond the pickets. I ran my fingers across rough crags of bark. Crawly creatures called this place home— itty-bitty ants and many-legged spiders. One of them was in transit from a tree trunk to my pants leg. I bent down and let it crawl across the back of my hand before returning it to the vertical trek up the oak. "Whoosh, Spidey, whoosh away."

Back at the novitiate, I sat down on the parlor sofa and ran my hand over the colorful needlepoint. The kind of fabric my brother took pride in choosing for his upholstery—silk damask magenta hummingbirds frolicked among gold and teal trumpet flowers. Heralds of heaven's glories. Perfectly coordinated striped drapes lined the casement windows. My attention fixed upon a tree, one of the old oaks, far in the distance. Its russet leaves embroidered the pale blue sky. My heart moved from this roomful of stillness to the tree rustling out there in the wild, unsheltered, yet giving shelter to anyone who came by.

An hour passed. I went out to the tree and breathed damp earth.

My last full day at Christopher House dawned clear, but cool enough for the woolen shawl and leather gloves I packed. I tried to follow Sister Loretta's advice not to worry about whether I would go home with an answer or not. But a tense ache kept riding across my back.

Where would I live my life without Andy, if not here?

On my umpteenth meditative walk, I followed the creek across the bridge to the low white fence, its rough wood coated in peeling paint. Slivers snagged the fringe of my shawl, causing it to tighten around me. A rush ran through me, remembering the warmth of Andy's firm embrace. The caught fringe snarled into a knot.

Sister Loretta met with me in the guest parlor after dinner. She settled into a high-backed chair. Her deep blue eyes inspected me. "This has been a hard week for you, no?"

I couldn't deny it. "I came to Christopher House eager and ready to move on with my life," I said. "But I've only found questions with few answers."

The setting sun backlit her graying hair so it appeared silver-plated. "Remember the Lord's promise," she said. "*Ask and you shall receive; seek and you shall find; knock and it shall be opened to you.*" She leaned forward. "Do not doubt the Lord wants to give you good things, Meg. You may not get the answer you were looking for, but much has happened this week."

I looked past her to the last rays of light touching the old oaks.

"You have sought the Lord's will with a sincere heart," she said. "He will honor that." Sister Loretta asked me to pray with her in the chapel.

We knelt in the front pew, made the sign of the cross, and squeaked on leatherette kneelers. After about a quarter hour, she pushed herself up as one with arthritis does and gamely limped to the altar. A narrow cut-glass vase with a single rosebud kept vigil next to the tabernacle. She brought it to me. "This is for you, Meg." Like chanting a prayer, she said, "The rose, once given ..." I waited for more of what sounded like the opening line of a poem, but that was all. "Good night. Sleep well."

I carried the gift back to my room. The rose, once given. I placed the bud vase on the dresser and nuzzled the soft edges of barely open petals. A moist spritz of honey met my nostrils. When I held my thumb to the ruby bud, I almost felt a pulse.

The rosebud could have enchanted me all night, but I needed to pack for the journey home. And my eyelids begged rest.

It seemed only minutes later when I awoke, startled, still half in a dream ...

A little girl wearing red Keds on a playground swing called out to me, "Higher, Mommy, higher!" I pushed her back and forth, back and forth. Taller, maybe older, children filled other swings. They pumped their legs to beat the band. An orange VW van pulled up. "Time to go home," I said. The girl in red Keds ran into my arms and gave me a big hug. "Did you have fun today, Rebecca?" She smiled a toothy grin. The driver came over, a man with ruddy cheeks and a hearty laugh. He held out his arms and everyone scooched off their bucket seats. When a squirrel ran by, Rebecca screamed in fright. "Don't be afraid," said the man. We all grabbed hands and skipped to the van.

I slowly replayed the dream. The little girl had called me "Mommy." I didn't tense. Whenever anyone called me "Sister," I tensed tight as a coil.

Rebecca? Rebecca was one of the kids in my class. She would be a year older by now. I missed watching the kids grow up, though I worried how their developmental delays would affect them as teenagers and young people. Who would love them?

Gray-blue morning light hinted at dawn. I rolled up the blinds and opened the window. The North Star flickered bright. A waft of air, soft as a silk scarf, touched my shoulder. Soon I heard Sisters chanting morning prayer in chapel:

Ave Maris Stella—Hail, Star of the Sea. Sailors' compass.

The rosebud quietly bloomed on the dresser. I slipped into my robe and thumbed a rosary bead as I pondered the bud's secret center. *Hail Mary, full of grace.*

When I took the rose out of its vase to change water, a thorn pricked my finger. Blood, a drop, tasted like warm melted copper. I was awake and alive—and awash in longing for the kind of love I had lived in my dream.

The rose, once given … I was the rose, and I had given myself to Andy.

Lord, how can I make a family now?

If Andy ever reached out to me again, I would go to him. I knew that. But did I love him enough to let him do his own searching? Find his own dream, whether it included me or not?

I needed to make a home. I knew that now for sure. With or without Andy. More than a want, more than a dream. That's how I loved best.

When I placed my rose in fresh water, a petal fell. *The rose, once given.*

CHAPTER 14

DEN

THE MORNING OF MY DEPARTURE from Christopher House, I rose early. Sister Loretta, the only one in the breakfast room, sipped a cup of tea. Her larkspur eyes focused on the faraway. As I approached, she motioned for me to sit down. I poured myself a glass of orange juice.

"You have a glow in your cheeks that I haven't seen all week."

"Sister Loretta, how do you know when a decision is right?"

She set her tea aside and folded her hands. "Have you made a decision?"

"Yes," I nodded.

"Are you happy?"

"Yes."

"Do you have any doubts?"

"Not anymore, Sister."

"Well then, it appears you have made a right decision."

My fidgeting fingers relaxed. "I'm surprised to be telling you this, because it's not what I expected to happen this week. I wanted to join the Christopher Sisters. I enjoyed working with the retreat team, and the quiet beauty here. But I would be running away from how I love best."

"How do you love best, Meg, or are you still searching?"

I shared my dream of the girl on the swing at the playground. "I need to make a happy home, a family ... someday."

Sister Loretta walked to the window overlooking the terrace below. She leaned on the sill, bracing her palms on it.

"If your plan is meant to be, the Lord will clear a path." She turned to face me. "But what will you do until 'someday' arrives?"

Her question reeled me back to immediate concerns. "I miss teaching and hope I can return to the school district next semester. In the meantime, I'll continue my work in the parish."

"You're going back to that den of celibates?"

I never heard the word 'celibates' before, much less the phrase "den of celibates." She did not say it as a compliment. "Do you mean the priests?"

Her face held as much care as her tone did irritation. "Yes, the priests."

I held my empty juice glass. Sister Loretta had drained my last illusion—the priesthood was not the benign patriarchy I once leaned upon as a bulwark of faith.

"My job is there." Her concern touched me, but she didn't have bills to pay. I could manage a couple more months at the parish. I wouldn't be confronted with the "den of celibates" very often with most of my time spent visiting sick and elderly parishioners.

"Are you hoping your priest will be waiting for you?" Her eyebrows arched.

"No, I'm not going back for Andy," I assured her as much as myself. I wouldn't pressure him. True, I would fall into his arms any day of the week—but only if he was sure. At this late juncture, I was ready to wait for someone else, someone without Andy's heavy baggage. Or go it alone if there was some other way to make a family. I wondered if single people could adopt. The little girl in my dream called me "Mommy," but she didn't call the man "Daddy."

Sister Loretta walked me to my car after breakfast. "I will worry about you, Meg. If you need to talk, or ever need anything—or if you change your mind—don't hesitate to call me."

I thanked Sister Loretta from the bottom of my heart, took one last look at the silver cross on the bell tower, and headed home. Christopher House had given me an oasis as well as a sense of the sacred—admittedly also an escape. I was depleted. With God's grace, I would have good things to give again. Time to replenish the store before moving on.

℘ ℘

I barely got to my office in the Parish Center Monday morning before Father Mack greeted me. "How was your time with the good Sisters?" His voice carried a joyful lilt.

"Wonderful." I neatened a few papers on my desk. "Leo said the priests took bets on when I would join the convent. Hope you didn't bet too much." I turned on the desk lamp. "I didn't make the cut. Seems God has other plans."

Father Mack's posture stiffened. He clasped his hands behind his back. His jowls twitched. "God's ways are indeed not our ways, are they?" He left muttering something about the problem with Maria.

I caught his reference to the *Sound of Music* and told myself to be on the lookout for a tall, handsome Austrian with a brood of children. Not an unhappy thought.

Ruth stopped by later in the day, teasing me with a lacy white head doily. "Will you be putting on the veil any time soon?"

"Not if God has anything to say about it."

She folded her arms and gave me a long look. "I could have told the Lord as much."

About a week later, Leo said he got a letter from Andy in Canada "sounding sunny as the Riviera." He tossed his arms in exasperation. "That guy wouldn't let on if they were plucking out his toenails. By the way, they're keeping him until Thanksgiving."

While I appreciated hearing my reprieve from Andy would be longer than expected, the scenario Leo described seemed overblown. "What's so hard about brushing up his French?"

"Oh, my," said Leo flustering his tuft of hair. "You must know it's not the nouns, but their gender that's difficult to master."

Leo's roundabout allusion confirmed my suspicion that Andy hadn't been sent away to work on language, but rather matters of masculinity and femininity. I nodded acknowledgment.

"Do you know what Sister Loretta, the novice director, called you priests?"

"Can't imagine."

"A den of celibates."

Leo slapped his knee. "Sister Loretta is a wise woman."

∞ ≈

Regular routines ticked off the days until Andy's return. I dreaded seeing him again as much as I looked forward to it. Thursday night, I threw a load of laundry in the wash and picked up a book to read. An hour later, a knock on the door startled me. Probably my neighbor wanting to use the washer. Or ... could Andy be back already? What to say?

I opened the door. The pit of my stomach knotted hard.

"Father Darren, what are you doing here?"

"Heard you're not going to be a nun after all. Wondered if you wanted to talk about it."

I held the door, speechless.

"Aren't you going to invite me in?

The door stood halfway open, halfway closed.

"Didn't mean to disturb you," he said.

My knees went to mush.

"It's my birthday tomorrow."

His breath smelled beery.

Darren pushed the door all the way open and wiped his feet on the welcome mat. The damp shoulder of his raincoat brushed my neck. He took off his jacket, shook it, and laid it over a dining chair. "You don't mind?" He made himself comfortable on the couch, drumming the cushion. "Come, sit down. We should celebrate my birthday—and you, free of the nunnery."

"What are you doing"—my voice cracked—"for your birthday?" I gripped the high back of the Cogswell chair.

"That's up to you." His lips that never smiled cracked into a grimace. "Maybe we could, you know, do stuff. Hey, why are you still standing?"

The sturdy frame of the old chair shielded me. *Do stuff?* His words hissed in my ear. Did he know about Andy and me? My throat went dry. "Not a good idea, Darren."

"Don't play innocent with me."

My nails dug into the chair's welt cord piping.

"Come here. I want to talk to you." His jaw jutted out over a maroon turtleneck. "I thought we could have a nice visit. Who knows? Maybe get a relationship going."

The absurdity of the situation made me want to laugh, but my mouth wouldn't move. I was absolutely parched. I braced myself against the chair back and prayed in desperation. *Oh, God—I need you—now.*

Darren pulled a black leather cigar case from his pocket and laid it on the coffee table. "Prayer group chipped in for my 30th birthday. Too bad you don't come anymore."

Water, I needed water. "Do you want a drink?"

"What do you have?" He slid a slim Winchester from its case, and a torch lighter.

"I'll go see." I went to the kitchen and quietly unlatched the back door to run upstairs to the neighbors. Stopped. Damn. Thursday—their bowling night. No one would be home.

I poured myself a glass of water, thirsty enough to drink a vat of the stuff. Without much thought, I reached in the cupboard for my largest stainless-steel mixing bowl and filled it with water. A vat of water. I stared into the liquid. What was I doing? As if looking into a crystal ball, other images surfaced: Jesus and the woman at the well. Jesus changing water into wine. Jesus washing the feet of Judas. I wrapped a towel around my waist and carried the bowl of water into the living room. I set it on the floor in front of Darren. "Take off your shoes."

Darren's eyes rolled cold toward me. "What do you think you're doing?"

"Isn't this how it's done?"

"In Lent." He moved the bowl of water aside. "It's not Lent."

His amorous pretense broken, I sat down on the edge of the chair. "When men and women 'do stuff,' as you put it, they're usually looking toward marriage. If you want to be a priest, you can't do those things."

Andy and I had gotten burned badly going in a direction we couldn't if he wanted to stay a priest. We agonized, but Darren only wanted to "do stuff"—like it didn't matter. As if he were entitled to give himself a "birthday present." To use me—without consequence. I wanted to throw the bowl of cold water at him and see him squirm. But I didn't want to ruin my couch.

Darren took a drag from his cigar. He propped his fore-arms on his knees and watched the tobacco burn. A couple of minutes passed. Flicked ash in the bowl of water.

"I knew a woman in Germany. A Belgian sister. Nicole. I was in seminary." He drew a puff on his cigar. Exhaled the smoke—straight at me.

"I asked her to take an assignment in the States. That way, we could see each other sometimes. But her nunnery wanted her in Louvain." He sneered the word. "She was an artist. They had good studios." He pinched the lit stub with his thumb and forefinger. "She went to Louvain."

His voice rasped as if a razor nicked his vocal cords.

The knot in my stomach loosened. "I'm sorry for your loss."

In the silence, I grasped a memory from months ago. The painting hanging over his bed. The "she" who wouldn't let him give it away. His anger toward her.

She had a name.

Darren got up and threw his cigar paraphernalia into his pocket without reassembling it. I retrieved his raincoat and gave it to him. He put it on as if covering himself in a thousand shadows. He stumbled toward the door. I laid my hand on the doorknob, but his tobacco-stained fingers grasped mine from behind. He spun me around, kissing me so hard my tooth bit the fleshy inside of my lower lip. "No. Darren, I'm not who you want."

"She was the only one I ever would have married. Shame you have her hair."

I locked the door behind Darren, pressing my forehead against it until a smear of sweat told me a long length of time had passed. The stench of his cigar lingered in the room. I opened the windows in the apartment and gulped damp air.

The round stainless-steel vessel filled with water rested on the floor. I emptied it carefully, watching the slow splash of salvation trickle away.

Lord, were you here? Am I safe now?

I sat down in my grandmother's rocker and rubbed the bowl dry with the towel from my waist. Mom used to sit in the rocker reading to Eddie and me from *The Wizard of Oz*. I begged her again and again to show me the picture of Dorothy dousing the Wicked Witch of the West. Would Darren have evaporated if I threw the water at him—or would I only have a soggy couch?

The evening's scene played like a scratchy needle on vinyl. The only sense I could make of it made no sense. He had barged in wanting me to be somebody else for him, for one night anyway. Why didn't he ask that nun to marry him? No wonder she went to Louvain. His story haunted me. How would Andy and I end up? At peace, or riddled with unfinished business?

Secrets. Did every priest keep secrets? They played fast and loose with a vow the rest of us thought meant not only remaining unmarried but also unbedded.

Sister Loretta's words crystallized. "Den of celibates."

I couldn't tell Father Mack about the uninvited knock. Though he never confronted me directly, signs indicated his awareness that something transpired between Andy and me.

Although I was sure Leo understood the difference between Andy and Darren, he was low man on the totem pole. Powerless.

Darren's knock on my door crossed too many lines. I couldn't stay silent. Not this time. He might have hurt me—in my own flat. Who would he try next?

My old German prof, Father Wilhelm, was generous to me in college. Had a good enough opinion of me that he arranged a nanny job so I could afford our class trip to Frankfurt. I didn't see him often anymore, but he never failed to offer a kind word.

He wouldn't know about Andy. I wouldn't have to explain the difference between a simple love and Darren's distorted actions.

I called to make an appointment to visit the faculty residence on Saturday. I would tell him what happened. I might have grown up on the wrong side of the tracks, but no one had the right to use me for a one-night stand—least of all a priest. Father Wilhelm couldn't make it unhappen, but maybe he could do something to get this bad apple out of the bin.

I rang the buzzer at the faculty priests' residence and held my breath.

"Who's there?" It sounded like a student's voice. I worked the reception desk one semester. One of the lighter tasks for work-study students.

"Meg Joyce to see Father Wilhelm."

Buzz. The terrazzo tile in the reception area was buffed to the same high polish as ever.

I held my winter gloves in both hands to keep my fingers from trembling. How do I tell Father Wilhelm one of his brother priests is knocking on doors expecting to get laid?

A slight man in a black clerical suit broke into a big smile as he walked toward me. "*Guten Morgen*, Meg. It has been too long. How goes everything? Come in. Tell me what you've been up to." He led me into a parlor furnished with easy chairs.

"Visiting the sick for St. Gabe's is good, but I hope to get back to teaching again. That's my true calling. Being a nanny for the family in Germany was good practice. How are they?"

"They're expecting another baby this summer. That will make three children under 5 years old. Maybe you want to go back?" He rapped the wide wood armrest.

"If only I could." My eyes stung, filled with memories of the sunny summer when I was part of a happy family.

The crease in Father Wilhelm's forehead grew deeper. "Everything okay?"

I looked down, shaking my head from side to side. "Do you know Father Darren?"

"From Campus Ministry? Sure. Why?"

"I don't know how to tell you this. There's no good way. I didn't believe it myself." I folded and unfolded my hands a dozen times.

"Tell me what, Meg?" Father Wilhelm leaned in close as if he was going to hear a confession. Oh, no, he thinks it's my fault.

"Thursday night ... he came to my apartment. I didn't invite him." My pulse raced. "He said he wanted a 'relationship' with me, but I don't think that's what he meant." I doubled over.

"*Mein Gott!*" Father Wilhelm fell back in his chair as if I had dealt him a body blow. His eyes shut into two canyons as he hit his forehead with the back of his hand. "He is such a *boy*."

A *boy*? At 30? Was I, at 24, a *girl*?

Father Wilhelm drooped. "Are you all right?"

My spine prickled. "I didn't let him do anything," I said.

"Good." He stood up like a sailor getting his land legs and ushered me to the parlor door. "Leave it alone, Meg. I will talk to him. And don't open your door to strangers."

That was the problem—Darren wasn't a stranger. We were supposed to trust priests. How did Darren ever slide through to become a priest in the Order of Clement? I hoped Father Wilhelm could straighten out this boy in a man's body, this choirboy who sang off-key.

Castrato.

I walked toward the edge of campus, to the arched wooden doors of St. Gabriel's church. I wanted to pray. But my hand froze encircling the brass pull.

Lord, I don't know where you live anymore.

CHAPTER 15

WOMAN & CHILD

ANDY LOVED ME AS A WOMAN—and abandoned me because I was a woman. Darren wanted me as a woman, in place of another woman.

Who am I to you, Lord? And what am I doing in this den of celibates?

When I heard Andy's voice for the first time since he returned from Canada, I stole away to the church at the end of day. Not that I believed God would be there for me, but because I needed a quiet place to collect my jumbled nerves. I took the indoor route through the mezzanine level dining room and past Josie's kitchen, hoping no one would be there.

As I entered the passageway, I noticed a door slightly open and glimpsed a prayer room with half a dozen scattered kneelers. A tabernacle and vigil candle set on a simple altar. I knelt and rested my head on my hands.

Lord, what am I doing wrong besides being a woman?

Gradually, I became aware of someone standing next to me. When I looked up, Father Cronin said, "This is the community's chapel." I nodded and continued praying. He took another step closer. He repeated in a loud whisper, "This is the community's chapel."

Many months had passed since I heard him tell Ruth, "This is the community's dining room"—but the echo and fracas that followed remained vivid. The hair on the back of my neck triggered flight—immediately—or risk having a tabernacle thrown at me. I held back a huge sob—a woman couldn't so much as be left to pray in a place where one of these men didn't want her. "Sorry," I said. "Didn't know."

The passageway broke into two wings. To the right, I would end up in the worship space left open for weekday Mass and devotionals. I turned left into the main church passage. The main church only opened for Sundays and ceremonies. It would be quieter there.

The nave appeared cavernous without any worshippers. Alone, I sat on the marble floor, very close to the altar. The table of the Lord was empty, save for a plain white cloth. I took a hemmed linen edge of the altar cloth and dried hot tears from my brush with Father Cronin.

Late afternoon sun poured through the stained-glass windows and spilled their images onto the veined marble floor. A large translucent crucifix appeared in front of me. The veins in the floor mixed with Jesus' savaged body—hurting on the outside like I hurt on the inside. His eyes seemed to see into mine with profound compassion.

My hands merged into the filtered light when I touched his feet. Nailed. Immobile. Stuck.

So, this is where you are, Lord.

Mom used to tell me stories about St. Teresa, her namesake. The saint said, "Christ has no body now but yours, no hands, no feet on earth but yours."

A woman's body?

Perhaps God's breath filled women every bit as much as men, but how to be Christ's hands and feet? Especially since I wasn't going to be a nun like St. Teresa. I studied the doors leading out of the church and thought of people going by—like the people on the other side of the fence at Christopher House. The ones who never found their way inside. I turned back to the crucifix, but the image waned in the dimming sun. My hands softened in the remaining light.

I wanted to hold children, make a home, love and be loved. Was that enough?

Deep in thought, I returned to the Parish Center to get my coat and go home. Andy was coming up from the lower level. Father Mack had let him set up a carpentry shop in an unused area. Andy was good at joinery. When we'd visited his family's home for Jenny's party, he'd smiled with pride, showing off a dovetailed bookcase he had made.

I eyed the wood-handled chisel he carried. "The tool man. Hi."

Andy smiled. "The visitor lady." He twirled the chisel by its handle. "Josie asked me to make a pencil groove in her recipe box."

"Sounds like a recipe for disaster."

"Nice to hear you laugh, Meg. Thought you must hate me."

I took the last step down from the mezzanine level. "No, *Alfons* Vogel, I don't hate you. I don't understand you—but I don't understand much these days."

"Want to sit down a minute? It's been a while."

We hadn't passed a civil word since before I left for Christopher House. We turned into the nearest meeting room.

He set down the tool and his hand brushed mine. The warmth of his touch brought me back to earth—with a thud. Whatever I had in me to give, I couldn't give it here, not in this Church, and definitely not with Andy.

My words came slowly. "When I prayed this afternoon, I remembered St. Teresa's poem about becoming Christ's hands and feet. I'm having a hard time figuring out how."

"Yes, I know the prayer." Andy clasped my hands and leaned toward me, raising them to his brow. I rested my head on our laced hands. We sat like that a few minutes. A memory of the way things used to be.

Andy released his grip. "He'll show you how. He'll show us how."

"The Lord seems to open doors only to slam them in my face," I said.

"I know what you mean, Meg. I wish I knew the answer."

"This isn't good for us to be thrown together every day, Andy. I need space—away from this Church where women don't belong. I need to be where I'm loved and can love back."

"I wish I could give you that."

I ran my finger across the sharp half-inch flat edge of his chisel. "You could, Andy. But you love other things more."

☎ ☧

My old department head slammed another door in my face: Mrs. Olson changed her mind and wouldn't retire in January after all. She asked if I was interested in covering a six-week maternity leave in the spring. Sure, but I needed a way out much sooner. I considered any job slightly related to teaching, maybe Day Care Coordinator or Museum Guide.

I shuffled to the kitchenette, hoping the coffeepot wouldn't also come up short. Father Mack poured himself a cup—the last cup. I took a Lipton teabag and immersed it in hot water.

"Why don't you join me in my office, Meg? Not good to drink alone."

I eased into one of the two oxblood side chairs and complimented him on his collection of Chinese indigo vases. "Lovely things."

"Blue is the color of Our Lady," he said. "One of her important feasts is coming up December 8—the Immaculate Conception." He shook his finger at me. "Now don't be getting it confused with the virgin birth. This feast is about Mary's coming into the world without sin."

I assured him I knew the difference, thanks to my 7th grade Sister. "Though it's hard to believe anyone besides Jesus was born without sin."

"She *had* to be preserved from sin if she was going to be the mother of Our Lord."

"Of course, Father Mack."

I didn't tell him about the first time I questioned the doctrine of the Immaculate Conception, nor that it took a Sunday School class of teenagers to make me question Mary's virginity. True daughter of Catholic schooling, I said "Blessed *Virgin* Mary" as if it were her middle name, not necessarily attached to meaning.

He opened the side drawer of his desk and pulled out a stack of photos. "Women are marvelous creatures, Meg. I don't say that lightly." He riffed through the photos, stopping at one. His features softened. "Delores."

Father Mack passed me the faded picture of a woman, perhaps in her mid-30s standing on a ladder to top the Christmas tree with a star. She was looking over her shoulder and laughing as if the Kodak Instamatic caught her by surprise. The small square print conveyed few details, but the happiness of the moment was evident.

"Sister Delores. She was full of grace," he said. "Wonderful woman. We served on a retreat team together. Trained community leaders on peace and justice issues one parish at a time. The Spirit was blowing in the wind."

"One night, we fell asleep in the lounge sitting up. We were that tired. When we woke, the lights had gone out. She let me hold her, and I held her—just held her—the rest of the night."

I studied the photo one more time before returning the memory into his hands. "Christmas is a beautiful time of year."

"Tis," he said. "Virgin and Child." He played with a corner of the photo's half-inch white border. "Makes us men wonder what we're good for."

Virgin. Mother. "They needed Joseph to make a family."

"Ah, so they did." He scanned my face. "Some young women pray to St. Joseph for a husband. Do you, Meg?"

"I haven't heard of the custom."

"You should pray to him … since other avenues haven't worked out."

Father Mack rose from his chair, letting the photo fall on his desk. The meeting was over.

His advice shook me. How much did he know? Why did he tell me, show me, that feelings between a man and woman were not unknown to him?

That night the first snowfall of the season thickened the sky. I watched white flakes come down from heaven, sparkling like stars on a thousand Christmas trees.

Immaculate.

Would Delores be "full of grace" if she let Father Mack do more than hold her? Did he cut his men slack because he knew his own longing?

Was I a Madonna or a whore—or simply a woman who had not been born immaculate?

$$\infty \, \wp$$

Winter white. Only pine trees showed any sign of green. The Parish Center opened its doors to desperate faces each day. Mothers barely looked up as Sue asked them what she might do for them. Always the same: "Could you put my kids on the list for a few Christmas toys?" The men hesitated, cap in hand. Sue covered for them saying, "Oh, it must be Father Andy you're wanting to see." Andy had become the go-to priest for handouts and a word of encouragement.

I saw him in the hall rubbing his forehead after a midday encounter.

"Rough case," he said.

A ruckus at the front door broke the moody moment. Sounded like a dog barking. We peered around the corner. A young boy held a rambunctious spaniel.

"I need to get my dog blessed for Christmas."

Andy smiled at boy and dog. "What's the name of this dog? And who might you be?"

"That's Ajax." The dog shook his curly mane. "I'm Tommy. If I get my dog blessed, maybe Mom will let him come with us to Midnight Mass on Christmas Eve."

Andy suppressed a laugh, but his eyes glinted. "You must obey your mom, of course. But I can tell you this—wherever Ajax is, and wherever you are, Baby Jesus will see you and smile." He proceeded to bless the dog with as much solemnity as he could muster: "*Ajax, may you be blessed in the name of the Father, and Son, and Holy Spirit. May you and Tommy enjoy life together and find joy with the Christ Child.*"

We all said "*Amen*" except Ajax—he barked.

Andy and I stepped outside to wave goodbye to Tommy and his hallowed dog.

"Kids. Always a surprise. Glad you didn't join the convent?"

I watched Tommy run after Ajax rather than look into Andy's hazel eyes. This wasn't a conversation I wanted to have. I leaned against the wrought iron railing that lined the steps.

"You wanted children, Andy. How did you commit to a life without them?"

He crossed his arms. "It's part of the sacrifice of being a priest, Meg. You know that." His eyes followed a dripping icicle.

The walls of my throat felt coated in ash. "I used to take that for granted, but now I wonder: Who asks this of you?"

"I gave that up to serve God."

"No. God didn't ask this of you. The Church asks this of you. You gave this up in obedience to the Church. God asks us to be who we are."

Andy edged closer to me. "Then why were you going to give up children? Why did you think about joining the convent?"

"Because I was listening to you instead of God. I was running away because it's too hard seeing you all the time. Making love is the way children come, you know." I turned away and grasped the iron rail, its spikes like spears that could cut my heart.

A shadow eclipsed Andy's face. "Come with me." He tramped down the steps to the sidewalk and waited for me.

I let go of the rail and followed his deliberate steps through the parking lot, wrapping my sweatered arms around myself against the cold. We paralleled the heap of bricks called a church, turned at the corner, and entered the vestibule. A shaft of sunlight narrowed as the door closed.

Andy led me to the stone baptismal font. He spread his hands over the golden dome that covered it and pressed his palms into the etched wings of the Holy Spirit.

"Each time I do a baptism, I quietly give the child an extra name." He turned to face me, the green flecks in his eyes drowning in their muddy brown pool.

"I give each child my first name … because I can't give any child my last name."

Someone opened the heavy wooden church door and let in a draft of wind.

From the shallows of my breath, I said, "Alfons is a good name for a child."

CANDLEWOOD

Spending extra time at the parish was not in my plan, but Eileen asked me to go with her to Saturday's *Advent Morning of Reflection.* Since my sojourn at Christopher House, I begged off her overtures for lack of feeling sociable. Though I hadn't told her about trying to join the nunnery, I did tell her that I made a retreat. She teased me, "Do you have to spend all your time being holy?" Her sister was a nun—Eileen anything but—so I appreciated the mile-long effort behind her willingness to spend time together doing something "holy" for the sake of our friendship. I agreed to join her and suggested lunch and a gabfest afterward.

When we arrived at the Parish Center activity room, I saw Ruth pressed into service as primary greeter and seater. She asked, "How did you get out of extracurricular duty?"

I winked at Eileen. "Said I was bringing a friend."

"Thanks for the tip. I'll remember that next time."

Ruth seated us at one of the round tables used for everything from fish fry to senior Scrabble games. White tablecloths, red poinsettias, pitchers of punch, and a plate of Josie's cookies on each table transformed the humble *Advent Morning of Reflection* into a festive gala.

Father Mack welcomed the attendees. He took pains to thank those who made the trip from the Twin Cities saying he hoped they'd return at Christmas to hear St. Gabriel's Angelic Choir—for which the parish was known.

I whispered to Eileen, "And bring your pocketbooks." She feigned shock.

Father Mack quieted himself. "It gives me great honor to bring you an extraordinary presenter today."

He walked over to a woman seated at the front table. Something was familiar about her. She wore a modest periwinkle blue dress that skimmed her figure. A wave of graying hair softly accented her forehead. Clear blue eyes widened when Father Mack took her arm, as if escorting a queen. His usual wan smile opened into a broad grin telling the group about retreats the two of them had given at parishes around the country.

Delores—Sister Delores—the woman topping the Christmas tree with a star in Father Mack's photo. I heard him ask Sue yesterday to buy flowers for the guestroom. Heat filled my stomach, and I crossed my arms tight around my midsection. Might Delores fall asleep in his arms again, as she had once upon a time?

Eileen must have noticed my reaction. She tugged at my sleeve. "Everything okay?"

I summoned composure from somewhere. "Just a little indigestion."

My mind spun. I assumed the relationship between Sister Delores and Father Mack flamed out long ago. How did this work? Falling in love was fine if one kept it at arm's length. *She let me hold her, just hold her.* Hugs and kisses, above the waist stuff. High school.

Or courtly love. Delores as Guinevere, bride of Father Mack's eternal King. Was this what they called "sublimation"? No problem peering or leering or lusting from afar. But to spark a bright light, tumble into each other's souls, touch, make love—damnation.

The den of celibates played by rules all their own. Women didn't make the rules—only ordained men made the rules. Women were supposed to play along. Some did.

If I could give up children, Andy and I could go about our business under the radar. The rules seemed to allow most anything—except having children. Legitimate children. Some popes had mistresses—and illegitimate children. Leo said he gave credence to those who claimed celibacy kept Church wealth intact. Medieval inheritance rules.

I didn't want to believe it.

Eileen was only too happy when I suggested leaving the *Reflection* at break time. At the diner, she shared the news that she was going to visit her sister the nun in New York.

"And—" she hunched over the table—"perhaps move there in spring."

I was dumbfounded. "What? Why?" Small-town Eileen in New York—unthinkable.

She leaned back. "Yeah, big move. But why not? A darn sight better than turning into a wrinkled old dollar bill working at the bank. I thought I might find a rich husband in finance, but they're all taken. I'm bored, Meg. I want to do more than count by fives and tens all my life."

I gaped at her. "What would you do? You don't know anyone there besides your sister."

"She said I could stay with her until I got settled. And earn my keep by helping with the kids at her school while I look for a job." Eileen wiped pancake syrup from her fingers and bit her lip. "What do you think of my plan?"

I thought she was crazy, but I said, "You're amazing."

"It's no more than the kind of thing you'd do, Meg. I would've been scared to death to go to Germany like you did junior year. *That* was amazing."

Eileen reminded me of a time before my wings got clipped. Seemed every time I tried to fly since then ended in disaster.

We spent the rest of the day shopping for things Eileen would need in New York—a cocktail dress, heels, evening bag.

"Do you really think you'll need these working with kids?"

"Well, I'll have dates at night. New York is a big pond."

Incorrigible.

𝄞 𝄢

I avoided Father Mack following the *Advent Reflection* with Sister Delores, but a week before Christmas, he asked me to sort the mail. Sue was out with a bad cold.

A heap of envelopes sat on Sue's otherwise neat-as-a-pin desk in the reception office. Much of it looked like Christmas cards. About as many were addressed to individual priests as to the parish at large—probably donations. I put them in Father Mack's cubby.

The slot for Campus Ministry staff overflowed. It was a student's job to pick up the mail, but not many were around during Christmas break.

Among the envelopes was a postcard for Darren. Intrigued by the intricate medieval drawing on the stamp, I looked closer. A crowned Mary lay on royal bedding holding her newborn Jesus. A chapel angel kept watch. Not the typical manger scene. Printed in the bottom of the frame, I read *BELGIQUE – NOËL*, and *KERSTMIS*.

Oh my God—hadn't Darren told me the painter, a nun who chose an art studio over him, went to a convent in Belgium? I restrained myself from reading the note but couldn't miss the single initial scrawled at the bottom: *N.* Nicole.

Darren had made the relationship sound dead as a doornail. Although a postcard was hardly intimate, she was reaching out. Was this an all-of-a-sudden thing, Christmas nostalgia?

When I heard someone coming down the main hall, I quickly stashed the card in its slot.

A man's voice whistled the tune for "Rudolf, the Red-Nosed Reindeer." Approaching Sue's office, he improvised the lyrics:

Suzy, with your eyes so bright,
Is there mail for me in sight?

Darren's voice. When he saw me, he did a doubletake, as if he'd seen a ghost. I wished I could disappear. He unbuckled his knapsack and threw it on the floor. "Getting CM mail."

"I'll get out of your way." I stepped over the knapsack.

Darren's fists clenched at his sides. "That's a good idea."

My head throbbed. "Look, you were way out of line to come to my flat."

"So I heard." He dumped the CM mail into his bag. "You went running to your buddy, Father Wilhelm." He glowered.

My voice rose. "What did you expect me to do? Roll over and play dead?"

Father Mack came out of his office. "What's this? Don't you like Father Darren's singing?" He gave Darren a hearty pat on the back. "Merry Christmas, my boy."

I wanted to strangle them both. "A misunderstanding," I said. "The mail's done." I left.

No sooner had I gotten seated in my office, but Darren thrust himself inside and closed the door. I armed myself with a paperweight, palming the heavy object.

Between his teeth, he said, "You might just be getting me killed."

"Father Mack likes you much too much to kill you."

Darren rolled his knuckles across my desk. "I'm supposed to go fix things with Nicole."

Nicole. Postcard. Belgium. Fix things? "Please take your hands off my desk."

"Listen. I want to tell you something." He broke into a sweat. "I *do* want to straighten out my life. But now," he nearly reeled, "my *dear* Nicole is on her way to Botswana."

Botswana? Africa? "I thought she was in Belgium."

"Was. They want her to set up some kind of arts co-op with the natives." He set down his knapsack and dropped into my side chair. "While she's weaving baskets, I'll be dodging border patrols." Darren set one elbow on the chair's arm and cradled the side of his head in his hand, eyes wild. "The only way I can see her is to go to the Clems' mission on the eastern border—in godforsaken Rhodesia." He stared at me. "By the time I get there … she could be dead."

I doubted she'd be doing arts in a danger zone. Darren dripped with sincerity—or was it whining? What did Nicole ever see in this hulk of a wimp?

"When do you go?"

"Soon, but not sure for how long. It's a temporary assignment."

Out of my hair. And certainly, out of his depth. "I'll pray for you."

Darren picked up his heavy knapsack and opened the door. "Thanks."

୫୦ ଓଃ

I needed to clear my head after seeing Darren. Outside in the wind, I looked up at the naked limbs of winter trees. Their structure uncamouflaged by leaves, boughs either embraced the sky or beat gnarled fists at heaven.

When Darren asked Nicole to take an assignment stateside, did he only want what Father Mack had with Sister Delores—an occasional visit for old time's sake? Is this how love affairs between priests and nuns, and other women, play out? Would God ask them to submerge their *human* love to show *His* love? It didn't seem to be working. God was not who I saw when I looked at these people. I saw brokenness, loneliness, fleeting moments. A high price to pay, no matter how noble the aspiration.

Men like Andy turned inside out.

It wasn't that I didn't see any happy, healthy priests and sisters. I saw many. I believed someone could choose to show their gratitude for God's steadfast love by putting themselves entirely, viscerally, bodily in his service. Rare, but not unknown. Others, like bachelor uncles and maiden aunts lived their lives and did their work. These people taught me in grade school and college.

But I also saw men and women, too many, neither happy nor healthy.

They hid a part of themselves, an open sore, a wound that never healed.

I decided then and there to make a clean break with Andy. Clean breaks heal better. I wouldn't keep the embers burning by sending postcards or visiting for long weekends pretending another purpose than snuggling for a night. No.

At a sunny clearing in the woods, I stepped on a patch of ice. It cracked. Rivulets streamed from underneath. Andy and I broke each other's hearts—cracked them open. Flowed into creation, the heart of God. We'd never be the same again.

Andy said the Clems promised him a wide-open kind of love would come in prayer—not from loving a woman. He pulled back from me like a guilty child with chocolate-stained hands. I hoped the Clems' promise would come true, or else he'd grow gnarled like an ugly tree.

Like Darren.

I wished God had opened my heart a different way. I didn't want to learn about love, intimacy, with Andy—an unavailable, taboo-laden obstacle course of a man.

But I wouldn't trade the months we had together for anything.

The sun's warmth caressed my cheek. I tucked my hands in my pockets. A smooth flat stone lay in one nubby corner, from the day Andy and I skipped stones at the boat launch. I made an indentation in an unmarked piece of snowless ground and buried it. Prayed for our transgressions. Not sure we sinned against God, but for sure we sinned against the den of celibates.

CHAPTER 16

LAST RITES

JANUARY BROUGHT A FULL ROSTER of hospital visits. Leo said many people willed themselves through the holidays but yielded to fate soon after.

Fate. Sitting in limbo seemed my fate. Waiting—for a husband to appear, for a job to open. Would I return to teaching in the spring to cover a six-week maternity leave, or wait for a more permanent offer? I came up empty-handed on other job applications. Everything seemed on hold. Even the snow piles stayed capped and crisp.

I didn't want to yield to the fate of waiting for my life to happen. Eileen's bold roll of the dice to New York made me want to rediscover my once gutsy self who crossed the Atlantic to live in a foreign country as nanny to unknown children.

Driving from hospitals to shut-ins, I muddled over my dilemma. The last time I felt a smidgen of my old self was when Beth and I visited her family on Long Island. I relished the days we went into Manhattan. Raw energy. People acted like they were going somewhere. Men in business suits, women dressed to the nines, pretzel vendors and card trick hustlers—all played at the top of their game. I wanted to find the top of my game—before I left this world accomplishing zilch.

Eileen was headed for New York. My best friend. I could visit her there. Or ... I bit my lip at the thought ... how might she feel about a joint expedition? We met for hamburgers and two days later, I broached the subject.

She spluttered her Coke. "And room together? Twice the fun at half the rent. Fabulous."

We spent the next weeks devouring *Mademoiselle* and *Cosmopolitan* magazines in an attempt to gain sophistication and savvy by osmosis. I set my sights on getting a job with *Sesame Street*. My students had loved the show. Kids. Yes, that's where my hands and feet belonged.

Lord, everyone sees the Holy Spirit as a dove, but I'm betting on Big Bird.

∮ ∯

Eileen and I talked almost every day about our gigantic plan. But before going anywhere, I wanted to settle a nagging score with my dad. Since the day at Christopher House when I let go of childhood disappointments, the desire to mend what I could with him had grown. If I was going to let another man into my life, I needed to deal with the first man in my life. If he had tried to be a horrible father, he couldn't have aced it better. The sad fact was that he wanted to be a good father but failed miserably—and he knew it.

Dad had visited Eddie and me before he and Sadie, his second wife, moved to Arizona a few years ago. In a last-ditch effort to make amends with his children, he admitted he drank too much, but said he changed. The drinking years robbed him of his corner grocery, his family, and his pride. He took a job as a used car salesman. Sold himself to the secretary at the car lot, Sadie. As if it would make up for years of missed birthdays, joyless holidays, and unremitting shame, he offered Eddie money to start his own upholstery shop.

"There's nothing like being your own boss," he said. "This is a loan. I want to give you a start, but I want you to be able to say you made it on your own."

Eddie said he was doing fine and didn't need it, but Dad pushed. Eddie took the money.

Dad smiled at me. "You'll marry soon. It'll be your husband's job to take care of you."

Who did he think took care of me when he stopped making child support payments?

Water under the bridge.

Botched as that last visit was, he'd made the effort. I had not given him an inch. I would reach out this one time. I called the phone number Dad scribbled in his Christmas card.

Sadie answered the phone. "Meg? Oh, Meg! Let me get your dad on the line."

Dad's gravelly voice greeted me. "Princess! You could only be calling your old dad for one thing—when's the big day?"

Oh, geez, he thought I wanted him to walk me down the aisle. "Hi, Dad. No, not engaged. I called because … in your Christmas card you said the desert was beautiful in late winter. Maybe I could come for a visit and see it?"

Dad took a breath, made a gurling sound, and coughed. "Visit? Is something wrong?"

"No, Dad, nothing's wrong. Everybody's okay. I've got some time off this winter." I figured I could whittle a week in Arizona before taking a bite out of the Big Apple.

"Of course, Princess. Would love to see you. Great." He talked in short bursts of breath. "March is nice, and April— that's when the flowers bloom in the desert. Could you come then?" He coughed, wheezing.

"Sounds good, Dad. I'll firm things up at work and call you soon."

His labored breath came again, and another. "I love you, Meggins."

It was the only time in my whole life I heard him say those words. I reached deep inside. "Love you too, Dad. See you soon."

After getting permission from Father Mack to use my remaining vacation time, I called Arizona to set the dates for my trip. Sadie broke down when she heard my voice. "Oh, darling, I looked for your number but couldn't find it in your dad's things. He was so looking forward to seeing you."

The trim princess model phone seemed to weigh a ton. He always called me "Princess."

"Your father was the happiest I ever saw him." She blew her nose. "He had a heart attack, dear. They couldn't save him."

My eyes burned as tears welled up. I didn't offer to come anyway. I wanted to remember my last phone call with him, not look at his grave. I wanted to hold onto that one last shred of evidence that he loved his daughter, not witness one more time he had someplace else to go.

I broke the news of Dad's death to Eddie.

"So, did he leave us anything?"

"No, Eddie, he didn't leave us anything, but as I recall, you got yours."

Eddie was only too happy to delegate the task of telling Mom. I met her for Sunday brunch, at a restaurant where we seldom ate.

I ran out of idle chit-chat as I poked at my poached eggs and jam-filled Bismarck.

"You seem distracted, Meg."

As I shared the news about Dad, she stared at the white cut-lace tablecloth and set her coffee cup on it. Her diamond-hocked ring finger traced the empty saucer's indent. Round and round, her finger rubbed the groove of time and worlds that once had been … and never were.

"So," she said, "I can call myself a widow now, not a divorcée."

I remembered the sawdust floor of Dad's grocery, and the day a mouse skittled across it. Mom screamed.

"Enough, Teresey!" Dad stomped the creature with his broom and crushed it underfoot. Red jelly crept out from gray splat edges. The auctioneers came that day. Sold everything. Nothing left but ten cents on the dollar to pay down the mountain of debt—and start over.

℘ ℘

By late January, Eileen and I had the nub of a plan for our New York foray. My friend would stay with her sister until she found a job. With her experience in a bank, she said it wouldn't take long; they always needed tellers. I would join her as soon as one of my resumes produced an interview. Too bad my teaching credentials didn't transfer for a license without extra courses.

I decided to unveil the plan at my January birthday dinner at Mom's house. Figured everyone would welcome a diversion from thinking about Dad. Apparently, Eddie and Hank also wanted to shake up the somber undertone. They brought fancy fringed blowout horns leftover from New Year's Eve to replace the ritual of blowing out birthday candles.

When Mom sliced my piece of cake, I blew the horn with gusto. "This will be an exceptional new year," I said—and proceeded to share the idea of moving to New York.

My news drew oohs and aahs from Eddie and Hank. "We're coming to visit you."

Seeing the pair together and happy eased my mind about leaving. Eddie had hit the six-month mark sober.

Hank named off museums I "must" see. His work at the art gallery took him to Manhattan for grants conferences. "Best 23 square miles on earth."

Mom wrung her hands. "Eileen's a flibbertigibbet—you can't be serious. What if something happens to you? Where will you live?" I spent the rest of the evening attempting to ease her mind with unfounded assurances everything would work out fine. I didn't dare tell her my own fears, nor why I needed to move a million miles away from St. Gabe's.

Despite Mom's fears, and my own, I patted myself on the back for taking steps toward a new life for myself. Andy could stew in his own juice.

Ⅴ Ↄ

Eileen and I announced our New York pipedream at Kelly's Pub in early February. Everyone wanted to know when we were setting out. Dates were tentative, but spring for sure.

Beth had become a regular at Kelly's. I credited her resilience moving past Flynn, the errant novice. She offered her parents as a way station any time we needed a hot meal. "Long Island is a short hop on the rails."

Going public made it official. No turning back. The flip-flop in my stomach alternated between excitement and fright.

A lanky newcomer to the ceili group sidled next to Eileen most of the evening. I had noticed him at the Christmas party asking her to dance—often. Obviously smitten. Bad timing that the object of his affection would soon be off to the big city.

I headed home from Kelly's with the Village People's "Y.M.C.A." blaring on my car radio. Snowplows had cleared the divided highway, but heavy winter blizzards left immense snow piles on both sides of the road. On sunny days, snow melted only to freeze at night. Traffic moved well, and I drove without a skitter.

Until a truck coming the other way crossed the median. Black ice.

"*No!*" I steered toward the shoulder. Stopped me cold.

My chest smashed into the horn.

I must have zonked. Sometime later, I heard sirens and opened my eyes. A fireman pried the car door open and eased my pinned body onto a stretcher. The pileup behind me looked like a drunken accordion, cars jammed helter-skelter.

Police kept asking me questions, and paramedics checked vitals. Someone said, "You're going to the ER, young lady. I'll call for a tow."

I roused when the paramedics hit a bump wheeling me into the hospital. In the ER room, a familiar face came into view. Hank.

"How'd you get here?" I asked.

"The police called me. Lucky you put my name as the emergency contact in your glove compartment."

My head throbbed. When I touched my forehead, my hand came back bloody red and wet. "Is the car okay?"

Hank ran his hand along the bed's siderail. "Don't worry about that now."

A scrub-clad doc tweezed shards of glass from my forehead and hair. I must have passed out. When I came to, the doctor called it a miracle I walked away without any broken ribs and told Hank he could take me home.

At their house in St. Paul, Eddie and Hank took turns easing my headache with cool compresses and changing bandages on my bruises. I ached all over.

After talking to the insurance company a few days later, I had more of a headache. The car was totaled.

Hank drove me home on Wednesday and I bussed it to work on Thursday. I would be bussing it for a while. Not great for a job that required driving from nursing homes to hospitals to old houses.

Josie baked cookies for my return. Father Mack oozed solicitous. Leo told me not to worry about a thing. He covered most of the week's visits.

Late in the day, I heard footsteps coming fast down the hall. "Meg, I heard about the accident. Oh my God, you're bruised. What happened?" Andy was literally out of breath.

I stared at him. I might have died. Should I have died? If I died, we'd both be free. "I'll be fine. My brother and Hank took good care of me. And Daisy the cat kept me company."

"Have you seen a doctor?"

"Yes."

"No concussion? You know, my sister, they watched her a few days …"

I relived the night Andy came to my apartment after the accident with his sister. He arrived a zombie—and left a new man. The first time we made love. We watched Jenny grow strong again and took it as a good omen for us.

"I remember, Andy." I wished he'd leave now. I couldn't hold it together much longer.

"Meg …"

"That's my name."

He stepped closer.

"Don't." I put my hands up for him to stop coming toward me. "If you come any closer, I may need you the way you needed me after your accident. That would be terrible, wouldn't it?"

He looked at me like a deer caught in headlights.

"Don't pretend to care. Please."

"I do care about you, Meg."

I turned away.

Andy backed out of my office slowly, leaned on the doorjamb a minute, then left. I heard his plod-plod-plod up the stairs to the priests' enclave.

I heard the door slam on his monk-like cell. Cramped, to remind him of his vow of poverty—not that he ever had worries where his next car, or meal, or roof would come from. Like the military, everything supplied so men could focus on mission. Exactly like the military, obedience the name of the game. Priests made a vow of it. That was the vow Andy kept. As long as he remained free of ballast like me and obediently went wherever he was sent, he could remain a commissioned officer. The vow of chastity? Irregularly kept. Me? Collateral damage.

With the insurance company dragging its heels, Ruth offered me the use of her car so I could catch up on visits to shut-ins. The priests only shared their cars with "the community."

⁀  

The Sunday after Valentine's Day, Eileen said she needed to talk. Since I was without a car, I asked her to come over. She hadn't seen me since the accident and gaped at my forehead.

"Looks worse than it is. I'll be down to Band-aids soon." With luck. "What's up?"

She blushed. "You know Mark—the tall one with deep blue eyes ...?"

Eileen could only mean the lanky guy who followed her around like a puppy. Why was she blushing? Did she like him? She hadn't said a word. "For sure."

"We've been seeing each other off and on since Christmas. Casual—I thought. But Meg, Valentine's Day ... a dozen gorgeous roses." Her arms swept up to encircle the huge bouquet in her dream-filled eye. "And we, you know ... How could I not?"

"Eileen?" My voice went up at the end.

Two donut-hole eyes widened. "Oh, Meg, he asked me to stay. Said he'd miss me too much if I moved to New York. I have to stay and give it a chance."

I wanted to be happy for her, but more than that, I wanted to wring her flibbertigibbet neck. She had no idea how much I counted on a new start in a new city.

"That's so romantic," I said.

I needed a car ... and a new plan.

₭ ₮

On Ash Wednesday, Father Mack invited me to meet in the upstairs living room. I wondered if he might offer a loan or a raise to help with buying a car. The insurance agency had left me aground—now nearly four weeks since submitting my claim.

"You've been somewhat stranded with us, Meg."

A less than subtle observation. I acknowledged it was taking longer than anticipated to get back on the road for visits. Out of the corner of my eye, I saw Andy rounding the turn up the stairs. A flashback to the night we stole past this room. The last time he held me—before fleeing from my tears.

"Ah, there you are my boy," said Father Mack. He motioned for Andy to sit with him on the couch. They looked like a father and son next to each other.

I would've understood if he asked Leo to sit in, but why Andy? He didn't make any attempt at eye contact with me.

A pain, sharp as gargoyle claws, dug at my chest—Father Mack knew. All those times I suspected he knew about Andy and me. Oh no, was this a belated counseling session for us?

"Besides the loss of your car, how are things going?"

"The bruises are nearly healed." Except for the fresh gash of Andy's silent presence.

Father Mack's eyebrows came together, forming a wrinkle between them.

I ventured to make this meeting about my work, not Andy and me. "Most of the visiting schedule remains unchanged. Ruth lends me her car part of the day for home visits. I bus where I can. Our volunteers offered to cover the outer ring of nursing homes until I find a new car."

"Lovely team of volunteers," said Father Mack. "Tell me, Meg, when you do make visits, are you leaving parish bulletins?" He crossed his arms and tapped one finger on his lips.

It seemed an odd obsession, not the first time he quizzed me about the poorly printed redundant scraps of news. Andy gripped the couch sidearm and seemed to squeeze it hard.

"I always leave the bulletin, Father Mack. You were so right that people would enjoy reading about parish happenings. Thank you again for the suggestion."

"Good. So … do you think they appreciate your visits?"

Why would he be sending me if he didn't assume parishioners appreciated the visits? When I hesitated, Andy sucked in his breath but didn't look up. My stomach got queasy.

"Why, yes, they do seem to enjoy the visits, especially receiving Holy Communion more than once a month on First Fridays when the priests go. The homebound folks say they don't know what they'd do without Ruth and me. When I learn of other needs during a visit, Ruth and I coordinate outreach efforts. For instance, she'll make sure a volunteer is available to shop for groceries if I flag someone who doesn't have family in the area."

As I prattled on, Father Mack listened, expressionless. Andy squirmed like a schoolboy.

"Also, as you know, I approached the nursing school to work with me arranging field work opportunities for student nurses. It's going well. They monitor blood pressures after a bout in the hospital. Homecare is an emerging field of practice, so it's been a great way for them to get their feet wet." I was impressing myself about setting up partnerships and developing a strong volunteer corps since coming on board.

A strained Andy lurched over to the wet bar. "Would anyone like a soda?"

Father Mack waved him off. "Do people you visit ever offer you something, Meg?"

I thought he was joking about Andy offering soda. Perhaps the meeting wasn't about us after all, though I still didn't understand why Father Mack asked him to sit in.

"Folks offer me coffee or cake quite often. Their way of saying 'thanks'—and making the visit last a little longer. They don't get much company."

"That's nice, Meg, but don't they offer you a few dollars for the Church?"

A glass Andy reached for tumbled on the counter but didn't break. I jumped, startled.

If any of the shut-ins offered money, I would have turned it over immediately given his earlier interrogation about the Christopher Sisters' stipend. But no one ever did.

"No. Hadn't occurred to me they should." Gargoyle claws gripped again.

"Odd." Father Mack cracked his knuckles. "When Father Cronin visits, he returns with pockets bulging. It's how people show their appreciation."

Andy looked on from the wet bar, staring into an empty glass.

"Very generous of them," I said. "Must be different when a priest comes to the house."

"Father Cronin uses the money to provide a dinner for the ushers once a year—a steak dinner—people give him that much."

His lilting phrases could curdle milk. "What do the ushers have to do with bringing Holy Communion to people?"

"That's not the point, Margaret. Father Cronin could ask to use the money for himself, or he could donate it to the general fund, but he said he'd like to do something to thank the ushers. Those are the volunteers he oversees."

Father Mack clasped his hands behind his head. "If you had some money from your visits, you could thank your volunteers. They're carrying the load for you these days."

"But I don't have any money." He was like a dog with a bone. The Inquisition. My voice thinned. "If I did have money, I would love to give the volunteers a luncheon or dinner."

"Exactly," said Father Mack. "You might want to consider the matter."

Was he asking me to shake down old women, and then give them Holy Communion?

Andy caught my eye, winced, then turned his back to the scene as he put his empty glass on the counter. My eyes burned.

"That's all, Meg. You can go."

As I left the room, Father Mack said to Andy, "On second thought, pour me a splash of something on the rocks … and one for yourself."

I wanted to scream. Say something, Andy. Stick up for me.

But why would Andy challenge the man who treated him like a son, gave him a carpentry shop to call his own, shared a splash of something over the rocks. Someone who probably told him, "Don't worry about her—she'll find someone else."

Soon after, Josie called the priests to dinner. She sounded like a den mother— "Boys, time for your supper." Boys … not men. When Sister Loretta called this place a den of celibates, perhaps she only meant many priests were still boys, cubs in a lion's den. A boys' club. Maybe Josie also knew that.

All this time I had spent wrestling with the obligation of celibacy, but that was only part of the picture. Celibacy may have been the fish skin that kept sperm in check—but the den of seminary and rectory kept their manhood at bay. Entrance to the lair was closely guarded. I had walked much too close to the entrance.

No, the meeting with Father Mack had nothing to do with my work—and everything to do with Andy. I hadn't stolen money from Father Mack—I had stolen the heart of his favorite son. But why punish us now? Andy and I hadn't been together in months. Father Mack probably had hoped that the convent would rid him of me. No fuss, no muss. Today was about giving me notice that it was time to go.

An official-looking envelope from the insurance company lay in my mailbox when I got home. Gingerly, I propped the envelope against the saltshaker on my kitchen table until I worked up the courage to open it. To my amazement, the payout for my claim was larger than expected—not enough to cover the cost of a new car, but enough for a decent down payment. Or, if I were Father Cronin, perhaps a steak dinner for every single volunteer at St. Gabriel's Parish.

Though foiled a few times looking for another job, now I had a way out. Tonight, *my pockets were bulging—the insurance company had given me that much*. Echoing Father Mack gave me piercing satisfaction. I would purchase my ransom, but I would leave on my own terms.

Ash Wednesday. Burn the past.

~ CHAPTER 17 ~

WINGS

AN ASH WEDNESDAY TUNA pot pie kept me company as I pondered how to exit St. Gabe's and land on my feet. All I had to do was figure out where I was going, and how to get there.

I needed a serious sit down. Looked around my apartment—dishes in the sink, laundry to be done, dusting. Too many distractions. Wished I could go to Christopher House, but no car.

In my early days at St. Gabe's, Father Mack sent me to a diocesan workshop on lay ministry at a retreat and conference center at the edge of town. What was it called? The Willows. I unearthed their pamphlet from a drawer: *A place for reflection, prayer, and solitude. Available for group trainings or private retreats.* The back page gave directions, including by bus. Perfect.

I arrived at the Parish Center on Thursday as if nothing had happened the day before. I called The Willows. Yes, they could accommodate me. I booked myself for the weekend package at the discounted rate reserved for parish personnel—I did still work at a parish.

I walked into Father Mack's office and greeted him as if any ordinary day. "I've been thinking about our conversation. I want to take some time to consider what you said. I'll be staying at The Willows a few days."

He leaned back in his chair and looked me straight in the eye for a long minute. "Whatever you say."

An old Victorian adjacent to The Willows' main building accommodated guests. Having slept hardly a wink, I found my room on the second floor and plopped face-down on the quilted coverlet of appliqued roses for a nap—though only 11:00 a.m. I touched the raised appliques and remembered the scent of the rose in Sister Loretta's budvase. "The rose once given …"

Andy held it tenderly, but only for a moment. He wanted its sweet scent without the thorns.

After lunch, I relaxed by the fire in the sitting room to begin serious planning. The big wingback chair held promise of a guardian angel. I would need one.

First order of business—when to give notice. I decided to assure Father Mack of my departure immediately, but setting a date depended on a plan. I opened my notepad and jotted my departure date: March 30. Appropriate. March 30 would close out the month, and most of Lent, but avoid Holy Week. Going through another Holy Week with Andy within range was beyond what I could handle.

I opened my notebook and wrote out options for careful assessment.

> **Option 1** – *Stay at St. Gabe's until a teaching job opens*
> **Pros:** Secure paycheck. Father Mack didn't fire me outright, so he'll wait for me to go.
> **Cons:** Father Mack's daily glare until I leave. Andy's presence. Would need to buy a car.

Option 2 – *Look for another job doing something in the Twin Cities*
Pros: Quickest route out of Shady Bluff. Bigger job market. Could continue applying for teaching jobs since my license is good anywhere in the state. Near Eddie and Hank.
Cons: Still too close to Andy? Would need to buy a car.

Option 3 – *Move to New York City in spring*
Pros: Far away from Andy. New pool of men. Chance to start life over. No one knows my past. I loved the challenge and excitement when Eileen and I were making plans.
Incredible bus, subway, and rail system—I could get around without a car. And use the insurance money to cover a few months' rent until my first paycheck.
Cons: Risky until I get settled, find a job, and learn the transportation routes.

Dizzy from contemplating the jigsaw puzzle of options, I put down my pen, sank into the wingback chair, and closed my eyes.

The receptionist soon tapped me on the shoulder. "Sorry to disturb you, but there's a call on the house phone for Meg Joyce. That's you, right?"

Who could be calling me? I hadn't told anyone but Father Mack my whereabouts. I stumbled out of the chair, half-asleep. My notepad and pen fell on the floor.

I followed the receptionist's path through the house. She pointed me to an old-fashioned wooden stand in the hallway. The black rotary phone sat on a crochet doily, its receiver off the hook. "Hello?"

"Meg. It's Andy."

"Andy? What's wrong?"

"That's what I called to ask you."

"Oh. How did you know I was here?"

"When I didn't see you Thursday or today, I got worried and asked Father Mack."

"Geez."

"I could come over there, Meg, if you want me to."

He could come over? To do what? Break my heart a little more?

"You don't need to come over, Andy. You were at the meeting with Father Mack. I need some quiet time to sort things out."

"You weren't the only one who got blindsided."

"But I'm the only one who's out of a job."

Long sigh. "Promise me you'll call if you need anything, okay?"

Where was he when I needed a knight in shining armor on Wednesday? "You're the last person I would call—Father Vogel." Click.

I went back to the room with the wingback chair, wadded up my page of "Options" and threw it in the crackling fire.

Pen and notebook lay on the floor. I picked them up and turned to an empty page. Only one thing to do. I would use the car payout money to move to New York. I needed breathing space more than anything else. As far away from this town as possible.

Dear Big Bird—

I enumerated compelling reasons *Sesame Street* should hire a teacher of students with developmental delays. A love letter to my new life. I would polish the letter when I got home, look up the address, and splash the mailbox with holy water for luck.

Andy called again the next day at about the same time. "Please don't hang up on me this time. How are things going, really?"

Gratifying to know he cared, but unless he was singing a different tune, nothing had changed. "You truly want to know? Things are looking up. The insurance check came in the mail on Wednesday. Opened up some options."

"Wow, glad to hear that. Now you can get a decent car."

Andy assumed the obvious option. "Yeah, maybe. A decent … car. Not one that would jilt me off the highway at the first sign of trouble."

"You deserve better, Meg."

"This is hard, Andy."

"Listen to me. I don't make the rules."

"I sure don't make the rules either. But you follow them. Some of them."

"I'm sorry, Meg."

As if he'd broken a china doll instead of a human heart.

I hung up.

⁞  

When I got home Sunday, Eileen had left a message on my answering machine about getting together for coffee. I wanted to share my decision and tug at her for some support, so I called right back.

Lanky guy answered the phone and gave it to Eileen. "Let's go to that place where they put those seeds in the coffee grounds that make it taste yummy," she said. "What are they?"

"Cardamom. Lots of healing properties."

She picked me up an hour later. I let her jabber about Mark until she was out of steam.

I was on my second cup of spiced coffee before she asked, "What's new with you, Meg?"

I stirred the spoon in my mug. "What would you say if I took the plunge and moved to New York on my own?"

She blinked a dozen times. "You always were the brave one. Me? I got cold feet."

Though I would miss Eileen's unfailingly upbeat company, I backed her decision to stay and give Mark a chance. If things didn't work out with him, she could come to New York later. As for making it on my own, I joked, "*If I can make it there, I can make it anywhere.*" We vied to outdo each other singing Liza Minnelli's line from *New York, New York.* Until coffeehouse patrons gawked, then clapped.

Eileen threw in a word of caution—"Be sure you don't fall in love with the wrong man, like Liza did with De Niro."

"*Moi?*"

Damn. Andy spoke French. I wouldn't make a mistake like him again.

"When are you going to make the move?"

"In the spring, like we planned. I've decided to give notice for March 30, leave in April."

Eileen smushed her Angel Flake coconut pie. "Wow, that's fast. What about your flat?"

"I'll put an ad in next Sunday's newspaper to sublet—and throw myself on my brother's mercy to store my stuff in their basement."

Eileen lit up. "Sublet? Hmm. Hey, what about me? You know my small apartment. I've been looking for a flat, but I hardly have any furniture. Your place is nice. I like the Victorian vibe. And you wouldn't have to store anything—unless you wanted to, of course."

My hunched shoulders relaxed. I was trying to sound like I had everything under control, but Eileen's desire to sublet lifted a huge worry. "Terrific by me. I'll talk to the landlord. Oh, and with Mark in your life, the shoveling and lawn mowing duties should be a cinch."

Things were starting to fall into place. I tucked into my pie and tasted luck.

An impish grin descended on Eileen's next volley. "Meg, did I tell you that I was going to visit my sister in New York?"

I gave her the side-eye. "Yes. And you were going to stay with her until you found a job in a big bank." We broke out laughing.

"I'm still going to visit her. She said Easter would be a good time because school is out. What if we fly out there together? We could shop, see the sights ..." My friend was on a roll. "About the rent, I'm willing to go half with you for April."

"Eileen, are you my guardian angel?"

⁣⁣⁣

Father Mack came to his office earlier than usual on Monday morning. Good. I could get this over with. He sat down in his swivel chair. He didn't suggest I sit.

"Good morning, Meg. Did you enjoy your respite? Visiting the sick can be draining."

Interesting spin. "Father Mack, when I visit the sick and homebound folks, they bring me closer to the meaning of life." I squinted into the sun streaming between the blinds. "They remind me of the shortness of life. You recall I was going to take a week's vacation in spring to see my dad? My voice cracked. "I'm afraid he had a heart attack. He passed on."

Father Mack sat up. "Sorry to hear that, Margaret."

I looked at him directly. "As it turns out, I have an opportunity to move to New York."

He slowly folded his hands across his midsection. "Tell me more."

"I've decided to go. I want to give you enough notice to make a smooth transition. My last day will be March 30th. I do hope I can still count on a week's vacation pay."

I had put down my marker for a bit of severance. I held my breath.

Father Mack lowered his hands and laid them flat on the desk. "Sounds like a change of scenery might do you good. March 30? Yes. Work with Father Leo on arrangements—and have him put in for your extra week's salary. We'll call it a going-away gift."

"As you say."

"Is that all, Meg?"

"Almost. If I could make a suggestion—perhaps if you send priests out more regularly to do the visits, you'll get a bonanza of contributions."

I did not wait for Father Mack's reaction.

℘ ℰ

When I received a response from *Sesame Street* inviting me to apply when I got to the city, I called Eileen—ecstatic.

Word about my imminent departure—solo—spread fast among the Kelly's Pub crowd. Before I knew it, St. Pat's Day fused into a going away party for me. Everybody seemed to know somebody in the big city. I collected more names and numbers than I would be able to contact in a month of Sundays—and more recommendations for Irish pubs than any one person should visit in their lifetime. Eileen bequeathed me the evening bag she'd bought for her would-be dates in the city.

Beth relayed her parents' invitation that I join them for Easter dinner.

I soaked in every sincere "Luck of the Irish to ye."

CANDLEWOOD

I told Leo that I planned to stay at the Midtown YMCA in New York until I got settled in a job and found an apartment. He soon appeared with a tome of a book.

"Take a gander at the listings for women's residences, Meg. You might find something more interesting."

The entry for New York ran five pages. It indexed every parish, charitable organization, rectory, and seminary—as well as Catholic residences for women. I didn't know such places existed and suspected this was Leo's way of looking out for me. One of the entries seemed promising: the Jeanne d'Arc Residence in Chelsea, lower Manhattan. Leo looked up more information and convinced me I would be in good hands. I booked a room for a month.

In the remaining weeks, I said heartfelt goodbyes to my regular roster of homebound parishioners and thanked them for the many life lessons they'd shared.

Most dabbed their eyes and said, "You've been like a daughter, Meg."

I suggested one of our volunteers for Leo to consider hiring in my place.

"Not sure if Father Mack is going to replace you," he said. "Not that you could ever be replaced." He stretched out his chubby arms to me and grabbed both my hands. "I'm so sorry things went south with that knucklehead Andy."

Tears welled up. "Thanks, Leo."

If anyone was going to speak the truth, it was Leo, my wise fool turned friend.

Only one day left before departing St. Gabe's, but no one was in the mood for a going-away party. The nation was in the grip of reports about a nuclear meltdown at Three Mile Island.

Mom used the incident to beg me one more time to stay. I showed her on the map that New York City was more than 100 miles from the disaster. Besides, I'd bought my ticket and was determined to get out of town.

Josie baked a cake for one last lunch with Ruth, the other staff, and the regular volunteers. "I hear New York is a grand city, Meg," she said, "but keep your wits about you."

In between bites of cake, Sue said that Father Mack would probably not make the party since he went to the car dealership an hour ago. "Isn't it generous for them to donate a car to the parish? Always the Motor Trend Car of the Year."

Josie wrinkled her nose. "I wonder how many sins a 1979 Buick Riviera wipes out?"

I was privately glad Father Mack had found an excuse to be away. I could not have managed a civil response if he attempted to make a show of wishing me a fond farewell.

Ruth put up a cheery front. "I suppose you'll be rooting for the Knicks now," she said, "but don't forget the home team." She gave me a teary hug. "I'll miss you."

Father Cronin slipped in before the party broke up. He handed me a St. Jude medal. Saint of the Impossible. "Good luck, Margaret." Father Cronin and I had our differences, but he did one thing faithfully—he gleaned the souls of the dead. Not his fault no one in seminary prepared him for new-fangled women working as lay ministers on his turf.

I was packing up the last of my things when Andy appeared at my office door. "New York is a long way away," he said.

"Only half-way across the country." I kept stowing knick-knack gifts from elderly folks.

"Do you know what you're going to do there yet?"

"I have a few ideas. One of them is sure to pan out."

Andy picked up a ceramic bluebird, the ones given out as premiums with Tender Leaf Tea in years past. "Leo said you found someplace in Chelsea to live."

I wondered if Leo had shagged him down here to say goodbye. "Yes, a women's residence. Should be safe. Jeanne d'Arc of something-something … let me look it up." I showed him the entry in the big directory Leo lent me. The long name was in French.

"Do you know what this says?" Andy was trying hard to stifle a howl. Reading from the book, he translated the entire name: "The Jeanne d'Arc Home for Friendless French Girls and Others." His raucous laugh grated like nails on a chalkboard.

"I must be one of the others," I said flatly.

"Didn't mean anything. I'm sure it's a fine place." He set down the bluebird.

The precarious nature of my exodus was all too obvious. "Andy, you know I'm leaving on a wing and a prayer. I've got to get out of here."

"I know, Meg."

"So, that's that." Why was he dragging out this good-bye? When would we ever be done?

"How's your brother doing?"

"He's working the program. Eight months sober. He might open his own upholstery shop. My dad gave him some money a while back before he died."

"Your dad died? When?"

"January."

He took a step closer and wrapped his arms around me. "No one said anything."

My anger melted away like snow in spring. I laid my head on his chest. I missed him, I missed us. I had grown brittle trying not to care.

"I'm a mess without you, Meg, but I don't want to stand in your way."

Our moist eyes said everything. I couldn't take one more minute of this. It was his own damn fault. If he asked me to stay in that second, asked me for another chance, I would have abandoned my plans. I waited—but when he said nothing more, I put as good a face on it as I could. I wanted to leave with some shred of dignity intact.

"Well, you're standing in my way right now. Help me outside with these boxes?"

Eileen was due to pick me up. Andy waited with me on the steps, under the gargoyle's downspout. When she parked, he put the boxes in the trunk of the car, waved goodbye, and soon we were out of sight of each other.

CHAPTER 18

AMAZON WOMEN

MARK DROVE EILEEN AND ME to the airport. I was afraid the plane might take off without us if the lovebirds didn't stop canoodling. Andy and I couldn't so much as hold hands in public.

Once aboard, Eileen relaxed. "You'll like my sister. Mary may be a nun, but she's cool. Tough enough to teach in the Bronx."

Sister Mary-Mary, as we flippantly called her, greeted us at LaGuardia airport with smiles and hugs. She braved her way through city traffic and snagged a parking spot in front of the Jeanne d'Arc Residence. Eileen followed me inside to satisfy her curiosity.

The receptionist ran her finger down the reservation list. "Perhaps under another name?"

"Didn't you get my letter," I asked, "and my deposit?"

She smoothed her collar and turned the page. "You've been waitlisted. Mother Clare would have sent you a letter."

Visions of homelessness. "I didn't get a letter." Any letter probably went to St. Gabe's and never got to me before leaving.

She tapped my deposit check on the counter. "We could give you a cot in the dormitory until a room becomes available."

My head throbbed. "May I think about this a minute?"

"Or I could refund your deposit toward alternate lodging until a room opens." She offered a short list of other women's residences.

Eileen rolled her eyes.

On my first day in New York, the only thing I wanted was a warm bed and a sliver of privacy in this cheek-by-jowl town. "Thank you. I'll try to find another place." I stuffed her list in my purse.

Sister Mary eyed us quizzically as we approached the car, suitcase in hand.

"Can you believe it?" said Eileen. "They wanted her to sleep on a cot."

Sister Mary frowned and checked her watch. "I need to get back for Holy Thursday services. Maybe you could stay with us tonight? The Sisters surely wouldn't mind."

I didn't want to be a charity case so early in the journey. "That's generous, but I could make some calls. The receptionist gave me a list." I hoped the Vanderbilt YMCA in Midtown might have a room. Why didn't I keep my booking instead of listening to Leo?

Eileen suggested finding an Irish pub to make the calls. "Luck of the Irish, you know."

Sister Mary latched onto the idea for lack of any other. "Indeed, I know a nice pub near St. Patrick's Cathedral. If I can find it. You can make your calls and we'll be off." Her words sounded airy but worry filled her face. After circling streets around the cathedral, Sister Mary spotted the pub. More circles yielded a parking meter.

I made a beeline to the pub's phone booth and rifled through a directory hanging on a chain from the shelf. Dialed the Vanderbilt YMCA—not on the Jeanne d'Arc list.

A harried voice said, "Sorry. Easter vacation. Booked."

CANDLEWOOD

The crumpled receptionist's paper listed Martha Washington Hotel for Women. I called. No rooms available for the next ten days. Maybe Allerton House? Nope.

I slowly walked back to our table. "What's that about Irish luck?"

When Sister Mary fretted about being late for Holy Thursday services, Eileen said, "Would the Lord not prefer we look after Meg?" Her high and mighty tone hushed her sister until we burst out laughing. Eileen ordered a round of suds.

"I might have to take you up on a room, Sister Mary. But it won't be for long."

As we clunked mugs, an order of fish and chips arrived—on the house. And—a second round. The bartender pointed to a man in a slightly rumpled suit at the bar. He raised his hand in a wave.

Did we look altogether desperate—Eileen wobbling on stilettos purchased for the big city, Sister Mary wearing a short veil in a bar on Holy Thursday—and me bouncing to the pay phone with my botched perm—cousin to Orphan Annie? Yes.

The suit man moseyed over to our table, a perfect part in his coffee-brown hair. "Mind if I help you celebrate the holy day?"

We invited him to sit down. Sister Mary took a swig of beer like a sailor and blurted out the whole story of my muddled reservation. Her cares about getting back to the convent in time for devotions evaporated like the froth on her brew.

I intervened with the information we were only at the pub so I could make a few phone calls to find another place.

"From the Midwest, aren't you?" he asked. "I can tell by the way you talk to strangers."

"Upper Midwest—St. Croix Valley, near Minneapolis." I felt my cheeks flush.

"Don't be embarrassed," he said. "I pedal women's magazines in Chicago, Milwaukee, and the Twin Cities. Love the Midwest. Can never figure out why folks come east."

I recovered by folding my hands and crossing my legs, sitting up a little straighter and evoking a serious tone. "I'm going to work in children's television. Best opportunities are here."

"More power to you." He winked and extended his card. "Charlie. Lemme know when you get settled."

I read his card: Charles Miller, Regional Sales Manager. If Andy had gone into business, his suit wouldn't be so well tailored.

Charlie buttoned his jacket. "Well, ladies, I must be on my way. He nodded to Sister Mary and Eileen. To me he said, "Give my regards to Big Bird."

"Looks like you've got a hot prospect already," said Eileen. Her sister urged caution.

We hungrily finished the fish and chips. As I licked my fingers, the greasy newspaper liner in the basket unexpectedly reminded me of another printed page. "Eileen, remember the last issue of *Mademoiselle* ?" She hadn't read it. "Big article on a book made into a movie—*The Bell Jar*. A New York City women's residence figured prominently." I pinched my lip trying to remember the name of the hotel. "It was called … Amazon? No, she called it Amazon in the book. The real place starts with a 'B' – 'B' – Barbizon – that's it."

I ran to the phone booth and found the listing.

A thin dime later, I had a reservation for a week. Cost a third more than Jeanne d'Arc, but worth having a roof over my head. And a place named in *Mademoiselle?* Priceless.

After toasts, Sister Mary dropped me at the corner of 63rd Street and Lexington Avenue—only a dozen blocks from St. Patrick's Cathedral and our lucky pub.

CANDLEWOOD

℘ ℘

The doorman ushered me into an expansive lobby of potted ferns and Oriental carpets. A porter took my only bag to a room with little space for more. I surveyed my piece of the world and went to sleep counting pink and green vintage floral blessings.

Eileen attended Good Friday devotions to keep her sister happy. I slept in until the promise of coffee, included in my room rate, lured me downstairs. I rode the elevator to the mezzanine and sauntered down a grand staircase to the lobby I read about in the magazine. I imagined *Love Story*'s Ali MacGraw did the same when she lived at the Barbizon, and Grace Kelly a generation before.

I enjoyed a breakfast of rice pudding, and then selected souvenir postcards at the front desk. For Ruth—the ornate mezzanine-level balcony wrapped around Barbizon's atrium lobby. I jotted, "Found a new mezzanine!" I wished I could hear her chuckling about the day she got reamed out by Father Cronin on the Parish Center's mezzanine. Mom's postcard showed a view of the hotel overlooking a park. *Sister Mary helped me find a safer place. Will call soon.* Only half a lie.

The desk clerk added postage to my room bill. He offered a map of the city and a color-coded schematic of bus lines and subway. Said the city was mine for a fifty-cent brass token.

The map showed Central Park only steps from the hotel. I let cool morning air banish well-warranted fears. What if I didn't get a job at *Sesame Street?* Worries for tomorrow. Today I wanted to enjoy the fragrance of white cherry blossoms. Beautiful place to forget about Andy.

Walking brought relief from monthly cramps—a timely reminder that wherever I lived, I would inhabit the body of a woman. Good Friday. Someone else shed blood this day, rose three days later. Promised new life.

The park's wide paths led me across a well-trod field named The Sheep Meadow and further to a lagoon. I sat down on its banks.

The Lord is my shepherd. Please lead me to green pastures and restore my soul.

After Eileen and I spent Saturday window shopping on Fifth Avenue, she wanted to see my room at the Barbizon. We made a pit-stop before meeting Sister Mary for an evening concert.

Eileen surveyed the chintz bedspread and matching curtains, a small club chair in one corner and writing desk angled into the other, a three-drawer dresser to hold my belongings.

"Meg, this is a tiny dollhouse. Our dorm room was bigger."

I sighed. "Tis. But I might have slept on a dormitory cot last night. This is a castle."

Eileen sat in the club chair and kicked off her shoes.

"You know, old friend, you could have moved to Minneapolis if you wanted a change of scenery. Why all the way out here?"

"You're the one who put the bug in my ear, *old friend.* Besides, people move to Minneapolis to find a job. People move to New York to reinvent themselves."

Eileen shrugged. "Why on earth do you want to reinvent yourself?"

I untangled myself from my prone position on the bed and sat upright on the edge.

"Can I trust you to keep a secret?" Instant chills. Maybe I shouldn't say anything.

"Meg, you always play it close to the chest. I never pry, but you worry me sometimes. We hardly saw you last summer—

always waiting for your *mystery man.*" She bolted over to sit next to me on the bed. "Oh my god, did something happen?"

I saw the question of whether I got pregnant plainly in her eyes. "I'm not in trouble—let's clear that up. But there was a reason you never met him."

"Okay, spill."

"He was, let's say, not available." I trusted my friend would translate my words to "married"—not think me naïve enough to fall for a priest.

Eileen sprang to her feet. "But you made yourself available for him all the time."

"Exactly. Bad habit pleasing everybody. Waiting forever for my mystery man to make up his mind. Before that, letting Sean call the shots. Trying to be the kind of fiancé who'd fit in with Jake's snooty family. Wanting to make my mom proud. Once upon a time, I believed if I was the kind of girl the Church said I was supposed to be, life would turn out fine, but…"

Eileen sat down on the bed again. "You really fell for him, didn't you?"

"Lock, stock and barrel." I wondered if Andy had this conversation with Leo.

"So … distance is your medicine of choice. Got it."

I looked out my window toward the Chrysler Building's sunburst crown. "I could have bought a new car, but—dreaming bigger dreams—I couldn't let the chance go by."

"What about marriage and kids?"

"Like you, I still want those things." I laughed. "Not very liberated of us, huh?"

Eileen crossed her fingers. "Mark had better pan out."

"The way he looks at you—no doubt. I want someone to look at me that way—and stay."

"You *are* worth it, you know." Her mascara started running.

"The reason I'm here, Eileen, is that I need to find out who I'm supposed to be for myself, not for anybody else. If a guy falls for me, I want him to fall for Meg, not for his vision of who he wants me to be for him."

"That's deep, Meg."

"And if I find Prince Charming—what if he reverts to frogdom? I need to know I can walk away. My mom stayed much too long in a bad marriage. I don't want to have to do that. Or in a bad job, either. I need to know I can make it on my own. For me, *women's lib* is knowing I have the choice to walk away—or walk towards. I don't want to be trapped—ever."

Eileen's eyes grew wide. "Meg, you don't need to totally reinvent yourself—trust me. But yeah, I get that you have to conquer the world and search for your heart of hearts."

"And maybe learn how to guard it a little better."

"The world or your heart?"

"Both, silly."

Eileen and I found Sister Mary paging through *Life* magazine in the sumptuous, if worn, Barbizon lobby—could have been borrowed from a Roman villa.

Eileen looked up at the faux atrium ceiling. "Is that a hole in the glass?"

Indeed, a shattered pane stared down on us.

Not the luxury sorority hotel of former years, I observed. "Back in its heyday, the Barbizon was all the rage for starlets, young writers and artists, pioneering professional women." I nudged Eileen. "Maybe they broke the glass ceiling after all."

She laughed at the phrase recently added to our view of the world. "As you will, Meg."

The joke seemed to go over Sister Mary's head.

Our womanly triumvirate took a cab to Avery Fisher Hall for the concert. The Lincoln Center complex of buildings seemed to float in an expanse of glass. Once inside the hall, the orchestra reverberated in a cocoon of rich woods. The Holy Saturday program hewed religious, but new. Bernstein's Chichester Psalms cascaded brooding, jazzy, and sweet tones all at the same time. I found myself in a world of possibilities far from St. Gabe's, a world away from Andy. Last year's Easter candle, with our names inscribed in wax as on a tree, melted away.

The three of us emerged into the neon night not wanting to say farewells. Eileen would fly home on Easter. She promised to write, and Sister Mary told me to call if I needed anything.

A cab pulled to the curb— "Need a ride, Sister?"

Sister Mary persuaded the cabbie to drop me off at the hotel before she and Eileen headed uptown to the Bronx.

Beth's dad picked me up for Easter dinner as planned. The Johnsons welcomed me like the long-lost daughter they'd gotten to know the previous Easter.

Mr. Johnson said once I got the job with *Sesame Street*, he'd help me move. Not that I had much to move but help with my luggage was better than juggling it on a subway or bus. Mrs. Johnson encouraged me to look for an apartment in Woodside, Queens. Reasonable rents, she said, and the subway connected with the Long Island Railroad, the LIR, so I could visit them easily and she hoped, often.

Ensconced in my little room at the Barbizon on Easter Sunday night, I counted friendly faces instead of sheep—the Johnsons, Sister Mary, the cabbie, the doorman. And a man named Charlie. The Big Apple was starting to feel like a small town.

֍ ֎

On Monday morning of the first week on my own, I read the letter again from *Sesame Street* inviting me to apply when I moved to town. A job with the Children's Television Workshop seemed too good to be true. Though not exactly an offer, certainly a shoe in the door.

I studied the color-coded transit maps and located their offices at 1 Lincoln Plaza, a short ride on the M66 bus that stopped a block from the Barbizon.

What to wear? Spring came earlier to New York than Minnesota, but cool enough for a tweed jacket. Paired with my sage green pincord skirt, I would look as stylish as any young woman in *Mademoiselle*. Perfect. With jeans, I might pass for a *Cosmo* girl. Did I want to be a *Cosmo* girl? Maybe part of my reinvention. Being a Catholic girl only brought me trouble.

When I arrived at CTW, I walked through the door as if I already had the job. The articles I read about interviewing said to appear confident. I found my way to the Human Resources office and unfolded the precious letter.

A thin man with an Afro at the main desk saw the letter and winced. "Oh, honey, we send that form letter to everybody who writes us looking for a job. Do you know how many dozens of people contact us each week?"

My stomach flip-flopped like a fish on the line. Though I talked as if the letter guaranteed me a job, I only half-believed my own blather. I stifled the enormity of my gamble.

But I wasn't going to be turned down without a fair shake.

I refolded the letter. "I can only imagine the hundreds of people interested in working here," I said, "but how many of them come in person to apply?"

In a weary tone, he asked, "Do you have a resume?"

I pulled out my carefully typed resume, stood tall, and gave it to him.

"An honest-to-God teacher type. Master's degree?"

His short burst of interest emboldened me. "No, but I'm very versatile. I also have experience coordinating volunteers. What kind of openings do you have?"

He pointed to a cork board on the office wall. "See for yourself."

At least ten job descriptions hung by bright pushpins: *Gaffer – Continuity – Support Crew*. I had no idea what any of these jobs did. I read the description for *Production Assistant*: Schedule meetings, coordinate resources, arrange scene charts. I could take a crack at that.

I removed the notice from the board and gave it to the man at the desk.

He chuckled. "Okey dokey. Let me see what I can do. Where can I contact you?" When I gave him my address at the Barbizon, his eyebrows lifted. "You're serious, aren't you? Give me to Thursday to see if I can get you in with somebody."

The next morning at breakfast in the Barbizon café, a petite young woman about my age smiled "Good morning" and invited me to join her. "New here?"

Her Southern drawl told me women from all over the country came to make it in the city. I welcomed a chance for conversation with a like-minded soul. "Fresh off the boat you might say."

She laughed. "Not for long. Everybody hits the road running here. But let me give you some tips: Don't talk to strangers—unless they're male, good looking, and wear a pressed suit."

"That's most of the population in this city." Charlie was only a little rumpled.

She wagged her finger. "Don't cry until your fortieth interview turns you down. Somebody warned me about that early on. Sure 'nuf, I got hired on my thirty-ninth audition—

Sweeney Todd: Demon Barber of Fleet Street. Isn't that delicious? I do hardly anything, a walk-on in a crowd, but I get to see everything and everybody and go to the parties. By the way, they called me their Georgia peach, so now I'm going by the name Georgia. Cute, huh?"

"I'm Meg—so far. Thanks for the advice." But I wasn't trying out for theatre.

With no word about a job by late Wednesday, panic set in. What if they didn't call? I couldn't move back to podunk town. Andy's territory. They had to call.

I barely scratched breakfast on Thursday. With mush for nerves, I checked messages at the desk—for the hundredth time. A pale blue note revealed an interview on Friday at 9:45 a.m. I ran to my room panting. I practiced my interview speech hour upon hour. Spent a restless night. In the morning, I tamed my hair, gulped coffee, and hopped the bus.

I checked in with the Human Resources man who had tried to wave me away. "Why if it isn't Miss Minnesota." He came round his desk and sat on the edge. "I convinced Mrs. Nelson to see you. She's a screener. If you get by her, you've got a shot." He pointed me down the hall. Surprised by his help, I thanked him profusely.

Mrs. Nelson glanced at my resume. "A teacher who applies for a secretary position." She peered at me with the benevolent gaze of a buddha. "I'm afraid you'd be bored with this job."

My grip tightened on the folder in my lap. "I realize I have to start somewhere."

"Although you're not cut out for this job, Henry, our front desk man, was impressed with your spunk. Not a bad quality. Unfortunately, I don't have anything else open. If you're serious about working in children's television, you'll need experience." Her manicured nails reached for monogrammed notepaper. She wrote a name and address. "Tell him I sent you. His employment service places people in ad agencies."

"Advertising? I don't know anything about ads."

"You know about kids. But if you want to get into television, advertising is the fastest way to learn the ropes. Each ad is a mini production. Said you have to start somewhere, right?"

She rose and shook my hand. "Good luck."

My stomach muscles tensed as I rose to accept the monogrammed note. "Thank you."

Outside, a beggar tossed breadcrumbs to the pigeons. Big Bird nowhere in sight.

Since this was my first, not fortieth, turndown, I decided to follow the advice of my fellow lodger and resist crying my eyes out. Instead, I beat strokes down a swimming pool lane at the Barbizon. When Georgia saw me poolside, she asked me to her show's afterparty. I passed, set on spending time in the common room watching TV for the "mini-stories" in ads. Perhaps this could work. I extended my reservation at the Barbizon for the sake of a stable address while on the hunt.

On Monday morning I mapped my way to the address on the monogrammed note.

Mr. Fischer, a balding man in a three-piece suit invited me into his office. "So, you want to break into the business. How fast do you type?"

I typed my term papers in college, and progress notes on my kids, but not much while at St. Gabe's. When Mr. Fischer's stopwatch dinged, I had only finished a third of the copy page.

"I owe Susie a few favors, but you're going to ruin my reputation. Tell you what—come here a few hours each day to practice. Once you're up to speed, I can place you."

My voice quivered when I asked, "Isn't there anything besides typing?" I was spiraling in a long detour from working with kids, their shows, or any of my hopes.

"Sweetheart, every woman starts in the typing pool. It's not so bad. You learn a lot, meet everybody, get taken to lunch on your birthday. Listen, I placed a young woman last year who came up with a good line about lipstick—*kisses on a tissue*—you probably saw the ad. She's got her own accounts now. Big bucks. Another filly got promoted to scripts."

I wanted to run back to Shady Bluff and shake Andy until he turned blue in the face. He breaks his vows and gets the keys to the kingdom—I trust him and get the keys to a typewriter?

By the end of the week, despite practice, Mr. Fischer declared me hopeless.

"Can you spell?" he asked. "I've got a temporary gig, part-time. Proofreading."

Finally, something I excelled at. Anything to pad my budget. I counted on the car insurance money lasting three months, but I was blowing through it with dwindling prospects. I wrote Mom that I was in line for a second interview. Didn't want to worry her.

Mondays through Thursdays, I proofread car maintenance instructions that droned like a Latin missal. On Fridays, my day off, I pounded the pavement to other employment agencies only to find Mr. Fischer told me the truth: women start as typists everywhere in the city. Galling. I never saw any men typing 65 words per minute as if their life depended on it. Scoured the want-ads and applied for everything from insurance jobs in the Wall Street district to bookshops on the Upper West Side. In a matter of weeks, I knew the color-coded transit system like the back of my hand.

CANDLEWOOD

As I hurried to work one morning, a woman of a certain age entered the lobby. She wore a hot pink shirtdress with a wide sash. I had seen her in photos. The front desk man said, "Good Morning, Miss Brown." I hesitated to take the elevator with famed *Cosmo* editor, Helen Gurley Brown, but she motioned for me to enter. Perhaps she recognized me as a fellow "mouseburger," the term she coined to describe women like herself who need to work hard to get noticed, and appreciated, in a man's world. She had done it through sex as much as savvy, but she had done it. I would need to find my own way.

Five weeks in, a couple dozen turndowns, and deep into my twelve-week budget, I called Eddie from the Barbizon's bank of phone booths. No phone in my room—only a crackly radio. After he agreed to secrecy with Mom, I told him I blew the interview for children's television.

"But you're the smart one, Sis. You always make it. Something will turn up."

I traced the phone booth door's glass panel. "Eddie, here's the truth. I've got a part-time job—temporary—proofreading car manuals." I sucked in my pride. "I may need a loan to tide me over until something better breaks."

"Why don't you come home?"

"With my tail between my legs? No can do."

He lobbed a wisecrack about tailfins, told me to enjoy the city until I came to my senses.

After supper at an inexpensive Greek diner, I picked up the *Irish Echo* at the corner newsstand. A reminder of familiar things like how to make a St. Brigid's cross. On the last page, it listed ads for apartments—and rooming houses. One in the Bronx said: *Clean sheets provided weekly, shared kitchen. Former home of the landlord. Reasonable.* What the Bronx lacked in safety, it made up for in cheap rent. Sister Mary survived there. I circled it.

The next day, the front desk clerk snagged me to deliver a phone message.

Meant to give you the name of an old acquaintance before you left. Harvey Girard. Art history department at Hudson University. Drop by and give him my regards. - Hank

Nice of him to give me something to do besides stew. I decided to find the professor on my day off and from there see about the rooming house in the Bronx.

Professor Girard, bearded and bespectacled, invited me into a room decorated with a timeline of historical eras and art examples to match.

"A friend of Hank's. Good on you," he said. "How is the bastard, anyway?"

I wasn't sure what to make of his greeting but told him Hank sent his regards.

"Never mind the niceties. Talked to him the other day. Said you needed a job."

That bastard sent me here on a ruse. "I'm working as a proof-reader."

"Waste of talent. They put the bright young things in dowdy jobs. Can't let the women outpace their sons and nephews."

I attempted a laugh. "It's either that or typing, and I'm better at proofreading."

"Hmm. Good diction, good spelling. I see why Hank sent you to me. Like art?"

"Can't draw with a straw," I said, "but love going to Hank's openings in St. Paul." Since Professor Girard seemed to know Hank well, I added, "A shame he can't draw either."

"Without Hank's fundraising, that little gallery would go belly up. He's a pro. Had the privilege of teaching at a summer art program with him in Chicago. Smart guy." The prof let his glasses dangle from their lanyard as he appraised his timeline wall. "Which era speaks to you?"

Though I respected Renaissance painters, I walked past them to the modern era. I pointed to a monochrome line drawing and one with splotches of paint. "Here."

"Remind me not to play three-card Monty with you, young lady. Just so happens, one of the galleries where I send my grad students is short-handed. The owner likes to show new artists, but most of my students want to work with dealers in Old Masters." He yawned. "Interested?"

Though a thrill went down my spine, I said, "I don't think I'm qualified."

"Leave that to me. They don't expect an expert, just a hard worker." Professor Girard gave me the card of a Midtown gallery. "Report for duty Monday morning. Nine o'clock sharp."

I called Hank soon as I got back to the hotel. "You're a sly fox. I owe you one."

"No," he said, "I'm paying a debt for the way you helped me with Eddie. I thought we were going to lose him last year. Let's say we're even."

I let myself cry. Tears of joy.

On the heels of getting the job, a letter came—with a generous check.

Don't spend it all in one place. – Love, Eddie & Hank

Following my change of fortune, I returned to Central Park and the Sheep Meadow where I'd spent Good Friday, my first day in New York. Sitting on the banks of the lagoon again, I thanked the Good Shepherd for my derelict brother and his partner in *crimen pessimum*. They helped me in my hour of need—unlike Father Mack, the man of God, who disposed of me like a used rag. My tabooed family wasn't so bad.

With a steady paycheck secured, I went on the search for a place to live in the neighborhood Mrs. Johnson recommend-ed—Woodside, Queens. Only twenty minutes from my job in Midtown. The third place I looked at for rent was a furnished apartment on the second floor of a spotless building only a block and a half from the transit station. A tall woman with a German accent led me through the galley kitchen to a modest living room, where two cane barrel chairs flanked a cushy couch. The sunny bedroom was big enough for a generous dresser and a slant-top desk made from an unusual dark wood. Chenille from bygone days covered the full bed. More than adequate for me. I signed the lease for June 1.

CHAPTER 19

TRAINING WHEELS

THE GALLERY PUT OUT A CALL for new artwork the week I started. Submissions soon poured in. My job entailed writing an acknowledgement note to each artist, mounting artist-provided photos of their work, and cataloguing entries by title, medium of execution, and dimensions. If the gallery director and curator saw promise in the submitted photo, they'd request the piece.

Stan, a grad student intern, wrote brief descriptions of each piece. I figured him for one of Professor Girard's few acolytes who appreciated modern art. He wore a daily uniform—black tee shirt and pants. With matching black hair and mustache, he could fade into any alley any time.

Among late arriving entries was a geometric print of many colors. "Mesmerizing isn't it?" asked Stan. "Living art."

I liked some pieces better than others but did enjoy seeing brushstrokes from a living artist. "Not a museum piece, for sure."

"Will be one day." He admired the circle and cube patterns.

Mr. Greene, the gallery owner, came into our workroom to review the latest submissions. He held up the circle and cube photo. "What do you think of this one, Stan?"

Stan donned the black linen blazer he kept flung over the back of a chair. "Stunning."

"And you, Miss Joyce?"

Did he truly want my opinion? "It's interesting."

"Stan, call him up and tell him to send the canvas." The owner left with no more picks.

"Wow, Stan, you've got a good eye. Maybe they'll hire you as a curator, or dealer."

Stan's pale cheeks blanched, but his eyes held steady. "That's my goal."

At the gallery's Solstice exhibit, Stan and I staffed the hors d'oeuvres table, drooling as much over tidbits on toothpicks as the art. He looked like he could use a good meal.

The people who came to view and buy art seemed cut out of movie frames. Vogue clothes and edgy haircuts mixed with hippie psychedelics and short stumpy codgers. Nothing like the folks at Andy's brother's art show—a lifetime ago. It would have been nice to share this new experience with someone other than my emaciated co-worker.

I wondered if Charlie liked art.

Busy getting a job and a place to live, I hadn't spent much thought on male companionship. I rummaged for the "call me Charlie" magazine exec's card. Turned up in a drawer with the list of women's hotels I kept as a souvenir of my first day in town.

What if Charlie didn't remember me? A one-off afternoon in an Irish pub almost three months ago—not an auspicious beginning. I read his card again. Midwest regional manager of a national women's magazine. If dating didn't work out, perhaps a job would. As a Midwest rep, I could visit home on the company dime.

I carried the card to work, but didn't call. My southern belle friend from the Barbizon had warned me about men in rumpled suits. On Thursday, I dialed his number anyway.

"You landed in the art world? I'm impressed. Bert and Ernie are overrated," he said. "Let's have lunch to celebrate." Pause. "Bloomingdale's? Meet me in housewares."

Low on glamour, but amazed he remembered me, I accepted.

In the June humidity, Charlie was even more rumpled than he'd been in April, but the Bronx accent hadn't changed. "How'd you get here?"

"Hopped the 6 train, Green line. Only took five minutes. Hello."

"A local already. How about lunch on the train?" He winked like it was an inside joke.

I wanted to trust his wide face with cheeks puffed out like *The Little Engine That Could*, but a hotdog in a subway station wasn't much of a celebration.

"Why'd you ask me to Bloomie's if you want to eat underground?"

Charlie pointed to a narrow, carpeted stairway at one end of the housewares department. A mirrored panel read LE TRAIN BLEU in gold etching.

"Where are you taking me?"

He sprinted up the steps. "All aboard!"

When we reached the top, an elegant train's dining car appeared on the roof of the department store, complete with waiters dressed like conductors. I stepped inside. "Wow."

"The place just opened. Thought you'd get a kick out of it."

"Are you always so full of surprises?"

"Depends on the company."

Lunch lasted longer than my lunch hour. When I returned to the gallery, Stan joked, "Hot date in the middle of the day? Covered for you. Warn me next time."

ꕥ

Sister Mary called me the weekend before the Fourth of July. "Eileen gave me your number. Said you hit the bigtime with—what was his name?"

"Charlie's a hoot," I said. "He took me to lunch to celebrate not falling on my face yet."

Sister Mary laughed. "Wondered, Meg, if you made plans for the holiday?"

"Not yet." Though I hoped Charlie might want to do something on the holiday, our lunch probably punched the ticket.

"We're having a cookout for the neighborhood kids in the afternoon." Her voice dropped. "I don't suppose you'd want to come?"

"Haven't been to a cookout in ages. And I'd love to see a few kids for a change."

She gave me directions that included changing from the train to a bus at 116th Street. "Better above ground coming into the Bronx," she said "Plan on staying overnight. Not safe around here after dark. I'll drive you back in the morning. Eileen would never forgive me if any harm came to you."

The bus ride through Harlem and into the South Bronx looked like a war zone—scorched houses and boarded up businesses. A stand of semi-tropical foliage obscured the convent's address, but the cross on the front door told me I was in the right place. I rang the bell and rubbed the deeply lobed purple leaves between my fingers while I waited for someone to answer. The plants, more like mini trees, sported bright red spiky flowers.

Sister Mary greeted me as if I'd come for afternoon tea. "Come inside. You look like you need a lemonade. But first …" She pointed to a guest bathroom. "You may want to wash your hands. Those pretty leaves you were admiring sometimes cause a rash."

"What kind of plant is it?"

"The gorgeous monsters are castor bean plants. We used to raise a pretty penny making rosaries with the seeds, but now we can't give them away."

When I returned, Sister Mary set a chilled glass of lemonade on the kitchen table—along with the most unusual rosary I ever saw. The beads ranged from about a quarter to half an inch, each gray or brown one uniquely patterned.

"Everybody got scared after a Bulgarian dissident was poisoned last year with ricin made from castor seeds. Headlines for days. Did you read about it? A spy shot the poison pellet from the tip of an umbrella. Can you imagine? But, honestly, these beads are safe unless someone chews a bead or crushes it into a powder. That's the only way the ricin poison is released. And who would ever do that with a rosary?" Sister Mary rolled her eyes. "Only in the James Bond world would anyone have the equipment to highly refine these beautiful seeds into a potent evil."

I cautiously fingered the beads.

"Go ahead. Take it. My gift to you for helping us out today." Sister Mary put her hands on her hips. "Grab a couple buckets from under the sink and take these small flags. You'll oversee relay races. I'll get the hula-hoops."

Kids steadily filled the schoolyard as afternoon hours slipped by. Moms set out bags of chips, M&M's, and buckets of fried chicken. Men brought grills followed by older kids carrying Lil' Oscars—soon to reveal hotdogs, ribs, and cans of Bud.

"I suppose the grills are the cue for the parish priests to come out," I said.

Sister Mary looked around as if to be sure no one would overhear her. "The pastor and his assistant were invited to the

Pelham Country Club. Sounds posh, but they're trying to rustle up money for a new boiler before winter." She covered a giggle. "Yes, I'm jealous anyway."

In the early evening, a couple of gangly men kicked into gear beating out drum rhythms on empty trash cans.

A girl about six years old sidled up to me and scrunched her shoulders. "Are they gonna shoot?" she asked. Her almond eyes begged for rescue.

I dropped down to her level and circled her with my arms. "No, honey, these are good guys. They're making music. Kinda loud, huh?"

"Too loud." She put her hands over low-set ears and her tongue rested on her lip. I recognized the features of a child with Down syndrome.

"What's your name?" I asked.

"JoJo."

I took her tiny hand and walked through the crowd, soon finding a frantic mom.

"JoJo, you need to stay by me." She hugged her hard. "Oh, thank you, Sister. I went to fill a plate for her and when I turned around, she was gone."

"No problem. The loud music scared her." I turned to my new friend. "Okay now?"

"This little one is afraid of everything. Aren't you, sweetie?"

Being the only white face besides the Sisters, the mom had made the obvious assumption that I must be a Sister. I explained I was a friend of Sister Mary's.

"The Sisters are nice," she said. "Good to us in the neighborhood, not judgy like others."

We sat down together with the little girl between us, showing her how to clap to the drum beat until she started laughing and munching potato chips from her mom's plate.

I stayed near them, and made sure JoJo got a sparkler at dusk. She hopped up to join the other kids singing "Yankee Doodle." We heard fireworks in the distance but couldn't see them.

As night neared, the crowd spilled into the street. Teens danced to a boombox.

Squad cars slowly circled. "Everything all right here, Sister?"

"Fine," I waved. He could have asked any of the neighbors.

Sister Mary said she recognized some of the teens from the eighth-grade class she taught a few years ago. As the party wound down, she approached the girls to help pick up, and of course, the boys stayed to help if the girls were there. Sister Mary had moxie.

Men packed up their grills, weary—and a few bleary. The moms rounded up the kids. JoJo ran over to give me a hug goodnight.

₭⁣⁐

Back at work a few days after the Fourth, Stan relayed a phone message. No name.

"Looks like somebody's back in business," he said. "The guy sounded eager."

Three weeks had passed since lunch with Charlie. I'd stopped expecting to hear from him again. "Did he sound like he was from New York—or someplace else?" Maybe my brother or Hank. Andy? Longshot, but Ruth might have given him my info.

"Pure Gotham City: *Tell 'er ta cawl me soon as she ra-turns.*"

A New Yorker. Charlie? I dialed the number.

"Have you seen the sculpture garden at MoMA yet? Free for lunch?"

I hung up and looked over at Stan. "Is MoMA the Museum of Modern Art?"

"Sure is. Lunch again? I'll cover for you. Have fun."

When I told Charlie that I spent the holiday in the Bronx, he nearly flubbed his iced tea. "No kidding. Went over to City Island with my buddies to catch some bass and bluefish. You'd hardly know it's part of the Bronx—so genteel. What were you doing there?"

"Braiding cornrows and eating ribs. Remember Sister Mary? She invited me to help with a kids' party."

"Nice woman. A mama she-goat." Charlie appraised Picasso's bronze goat in the garden.

"I don't know how those families manage to keep it together," I said. "Terrible rash of fires. The whole place seems held together with duct tape and barbecue sauce."

Charlie skewered his nearly raw steak. "Don't tell me you're a bleeding-heart liberal?"

I stabbed a forkful of salad greens. Andy would have been thrilled I refereed relay races for kids wearing secondhand shoes. He would've wanted to be there himself. He would've been great with the kids—like with the ragamuffins at St. Gabe's last Fourth of July.

"You're not a barbaric vulture, are you?" I wanted Charlie to know I could swing back.

"No need to get on your high horse," said Charlie. "This Brooklyn boy worked to get where he got—started in the mailroom—and sure wouldn't burn down my own house."

"That's what you think?" I gasped. "Sister Mary said the city closed dozens of neighborhood firehouses to fix the budget. What do you think is going to happen to the rattletrap houses poor people live in when it takes a while for a firetruck to get there? Faulty wiring, trying to keep warm with space heaters or stove ..." I took a breath. "Nobody sets fire to their own house—except maybe landlords wanting to get insurance money for their dilapidated properties—no questions asked."

Charlie ordered a martini. "If they worked a little harder, they could live better."

"Whoa."

"Take you, for instance. When your *Sesame Street* plan fell through, did you cry uncle? No. You're working hard and making a go of it. That's what I admire about you, Meg."

I wondered what Charlie saw in me besides a green-as-grass Midwesterner. Plenty of pretty young women in the city for lunchtime dalliances.

"I'll take that as a compliment coming from you, Charlie."

"Barbarian though I may be, I'm no vulture. You might be interested to know I hired a black woman last summer to cover sales on the northside of Milwaukee and the southside of Chicago—my Brooklyn accent was getting in the way." He downed his martini. "Picked her from the typing pool. Always on time, always organized, always delivered. She's making good money now."

I looked at Charlie in surprise. His actions spoke louder than words. I offered him an olive from my salad. "Sorry I don't have a whole branch."

—— ❦ ❧ ——

Lunch dates soon expanded to after-work dates. One night, we met for drinks at the Top of the Sixes, 666 Fifth Avenue. The Empire State Building soared a mile south. "Fabulous view."

"Get used to it." Charlie went on to brag about a big contract he hornswoggled with a grocery chain for his magazine, elbowing out the competition for shelf space.

"Ladies' magazines live or die by cutthroat tactics?"

"You got that right." Charlie ordered Dewar's with a twist. "What'll you have?"

I mimicked a guest at the gallery show and ordered Jack on the rocks. "Rhymes with Jack in the box."

Charlie howled. "My little girl couldn't have said it better."

Pop goes the weasel. He had a little girl? What was I doing having drinks with a married man? Divorced? Must be divorced. Or maybe this was a business meeting. Testing my rapport with would-be clients.

I let it ride. And avoided the niggly hunch of why he only saw me on weeknights.

Lunches, drinks, and dinner became a regular thing. I looked forward to seeing Charlie. Could count on a big smile. Squired me to fancy and not-so-fancy haunts—saying he hadn't been there in a while. Asked my opinion about the news, about a business deal he was rigging, about office politics.

He seemed to enjoy hearing my lowbrow take on "new" art, and my imitation Southern drawl sharing backstage gossip from my Barbizon friend. Beamed when I laughed at his jokes.

The last Friday in August, a spray of exotic flowers landed on my desk with a note:

La Caravelle – six o'clock? – Charlie

"Whoop-di-doo," said Stan. "Ready?" His wrinkled forehead reminded me of Father Leo.

Charlie's goodnight pecks had grown warmer. An arm around my waist became a long hug before hailing a cab to send me home. Charlie was ready. Me, not so sure.

I met him anyway. Why not? For most of human history, marriage equaled a contract to ensure heirs, economic advantage, or diplomatic relations. Breeding and pleasure didn't necessarily occur in the same bed. Romantic relations? Saved for brothels and mistresses.

At least Charlie wasn't a mixed-up priest. He knew what he wanted—and was willing to pay for it. Why not enjoy a nice meal at a posh French restaurant in New York with a man who could afford these things?

What was I worth?

Sundrenched murals of Paris parks lined the walls of La Caravelle. We scooched into a plush red velvet banquette. Massive bouquets hid other diners from view. The restaurant was conveniently tucked into the ground level of the Shoreham Hotel.

After ordering champagne, Charlie pulled out pictures of his kids—a Little Leaguer at bat and his "princess" on her new bike. His task that weekend was remounting her training wheels.

"She nearly fell when I took them off a few days ago. Can't have that."

I flaked my *Salmon au Pernod* with a fancy fish knife. The licorice sauce licked pink flesh. After dinner, we emerged to the heat of saturated summer air.

"Let's take a carriage ride," said Charlie. We strolled arm in arm to Central Park. Charlie surveyed the horses lined up at the curb of 59th Street and Fifth Avenue. He pointed to a chestnut mare. "That one's a beaut."

We climbed into the buggy and nestled into its ample leather cushions. The horse clip-clopped along, sultry as the night.

Charlie pressed close. "I want to kiss you, Meg."

Charles Miller had Andy's build, his easy laugh and strong hands. I didn't refuse him.

The Brooklyn boy's kiss lingered in my mouth, tongue lapping mine, cognac lips warm. Searching. Hungry. He caressed my breast. "Oh, Charlie." I wanted him.

The chestnut lifted her long neck and neighed. The driver coaxed the mare round a turn. I slipped my hand under Charlie's rumpled suitcoat and stroked his back. He touched my chin so that I looked into his eyes.

"I shouldn't string you along, Meg."

He smelled of warm amber.

"My wife is a lovely woman. Gave me two great kids. I can't leave. But she was born with a silver spoon. Doesn't understand me."

Our horse gamboled past Bethesda Fountain. The Angel of the Waters statue spread her wings. How many times, I mused, did she hear a lonely man ask a woman not his wife for a kiss.

He whispered, "Would be nice if you lived in Manhattan. I could see you more often."

The chestnut softly whickered.

"There's a swell place in SoHo. Artsy neighborhood. You'd like it." Charlie looked at me with the hopeful eyes of a soul in purgatory.

The coachman flicked the reins of his horse.

My body twitched.

Love and marriage weren't going together like a horse and carriage for me. Charlie was inviting me to another kind of life. SoHo, on the way home to Jersey for him, an easy tryst. I knew from a secretary at the gallery, from Stephanie in *Saturday Night Fever,* and from my Barbizon friend who'd moved on—what any woman knows: men like Charlie treat their mistresses well. A pied-à-terre, money on the dresser for shopping, the occasional bauble—the only thing I had to do was be there for him. We had sparks. It wouldn't be an effort.

I struck out with Jake. Sean. Andy. Three strikes. Was I out?

Be a *Cosmo* girl.

But that kind of life wouldn't give me children.

The carriage's leather bench was moist with our sweat. I slid a few inches away from him. "Charlie, I like you. I like you so very much. But when you talked about your kids tonight … a family is what I want more than anything."

Slow breaths passed between us.

He entwined his fingers in mine and squeezed my hand. "I was afraid that's what you'd say, but I had to ask."

I squeezed his hand back and thanked him for asking. He wanted me and I wanted him. Warm, easy. For a while. But his wife would get hurt. I would get hurt. Kids would get hurt.

The carriage driver deposited his crestfallen riders back to 59th Street. Charlie hailed a taxi and gave the cabbie enough for my fare. He ran his fingers through my hair. "It's been sweet. Take care of yourself."

I reached up to kiss him on the cheek. "Thanks for the training wheels, Charlie."

∞ ∞

Kids.

I called Sister Mary to ask about helping with weekend programs in the neighborhood.

She hesitated. "The Bronx is too much trouble. But I saw you with our JoJo last month. You're a natural. Most folks don't know how to handle a child like that."

"Guess I always had a soft spot for the ones left out."

Sister Mary asked me to wait a few minutes while she looked for something. I doodled on my address book.

"Let me run something past you. I have a friend, Sister Camille. She works at the Balto Center—one of the first places to teach young children with special needs. You'd be good there."

My heart sank. "I'm very interested, but if you're suggesting I look for a teaching job, I can't. My license isn't valid in New York."

"Never mind," she said. "Start by volunteering. Take some night courses. Who knows?"

The notion intrigued me. "Where is this place?"

"That's what I was looking for. Here's the phone number and address—Upper East Side. Can't be far from your art gallery. Convenient, yes? Call Sister Camille."

CHAPTER 20

SHEETS

VOLUNTEERING WITH PRESCHOOLERS at the Balto Center on weekends while staff met with their parents renewed my sense of purpose. Cutting into time for home chores, however, proved a challenge. I was working a lot of late nights at the art gallery since more fell on me when Stan cut back hours for classes in September.

Stan's choice of clothing also changed in September. Instead of the man in black at the desk catty-corner to mine, a natty range of browns appeared. I mentioned the new duds.

He flipped the collar of his tan corduroy jacket worn over a chocolate turtleneck and stuck out a foot revealing brown argyle socks. Stan looked at me as if I was his mirror. "Like it?"

"Spiffy."

"Not too much? Meeting somebody later." Stan asked if I could cover his last half hour.

"Time for me to return your favors from summer?" I missed Charlie, but not the guilt.

"Who's the lucky lady?"

Stan ducked his head and made a quick excuse to see one of the dealers.

The *New York Times* lay on Stan's desk. A headline announced Pope John Paul II's upcoming visit to the city. Reporters speculated the Church's teaching on contraception might dog him. Though very aware of the unpopular ban, I had never read the contentious 1968 encyclical. On my lunch hour, I picked up a copy at a nearby bookstore out of curiosity.

When Stan saw the paperback *Humanae Vitae* in my open tote, he slowly spun around. "Are you Catholic?"

"Worse. Irish Catholic. I'll never understand how popes can say such beautiful things about married love and then choose celibacy." A bitter taste was all Andy and I had to show for it.

Stan bit his fingernail. "Popes aren't the only ones with strong opinions."

"What's your background, Stan?"

"WASP—by way of parents, prep school, and 'pisscopalians." Stan shifted in his chair and tossed a paper airplane nowhere in particular. "Now take Little Italy Catholics—they know what holy stuff is about. Have you visited the cannoli neighborhood yet?"

"On my list, but no."

"Come with me to the San Gennaro festival. Best arancini balls this side of Naples."

With Stan smitten by a new girlfriend, I felt safe to join him. Not like encouraging him. The night of the festival, we walked in a candlelight procession behind a float decorated with sheets of dollar bills for the poor—and carrying a huge statue of Naples patron San Gennaro.

Holy cannoli.

When Sister Mary said she had an extra ticket to go to the papal Mass October 2 at Yankee Stadium in the Bronx, I begged off. Little Italy inspired me more than big Rome.

80 03

Back-to-back weeks of parades for the pope, followed by protests against Fidel Castro, vexed the city with blocked streets, frenzied news cycles, and swelling crowds. The city breathed a collective sigh of relief when the United Nations' invitees from both sides of the spectrum left town.

By mid-October, I looked forward to an easy ride to the Balto Center on Saturday morning. But the phone rang on my way out the door. I picked it up in case of another snag.

"Father Mack said you moved to New York City."

The back of my neck crawled with a thousand spiders. Darren's voice.

"I didn't believe him, but Ruth gave me your phone and address. Said to say hi."

My mind churned. "When did you get back from Africa?"

"Long story. I'll tell you about it later."

Later? "Where are you?"

"I'm in New York for a conference. How'd you like to show me around?"

Sightseeing? "Sorry, but I've got a million things to do today."

"That's no way to treat an old colleague." Darren dripped recrimination.

If I didn't leave in the next few minutes, I would be late for the kids. "Really, I'm totally booked. I volunteer on Saturdays."

"Good golly, Miss Molly. You could volunteer a few hours with me. I leave tomorrow."

I had to get him off the phone. "Gotta go. Give my regards to St. Gabe's." I plunked down the receiver. My hands shook.

I said a rosary on the train to calm my nerves. Whatever happened in Africa brought Darren back cocky as ever. I'd hoped the trip would banish his ghosts.

It didn't take long for the Balto Center kids to revive my spirits. Darren receded into no man's land. Before heading home, I browsed Egyptian goddesses at the Metropolitan, noticed Dürer's *Eve* getting friendly with a snake, and discovered not even Mona Lisa could escape the Warhol treatment.

Touring the cathedral of art took longer than I meant to stay. I caught a train home to Woodside hoping to grab a sandwich before getting together with new friends at the neighborhood pub.

ଓ ଔ

The smell of Mr. Clean greeted me upon entering my apartment building. Mrs. Bremer liked to keep her terrazzo hallways free of dirt and inhospitable to cockroaches. I approached my second story abode and smelled something else. A cigarette? Frau B. wouldn't be pleased. Out of the corner of my eye, I saw someone huddled on the next landing. Guessed someone's boyfriend was locked out. Pretended not to notice and opened my door.

"Beginning to wonder if I had the right place."

I turned. Froze.

The familiar outline of Father Darren. He crammed a book into his duffel. "Could've read this thing twice through. Thought you'd be done volunteering hours ago." He stood and took a drag. Scrambled down the steps and stubbed out his little cigar on the clean floor.

I struggled for air. "What are you doing here?"

At my heel, his breath smelled of smoke and foul eggs. He stumbled past me into the apartment and dropped his duffel. "Nice pad."

Pinpricks like tiny shrapnel raked my back.

Darren threw his jacket over the duffel. "Checked out of my hotel. Knew you'd come home sooner or later—after your *so busy* day."

"It's late. You shouldn't be here."

"Looked on a map and saw your place was closer to LaGuardia than the hotel, so ..."

Flares burst in my stomach. "You can't stay here, Darren. What were you thinking?"

"Little Meg." His voice caved. "Please. I need somebody to talk to tonight. I fly away in the morning. Lemme crash, okay?"

He already crashed. Jekyll and Hyde.

A million scenes went through my head. If I screamed, the neighbors would come running. Like they did when my mom screamed. What would they see? A woman who didn't know how to handle a drunk. They'd close their doors and mutter about "the woman who screamed." Darren needed to sleep it off. He wouldn't do anything to me—I knew all about Nicole. If I sent him out to a cab, where would he end up? He might never leave town.

Said he would "fly away in the morning." I had to get him on that flight.

I stepped into the apartment and closed the door behind me. "So, talk. What happened?"

"Gotta beer?" He sat on my couch like lord of the manor.

I popped two beers and sat across from him.

Darren rubbed the cold can between his palms. "Africa is a very dark continent."

I waited at least ten minutes while he disappeared into his own thoughts.

"Never got to see sweet Sister Nicole—or her wet paint-brush either."

Wasn't expecting that. I avoided eye contact.

He swilled his beer. "Should've been easy. The Clem's mission was right across the border." His hand sliced lines in the air. "Rhodesia here—Botswana there."

"Why couldn't you get there?"

Darren grunted and leaned forward. "Bush War guerilla rebels didn't much care about visas, passports, permissions, any damn thing. Just as soon blow your head off." He gulped the rest of his beer. "Your fault they sent me to that hellhole."

Molten metal shot through my veins.

He crushed the can in his hands. Aimed for the wire basket in the kitchen more than ten feet away. Missed. The can clanked against the fridge. "Gimme another."

I slid my beer over to him.

"A damn bust."

I quelled the fire roiling in my belly and went into the kitchen, picked up the can, and disposed of it in the basket. When my kids acted out, sometimes it helped to break the chain. I needed to break Darren's mounting barrage.

I walked to the linen closet. "I'll get some sheets. You can sleep it off on the couch."

When I returned with an armload of linens, Darren grabbed me from behind and pulled me down onto the couch. "Pretty little Meg."

Pillow casings tumbled to the floor and folded sheets lay like land mines. I struggled to my feet. "Don't, Darren. Don't."

He lurched toward me. "You smell good." Stuck his hands under my breasts.

I slapped him hard.

"Ooch, little Meg. You want it bad, don't you?" He pressed against me. Urgent.

I wanted to cut Darren with a thousand knives. No one would believe I hadn't "wanted it." I wasn't a virgin. How could I have let him in? Stupid. Trapped.

"I don't want it."

He cranked my arm behind my back and pushed me into the bedroom. "Don't make me beg." The second I tried to make a run for it, he barred the door with his body. I dodged under one arm, but he caught me with the other and swung me down. I hit the floor hard, grabbed his ankle and bit it. But that only brought a swat across my back. Winded me.

It was going to happen one way or the other. I couldn't afford to land in the hospital. I had to go to work, pay bills. I didn't want anybody asking where I got that bruise. I opened my mouth to scream, but the sound caught. Nobody would help me anyway. When my mom didn't do what my dad wanted, she bore the marks. I knew now why she screamed.

I didn't scream. I only wanted this night to end.

He unzipped his pants, then dropped black Speedo shorts. Not boxers or briefs.

"Can't do it with your clothes on. Lemme see you, little Meg. Get up."

I stood up, woozy.

He surveyed the perfume bottles on my dresser—L'Air du Temps, Muguet des Bois, Chanel. He picked up the kissing doves bottle of L'Air du Temps, turned, and sprayed it in the air. "Not undressed yet?" Standing naked and erect, he pointed the nozzle at me. I unbuttoned my blouse—spray. Jeans—spray. Bra—two sprays.

Panties. I crawled under the sheet.

He ripped the sheet off the bed. Got on top of me. Didn't look at me. Nothing. Pound-pound-pound.

Cold. So cold. Like hell coming down on me. Hell, but not hot. Freezing. Empty.

My own eyes stared at me from across the room, watching what was happening.

It hurt. I was dry.

He finished.

And then he looked at me … disgusted.

I couldn't move.

He turned away.

I shuddered. My body cold as ice.

Warm tears dripped down cold cheeks.

I lay there, frozen. Hollow.

He rolled over. Breathing hard. Scratched the mattress. Muffled— "Goddammit, Nicki."

At first light of dawn, I took a long, long shower. Put clothes on. Measured coffee grounds, over and over.

He got up, washed, dressed—full clerical suit, ivory collar band and all—as if he hadn't unleashed his demons on me in the dark night.

Hardly a word passed between us. He was ready to go to the airport. I insisted on going with him. He didn't want me to, but I had to make sure he was gone. He was sober now. He didn't hit me when I called the cab. We careened to the airport.

He seemed to walk in slow motion to the terminal. I watched him get on the plane. I stayed to watch the plane take off.

Found a bathroom. Puked.

Once home, I took more showers. Sat on the bedroom floor, a hollowed-out shell. Stayed there long into the night.

Woke up in a sweat. When was my last period? Not likely pregnant, but if—

Tears flowed. I couldn't burden a child with this. Couldn't let sin explode inside me and scar a child. Couldn't watch Darren's cells multiplying, bloating into a daily reminder of a horrible night. Bad enough every cell of my body already bore the scars.

God forgive me, but if … I will join the sisterhood of vacuumed wombs.

☜ ☞

Routine. I went through the motions at work. Numb. The white noise of the city filtered the chaos of my world. At night, I curled up on my side on the living room floor swaddled in a blanket, clinging to a throw pillow. Slept little.

On Friday, Mr. Greene, the gallery owner, came into the workroom carrying the catalog binder I had prepared. "Miss Joyce, your work is always meticulous. What is this?"

He opened to a page and read Stan's description of an abstract expressionist painting. The photo I mounted showed a realistic nude. Another page described a landscape—not a portrait.

As I turned the binder's pages, my errors blurred into a black sea.

"I'm so sorry. I'll redo it. Sorry." I beat my breast. "*Mea culpa.*" The room spun.

"All right, Miss Joyce. Settle down. Sort it out and bring it to me later."

Stan came over and put his hand on my shoulder.

I bolted my hands up into the air. "Don't touch me."

Stan stepped back. "Okay, I won't touch you." He crouched down. "Meg, it's me, Stan. I won't hurt you."

I burst into tears. Stan reached for his hanky.

"Sorry, Stan, I don't feel good."

"Enough with the sorry stuff," he said. "You've looked awful all week. Do you want to talk about it?"

"No." I blew my nose. "Need to fix this book." Shaky hands fumbled pages. It dropped.

Stan picked up the book. "May I help?"

I said nothing, but as I tore out photos, Stan matched them with the proper descriptions. A couple of hours later, the binder was ready for Mr. Greene's desk.

I powdered my nose. In the mirror, my eyes looked like two burnt holes in a blanket. "Will you bring it to Mr. Greene for me, Stan?"

"No, it's important you show Mr. Greene you've got what it takes."

When I handed the binder to the owner, he appraised random pages. "Nicely done, Miss Joyce." He looked over the rim of his glasses. "As usual." He invited me to sit down in one of the molded black leather chairs across from his desk. The chair with wheels on its legs and a swivel base presented difficulties for sitting still.

The reserved Mr. Greene laughed heartily. "Mr. and Mrs. Eames designed not only for comfort but fun. Take it for a spin, Miss Joyce."

I let the chair spin a bit, but not too much.

"See what I mean?"

I nodded.

"I like these chairs. They remind me life is unpredictable. Can't control everything, try as I might." He leaned across the desk. "Isn't that right, Miss Joyce?"

"Indeed." Surely couldn't control what happened last week.

Mr. Greene removed his glasses and looked at me intently. "Let go of what you cannot control, Miss Joyce. Do your best with the rest."

Realizing the owner had observed my dreary self all week, I murmured, "Thank you."

"Enjoy your weekend, Miss Joyce. And for God's sake— and mine—have some fun."

Fun. What was that? But I did need sleep. Desperately. After work, I went to Bloomie's to shop for sheets. Maybe clean new sheets would do the trick. Picked through cases of white sheets, light blues, pale yellows. I couldn't decide. The next display held sheets in crayon box colors. Exuberant poppies praised the sun and caught its rays. Huge yellow butterflies danced among violets in another. I had never seen sheets like that. Vivid. Bold. Strong. Brave.

Joyful.

I bought a set of happy sheets. Paid for four corners of brave joy.

At home, I yanked the sheets off my bed and everything that happened in them the week before. Stuffed them down the garbage chute.

CANDLEWOOD

I knew Darren's warped actions weren't about me. Probably thought any woman living in the big city was on the Pill and having sex every other day. He used me the way men use women when they need to control something, anything—dominate someone, anyone—show how macho they are—need a punching bag but can't hit the boss, the customer, the guards, the Church.

He had to get it out of his system, and I was there.

Father, forgive him for he knows not what he does. None of them do.

I tucked in the corners of my new sheets. Reclaimed my bed.

Reclaimed my life.

Slept.

CHAPTER 21

FUMES

IF MY DAD COULD CHANGE, maybe there was hope for Darren. Wish I had gotten to see Dad's desert cactus in Arizona. I gave my Christmas cactus plant its scant once-per-week watering. If I coddled it through Thanksgiving, maybe it would bloom by the holiday. Rather than interrupt the ritual when my phone rang, I let the answering machine take the call.

"Meg?"

I doused the cactus and grabbed the phone.

"Andy?"

"How are you?"

His breezy voice betrayed no knowledge about last month's Darren incident.

"Fine. You?"

"Saw Beth at Mass Sunday. Told me you found a job and a nice apartment."

Ah, Beth prompted his call.

"Beth's parents are great. Mrs. Johnson tipped me off about this neighborhood. The apartment is incredibly reasonable. My landlady said the furniture came from a hotel she and her husband used to manage. The wood in my dresser and writing desk is loaded with character. She called it burled oak." I could hear myself blathering and came to an abrupt halt.

"Burled oak is gorgeous, but hard to work with," said Andy. "Not sure I would have the skills."

I pictured his intricate dovetail work. "You make beautiful things, Andy. You could make a burled oak desk any day of the week if you wanted to."

"You sound happy, Meg."

It was true. I had suddenly become happy in the last five minutes. This man's choices infuriated me, but I never doubted he loved me.

Andy asked if I had much time to see the sights.

"Everything is a new sight. I'm working through Hank's long list of must-sees. Haven't yet gotten to the Statue of Liberty."

"Ah, Lady Liberty and her torch. Can you walk up into it?"

Eileen asked the same thing when I sent a postcard of the colossus woman.

"Part-way, but not into the torch." I chuckled— "Might get scorched."

Andy burst into laughter.

A quiet stream bubbled through me at the sound of his laugh. "What are you up to?"

"Not much. Helped Ruth harvest the last carrots in her community garden. Sue put down her knitting to crunch dried thyme. The whole place smells like a French kitchen."

"Ruth wrote me about her project. She said the senior citizens had a hard time affording fresh produce, so of course she got planting. It started with the potting shed you built for her, you know." I paused. "Nice of you to help."

"Purely self-interest. I 'donate' to Josie. Could say, I eat what I reap."

Andy at his self-deprecating best. "The mama-san from the Asian market must have decided I'm a local—she smiles and puts a Chinese pear in my bag. Much crispier than ours."

"Sounds like you're getting on just fine."

"Beth probably told you I got a job at an art gallery. Not the work I expected, but interesting. And every other week, I volunteer with preschoolers. I plan on taking night school courses for certification to teach in New York."

"Yeah, Leo told me something about that. Kids with special needs, right? Sounds right up your alley."

Hearing myself talk about plans and a future—with someone who blew all my plans and future—gave me confidence that the medicine of time and distance was working.

"Beth's folks often invite me for dinner, but between the gallery and the kids, I need a little time to do chores. I'll join them for turkey day, though."

Andy sighed. "So, you won't be home for Thanksgiving."

After all we'd been through, I thought he'd be glad to be rid of me.

"Maybe for Christmas. Not sure how much time I'll get off. We have a big show coming up at the gallery. Lots of receptions for well-heeled patrons. Last week, I discovered caviar. Little black beads of juicy goodness. My boss marched over to say the hors d'oeuvres were for guests, not staff. I wasn't the only one—we slunk away like a school of fish."

"It's good to hear your voice, Meg."

Geez, I missed him. "We haven't talked like this in a long time."

"Too long."

My heart pumped faster. "Let's not go there."

"Yeah. Well, I just wondered how you were doing. Darren said he had dinner with you when he was in town for a conference. Gave a good report. Wanted to hear for myself."

Oh, my God. My throat tightened.

"Andy, maybe I shouldn't tell you this."

"Meg, what's wrong?"

I blurted, "Everything."

"Wait, a minute ago you sounded happy. What's going on?"

"We didn't go to dinner." My voice shallowed out. "I don't want to talk about it."

"Meg? No. Tell me he didn't— God."

Andy knew Darren. Not hard to put two and two together.

"I feel so stupid. I thought he might have changed in Rhodesia or Botswana or wherever the hell he went."

"Meg, it's not your fault."

"What's wrong with you men? None of you know which end is up."

Silence.

I put the receiver back in its cradle. Stared at the phone. Replayed our conversation. How could the same act of making love with Andy be a thing of violence with someone else? A bunch of "celibate" men easily blamed the woman. Blind to the difference.

But now Andy knew one of his own hurt me. Violated me. How could he live with that?

I wiped my tears and soaked up the spill from overwatering my Christmas cactus.

80 03

As much as I looked forward to seeing friends and family at Christmas, I held my breath against a hijacked flight. Iranian students had seized the United States Embassy in Tehran and taken more than fifty hostages. Anything could happen.

Mr. Greene let the non-sales employees leave the art gallery early on Friday. I went home to pack for my Saturday afternoon flight. Nice to have a few days both before and after Christmas before plunging back to work at the gallery's New Year's gala the following weekend. I jammed an extra pair of shoes into my avocado green Samsonite suitcase. Close to the color of a grenade. Wished I had room for a grenade, just in case.

The latch locked as I remembered that I hadn't packed a rosary. I always carried one on trips. The castor bean rosary Sister Mary gave me would be interesting to show around. I found it on the dresser next to my perfume bottles—unused since sleazy Darren sprayed me for kicks ... the night he took me hostage. Eight weeks ago.

All the rage I thought gone surfaced. Easier to forgive at a distance. Would I be in danger back home? What if he found a way to capture me, harm me? If I saw him, I might shoot him— I wanted to—so he could never again hurt me or anyone else.

But I didn't have a gun.

The rosary bulged in the side pocket of my luggage. I tried to push it flat, but not so hard that the bean might crack and release its poison.

Poison.

I sat at the kitchen table, shocked at the thoughts racing through my head. How to extract the poison ... how to get it to Darren. Without exposing myself.

Sister Mary claimed the hard-coated beans only proved dangerous if chewed—which meant they could be crushed somewhat easily. But that would also release the castor oil inside the bean. Sludge. Not enticing. But what if I gently cracked the shell and removed the soft insides? Then, I could collect the shell fragments. Put them in something. Disguise them. How?

Two hours passed.

9:00 p.m. I needed to act fast before the grocery closed. List: rubber gloves, plastic tablecloth, plastic cutting board, aluminum foil, coffee filters, paper plates and bowls, can of baking powder, tiny condiment spoon, Xmas wrap and ribbon. Gift tag. Pack of Winchester little cigars.

I got home and unpacked my bag.

Covered the kitchen table with the plastic tablecloth. Placed the plastic cutting board at one end. Emptied the baking powder into a dish. Covered my hand iron in two layers of foil with coffee filters between each.

Removed little cigars from the Winchester pack. Fit as many as would go into the baking powder tin. Tied them in a red ribbon. Selected one cigar and loosened some of the tobacco with an ice pick. Divided the shreds between two small bowls.

Donned rubber gloves and tied a bandana around my nose and mouth. Opened the window for ventilation. Wouldn't be smart to chance breathing the poison myself.

Cut three castor bean beads from the rosary. Placed them on the plastic cutting board with coffee filters underneath to absorb any residue from the oil-rich pulp inside.

Ready to crush.

With the iron, I eased pressure on one of the beans.

Success. The poisonous shell cracked, exposing the soft inside packet of castor oil. A slick of oily residue soaked into the filter. I separated the inner bean from the hard outer shell.

I repeated the process with the other two beads and shook about a tablespoon of baking powder on the plastic cutting board to absorb the sediment. Poked dry shell fragments onto a clean filter.

Crushed the shell fragments again, pulverizing them to release as much of their poison as possible.

I lifted the dry powder with the condiment spoon and mixed it into one of the tobacco bowls. Stashed the rest of the residue, filters, and cutting board into the garbage.

Sat back to rest. Dead tired.

Last step. Wearing rubber gloves would be challenging to do finger work, but I couldn't take them off and risk the junk seeping into my pores.

I held the selected cigar at an angle and spooned the laced tobacco back into it. Pushed ever so gently. The brown cigar paper broke. Dammit.

Prepared another. Okay.

Plugged plain tobacco at the bottom. Nested the laced cigar safely among the plain ones in the baking powder tin. The coffin sticks made a respectable bundle of dynamite.

I dropped the gift note inside:

Your sermons are dynamite! Enjoy ~

3:00 a.m. Done.

I tied the garbage bag. Gathered up the plastic tablecloth with the remnants. Carried them to the incinerator. Tossed my bandana and rubber gloves down the shaft.

The loaded tin, wrapped in nutcracker-printed silver foil, slid neatly into my suitcase. Though my crude handiwork was unlikely to be lethal, inhaling his favorite fumes would soon be followed by wheezing, coughing, respiratory distress. He'd never know what hit him.

ॐ ଓ

Mom said I was wasting away to nothing in the big city. She went all out fixing a Christmas Eve feast including apple stuffed pork roast and pecan pie. Eddie and Hank dug into the huge dinner, saying I should come home more often if it prompted this kind of meal.

It was hard to savor. My preoccupation delivering Darren's "gift" drove me crazy.

Mom fretted about my lack of a young man. "Whatever happened to the fellow who took you such nice places?"

"Charlie was fun, Mom, but not the serious type." What else could I say?

"If your flighty friend Eileen can get herself a steady boyfriend, I fail to see your problem. You're much prettier and smarter ... and ..." She eyed Eddie and Hank. "No offense, but a few grandchildren would be nice."

Mom never beat around the bush—but romance was the last thing on my mind.

"I'm dating, Mom. One of these days, it'll happen. For sure." I gave her my best gingerbread smile. "I like kids. That's why I'm spending my spare time at the Balto Center. Someday I'll have my own." I dug for another defense. "By the way, did you forget the guy who took me to the Italian festival?" Didn't matter Stan wasn't a contender.

Eddie came to my rescue. "It takes two to tango, Ma. She'll be fine."

"All right, I'll give it a rest. Just want to see you happy and settled."

Hank changed the subject by quizzing me on museums, Jewish delis, my work at the art gallery, and his old friend Professor Girard. Eddie needled me about wanting to come to the Big Apple for a visit over the Fourth of July weekend. I said only if he promised to be as good a guest as the daughter of Mom's friend who stayed with me on her way to a summer abroad program—and brought back ouzo. He reminded me that he didn't drink anymore. The good-natured way he said it let me know he was truly working the program.

Visions of family seated around the holiday table used to fill me with light and love. But now that happy family was seated with someone capable of the darkest of arts.

ℂℂ

Beth came to Midnight Mass at St. Gabriel's. I hid behind a pillar to avoid eye contact with Andy. After Mass, Beth invited me to a traditional St. Stephen's party on the 26th. Said she wanted to show off her new digs in Minneapolis since getting a music therapy job at the hospital. She pressed me to bring a favorable report back to her Long Island parents.

When she said a few friends from Campus Ministry would also be coming, I cautiously asked if she expected Father Darren. With only two more days before my return flight, I could go undiscovered dropping off the "gift" at Campus Ministry at a time Darren wasn't in the building.

She glanced sideways. "I probably should keep this hush, but you'll never guess what happened, Meg. Rumors flew about him with a pretty co-ed. All of a sudden, poof, gone. Everybody called her a slut, but I knew her from choir. Seemed a little naïve to me."

"He's gone? Gone where?"

"Transferred him. That's all I know."

Damn. My careful work for nothing. The jerk must have gotten careless. Like my brother once said, the priests can go after women, or men, but not students.

I wanted to find out the rest of the story and knew Andy could tell me, but I didn't go see him. I couldn't bear another bout of silence like his call at Thanksgiving. Worse, I couldn't chance another happy conversation. Not that anything could ever be the same again. I was defiled … and I'd wanted to poison a man.

Though relieved Darren was found out at last, I believed he was banished more to prevent scandal than to prevent him from hurting another woman. The priests banded together like glue. Rather than admit one of their own could prey on and rape bodies and souls, they chalked it up to "woman trouble." Still a priest. I tried to stop him. But I was too late.

At the airport, I tossed the cigars into a trash bin.

CANDLEWOOD

My apartment was bitter cold when the cab dropped me off from the airport. Forgot to close the kitchen window. I kept my coat on and stood looking out the window at specs of snow melting on the sidewalk below. White stuff gradually making everything icy. Icy as my body felt the night Darren raped me.

Icy as my soul today. *Lord, what's become of me?*

I only wanted to stop him from hurting me again, or anyone else. But poison? Like they say, *The road to hell is paved with good intentions.* I am no better than he.

Like the white snow smudged into black ice, my fear had curdled into evil.

Like Darren's desperate want of love, any goodness in him soured.

Satan was as real as God.

Quiet tears washed my cheeks. As evening fell, I found the phone number for the Christopher House and asked for Sister Loretta. I told her my story. She did not hang up on me.

"So now, dear Meg, you have eaten of the tree of good and evil. Which do you choose?"

My voice choked. "I can only choose good because God prevented me from doing evil."

"Are you thankful, maybe relieved? Or are you angry that your plan failed?"

"Relieved."

A long pause. "That's a start," she said. And then, she told me to say three Hail Marys each day for the three castor beans I cut from the rosary. "Light will return. I promise."

Lord, I will not let anger kill my soul any longer. But you, Lord— you must open the eyes of blind Churchmen.

CHAPTER 22

EPIPHANY

MY VISIT HOME TO SHADY BLUFF at Christmastime confirmed the wild bet I'd made in moving to New York City. I needed to live somewhere bigger than a four-corner town if I wanted to avoid the man with hair the color of late season dune grass, a thatch of it forever falling across his forbidden forehead. For six months, the Big Apple had proven its worth in distractions.

After a rush of champagne receptions for gallery patrons to close out the 1970s, I expected to have the office to myself for a while. Stan wasn't due back until mid-month. But, he showed up the day after New Year's.

"Did you miss the skating at Rockefeller Center or the screeching trains?"

"Albany wasn't good for my health."

When he took off his galoshes, I noticed the otherwise neat-as-a-mannequin Stan wore mismatched socks. In fact, nothing matched. I didn't probe.

"Ever hear of a Twelfth Night party, Meg?"

"Sure. Celebrates the feast of the Magi—Epiphany—the twelfth day after Christmas."

Stan fidgeted with his desk calendar. "My grad advisor, Professor Girard, is hosting a Twelfth Night party on Sunday and said I should bring you along. Didn't know you knew him."

"Friend of a friend." I hadn't seen the professor since he set me up with this job. Was he setting me up with a date now?

Did I want it to be a date? Stan was friendly but not my type. "Won't it be all artsy grad students?"

"Mostly, I guess. But you could run circles around a lot of them. Your museum visits are paying off. You used to say a piece was 'interesting.' The other day I heard you admire one of Calder's mobile sculptures— 'floating like gems in the sun,' you said. Impressive."

"Your influence." The owner recently promoted Stan to drafting wall panel descriptions for new artwork and invited him to a valuation meeting with dealers.

"So, are you in or not?"

Whoosh. "Okay. But no need to take me. I can get there on my own."

He broke his pencil tapping it hard on the desk. "Meet me at Zabar's Emporium Sunday at five o'clock. We can walk to the Professor Girard's apartment from there. They live on the Upper West Side."

Stan found me late afternoon on Sunday debating between Zabar's marble or pistachio halvah for the party.

"Can't you hurry up?" He scowled like an angry cat, snatched the pistachio chunk from my hand, and marched to the cash register.

This wasn't the mild-mannered Stan I knew. "We don't have to go if you don't want to."

"Of course, we'll go. Doesn't matter whether I'm feeling festive or not."

"Okay, all right. Let's go then." My fingers tensed tight.

Professor Girard greeted us with wassail. "Glad you could make it, Meg. Bring Hank around when he comes to town."

Stan shot me a quizzical look, but I pretended not to notice.

Mrs. Girard held out a velvet-lined basket filled with Venetian eye masks. When Stan took a gilded one, she dubbed him King Melchior of the Magi trio. Turning to me, she selected a mask sprinkled with sparkly crystals. "Let's make you the Star of Bethlehem."

After dinner, Mrs. Girard served the traditional almond custard cake with prizes baked into it. Whether tiny trinkets or old-fashioned beans, she didn't say.

Stan nearly spit out his first bite. He held up a red kidney bean on his fork.

I soon encountered a large lima.

Professor Girard proclaimed that our "elegant legumes" bestowed regal authority upon us to decide and declare winners and losers of the soon to be played mask-inspired charade games.

At the end of a delightful evening, save for Stan's forced smiles, Professor Girard told him to be sure I got home safely to Queens.

"Please don't feel obliged," I said.

He grumbled something under his breath. "Woodside, right? Won't take long."

Good to know he didn't intend to stay at my place.

After a long silence on the subway, Stan looked at me curiously. "Fess up. Who's Hank, and what's your connection to the professor?"

Hmm, how near to the truth did I want to tread?

"Hank is like family—a good friend of my brother's. A close friend, you might say. Hank and the professor worked together one summer. When I moved to the city, they helped me get a job at the gallery." I paused to consider how much further to venture. "Before I knew there was a Mrs. Girard, I assumed the professor wasn't ... the marrying kind ... like Hank and my brother." I hoped Stan would get the gist.

Eyes wide, Stan's face went beet red. He turned away, saying nothing.

On the sidewalk outside my apartment, he checked his watch. "Almost tomorrow." He turned around and hightailed it back to the transit station.

I decided to keep my private life private in the future.

Although working in the same room with me, Stan kept his distance—until Friday, nearly a week since the Twelfth Night party. After lunch, he asked me if I had gotten to a Broadway play since moving to the city.

"No. Why? Does Professor Girard think I should see one?"

Stan lowered his head. "You're okay, Meg. I was a lout at the party. Preoccupied."

"I'll say." Though not romantically interested, I missed his camaraderie.

"There's a play I thought you might want to see."

"Broadway is on my list, but tickets are pricey."

"Don't you know about the kiosk in Times Square? As much as half-off for same-day shows. Interested now?"

I perked up. "That changes everything."

A long line straggled around the kiosk when we arrived after work. Stan was convinced we'd get cheap tickets for a play called *Bent* because it opened to mixed reviews. I didn't know anything about the play but lead actor Richard Gere got raves. I had seen the broodingly handsome Gere on the big screen as a hustler in *Looking for Mr. Goodbar*, so I willingly agreed with Stan's choice.

We waited in line forty-five minutes, only to find tickets were minimally discounted.

"No problem," said Stan. "Remember, I'm Melchior—the king whose gift is gold."

"The Star of Bethlehem owes you."

Hours later, Stan and I emerged from the New Apollo Theatre shellshocked by two hours of storm troopers taunting and torturing "bent" men—homosexuals—in Nazi Germany.

"Let's get you home," said Stan.

The subway rattled like the boxcar where Nazis threw Gere and his gay lover. As a survival strategy in Berlin, Gere's character wore a yellow star, slightly less loathsome than the pink triangle worn by his companion. When the guard ordered him to strike his friend, Gere denied he knew him. But under the guard's threat, Gere hit his friend hard, then harder and harder as if proving to himself his drunken rant from earlier in the evening: "Queers aren't meant to love." He left his friend bloodied.

I turned to Stan and blurted out, "Why in the hell didn't Gere do what his family asked—get married and hide his gay side, play it safe?"

Stan sucked his lower lip beneath the upper as if he had no teeth. When the subway doors squeaked open at the next stop, his jaw slackened. "That's what my family asked me to do at Christmas. Sent me to our minister—counseling. Should I play it safe?"

"Oh, Stan." I felt heat rising in my cheeks. "Weren't you crazy about that girl you dated?"

Stan looked away. "You mean, that *guy* I was seeing. Yeah, I was crazy about him. Made the mistake of telling my parents. Wanted to bring him home to meet them."

I twisted the chain handle of my purse.

"The parents needn't have worried. He turned out to be a two-timing jackass. Found him fucking a mutual friend. Shouldn't have said anything to my family. Lost a lover—and my kin."

I ached at the memory of my brother's coming out. Mom's tears, my lack of understanding at first. "They need time, Stan. They'll come around … you'll see."

Stan looked up at the dark night sky as the subway rolled to its above-ground deck. "My parents offered a grand bargain. Said I could keep my trust fund if I didn't embarrass their Albany crowd by bringing any 'fairies' around."

"That's a lot to ask, and a lot to give up. What are you going to do?"

Stan sat up straighter on the thinly padded plastic seat. "I refuse to lie to a woman to get married. Wouldn't be fair to her. How would you feel, Meg? My god."

I nodded. "You're an honorable man."

He reached in his pocket and flipped a coin. "But a guy's gotta live." The coin came up tails. "Now you know how Melchior got his gold."

The crescent moon smiled askew at us. I gazed at the stars outside our graffiti splayed window. "The Star owes you a wish."

"Like a diamond in the sky." Stan's eyes implored mine. "Maybe queers *can* love?"

"Yes, Stan, you'll find love." I looked down and saw his mismatched socks. "And I hope soon, so you can find matching socks again."

He laughed. "Here's our stop." The station sign hovered over snowy tracks.

I tugged at Stan's coat lapel. "Thanks for seeing me home, Melchior."

"Shine on, Star, shine on."

Stan and I became regulars at the ticket kiosk in Times Square. Compassionate friends, without the worries of passion. I confessed my ill-fated romance, and Stan declared me absolved.

Enlightened by our missteps, we made a pact to cheer each other on and promised to follow our hearts to a brighter place.

For Valentine's Day, Stan introduced me to Ferrara's bakery in Little Italy, where we made a meal of tiramisù with espresso. On Sundays, we worked through Hank's list of must-sees. Stan added his Murray Hill neighborhood gem—the J. Pierpont Morgan Library. As we viewed Mr. Morgan's illuminated *Gutenberg Bible*, we agreed to believe God would guide our wanderings.

℀ ℅

When I told Stan about my Saturday mornings at the Balto Center, he asked if he could help. He proved immensely patient with preschoolers who had disabilities.

Sister Camille invited us to stay for lunch with the staff one Saturday in early March. During dessert, she asked, "Would you like to join us next week for the St. Patrick's Day Parade?" "We're hosting the 14th Street group home."

Stan and I looked at each other. "We were going to ask you about switching our Saturday," I said, "so we could go watch it."

"I can offer you a prime location. We're only three blocks from the Parade route down Fifth Avenue. It goes from 44th Street to 79th Street. The marchers should be in fine form by the time they reach us."

"Won't we be in the way if you're having guests?" Stan asked.

"Honestly, we could use some help with the gang," said Sister Camille. "The kids always want to be in the front row. Silly me, I call them kids, but the residents at the group home are grown up. We knew some of them as children when they came here early on. Hardly anybody else was doing special education then. The parade and holidays are occasions to get together."

"And now they're in a group home? What is that?" I asked.

"Once upon a time, not so long ago," said Sister Camille, "the only options for adults with disabilities were institutionalization and sheltered workshops."

"You wouldn't believe some of the conditions," said another Sister. "Parents began looking for better alternatives. The movement gained steam when they found an ear in the Kennedy administration in the 1960s. The president's sister had an intellectual disability."

"I wasn't aware of the history," I said. Guess I hadn't thought about what happened beyond school years.

"Community living places like the 14th Street group home foster as much independence as a person with disabilities can handle." Sister Camille pointed to a photo of two smiling young women. "One of our former students takes the subway to her job at the post office. Her friend keeps coffee cups filled at a diner. They're proud of their work, out in the world, not shut away like they don't belong."

"Utopian," said Stan, "but is it practical?"

Sister Camille acknowledged bumps in the road. "Funding is always an issue. People are experimenting with different models. Practical? I don't know, but dreams are possible."

As Stan and I approached the Center on parade day, I got the jitters. "I don't mind telling you—I'm nervous. I only know how to relate to kids, not adults who are, well, *challenged.*"

Stan did a double take. "Aren't you the one who said you didn't know anything about visiting elderly shut-ins for your parish—and now you miss them? Don't worry about it."

Why did he have to remind me of the parish ... another St. Pat's Day. Andy's first kiss.

At brunch, the Sisters served warm Irish soda bread, ham, eggs—and plenty of jokes.

"Cardinal Cooke offered us tickets on the reviewing stand at the cathedral," said Sister Camille. "He's a saint." She lowered her voice to a soft chuckle. "But I would rather be within walking distance of a restroom for a five-hour parade."

Stan nudged me. "Geez, we could have been in the thick of it—*at* St. Pat's *on* St. Pat's."

"We're here now, Stan. Pipe down."

One of the guests from the 14th Street residence, Maddy, cleared dishes with me after lunch. Her housemate Greg washed plates while Stan dried. Grown up versions of my students. Greg pointed to Stan's green tie. "Mine better." He pulled at the corners of his green bowtie.

Maddy jangled the green beads around her neck. "Better than everybody."

"Wish I'd brought my kazoo," I said. "Used to march in a kazoo band for St. Pat's."

"What's a kazoo?" asked Maddy.

"It's like a funny whistle. Hard to explain."

"Show me," said Greg.

"Yes, do." Stan extended his arm as if giving me the floor.

I was on the spot. Looked for something to fashion into a whistle. I pulled a tin foil sheet and rolled it tight.

"Like this." I tooted into the makeshift whistle.

"That's weird, Meg." Maddy laughed. "Can I do it?"

When she "whistled" with abandon, everyone in the kitchen erupted into claps and toots.

Sister Camille poked her head in the door. "We need to hurry to get good spots."

"C'mon, band," said Stan. "Let's be off." Our merry band tooted imaginary kazoos all the way to Fifth Avenue.

CANDLEWOOD

We left the party exhausted at the end of the day. Stan mused, "Are we normal? Is anybody?"

I glanced back at our happy crew. "Those tossed aside people are normal for sure. And Sisters who prefer restrooms to reviewing stands." I put a green carnation in Stan's buttonhole. "Fallen-away Catholics and queer WASPs." Stragglers from the Parade dawdled on the Avenue. "Also, women who dye their hair green, and of course, men who wear kilts. Completely normal."

Stan grinned. "Don't forget kazoo players."

৪০ ৫৪

The scent of cherry blossoms in Central Park meant a season of lovely walks after work. Though days were lengthening, I got home just before dark. The phone was ringing off the hook.

Eddie didn't often call. Got most of my news from Mom.

"Meg, are you sitting down?"

His flat tone worried me. "What's happened?"

He asked when I last talked to Mom.

"Sunday morning. Easter."

"Okay, Meg, brace yourself."

His hesitation felt like an eternity.

"Mom had a stroke."

The world stopped. "Stroke? How? When? How bad? Is she ... oh, God, Eddie?"

"She's going to be all right, Meg. It was a small one. The doc called it a warning stroke, a TIA or something like that."

Mom. Memories swarmed. Coloring Easter eggs. Putting talcum powder on her slippers to make bunny footprints leading to our baskets. Kissing my scraped knee. Always there for us.

"Is she in the hospital?"

"They treated her in the ER. Gave her something to dissolve the clot right away." He coughed. "They kept her overnight and did a bunch of tests. Said her symptoms were mild and resolving quickly. Sent her home with orders to see her doctor for follow-up."

"I don't get it. She had a stroke—and they sent her home? How did it happen?"

"I don't know how to explain it. Hank and I took her out for Easter dinner. She was fine one minute—then slurred her words. We joked about her getting sloshed even before drinking her Brandy Alexander dessert. She just slumped to one side of her chair. Rushed her to the ER."

"Thank God she was with you guys." My sweaty palm gripped the phone. "Now what?"

"Hank took Mom to her regular doctor on Monday. He gave her meds for high blood pressure and told her to quit smoking. That'll be the hardest part."

As I put the pieces together and the timeline, I shouted, "Why are you only calling me now? It's Wednesday—and this happened Sunday?"

"Calm down, Kitten. We didn't know what to say, and Mom didn't want to worry you. You couldn't do anything, being in New York." Eddie paused. "Meg, you should come home."

"Of course, Eddie, my boss will understand. I'll get home by the weekend."

Another hesitation. I could hear Eddie taking a deep breath. "What I mean is, you should move back home. If something happened to Mom, Hank and I would do everything possible—but she couldn't come live us or anything like that. Our lifestyle, you know, it wouldn't work."

Cards were on the table—all face up but one. It was my turn. "I'll call Mom."

Mom told me she went back to work and that I shouldn't fret. "Honey, these things happen. It only lasted a few minutes. Should have listened to the doctor years ago, but they're always saying: Lose weight and quit smoking." She laughed it off. "Now I have an incentive."

I looked up "TIA stroke" and discovered she wouldn't have permanent damage, but the likelihood of a more serious stroke loomed large. Eddie was right—I should come home.

Where was home? Once upon a time, I thought Andy and I could make a home. Didn't happen. For my friends, home meant family. But I came from a broken home. Broken by so many things—Dad's boozing, Mom's crying, Eddie's struggles. Those days might be in the past, yet my pattern of finding "home" away from home was set. New York was mine, the home I had the courage to make for myself. Despite a rough start, my feet were on the ground, my apartment filled with houseplants and macrame. I was making new friends. Stan would be hard to leave behind. I had a good job at the art gallery. And, I already signed up to start classes toward teacher certification in the fall. I didn't want to leave. Not right away. Maybe I wouldn't have to. Getting a job in Shady Bluff would determine how soon I could leave. Given my attempts the previous year, I wasn't optimistic.

A week later, I called my old department head. She greeted me with the news that Mrs. Olson finally decided to retire. The district needed a replacement. When her offer sunk in, I stammered my acceptance. Fate was sending me back to the bluffs of the St. Croix River.

Eileen's letters had become more frequent of late. A redhead had captured Mark's interest. When I told her about my mom and moving home, she declared—without me having to ask— "You know you have a ready-made flat, complete with roomie, don't you?" I shouldn't have been glad Mark went AWOL but was thrilled to have a familiar place to sleep. I wouldn't have to squeeze into Mom's downsized flat or crash with Eddie and Hank.

When my landlady let me out of my just-signed lease renewal, I set a date to depart at the end of the month. Stan wouldn't let me leave the city without taking in the Statue of Liberty, and I gladly obliged. Up close, the Lady rose gracefully, calm but determined, her torch ablaze as dusk fell.

"Stan, look at her feet. She's not standing still." Never noticed that detail from pictures.

"A woman on the move. Like you, Meg. Free to choose her path."

I hugged my friend. "Promise me to remember you're rich in every way that matters."

∞ ☙ ☙

All packed, I opened my large bedroom window and climbed out on the fire escape to get some fresh air. Across an expanse of telephone wires and alleyways I listened to the cooing of mourning doves. Dozens of them in the neighbors' mishmash of coops. An Italian tradition.

New York gave me distance from Andy and time to get him out of my system, start over, find a new life. Now I knew Andy would never be out of my system completely, but I safely tucked him into a corner of my heart, as in a dovecote. I had made it in New York, in a manner of speaking. I could make it anywhere—maybe even back in the same city where Andy lived.

On the flight out of the city that never sleeps at night, I caught a glimpse of Lady Liberty, her torch lighting the way home.

CHAPTER 23

TIME AND DISTANCE

RUTH INVITED ME TO SEE HER pet project, the community garden, soon after my return to Shady Bluff. When I arrived at St. Gabriel's Parish Center, I noted the gargoyles hadn't moved an inch from their precipice. I scowled right back at them.

Sue said she'd love to visit but was breaking in the new pastor. Father Mack had transferred to a parish in Iowa. She rang Ruth and Leo. Also, Andy. Ruth welcomed me with hugs before apologizing she needed to give someone a ride to the doctor—hoped we could get together for dinner soon. Leo yammered like a parrot for a few minutes, then begged off for Confessions.

"Looks like I'll have to do," said Andy.

I surmised a setup to give Andy and me some time together. After all, Leo knew about our failed relationship, and Ruth wasn't born yesterday. Andy escorted me to a meeting room, newly replete with cushy chairs.

He sucked in his breath. "I'm so sorry about what Darren did to you."

I slowly nodded. "Not only to me. Beth told me the rumors."

"Yeah. Geez."

"How was it they believed a co-ed? When I tried to warn them, he got a second chance." I turned away. "They always think it's the woman's fault."

Andy pursed his lips. "They didn't believe her either, Meg. But I told our superior I knew it wasn't the first time he did something like that. I didn't tell him how I knew for sure, and he didn't ask, but he believed me."

My heart sank that he didn't speak up sooner. "I don't understand you men. If you had married me, you'd have been booted out no questions asked. But Darren violates me, and others, in the worst way—and he remains a priest in good standing." My hands trembled.

Andy shrank back. "We're not perfect. The Clems removed Darren from active ministry. In his desk job, at least they'll be able to keep an eye on him. Listen, we try to give each other the benefit of the doubt. Some women throw themselves at priests. You know that."

"And others don't. They trust." I steeled myself.

"We're just like other men," he said. "We make mistakes."

His words hit like gasoline on hot coals too long under the grate. "No, you are not like other men. Other men don't claim to act *in persona Christi* at the altar. Other men don't claim to be set apart, specially chosen by God to absolve sin—or deny absolution. Other men don't claim to be the only ones who can bring God's Son into the world, Body and Blood, each day. When other men make sacrifices for their families, their work, the world—it doesn't count for beans. When other men—and women—*forgive*, you say only a priest can free them from sin."

Andy covered his ears. "Meg, stop."

But I didn't stop. "Other men don't protect each other the way you men do for fear the whole house of cards will fall if believers don't keep believing in your specialness."

"Are you finished?" Andy set his jaw, but his eyes brimmed with sadness.

"Yes."

"Listen, I don't understand a lot of things either. I try to do some good. That's all I understand. Do you see that?"

The dark lump in the pit of my stomach had burned itself out. "I've always seen that part, Andy. But when you shield men like Darren, maybe thinking you're protecting the Church's reputation by protecting his—my fear is that your good work, your good name, will be torn from top to bottom like the veil in the temple when believers learn, as I have, that the Church cares more about the institution and its priests than about people like me."

Andy took my two hands in his. "I've never told anyone this, Meg, but I carry the same fear. That's why I finally had to speak up. I want to do better. Make things better."

We faced each other.

I leaned in. Could I forgive him? He hurt me too, just differently. The Church had hurt us both. Needlessly. For an ideal few achieved.

"I know you want to make things better."

I sank back in the soft chair. After several minutes, I opened a box of candy for what was supposed to be a crowd.

"Don't take them all," I warned.

"I'll mind my manners." Andy bit into the soft confection. "What's this?"

"Halvah, a sweet sesame seed cake from Zabar's, an amazing emporium on the Upper West Side. Long story how I got introduced to the place. Addictive, huh?"

Andy grew quiet and took a long look at me. "You've changed, Meg."

"Have I? How?"

"You seem surer of yourself."

I laughed. "Wouldn't have survived in the Big City if I didn't act as if I knew what I wanted. A person would starve if she didn't have her order ready to yell at the deli guy. Getting on the subway, hesitancy might have crushed me between the doors."

I told him about the daughter of my mom's friend who stayed with me on her way to a study abroad program in Greece. "The nervous teenager returned a confident young woman who could navigate the world. We drank ouzo she smuggled back. When you stretch, you change."

Andy sat on the edge of his chair, not only listening, but champing at the bit.

"What's happening in your world?" I asked.

"I'm glad I got to see you before …" He clasped his hands. "They've asked me to do some mission work."

So, this was why Leo and Ruth made themselves scarce—a chance for Andy to say goodbye. Ships in the night, our comings and goings. "What will you be doing?"

"The Clems adapted a 12-Step program with the Plains Indians. Word's getting around it's working. A bishop in Nevada asked us to come out there. I'll be gone about a year."

A year. A reprieve from worrying about being back in the same town together.

"I didn't know you worked with alcohol or drug abuse."

"I don't know anything about it." He shrugged. "Don't know why they're sending me except being short of guys."

"Do you want to do this?" I asked.

"I want to help people. That's what I signed up for."

I saw the furrow in his brow. "You'll do fine."

"Thanks for the encouragement. Terrible disease, alcoholism—as you know. Wish I understood it better. Wish I understood Native Americans better. Wish they asked someone else who could do a better job."

On my way out the door, he asked, "Will you pray for me? Maybe write? You always tell me the truth, even when I don't want to hear it. But I need to hear it. I've missed you."

CANDLEWOOD

☙ ❧

Summer mornings with a roomful of third graders brought me back home like nothing else could. The half-day schedule gave me time to reacclimate to teaching and try techniques I learned at the Balto Center. One little girl learned how to make her name with blocks. She'd be in my class in September.

On sunny afternoons, I hiked the bluffs of the St. Croix Valley, enjoying birdsong and waterfalls the big city couldn't offer. On long-lit nights, Eileen coaxed me into double-dating. To make the straying Mark jealous, she talked her handsome cousin and his friend into going out with us. "Let Mark get it out of his system now," she said, "but if he's not begging to come back by the holidays, he'll be history. Until then, I'm not going to sit and sulk." Her no-nonsense attitude surprised me. We went to concerts at the Levee and invited the guys to Kelly's Pub where the bartender welcomed me back by offering a new set of wheels for a song. We cooled off from the July heatwave watching *Airplane!* in super air-conditioned theatres, more than once.

On weekends, I helped Mom clean cupboards, wash windows, and paint the living room—excuses to spend time with her. She never talked about dying, but one afternoon she sent me home with grandma's prized set of Depression-era glass dessert plates. When I was little, the delicate cameo ballerina pattern made me want to be a dancer.

By October, I settled into a steady rhythm of work and social life—sans double-dates. Mark returned to his senses after his summer fling, but Eileen was putting him through his paces. I expected he'd propose by Christmas. Probably time for me to move out, but I didn't want to relocate again just yet.

Evelyn Ann Casey

After school each day, I detoured through the park on my way home. Loved hearing the rustle of Jack Frost's masterpieces. On a very windy day, a bunch of colorful leaves blew inside the front door with me. As I picked through mail, a letter fell out of the pack.

Dear Meg,

Got through orientation and now have an address, although around here the place is known as the stone house by yonder creek.

Learned a lot the last few months. Native American elders speak softly, without much inflection. Took me a while to understand they were saying the same thing in a hundred different ways—AA wasn't working because it's about focusing on yourself. The Indian way is about relating to family and tribe. Big a-ha!

We're working with the tribe to adapt AA Steps to Native rituals like the sweat lodge and talking circles. Hope I'm not entirely useless here. Pray for me!

I imagine you're enjoying being back at teaching. You were made to be surrounded by a bunch of rug-rats.

Andy

Eileen juggled groceries as she entered our flat. "Why are you sitting in the dark?"

I was on my third reading of the letter by waning daylight. "Just about to turn on the lamp."

Dear Andy,

Sounds like you've got your work cut out for you. Eddie said he felt awkward at AA meetings before he found a group with other gay guys. Guess that's a culture too with its own understandings.

Yes, the kids are precious. The ones with Down syndrome are always eager for hugs—they press their little faces against my belly, and I yield every time. But I need to encourage them in their work. They can learn and do much more than we sometimes let them.

A few of my kids were born with fetal alcohol syndrome. Incredibly sad. Some days it takes all my patience to quiet them. They're hyperactive and some can't follow more than a one-word direction. I wonder if their moms knew what harm they were doing by drinking while pregnant— might have been enough to make them stop. Maybe next time, you guys could send somebody across town????

Praying for you~ Meg

Our letters flowed back and forth. Andy told me about learning to ride a horse, the need for blankets at night after hot, dry days in the desert, and the vacant eyes of men and women hollowed from addiction. I shared stories with him about using talking circles with my kids when bad things happened—with a small bean bag instead of the traditional stick. Yes, they could learn to take turns. My kids might not comprehend why other kids bullied them on the playground, but they knew when people made fun of them. Talking circles gave them a way to express their anger. I did what little I could to make a safe haven for them.

Nothing I could do to make Andy's days any easier, but I hoped my letters were something like a haven for him.

Andy's letters showed another side of him. He was the good man I had fallen in love with once upon a time, but I was learning to appreciate his desire to be totally dedicated to his work. Grudgingly, I found myself accepting the practicality of being unmarried, but I hoped the harsh conditions didn't rob him of joy. Without joy, how could anyone give much of anything?

Dear Meg,
Tough day—heard about John Lennon. Guess no one lives forever. Imagine. I'm trying to make the world a better place. Trying. It's hard.

Andy

Miles away, we were growing closer to each other than ever. I couldn't deny the twinge at the center of my heart each time his scrawly handwriting reached into my mailbox.

I looked forward to Christmas when he'd be home for a week. In the meantime, seasonal traditions filled my days— taking the kids to the pumpkin patch, coloring hand-turkeys for Thanksgiving, and decorating gingerbread men for the tree in our classroom.

𝕏 ᘓ

Andy surprised me by showing up at the school just before Christmas. He asked the kids, and me, if he could hang an ornament on the tree.

We took a vote, and he added a wax candle angel to their gingerbreads. Andy told them the angel's name was *Chandelle*, and he winked at me. Eager faces vied for his attention. Their teacher was ready to melt.

After school, Andy and I took a snowy walk downtown. He looked entirely out of place with his cheeks browned by the intense Nevada sun. Carolers on the street corner didn't notice.

"Let's go home for hot chocolate," I said. "You can meet my roommate."

We arrived home to an empty house. Eileen had left a note on the kitchen table: *Gone tobogganing with Mark!*

"Sorry, Andy, Eileen's flown the coop. Maybe next time."

I pulled hot chocolate makings from the cupboard and fridge. Cinnamon filled the air. I poured steamy milk into honeyed cocoa. We wrapped our hands around earthenware mugs and drank deeply.

"It's good to see you, Meg." Andy's eyes met mine across the kitchen table. He raised both hands, reaching out, as if asking me to dance. We rose and held each other, swaying to music only we could hear. His fingers caressed the nape of my neck.

Cinnamon and chocolate and warm milk flowed through my body.

I tugged his flannel shirt free. The muscles in his back fit the palm of my hand.

My cycle was far from a fertile time. We could have this moment. *Thank you, Lord.*

Our hands clasped and we walked together to my bedroom. "Are you sure, Meg?"

"Yes."

My breasts swelled at his kiss. Our bare bodies curved into each other, closer, closer. Rolling like potter's putty. The wheel turned, turned, turned. He slipped inside, plunged into me, deep, sure. Wet clay walls at the center of my being opened wide, welcomed him, held him.

Sweat glazed our bodies.

We fell back in love ... if we had ever fallen out of it.

On Christmas Eve at Mom's, my brother wasted no time grilling me. "Okay, who is he?"

Hardly less subtle, Mom said, "You know any friend of yours is welcome for dinner."

I passed off my glow to holiday cheer and turned the conversation to congratulations on Mom's nearly six months off cigarettes. Went on to share the news Eileen and Mark were engaged—and so, I needed to enlist Eddie and Hank to help me move.

The glow lasted—catching myself in mirrors, smiling for no reason.

But it was early February before I heard from Andy. I hadn't written either. What does one say when something simply is? We were as real as ever. Nothing had changed, yet everything had changed. The tune hadn't changed, only the chord. The chord was deeper, stronger. Clearly, our early attempts at love hadn't been a flash in the pan, a fluke. Not a mistake.

We loved each other. Our bodies spoke this truth. We cared about each other, leaned on each other, strengthened each other. We sought each other out to tell exciting news or share a disappointment. Time and distance had weighed and measured us, and here we were.

> *Dear Meg,*
> *Thank you.*
> *Andy*

A week after Andy's note, I still hadn't written. I picked up the phone and called him. Someone else answered. "Yeah, he's around. Wait a minute." In the background, I heard the phone answerer say, "I think it's your sister."

"Oh, Meg, it's you," said Andy. He paused before asking, "Did you get my note?"

"Yes." Tongue-tied like the first days of new lovers. "I started writing a few times, but I could only say the same thing. It was good to see you too."

"My sister's coming to visit next week. That's why they thought you were her. Hey, why don't you come for a visit? I could teach you how to ride a horse ..." Andy's voice trailed off.

I would have given anything to visit Andy, but what would his houseful of priests say? We ricocheted back to square one. By ourselves, everything was wonderful. With others, we posed a forbidden question.

Andy answered my silence by saying, "No, I guess you couldn't do that." Breathing fast, he said, "It would be hard to get away in the middle of the semester, right?"

I couldn't squelch my hopes, nor my fears. "When will you be home again?"

"In the spring."

"We have a lot to think about, Andy. Let's talk then."

CHAPTER 24

GARDEN

THE MAPLE TREE IN FRONT OF my apartment broke dormancy early in the week. Blood red buds burst with the unlikely promise of green leaves. Through the tree's crisscross branches, I saw Andy looking for my new address. His arms were brown as winter wheat. He looked thinner than at Christmas. The months apart had given us a chance to think about where we were headed. I told myself that if he walked up the stairs with a heavy heart, I would know it was over.

Andy bounded up the three flights of stairs in my elevatorless building, four counting the garden apartment. My heart skipped.

"It's a long way up here, Meg."

I laughed. "I do it every day."

A warm hug followed, and a kiss as if it was our first. A new beginning. He brushed my cheek gently, and I took hold of his hand as we entered the apartment.

The windows were open, and his words rested on the breeze as he told me everything he'd written in his letters about the tribal mission—the poverty of people who lived on the rez, their joys and sorrows told in beads and dust, the woven baskets he used at Mass, the fall from his horse. Stories of a man who was a priest.

We didn't make it to dinner. A pause, a touch, a kiss ... not so much a kiss with a beginning and end, but the pressure of lips meeting and breath moving into one another. My forehead found a niche at his temple. When our eyes finally dared to ask the question, there was no more question. We undid each other's buttons, and burdens too. We caressed every limb, curve, muscle.

Once, I let Andy go. He wasn't sure. Now he'd come back. He was here. He wouldn't have come back to me, not this way, unless this time was different.

I wanted to give Andy a child more than anything, and it was a ripe time of month. I could let it happen. I wanted it to happen. But I would wait. I had prepared, so that if he came back to me, we could be more sensible than in our first flush. He'd be teaching at the university in town. We'd be making love. The diaphragm lodged inside me assured safe passage.

It wasn't that a child conceived tonight wouldn't be conceived in love, but I wanted to wait until our child would also be conceived in wedlock. I didn't want to trick Andy. I didn't have to. He wouldn't have bounded up the steps if he didn't want the same thing.

By this time next year, we'd be making love in our marriage bed, our families ready to welcome a child. Wishful thinking? Not after all this time.

The rest of our lives seemed only a moment away.

₮ ₳

The sun, low in the sky, suffused everything in afterglow. Andy's arm encircled my head on the pillow. His fingertips touched my damp shoulder. His eyes were closed. I lay wide awake drinking in the gentle light.

I rolled toward Andy stroking his chest, feeling the rhythm of his heart. He roused and yawned like a contented lion. I smiled. He put his hand between my breasts, resting on my heart.

"Hey," I whispered.

He opened his eyes, the green and brown flecks merged into a hazel pond.

I held his gaze softly. "Andy, I don't want to have to *protect* myself from having children."

He blinked and blinked again. His eyebrows made a deep ridge, as if he wasn't quite sure he heard right. His eyes opened wide. They flashed like a deer in headlights.

He sat up and swung his legs over the side of the bed. He turned around, toward me, searching my face.

"I have some friends," he said. "They've found a way."

Some friends found a way? He must have misunderstood. Oh no, did he think I was asking him to have a vasectomy? I must have said it wrong. I would say it better.

I stroked his arm. "Listen. What I mean is, I want to have children, *your* children."

His body tensed, eyes tight shut. His knuckles sunk into the edge of the mattress. After a few minutes, he faced me. "Don't you understand I have to confess every time I'm with you?"

I gasped. "I'm sin? This is sin?" Stunned, I got up and put on my robe. Covered my nakedness. Everything I ever knew about sin meant turning away from God. I was thanking God for bringing this man into my life. Until a few minutes ago, he was thankful for me.

He put on his shorts. "You know what I mean," he said.

"No. No, I don't. Not today. Not anymore. Making love with a woman who's telling you she's ready to marry you and let children come? This is as far from sin as anything could be!"

"Meg, I do love you …"

I pulled my robe tighter. "Did you think this was an affair?"

"I don't know," he said.

I was ready to shout from the rooftops that a rare and wonderful thing had happened—a man and woman loved each other—and he was telling me he didn't know what was happening?

"Andy, sin is saying no to this good thing. Please don't say no, not this time."

It was the dark side of twilight now. He dressed slowly. Started to pace. Mumbled to himself. He looked at me, eyes pleading, words incoherent. The mumbling grew louder: *To him whom much has been given, much will be asked.*

I recognized the line from scripture. I turned away from him. "And of her to whom nothing has been given, everything will be asked."

"It's for the Kingdom," he said. "I have to love the many."

I stood silent, having made love with this man, this man whose child I hoped to carry, this man who I thought had come back to make a life with me. I prayed, prayed hard, that I'd put enough spermicide into that damn diaphragm.

To love the many? Did he know what he was saying? He was repeating lines—someone else's lines—lines he'd practiced over and over. Lines he was told were the reasons he was a priest. But they weren't his lines, not his words.

What was simple and beautiful to me was a ring of fire for him. Simple and beautiful for him too—until I held up my lamp to shed light on the question we had avoided. I didn't think it was a question anymore—maybe he didn't think it was a question anymore either—but we had arrived at different answers. It was like a drop of hot oil spilled on us from that lamp scorching our separate truths.

He collapsed on the couch. I sat down next to him. Long minutes passed before we could bear to look at one another. This time he said, "They invited me to Oakmanship."

At last, his own voice, his own words. The sound of truth, but a word unknown to me.

"What do you mean, *Oakmanship?*"

"The men called upon for the hardest service. I only need to recommit to my vows."

I still didn't understand. But it didn't matter. I heard something else in his voice—*want*. They invited him to Oakmanship, apparently an elite corps of the Order of Clement. I invited him to a different order of chivalry, a different kind of fatherhood. I had told him my choice. He could no longer put off his. Andy's words: *But they invited me.* He had made his choice—to be a Knight of the Roman Catholic Round Table. Only one obstacle: no women or children allowed.

"Then what are you doing here?"

He doubled over, staring at the carpet a very long time, holding his head in his hands, taking labored breaths. After a while he reached for his socks and then his shoes. He said nothing. I said nothing. There was nothing to be said.

Andy walked to the door. I never saw eyes so sad. Maybe they reflected my own.

His step was heavy going down those three flights, four counting the garden apartment. Death has a sound. I hadn't known that. Each footfall on each tread echoed gone ... gone ... gone.

I sat on the upper step of the landing, suspended in space. Was I dead too, or only wounded? A wound bleeds. Blood is warm—it moves, oozing quietly under the skin. I put my thumb on my pulse. Tiny throbs pressed back. Wounded, but alive.

I should have hurled plates or broken glass at him. Then he too would only be wounded, bleeding but not dead. The worst kind of dead—a half-life. His body appearing alive, but his spirit dead. A zombie. Body and spirit split. Too many years of people telling him the only way the spirit could live in a priest was if he sacrificed his body. But when you kill the flesh, the spirit goes homeless.

CANDLEWOOD

Time passed. Gradually I became aware of myself in the hallway, shivering in my robe. If a neighbor opened their door, I would have to say something, but words failed me.

I stood up and went inside my apartment.

Dark now, true night. I hunched over the back of the couch trying to grasp what had happened, envisioning everything that transpired. Reliving it.

All at once the feeling I wasn't alone startled me. I looked up. A shadow materialized on the opposite side of the room. I focused, trying to make out who or what it was. I heard a guttural, smirking sound— "Luvvvv!" The raspy gray thing mimicked my own thoughts but with a sardonic twist. "What did you think would happen? How did you think this would end?"

An image of Andy and me emerged translucent between myself and the snarling shadow—like the afterimage of something bright looked at too long and burnt into the retina.

I burst out loud, "No. I will not stop loving him!"

The shadow disappeared.

We would not marry, but no one had the right to mock us. We may have failed, but we tried. Love is not a fairy tale.

ಸು ಧಿ

I must have fallen asleep on the couch because dawn filtered between the blinds. Church bells chimed the hour from the nearby Methodist steeple—not Catholic. I thanked the universe for that small favor. My world had turned upside down, but apparently no one told the sun about it. I got up and looked out the window assessing whether anything at all had changed. Nothing. Yet everything looked different to me. What would Andy see when he awoke?

I took the sheets down to the laundry room. They smelled of Andy. As did I. Why does a person's scent have to linger? I showered while the sheets agitated. I wanted to cry, but no tears came. I said a wordless prayer for Andy, the only way I knew how to love him now. It was out of my hands—maybe God could empty the bilge.

I walked to the diner down the block. The kind of place where veteran waitresses knew their tip would be the same whether serving plates or filling cups. People went to buy time. The coffee provided me with a needed jolt. I messed with scrambled eggs and toast. Mostly, I hid behind a newspaper, trying to find meaning in the hieroglyphs. If there was any meaning, it eluded me. I put a tip on the table.

I wasn't yet ready to go home, so I walked along the bluff above the shoreline. A chilly draft combed through my hair. I imagined myself one of a thousand ants in the layer between water and sky. Did it matter what happened to me or any one of us? Do things just happen, or is there a reason?

Back at my apartment, the space became an echo chamber for Andy's words: "I have some friends—they've found a way." Had he hoped I would be okay with an affair, living under a rock, slithering through stolen moments? No, he knew me too well. Maybe he hoped we could go on a little longer if we didn't put a name to it. We had fallen into the pattern his friends had found, living one truth secretly and another outwardly. Their way to keep body and soul together.

Until I asked him to choose.

I thought of our old family friend, Father Jim, a priest like Andy who wanted to do good things. Carol stayed with him, but she was past childbearing age. I always imagined their situation was the exception, unusual. But Andy's words belied another story—relationships had become accepted, a new norm—if one kept them quiet.

Ours was not a story about two people anymore. This was happening all over the Church—an open secret.

Ave Maria, ora pro nobis.

☯ ☯

Late. I was never late. I was regular as rain.

I wrestled with telling Andy.

Would I be able to keep my job? Schools didn't want an unwed mother. Until recently, even wedded mothers had to leave their job. If I got fired, I wouldn't be able to support a child. Could I tell my family? Mom lived in a modest apartment on a limited income. Dad already left this earth. My cousins stretched to raise their own families. My brother? I was supposed to know better. I was the first one in my family to go to college. I was the smart, sensible one—ha!

This was no way to bring an innocent child into the world.

I called Planned Parenthood. I needed to know how soon I could be sure if I was pregnant. A clinician talked to me for quite a while on the phone, answered my questions, told me signs to watch for—I felt foolish for not knowing them all. She offered to make an appointment but since it was too early for a reliable test, I decided to wait.

If I was pregnant and Andy married me, I would always know this wasn't what he truly wanted. I hugged myself across my womb in case there was anybody in there who needed a hug. I wanted a child, Andy's child, very much. This wasn't the easy choice like when I feared Darren's DNA multiplying in my belly, tainting a child forever.

Another day passed, and then a week.

I made a plan to move away before I started showing. Went to the library to copy want ads in out-of-town newspapers—Duluth, La Crosse, Eau Claire, Wausau, Milwaukee. Made up a story about my husband dying in a car crash. Looked up adoption information. Waited.

And then, cramps. I bled heavily.

Relief. Tears.

☙ ❧

It was the last week of school when a heavyweight vellum envelope arrived in the mail:

The honor of your presence is requested
on the 28th of June in the year of Our Lord 1981
at 2:00 p.m. in the Church of St. Gabriel
to witness the induction of
Father Alfons Vogel
into the grave responsibilities of holy Oakmanship.

I carefully tore the affront to my heart into a hundred tiny pieces.

A few days later, one of the kids in my class got shoved down on the playground and broke his arm. I didn't expect to see him at our end-of-year party, but his mom said he begged her to come. I watched as he showed off his cast like a monument to bravery.

He would heal.

Would I?

I decided to attend Andy's ceremony, my heart in a cast, a monument to bravery. I needed the finality of it, to mark a death, and to remember I was still alive.

The bishop led a procession of priests down the aisle of St. Gabriel's. Andy walked alone in last place, save for an altar boy carrying a two-foot wooden cross. All at once, I recognized it was hewn of burled oak. Its distinctive grain resembled markings on the Shroud of Turin, the Lord's burial wrap.

CANDLEWOOD

Frankincense filled the sanctuary. I wondered if Andy felt like he was back in the mission's tribal sweat lodge. Scripture readings and chants circled overhead like the cawing of black crows. After the bishop blessed the oak cross, Andy knelt and recited his solemn pledge in Latin. As if he was wielding a sword, the bishop tapped the cross down on each of Andy's shoulders. Then, bringing the cross within Andy's reach, the bishop invited him to take hold of it.

Andy almost touched the cross, but then drew back his hand. "Not worthy," he said, and again, "I am not worthy." Overcome, he kept repeating "not worthy, not worthy."

In the front pew, a woman reached for her husband's arm. Andy's mother, her eyes pained at the sight of her son in distress. Everyone squirmed in their seats.

The bishop put his arm around Andy's shoulder. "Rise and receive the cross."

Andy stood and took hold of it.

I didn't stay for the reception. I took one last look at the marble altar. For some men, like Michelangelo, human forms emerge out of marble slabs, hearts beating with life. Others chip away at the stone day after day, turning into workaholics with little of lasting value to show for their effort. And there are those for whom the altar is a millstone, grinding them to dust with no breath of life left at all. Which would Andy become?

Sacred Heart of Jesus, pray for us.

CHAPTER 25

ASPIRATION

KEEPING BUSY PROVED THE best antidote to my malaise. I had a dinner date with the fellow art enthusiast I began seeing since frequenting area museums. But first, I needed a shower after flying kites all afternoon with the fun guy I met at Beth's Fourth of July party. Nice bloke. I soaped the washcloth and practiced semi-intelligent things to say about the current Miró exhibit.

Scrubbing the sweat under my arm, I felt an odd bump on the side of my breast. The globule moved back and forth like a blob of gel paint. Had it always been there? I checked the other breast. Nothing. Maybe something got out of whack goofing around with kites. Decided to check again in a day or two. There were more pressing matters, like what to wear for dinner.

A few days later, the blob hadn't gone away. I thought about seeing a doctor, but I was too young for the big C. Besides, a blob is not a lump. I called the clinic out of curiosity.

The doctor said my blob was nothing unusual. Best bet—a fluid-filled cyst. I made an appointment for him to aspirate it in his office.

On the appointed day, his nurse applied a local anesthetic, and the doctor poked a needle into my breast tissue. Again. One more time. "Apparently this one is solid. Most are fluid-filled. I'll need to make a small incision to remove it. Hanging in there okay?"

Did I have a choice? Closed my eyes and said a Hail Mary.

The doctor wrapped up the procedure. "I'll send it to the lab for a biopsy. Just routine." He put a bandage over the incision. "We'll have the results in a few days."

The results didn't come by mail, but by phone. "Margaret, the lab found something in your biopsy. Nothing to be alarmed about, but some suspicious cells trailed from the cyst. I want to make a wider margin, be sure we got everything. We can do it at the outpatient clinic."

"Suspicious cells?" My chest tightened.

The doctor said he'd know more after the next procedure.

I wanted to call Mom but was afraid of giving her another stroke. My brother—useless in a crisis. I kept things under wraps.

Museum guy gave me a ride to the clinic for the 8:00 a.m. procedure. I didn't tell him the whole story, not yet. He returned on his lunch hour to take me home but couldn't stay. Had to catch a flight for business. Made me promise to ask a friend over later.

The discharge nurse said I could expect some soreness, but pain pills would help. Since I felt nothing on the way home, I didn't ask to stop for the prescription.

Eileen called early evening to check on me.

"I'm fine. No need to come by." Nothing more than a teensy cyst, now surgically removed. The doc said no abnormal "precancerous" cells had invaded other tissue. End of story.

Secure in the knowledge the ordeal was over, I slept soundly. But when morning came, my whole body ached. My breast throbbed painfully. Oh God, why didn't I fill that prescription? I climbed out of bed. Maybe if I sat up awhile it would go away. Nope. Ate a plain piece of toast and prayed I wasn't dying.

Though only two blocks from a pharmacy, I was weak as a kitten.

Who could I call to get a prescription filled at 9:30 a.m. on a Friday morning? Everyone worked. Besides, they'd want to know why, and I didn't want to say.

The one person I knew with a loose schedule was Andy. Wasn't this priest thing about helping people? He could be a priest—and not worry about being a man at the same time.

"Meg?" He barely recognized my foggy voice.

"Sorry to bother you. Wouldn't have called, but it's important."

"You all right?"

"Pretty much, but ..." Andy interrupted before I could make my request.

"There's nothing I can do."

"Wait, I ..."

"Meg, there's nothing I can do. Truly." Click.

I held the phone in my lap until it started beeping. Didn't bother hanging it up. I pulled myself to the bathroom. Clung to the edge of the sink and saw myself in the mirror. Two blood-shot eyes on pale canvas. Cracked lips he once kissed when they were full and rosy. Matted hair he caressed when smooth and shiny. A wretch looked back at me.

"I thought you wanted to be a priest to care for wretches like this," I said to an absent Andy. Stupid of me to call—I was the one person in God's wide world he couldn't be there for. Had to be there for "the many"—not me. He was an Oakman, called on for "maximum service"—not picking up a dinky prescription.

I flopped into a T-shirt and old jeans, gripped the banister, and descended step by grueling step. By the time I returned with the prescription, the phone was dead.

The nurse explained my body's reaction to the relatively minor procedure had probably been the result of shock to my system. Considering the level of pain on the day after surgery, I rebounded quickly. Back to work on Monday. Accepted museum guy's invitation for dinner and a concert on Saturday. The whole episode was fast receding into a blip on the screen.

Felt like an idiot for calling Andy. My pitiful voice would be his last memory of me. Did I dare try changing the scenario? Why bother, much less how?

As much out of vain pride as anything else, I stopped by Andy's office at the college. I wanted to show him I was well and strong—and did not need him after all.

I thought he might slam the door, but he let me in.

The color drained out of his face. "What happened … when you called?"

I rubbed my cuff bracelet, de rigueur since *Wonder Woman* hit TV. Eileen made me buy it on our last shopping expedition. I hoped a bit of superheroine strength might rub off on me.

"It was nothing. Needed some pain pills, and you were the only one I knew with flexible hours. After-effects of surgery were worse than expected."

"Surgery? I tried calling back, but the phone was dead."

So, he tried to reach me. "Wait—the phone was dead, and you didn't do anything?"

"All right. I didn't want to know. I was sure you hated me. And you sounded drunk."

The lasso of truth gripped us. I needed to be honest. I had held it in too long.

"I was in pain, not drunk. And I never hated *you*, Andy—I hated what you'd become. I hated what the Church let you become—you and your friends. I hated how you wanted me to go along with living two lives. I never hated that you wanted to be a priest—heck, I went to your vow ceremony. I hated that you wanted me to compromise my life. I want to make a home with someone and raise children. That's who I am—it's what I'm about. Don't ask me to compromise my dreams for you. I can't."

"Oh, Meg. I never meant to hurt you. You're the last person in the world I would ever want to hurt. Can you forgive me?"

I believed Andy, but the rollercoaster ride had taken its toll. "I know you never wanted to hurt me. I never wanted to hurt you. I want to forgive you, but I don't know how."

Neither of us said anything. It was hard ending up on opposite sides of the moon.

Andy asked, "Did you come to tell me what's going on? Surgery?"

I explained about finding the cyst. "The doc said some early-stage cancerous cells tagged along for the ride when they removed it, but I'm fine now. Good catch, before any real damage was done. I admit I must have sounded awful on the phone. That's why I came here today—I wanted you to know everything was okay."

Andy's eyes fell on the oak cross on his wall. "I should have been there for you."

I looked at my watch. "I have to get going. Dinner date sort of thing."

"Dinner date? Oh. A boyfriend. Sure." Andy stood. "Is that what you really wanted me to know?" Looming over my chair, he said, "Don't let me stand in your way."

The same words he said as I left for New York. His words did not match his actions.

He watched me go out the door. "Nice bracelet."

                             ಬ ಅ

The doctor checked the incision at my follow-up visit. "Healing well," he said. "You may have a small scar, but it'll fade over time."

He laid out brochures on diet and exercise and told me to be sure to eat lots of fruits and vegetables high in antioxidants. "I also want you to come in every six months for a mammogram. We want to keep an eye on this. Five years is the benchmark—if nothing recurs in that time, you'll be back to baseline risk."

"Why do I need to be followed so closely?"

The doctor cleared his throat. He peered at me as if I was a little girl who lost her dolly. "Margaret, I don't want to frighten you, but I would be remiss if I encouraged you to have children. In fact, it would be better not to."

I did a double take. "What did you say?"

He shot words like bullets about estrogen flooding the body when a woman becomes pregnant. "Increased hormonal activity in someone like you is likely to trigger tumor growth. Better to let sleeping dogs lie."

I drooped over, wailing.

The nurse gave me a tissue.

"There, there," said the doctor. "Don't worry. I'm not telling you to avoid a relationship. I'm only advising against pregnancy. You can present yourself to a man."

I rolled the diet and exercise brochures tight, like the barrel of a gun.

"No need to fret, Margaret. You can lead a perfectly fine life."

I got lost on the way home. Finally in my kitchen, I stared at the clock and saw why people stop the hands of time when someone dies. Time stood still.

What was this body for, this woman's body? I had taken care of myself—ate right, drank little, exercised, probably the only one of my generation who didn't smoke pot—all so my body would be ready to love a man well, ready to make a healthy first abode for a growing baby.

Who was I now?

⁀ ⁁

September slid into October, the month of ghosts. Echoes from a past autumn, on retreat at Christopher House, shredded my soul: *Make a home.*

Lord, when? Five more years? The day after never? What kind of life is this?

Each little face in my class reminded me I wasn't, and might never be, a mother. I sat on the park bench after school, picked up a fallen leaf, and crumbled it.

Museum guy was growing cool with my lack of interest in taking things to the next level. I couldn't attempt the necessary conversation. Better to be labeled an ice queen than a cancer candidate.

I didn't want to tell anyone. The whispers would sting far more bitterly than waiting five years: *Poor Meg, she's so good with children, but she can't have any.* No. I was practiced at keeping secrets. If I told Mom, and she shared it with even one of her friends from the Irish Club, news would spread. Eileen could keep a secret—kept a three-month vigil before popping the news she and Mark were expecting. No sense for me casting a pall on their happiness.

One person would understand—the only other person in my world who wanted children but couldn't have them. Different reasons, same effect. But I didn't want Andy to feel sorry for me. Pity, the worst humiliation.

Wet leaves slipped underfoot, like layers of peeled skin drowning in tears.

A few weeks later, I drove home from school and searched for a magazine article the nurse had given me at my last visit. She told me to take my time reading it.

The article explained promising research—especially on younger women whose breast cancer was often more aggressive. A team of doctors were following two women who became pregnant before knowing they had carcinomas. The one with early-stage abnormalities—like mine—had a mastectomy. She and the growing baby were doing okay by second trimester. A woman with more advanced cancer had to choose between chemo or keeping her baby.

I folded the article, set it aside, and screamed.

No, I couldn't endure the anxiety or make the choices these women faced. I would wait the five years. Live on hold. If I tested clean on all my mammograms, I would still be in my thirties. Plenty of time—if any man in his right mind would marry a woman who'd been intimate with cancer.

Five years. Could any good come of it?

Restless that night, I rose and searched the sky for answers. The cratered moon hung low.

Lord, take these five years in sacrifice for Andy. Turn them into grace and put them in the bank for the days he wrestles with his vows.

CHAPTER 26

CANDLEWOOD

WITH WINTER SNOWS FAST approaching, I needed to get my boot zipper repaired. The cobbler shop bells sounded their familiar ting-a-ling as I opened the door. Another customer stood at the well-worn wooden counter—a man with a strong back, wearing a bomber jacket across his broad shoulders. Wheat straw hair. My heart beat quickened. Andy.

The last time we met, I was on my way to a dinner date. Andy made the news of a boyfriend sound like an affront to whatever shambles of love existed between us. Wasted envy. Only a week later, the doctor told me not to have children.

"Meg?" Shades of red splashed his face. He dropped a shoe.

"Hello, Andy."

He lowered his head and focused intently on a pair of black oxfords. "My department chair sent me to get these scruffy things re-tipped."

"I can see why."

He looked in the direction of my boots as I laid them on the counter.

I ran my finger across the off-track rail-line of a broken zipper. Two facing paths designed to catch each other and hold on tight. "Busted zip. Otherwise, fit perfectly."

Andy searched my face. His hazel eyes flickered. "Worth fixing."

The shopkeeper busied himself sorting laces until our voices paused. He wiped both hands on his cobbler's apron. "What can I do for you folks?"

"You were here first, Andy."

"I'm not in a hurry. Please."

The old man peered under his visor from one to the other of us, then at our leather offerings. He scratched the bald spot on his head, sighed, and picked up the oxfords. "New tips and a shine will set these shoes aright." He tore off half a claim ticket.

Andy put it in his pocket.

After a thorough assessment of my boots, the cobbler said, "If you give me ten days, Miss, I'll do what I can to fix the track."

I thanked him and took the half-ticket he extended.

Andy opened the door for me. Shop bells consecrated our departure. Scuffed and broken things left on the counter.

A wild wind met us outside. Matched the restless hope tossing deep in my chest. Not to try and fail again, but for peace, for blessing. Closure.

Andy pulled his cap down over his ears. "Chilly."

"There's a coffeeshop across the street if you want to warm up."

His eyes followed mine to the Cuppa Joe Café. He reached for my hand. "Join me?"

My fingers filled the space between his. We didn't bother walking to the corner or waiting for the light but dashed at the first break in traffic. Two people rushing between stop lights. Hurtling toward something, anything. I longed to be on the other side of our past.

The café door blew open to reveal a crowded scene. We tucked into the last booth. Mini lights framed the plate glass window next to our table. Glimmers of holiday cheer.

Milky coffee mimicked the gray-brown sundown hour of this mid-November day. Andy offered clipped bits about the weather, goings on at Ruth's senior card games, Leo's latest foibles with nursing home volunteers—his voice cracked after a few gulps of his cup of joe.

"Meg, I acted like a jerk. If you want to beat me over the head with it, feel free. I wouldn't blame you. Really, I'm truly happy you're dating a nice guy. I want you to be happy."

I stirred my coffee to avoid Andy's eyes. After the doctor's news, I canceled a series of dates with said boyfriend. The phone stopped ringing. Easier to keep my barren future a private matter. But I could never lie to Andy. I stopped swirling my spoon and glanced up at him. No words came. Just a burn stinging my eyes.

"Please, Meg, say something. Yell at me. Whatever."

"It's not about you. Or anybody else."

Questions covered his face. "Meg, talk to me."

The words stuck at the back of my throat. I hadn't spoken them aloud to anyone. "Nothing's wrong, but nothing's right either."

He leaned in, waiting.

I held my hands tight around the hot coffee mug. Steam rose like incense from a sulfur lake. I looked across the expanse at Andy.

"Do you know what it means to let sleeping dogs lie?"

He neatly folded his napkin. "Right. I shouldn't bother you. I'll go."

So near, yet miles off the mark. I touched a tangle of mini lights around the window. How could I tell him the awful truth?

He picked up the check. "Let me get this."

As he pushed back his chair, the pit of my stomach ached. A bellyful of denial.

"Merry Christmas, Meg." The mellow timbre of his voice offered a branch to hang onto.

"Andy." I took hold of his wrist. "*Let sleeping dogs lie* is what the doctor said."

"Doctor?" He sat down.

"At my follow-up visit, he said I shouldn't trigger the hormones in my breast. Having kids would do that. *Let sleeping dogs lie* —that's how he put it."

Andy cupped his hands over mine.

I said the dreaded words: "I can't have kids."

Miniature white lights lit the cave in those words. A singular fact. A vowed fact in Andy's life. A shattering fact in mine. I cringed at the sound of my voice. As soon as I said it out loud, I heard the lie in it. Biologically true. But not the whole truth. I had lots of kids. A dozen half-pints looked to me each day in my classroom with eager faces, waiting for me to love them. Flesh and blood. Just not from my womb.

Andy jostled for his wallet. I thought he was going to throw a few bills on the check and leave. He might wrestle with this fact of his life, but he could meet a woman tomorrow and let down his guard. He could have kids. He wouldn't die from barking dogs.

The man with options I no longer had flipped through his wallet looking for something. A lost claim check, a novena card, quarters for a tip?

Andy pulled out a picture of a newborn. "My nephew."

My head spun in disbelief. Of all the things he could do or say about not having kids, he shows me a baby. I peered at the scarlet cheeks swaddled in a yellow blankie, his tiny, curled fingers, pouty lips—like every newborn I had ever seen—except smaller, with silky brown hair on his forehead and across his little arms. Distinct sideburns. "Is he okay?"

Andy stroked the edges of the photo. "Josh was a preemie, born before he lost the hairy covering that keeps kids warm while they grow inside." He looked tenderly at the photo. "Quite the hairy mess. But get this—now, six months later, the poor kid is bald as a coot. And eats like a horse." Andy's rich baritone laugh broke through my pain. He took hold of my hands. "Our family loves him no matter what package he came in."

"He's beautiful," I said.

I gave Andy's hands a squeeze and rummaged in my purse for the Kodaks of my kids at the pumpkin patch. Little faces grinned so wide their eyes became slits.

"Noah wants to be a fireman—after he learns to tie his shoes." Another hugged a pumpkin big as himself. "Here's Sally. It takes her a while to print the letters in her name. But she's happy as a lark. Believe it or not, she has a laugh just like yours."

We looked up at each other over the many images of God strewn on the table. Andy's eyes shone. I smiled for the first time in a long time.

"We have lots of kids to love," he whispered.

Damp air formed stray snowflakes outside the café window. "I don't have the heart to tell the kids there won't be a Santa Claus this year. Mr. Grinke bowed out."

Andy's face brightened. "How about Uncle Andy? I've got a pair of big black boots."

There was a time I believed only perfect packages deserved to be called love—perfect marriages, perfect families, perfect homes. Not true. Here was Andy offering to love me and my kids whatever way worked. Asking me to forgive him, love him if I could. My mom loved my dad, though she couldn't live with his alcoholism. Eddie and Hank loved each other.

Seemed God sent us hairy messes—and grace to love anyway.

CANDLEWOOD

❦

True to his word, Andy showed up at my classroom door the day before Christmas recess dressed in a big red suit and a pair of black boots. The kids squealed at every "Ho, ho, ho." Jonah pulled Andy's beard, but let go when Santa bellowed "Naughty or nice?" Santa winked, reached into his burlap sack, and gave the boy a present. My cheeks hurt from laughing. When parents came to pick up their boisterous kids, Andy made a quick exit "to feed the reindeer."

Sally Ingle twirled toward her folks, promptly falling on her behind. Mr. Ingle picked up his daughter and swayed her over to me. The Ingles looked at each other, wrinkles mirrored on their foreheads. "Mrs. Ingle and I were hoping you might have a few minutes?"

"I love having Sally in class," I said. "Today with Santa, her joy knew no bounds."

Sally's mom smiled. "She's a happy child."

"We've accepted Sally's never going to catch up with other kids," said Mr. Ingle. "We love her just as she is but worry about her future."

A shadow crossed Mrs. Ingle's face. "Sally came along mid-life. A surprise child. I'll be in my 60s, her father in his 70s when Sally's in her 20s. What if we can't care for her?"

The Ingles weren't the first parents to confide their fears. My heart always panged at their distress. I usually noted their child's small steps of progress and offered platitudes about hope and courage. But since spending the day in New York with the young adult "kids" from the 14th Street House, I could offer a glimpse at new possibilities.

"I'm in the learning stage myself about the options, but I truly believe by the time you'll be making decisions about Sally's future, you and she will have choices."

Shortly after the holidays, I made time to see the school social worker. She explained transition planning for post-school years. "Students and their parents usually need guidance and resources to be successful." She lamented the limited opportunities in Shady Bluff.

"For those families who can manage it," she said, "the young people remain at home and a case worker tries to find activities or some sort of employment or sheltered workshop."

When I told her about my experience in New York, her ears perked up. "A parent group in the Twin Cities has been active for a while. They might be plugged into the same national organization as people in New York. They've had success advocating for services. Recently got legislation passed providing funds for group homes, day programs, and employment training."

I got goosebumps listening to her. "Sounds like things are hopping," I said.

She offered to put me in touch with the Department of Human Services. "Be nice if somebody from around here got involved." Her eyebrows raised and she pointed toward me.

Winter weekends whirled in a round robin of meetings in the Twin Cities. Each meeting led to new contacts. Parent groups pointed me in the direction of vocational programs and emerging housing models. Wasn't long before I started volunteering at a group home in St. Paul on Saturdays.

On Sunday mornings at brunch with Mom, I shared tidbits about my new endeavor—just enough to pique her curiosity while letting next steps percolate.

I invited Andy to go ice skating in St. Paul after my volunteer shift—to be a sounding board. Over mulled cider in the park shelter, I shared my conversation with Sally's parents and told him about subsequent meetings with multiple agencies and programs.

"Seems group homes are much more than an experiment—a movement is growing nationwide to keep people in the community, not hidden away like they don't belong."

"Sounds great," he said.

"Nobody in teacher ed ever talked about what happens to *special students* once they grow up. We say other kids have their whole life in front of them. What about my kids?"

"Meg, I haven't seen you this excited—maybe ever. What's going on?"

"Think about it—a real home with respect, friendliness, love—that's the kind of place Sally and Jonah and all the kids deserve."

Andy nodded.

I couldn't hold back my dream a moment longer. "I want to start a home like that."

My friend blew on his cider. "Ahh." His eyes narrowed. "But sometimes folks get hyped, and then it doesn't last. What then? How do they support themselves?"

I slapped my wet mittens on the table. "Thanks for throwing cold water on the idea."

"Don't go off the deep end, Meg. I only want what's best. You're rushing headlong into this. Huge effort. How many people in a house—three? four? eight? How long do they stay? Would you live there? What about the hundreds of others? You can't save everybody."

I unlaced my skates and hit the blades together to loosen snowy ice. "Don't you think I've been asking myself those same questions? I'm not a nitwit. I'm okay with starting small. Let me ask you—if your Clems or some order of Sisters wanted to offer a better way of life, a home, for people with disabilities rather than stand by and watch them deteriorate in inhumane warehouses—would you throw cold water on them?"

Andy shook his head. "That's just it. We have resources, built-in-systems, partners. I rely on that. Without it, I couldn't do much. Would probably still be chopping cabbages for kraut."

Andy was different from me. He needed to do big things—and the Clems gave him that chance. He itched to go back to the missions. I knew from the way he simmered whenever St. Gabe's hosted a guest missionary. The man had a bad case of wanderlust.

"The people I'm talking about need a home—and I need a family. Families find housing, work, and a way to keep meals on the table. That's enough for me."

He twisted the fringe on the plaid scarf I gave him for Christmas.

"I wouldn't be doing it by myself. These places need a lot of people with big hearts. Families get involved, sometimes churches, local organizations, volunteers. If they can do it in the Twin Cities, or New York, why not in Shady Bluff?"

Skaters circled the ice, scratched the surface, glazed by. Andy stared at them a few minutes before facing me. "I spoke out of turn, Meg. You're braver than this guy." He poked a thumb at his chest. "When you get this thing going—yes, when not if—maybe I could help?"

I scrunched my Styrofoam cup. I wanted this tussled skeptic on board. "It takes all kinds."

𝕭 ℭ𝕭

At the group home in St. Paul the next week, I prepped lunch with Mamie, one of the residents. She peeled potatoes in fast, short strokes compared to my long ones. "No," she scolded, and turned up the radio. "Listen."

CANDLEWOOD

Dolly Parton's spunky "9 to 5" bounced forth. Mamie peeled in sync to its insistent beat. I took the cue. Other residents and volunteer helpers quickly crammed the kitchen, repeating the chorus. Mamie and I put down our peelers, joined hands and swung to the rhythm.

When we went to the dining room for lunch, Mamie tapped me on the arm. "Sit by me?"

The helper on her other side caught my eye.

"My brother, Jay," she said. "He needs a wife. You should marry him." I laughed and said I would think about it. He winced and asked her to say grace:

> *Dear God,*
> *Bless everybody,*
> *Make everybody happy.*
> *Dig in. Amen.*

I often stayed after lunch to talk with the houseparents about how they got a group home started. One week, they sent me off with a box labeled: The Nitty-Gritty. Reams of legalese on nonprofit management, Social Security Disability and waivers proved daunting. I verged on tears reading City Council minutes where neighbors brought zoning objections for "imbeciles" moving into their block. Maybe Andy was right—maybe I was in over my head.

I decided to call in a favor from Eileen and tap her accountant husband's business acumen. She and Mark not only offered practical help but asked about volunteering.

When I got back in touch with Sister Camille in New York, she forwarded my questions to the 14th Street House. Stories from people in the trenches who overcame many obstacles bolstered my confidence. Whenever I felt faint of heart, all I had to do was look at Sally and the other kids in my class to know the effort was worth it.

Andy called me a few weeks after our skating rink scuffle. "How about if I start doing some things now? With the kids in your class? It was fun being Santa."

Surprised, but warmed by his change of heart, I said arts and crafts offered a challenge. Andy became a weekly regular wielding construction paper and refereeing crayon fights.

"You don't have to do this stuff," I said.

"I want to." And that was that.

Finger-painting week I protected all stainable surfaces. Well into chaos, someone kicked at the door. Jonah announced, "Uncle Andy." The kids rushed over while I gaped agog at the sight of my friend juggling a slat-back chair and three paint cans.

"Are my artists ready?" Andy grinned at his welcoming committee. "And Miss Meg?"

"Sure." I laughed and directed the action to a swath of canvas cloths. "Neat chair."

Andy pointed to the dovetail joinery. "Made it myself."

The kids swarmed him like bees. "Who wants green - blue - red?"

"What's the plan, Uncle Andy?" I asked.

"Thought you and the kids might have some ideas."

The kids whooped with delight as they pressed colorful handprints all over the chair.

After school, Andy hung around to help me clean up paint and fold drop cloths. "Been wondering, do these group homes have names?"

I hadn't given it much thought. "Some do, some don't."

"Might be good to have a handle—a shorthand when you're on the stump."

I conceded he had a point and mulled it over. "If I gave the house a name, I'd want it to convey warmth and light, hospitality for sure, but also strength."

"Ah, *Chandelle*, you'd be the warmth and light of the place—and its strength."

The name Andy used to call me. I took my time folding a drop cloth.

"That's sweet, *Monsieur*. But English, please."

"Don't you know *chandelle* is a French word for candle—as in warmth and light?"

I guessed that long ago. "But Andy, wax is not very strong."

"Right. Hmm, the beams of a house are strong."

Andy was putting too much effort into the word game to be spontaneous. I could tell he'd been plotting a name, but I went along.

"Beam House? That'll make people think of Jim Beam whiskey. No, won't work."

"But *Chandelle*, beams frame a house, bear the weight and provide structure. Strong as the trees they come from."

"Okay, but names like Larch House or Cedar House sound like we're out in the woods."

A puckish grin tweaked Andy's face. "What about The Wooden Candle?"

I laughed. "Might go with Candlewood, but The Wooden Candle? Good name for a bar."

"May I have a drink at Candlewood House, please?"

My heart leapt. "Andy, that's it—Candlewood House."

When I relocated the hand-splotched chair to a brighter corner of the room the next day, a carefully painted A-frame house was on the single wide slat-back with a yellow candle glowing inside.

Candlewood House.

I placed my invisible handprint on Andy's gift.

ഇ ൦ൔ

Winter melted into spring. I hosted Easter dinner for my family. I wanted the security of my own zone to unveil my idea of opening a group home. I finagled Mom's baked ham recipe and didn't skimp on pineapple. When we sat down to eat, I said Mamie's grace:

> *Dear God,*
> *Bless everybody,*
> *Make everybody happy.*
> *Dig in. Amen.*

Eddie carved the ham. "That place in St. Paul has made quite an impression on you, Sis. You've been spending a lot of time there."

I could fudge this, put off telling them my dream, or I could come out with it and let the objections rain down. "I've been thinking ..."

"That's dangerous," said Eddie.

"Yes. Slightly." I had their attention. "Places like the one in St. Paul are starting up all over." I made eye contact with Mom, Eddie, and Hank. "Why not here?"

Mom selected a slice of ham and passed the creamed corn.

"You really love those kids, don't you, Meggins?"

"Lots of people love them when they're little, but not so much when they grow up. I don't want people with disabilities to lose their sense of home and belonging, but it's healthy to let them gain some independence as young adults. Group homes provide both."

Mom dabbed the corners of her mouth with her napkin. "Sounds like we need to do whatever it takes to help you make it work. Don't we Eddie? Hank?"

Perhaps I hadn't been so secretive at brunches with Mom after all. She saw right through me.

As if on cue, my brother and Hank began talking at once. Eddie won out. "You'll probably need to get a fixer upper. I've got friends in the trades. We can make a place homey."

Hank said, "You'll need to build more than walls. Building donor bases is my specialty."

"What's the game plan, Sis?"

The way they were chipping in took my breath away. I told them the St. Paul house invited me to spend an immersion week living with them in the summer.

"The rest depends on funding." I winked at Hank. "With the wind at our back, we could open in a year or two. I'm thinking of calling it Candlewood House."

"Great name," said Hank. "I can sell donors on that."

I served Mom's custard pie on the glass dessert plates she handed down from Grandma.

The guys begged for a slice to take home before they left, and I obliged.

"I'll drive Mom home later," I said. "Give us some girl-talk time."

Mom offered to wash dishes. I dried.

"I love Grandma's plates," I said.

"You be careful with them. They're yours to pass down now."

I ached at her easy assumption about grandchildren.

"Mom, you know when I got that cyst removed last summer?"

"Everything's okay now, right?"

"Almost." The truth spilled out. "You see, a small cancer attached itself to the cyst."

I could hear alarm bells in Mom's response. "Cancer?"

"I went back for a second excision. They got it all. But … the doctor said it might be better if I didn't try to have kids. No need to excite the hormones, estrogen you know."

"What? Honey, why didn't you tell me?"

So many reasons. "I didn't want to believe it. And, honestly, I was afraid if you said anything to anybody at the Irish Club, I'd be labeled forever."

Mom dropped her dishcloth. "Precious, I wouldn't say anything. I love you to pieces."

I told her about the five-year threshold and every six-month mammogram. "After that, I'll return to average risk. With close monitoring, maybe I could try for a child, though probably better not to." I forced a smile. "Couldn't do it without a husband anyway."

Mom gave me a long once-over. "So, you'll be a housemother for the group home."

"I'll probably never be a mom, but housemother is fine with me. Sorry you won't get to be a grandma."

She held up one of the dessert plates and let the overhead light play on the etched glass. "Honey, aren't you going to need a grandma at Candlewood House?"

ᛒᚩ ᚲᛉ

On a walk in the woods after school, I told Andy how my family jumped on the idea of Candlewood House. "Things are taking shape."

"You're on a roll, Meg. A real missionary."

"Nah, missionary is your gig."

Andy shrugged. "Was." He hacked off a pussy willow branch with his Swiss Army Knife.

"Hey, can I have that? The kids will love the furry buds. We're reading the Little Golden Book about the kitten who searches for his lost catkins."

Andy simpered: *"Have you seen the gray furry flowers that look just like me?"*

I roared. "If that was an audition, you're hired."

The next day, he appeared at my classroom door with Leo in tow to read the *Pussy Willow* book. The kids dramatized with much meowing. I took a dozen instant Kodak photos.

As days warmed, I gave Ruth a hand planting her garden. She teased me about *Pussy Willow Day*. Said Leo showed her photos. "Word's gotten out you're serious about starting a group home for kids like yours as they get older."

"The idea's catching on like wildfire, but legal stuff is a tall order."

Ruth laughed. "I'm an old social worker, remember. Well-versed in government jargon."

"Thanks. Volunteers seem to be coming out of the woodwork. Finding staff, a couple of people to work alongside me, might be harder. If you think of anyone, let me know."

"Meg Joyce, is that your roundabout way of asking if I might want to get more involved? You know you only have to say the word."

For sure, I could count on Ruth. She came to mind whenever I considered who to hire for day-today responsibilities. Her quick response took a weight off my shoulders. I asked her to join me for the summer immersion week at the St. Paul group home to be sure she knew what she was getting into.

I remembered Sister Loretta's words from Christopher House: "When things are meant to be, the Lord clears a path."

Lord, have I found my path at last?

CHAPTER 27

DUSK

AUGUST. THE LAST MONTH OF summer. Only a few weeks ago the choir director led Andy, Leo, and me up creaky steps to the steeple for a panoramic view of fireworks. Seemed like it would never get dark enough to start. Now, dusk came sooner each night.

Andy tended Ruth's community garden for her the week she came to live at the St. Paul group home with me. Our plans for Candlewood House were rounding out like tomatoes. We learned much, and it was hard to return. The following week, I arrived at the community garden on Saturday morning as usual, ready to fill bushel baskets. As I knotted a bandana kerchief around my neck, I noticed many rows already picked. Andy appeared from between tomato poles and wiped sweat from his forehead. "Hot day." As I chattered about ripe fruit and smooth beans, he nodded and picked, quiet.

"Penny for your thoughts?" I held up a plump radish.

He surveyed the land. "Let's take a break." We crossed over to the big linden tree on the far side of the hill and sat down in its shade. "Ever hear of a guy named Rother?"

"I don't think so. Wait ... something on the news a while back."

"Yep. Last year about this time. He's been on my mind lately."

The story came back to me. A missionary in Guatemala. Killed. "Did you know him?"

"Would've liked to know him. Tried to protect his people during the civil war there. Shot dead in the rectory. Could've gone home, but he said, 'The shepherd cannot run.' He didn't."

Andy's face was drawn, eyelids puffy.

"Looks like you've been missing sleep."

"Yeah."

His hazel eyes searched the long stretch of land that ran down to the river. "Meg, I talked to my superior a few months ago about upping my game."

Upping his game? When was a few months ago—in May as we planted the garden? In April—painting with the kids? A chill ran through me. He couldn't mean following in Rother's shoes. Why hadn't he said anything? We shared everything.

"Is that what you're tossing and turning about?"

Andy's faraway look returned to our spot under the linden tree. He pressed my hand to his cheek. "No, I'm not going to Guatemala. Don't speak enough Spanish."

I breathed a sigh of relief.

"While you and Ruth were away, my superior told me about a post in Rome with Caritas, a Catholic charity that works worldwide."

"Rome? The mothership?"

"Home of pasta and popes."

"What do they want you to do?"

"Be part of the team that goes where people are in desperate need. War, drought, famine. Do airlifts of food and medical supplies. That sort of thing."

"Why you, Andy?"

"They're short a guy who can speak both English and French—and has some missionary experience. That would be yours truly."

"For how long?"

"Stints run five or six years."

Pinpricks. "Five or six years?" May as well be forever. "That's a long time, and dangerous work." Airlifts in the middle of wars and droughts? I might never see him again.

"It's dangerous walking across the street these days. Don't worry, I'm not holy enough to be a martyr."

A tear traveled down my cheek. "When do you leave?"

"Gotta pack, get vaccinations, do orientation. Looks like month's end."

Too soon. Harvest wouldn't be done. Not enough time to meet my new class of kids. Who'd play Santa Claus? I buried my head in his chest. My heart throbbed like a leaden gong. I wanted to beat him with both my fists. I wanted to throw my arms around him and hold him. I wanted it to be yesterday.

Andy pulled me close. "I shouldn't ask this of you, Meg, and if you can't, you can't. But ... I want to spend time with you before I go. Real time. Like real people would."

I heard the longing in his voice. "What are you asking, Andy?"

"My family's place at the lake. I'm going to spend a few days there."

The lake. His favorite place.

"Would you meet me there? Could you ... think about it?"

A low-lying bough brushed my cheek. I touched the linden's heart-shaped leaf. Last May I drank the fragrance of its white blossoms. A lifetime ago I gave this man my heart. I still loved him, wanted him, remembered the flush of his kiss since our first time together. Desire surged through me like a storm filling the dry rock bed of a riverbank.

"Did you know Leo once offered to marry us?" I asked. There was a time when loving this man made sense. Loving him now made no sense at all. Our lives, like the tree branches above us, grew in opposite directions from a single starting point. And yet, I yearned for his touch one last time.

"Oh, Meg, I shouldn't have asked."

I plucked the heart-shaped leaf off its bough and tore it slowly down its central vein. I closed my eyes a moment.

Andy lifted my chin, and I saw his face, earnest, asking, wanting as much as I wanted.

My lips refused to say *not now, too late*.

"Yes. I'll come."

Andy agreed to wait for me to name a good time to visit him at the lake. The calendar hung on my kitchen wall, begging a last counting of days between cycles. I couldn't use the Pill—hormones didn't mix well with my womb on hold. The diaphragm, fitted when I hoped Andy was coming home to marry me, tossed and not replaced.

I recently finished a period. I checked my cervical mucus, several times to be sure. Washed my hands and diddled a finger in my vagina. No discharge. I could meet him right now.

But I wasn't ready. I wanted him, and I hated wanting him. I hated wanting to be with him only to see him leave. I hated loving him. I wasn't ready to say good-bye.

Daily discharge checks: white, yellow, cloudy. Clear, slippery. Too late. I would soon be ovulating. Stretchy, like egg whites. The perfect runway for sperm. I wanted to run away. Why did women have to take all the risk?

Thick, cloudy, gluey.

I called Andy to say the coast was clear.

ॐ ൙

On a balmy morning in late August, I slipped a bright saffron-striped sundress over my head. Bundled a bouquet of ivory hydrangea blooms in a damp towel to keep them fresh. Practiced saying a breezy "Hey, best wishes. Bon Voyage."

I wanted a happy ending.

As I drove the distance to the cabin on the lake, miles of crimson-tinged leaves lined the road. One last burst of life before their edges curled and crumbled, tumbled, and were gone. We could have been together every day of our lives—*now* he wanted one more taste of what might have been? On the eve of never seeing him again?

I nearly turned back. But I wanted this day as much as he did.

Andy came into view sitting on the cabin steps as I drove up the gravel driveway. Swim trunks, loose shirt.

He leapt to meet me at the car and hugged me tight. "You came." He ran his fingers through my hair, untangling the knots made by sunroof drafts. "Wasn't sure if you would."

I told him that I hiked the bluffs overlooking the river the day before, but it started to rain. True. Rain fell like tears from the sky to keep me company. I brushed away the thatch of hair that always fell across his forehead and traced the arch of his brow.

He touched my cheekbone and my body relaxed like a stream splashing over rocks.

"I'm here now." I reached into the car for the hydrangeas. "Look, these made it too."

Andy showed me into the lake house and rummaged through clapboard cupboards to find a makeshift vase. "Will this do?" He held up a Mason jar.

We could have been any young couple setting up house with odds and ends. Instead, we were the odds and ends.

"It'll do fine." I arranged the mophead blooms and trimmed them to fit the jar. Set it in the center of the pine board kitchen table.

He took my hand. "Let's go catch some fish for dinner."

From a distance, the water rippled like silk in a breeze. Gentle waves gurgled as we approached a small jon boat snugged on the shore.

"That's a pretty dress to go paddling in," he said.

"Glad you like it, but I did bring a swimsuit and shorts."

Andy laughed. "More practical but spin around once first." As I spun, he held out his arms and we danced in the sand. Slowly, he gathered me to him embracing me like a sheaf of flowers. He kissed me softly. "Thanks for coming today."

I touched his collarbone. "I'll go change."

We navigated across the lake the whole afternoon. Andy's jig in the weeds caught a walleye. When we idled in open waters to let the sun play on our skin, I eased over to Andy's seat and sat on the flat bottom of the boat, leaning my back against the coarse hair on his shins. A mackerel sky of cirrus clouds drifted above. "What does that cloud look like to you?"

He scanned the sky. "A plane, cargo plane. Lots. That one's about to fall in the ocean."

I saw Andy bronzed and alive one minute, flesh burning off his skeleton the next. Stifled a scream and turned to face him. "There are other ways of being a hero. Is that all you Clems care about?"

He stared over my shoulder, not into my eyes. "Being a Clem is the only thing I know how to do. And I'm no hero."

"You were a good Santa, good at finger-painting with the kids. You were a hero to them." I bit my lip. "Andy, you knew how to be with me."

He blinked his eyes tight. "You and the kids were easy to be with. But doesn't God ask hard things? I always feel like I should be doing more."

We sat silent until he asked, "What do you see in the clouds, Meg?"

I feared looking up and seeing cargo planes falling.

He asked again, "What do you see?"

I fixed on an oval cloud with short tentacles. "Sea turtle."

Andy smiled. "Native Americans say the world was created on the back of a giant turtle."

"In the beginning," I said, "creation dawned with the slowest of creatures."

"A long-lived and persevering creature." He trickled water drops down my back.

I raised my fingers in *Star Trek*'s Vulcan salute. "Live long and prosper."

Andy roared with laughter. "I've kept you in the sun too long."

We headed back to shore and scaled the catch for grilling. Gentle light danced on our limbs as we took one last splash in the water before building a fire.

The sun slipped into the lake, and we curled into each other on an old plaid blanket. Embers crackled on the birch. Lake water lapped the shoreline.

Andy stroked my cheek. "Your hair sparkles in the dark."

"No, yours does," I said. "My brown locks disappear in the dark."

"None of you could ever disappear, Meg. Not ever. I will always see you in my heart, no matter where I am."

I kissed his heart and rested on his chest. His chin caressed the crown of my head. The scent of woodsy earth and citrusy sassafras filled the air.

CANDLEWOOD

One strap of my swimsuit drooped off my shoulder.

"Is there a scar, Meg, where they cut?"

I tugged the strap until my breast lolled out. Andy touched the round underside lightly.

A summery flush coursed through my body. He rubbed his thumb across the faded pink row of railbed stitch scars and pressed his lips to them. I breathed in all the stars in the sky.

I smoothed his glinting hair towards one temple. "Where do you hurt, Andy?"

He tapped his heart.

I shook my head. "Your heart is good."

"Oh, Meg." His eyes opened wide, incandescent. He reached for my left hand and kissed the fourth finger. "I would have married you except for the rules."

I never expected to hear the words. I looked into the light of his eyes. "I know."

Our lips pressed into each other, holding our breath for dear life like underwater drowning divers. When our lips parted, we breathed. Clear, blessedly clear, air. The moon painted our bodies in an alabaster glow as we undressed. He traced each inch of my face as if memorizing it. I nuzzled his neck and tufted the hair on his chest, ran my hands the length of his body, kissed every muscle and sinew. Our lips met and we melded into each other. My hips lifted to meet him, and he rose. Wide and deep, I opened to him, rolling waves. Full.

We left the midnight beach for a calico bedroom and fell asleep in close embrace.

Like morning chimes, a lake loon called me out of slumber and asked its haunting question: *Where are you?*

I lay next to Andy, the man who would have married me— except for the rules.

The curtain fluttered. Soft morning light flickered across my body, shadowed the crevice between my breasts, and held vigil over my womb.

Andy's hands had gotten tangled in the bedsheets overnight. Bound. Like on the day of his ordination when the bishop bound his hands in linen cloth. Tied him to a promise he couldn't keep. Here we lay, as married as two people ever were. The catechism says a couple marries each other—the only sacrament witnessed, not conferred, by clergy.

I gathered my things quietly and set them on the kitchen table. A photo fell from my bag—Andy pressing my kids' hands in paint to grace the chair he made for Candlewood. Open hands. Unbound.

This was how I wanted to remember him. I wrote a note on a scratch pad:

> *Remember me, as I will you, but please don't write.*
> *Love, Meg*

If he wrote, I would wait for him. All over again. I couldn't do that this time—wait, longing, missing him, my heart brimming—but not able to say a word out loud about our love. If his plane fell from the sky, who would tell me?

Where are you? asked the loon again.

I am here, and he is not. My mind echoed the loon: "Where is he?" My answer: "He is across the ocean, and I am not."

The cabin window framed the sun rising out of the lake. Red rays streamed across the horizon. Blood on water. Dawn. A new day.

I lifted the screen door latch and walked down to lake's edge. We had skimmed the lake for an afternoon and named constellations in the night sky. Now it was time to create new lives, to name ourselves.

The loon's wail sliced through the mist.

Lord, thank you for a few moments of love. Thank you for opening our hearts.

The loon skittered across the water and took flight. I skipped a stone in its wake as if tossing a coin into a wishing well.

"For the journey."

- END -

AUTHOR'S NOTE

From *The Scarlet Letter* to *The Thorn Birds* to *Fleabag*, the star-crossed love between women and clergymen is a well told tale. I had no intention of writing another book on the subject. Growing up Irish and Catholic, priests were plentiful and woven into the fabric of neighborhood life. More than a few were sons of the neighborhood. One was a friend of my parents and a frequent visitor to our home. Only later did I understand the whispers about "his woman." The pair appear as a cameo in this book, though much fictionalized. They both have passed. As I got to know the woman, I was sad that she and our friend couldn't marry unless he left the priesthood—but never questioned the rule. Many priests and also sisters did leave to marry, so I assumed the couple must have had their reasons for living in the shadows. I didn't ask. Discretion and turning a blind eye kept the status quo humming.

More recently, the culture of secrecy and denial in the Roman Catholic Church has been shown to protect not only those who break their vows of celibacy, but also predatory priests including those who abuse minors. I am grateful for the candid insights of the late Father Donald Cozzens, a seminary rector, counselor, and respected presence in the Church who brought the plight of guilt-ridden priests and their partners into the open with his book, *The Changing Face of the Priesthood* (2000). He also pointed to the pitfalls in clerical culture that protected immature and deviant sexual acting out behaviors. When the abuse crisis exploded, I was as stunned as anyone, and angry about the cover-up. How could this have happened on the watch of priests, bishops, and popes I respected?

As I searched for answers, one thing became increasingly clear. Sadly, multiple sources show that the prevalence of priests involved with minors closely tracks that of men in the general population, about six percent (Plante, 1999). But inappropriate and sometimes abusive relationships with adult women and men were far more common. Based on 1,500 interviews, psychologist Richard Sipe estimated that in a system where priests are expected to be chaste, no more than half of them were leading genuine celibate lives (Sipe, 1990). The relationship between our family friend and his partner was not the exception I presumed it to be. Nor are affairs, harassment and misogyny confined to the Catholic Church. Baylor University's long-running studies on clergy across religions and denominations found that more than 3 percent of adult women who attend religious services at least once a month have experienced sexual misconduct, and 8 percent of churchgoers are aware of incidents in their communities of faith (Garland, D. R. and Chaves, M., 2010).

Focus is turning to factors that set the stage for inappropriate clergy behavior as well as efforts to both heal survivors and change a church culture that fosters coverups. The Santa Clara University Study, *Beyond Bad Apples*, debunks the assumption that these behaviors are the result of a few "bad apples," instead naming social structures of sex, gender, and power as drivers in a system that "isolates clergy and sets priests above and apart." (Rubio, J. H. and Schultz, P. J., 2022). The study is part of a wider initiative funded by Fordham University as part of the *Taking Responsibility* project. The National Association of Social Workers conducted a nation-wide study highlighting the experiences of women and factors related to healing in their recovery. They developed a model of resilience, and though I didn't expect it, faith in God proved to be the most salient feature in their recovery (Pooler D. K. and Barros-Lane L., 2022).

Women's voices are a seldom heard sound in the life of the Catholic Church and the patriarchal society in which we live. In *Candlewood*, I have tried to be faithful to the experiences of women, and to give them a voice through the character of Meg. Though she is a fictional character, many readers tell me that they "know" her. I am hopeful that as we grow in awareness, and the humility to listen to each other, change for the better is possible in our communities.

Acceptance of LGBTQ+ sexual orientations has grown considerably since the 1970s setting of *Candlewood*. Until 1974, homosexuality was classified as a mental disorder by the American Psychiatric Association. Hence, the angst of the Joyce family in this book. Catholic teaching makes the distinction between the inclination, which is not considered sinful, and the behavior which is deemed "intrinsically disordered." Pope Francis caused controversy in 2023 when he allowed priests to bless gay couples, although he clarified it was not as an expression of marriage.

In the book, Meg's first year of teaching is interrupted by a strike. From the late 1960s through the 1970s, school districts across the nation witnessed hundreds of teacher strikes. It is historically true that Hortonville, in neighboring Wisconsin, terminated employment of striking teachers in 1974. Meg's fears were realistic.

As a teacher of students with developmental disabilities, Meg's volunteering at the Balto Center came naturally. I styled the program after the Kennedy Child Study Center, then located on East 67th Street in Manhattan. At the time, few places offered diagnostic services for young children and counseling for their parents. I chose the name "Balto" after the statue in nearby Central Park honoring the Alaskan husky who led a team of sled dogs to deliver medicine to combat diphtheria, a deadly child-hood disease prior to vaccines.

I must also credit historian Paulina Bren for details and social narrative about *The Barbizon* (Simon & Schuster, 2021), the iconic women's hotel where Meg spent her first weeks in New York City. Indeed, in its heyday, it was "the hotel that set women free."

Meg's interest in making a group home aligns with the times. Following their success improving access to education for their children, parent groups advocated for legislation enabling the establishment of group homes. Meg's journey is loosely based on the Dungarvin model started in St. Paul, Minnesota.

Regarding the making of poison—while it is true that ricin is derived from castor beans, a much more sophisticated process is involved than Meg's efforts. Nevertheless, do not experiment with ingesting them.

For those who may wonder, there is no Order of Clement nor an Incarnatus University. While many organizations take the name of St. Christopher, the retreat house and religious sisters in this book are completely fictional. To the best of my knowledge, there is no town of Shady Bluff in Minnesota, although the St. Croix River Valley is as scenic as depicted. Though churches dedicated to St. Gabriel the Archangel are too numerous to count, the angel's message is always the same: *Fear not, the Lord is with you.*

BOOK CLUB
DISCUSSION QUESTIONS

1) The book opens with Meg believing her conventional goals of "husband, children, home" will be simple to attain if she follows the rules. What are the obstacles to her goals?

2) The novel is primarily set in a once prosperous Victorian college town along the St. Croix River settled by Irish Catholics. How do the historical and cultural details shape the characters in this story?

3) Meg lives in three different apartments in the book. What does each reveal about her? How does she react when Father Andy visits? And when Father Darren is there?

4) What draws Meg and Father Andy to each other? What pulls them apart besides the rule against priests marrying? Would their relationship have lasted under other circumstances?

5) When Father Andy distances himself from Meg, she goes on retreat to pray about becoming a nun. Others might have decided to leave the Church for good. How does Meg retrieve new life from the ashes?

6) Why do you think Meg could reveal her deepest sorrows to Father Andy but not to any of the women in her life, not even Sister Loretta during her retreat at Christopher House?

7) Meg determines that time and distance are the best bets for healing her heart and finding her true north, so she moves to New York. What does she discover – about herself, others, and God?

8) At one point, Meg prays, "Father, forgive them for they know not what they do. None of them do." Describe her

struggles with forgiveness – with her own father, with Father Darren, and Father Andy.

9) Father Darren is a danger to Meg. Have you been in a situation where you denied or questioned your instincts about a person?

10) The novel takes place in the 1970s. Did you learn anything new about historical movements of the time such as the sexual revolution, gay rights, or civil rights?

11) Meg begins as a teacher of children with developmental delays. Describe her journey to planning for a group home.

12) Were you satisfied with the ending? How has Meg changed? How has her faith changed? What do you think might happen to the book's characters going forward?

ACKNOWLEDGMENTS

This book would not have been possible without the men and women who generously shared their stories with me. You have taught me that finding your true north is a lifelong process. I am indebted both to those who decided to stay the course and live within the Catholic Church, as well as to those who pushed the boundaries of their lives by leaving. Thank you all for your courage.

Immeasurable appreciation goes to Kira Henschel of HenschelHAUS Publishing, Inc. for believing in this project and bringing it to publication.

From the tentative beginning to the final manuscript, I owe more gratitude than I can possibly express for Laurie Scheer's constant encouragement, listening ear, and invaluable insights. She is the epitome of a gracious teacher and an amazing person.

Tim Storm's early developmental edit and his Storm Writing School workshops kept me from many pitfalls as I embarked on my debut novel. The wise counsel and remarkable final edit by Susanna Daniel makes this story richer and deeper than it might otherwise have been. She works magic not only in her own writing, but lets it rub off on others.

Having a community of writers to rely on for comradery, honesty, and many cups of coffee made all the difference in this journey. I am grateful for time well spent with authors Kristin Oakley and Anne Tigan at libraries, bookstores and lunches. For faithfully bringing together a talented group of writers for support and trading tips, I must thank the incomparable trio of authors Christine DeSmet, Peggy Joque Williams, and public radio veteran Carol Larson. Likewise, critique group feedback proved invaluable, especially under the guidance of Angela Rydell of Writers' Inlet. And when quiet time was needed to sort and reflect on what to keep in the book and what to let go of, Julie Tallard Johnson's countryside retreats were just the tonic.

Most of all, I want to thank my better half for his warm presence and ever patient ways. He keeps the love light shining.

Finally, I would be remiss if I didn't acknowledge you, the readers, who trusted me with your time and interest to delve into the world of Candlewood.

ABOUT THE AUTHOR

Evelyn Ann Casey's award-winning poetry, as well as book reviews, short stories and essays appear in *Midwest Review, Potato Soup Journal,* Medium.com, *Windy City Reviews,* and elsewhere. She earned a graduate degree in education at the University of Wisconsin-Madison where she managed outreach programs in healthcare. When not exploring locales near and far with her husband, Evelyn enjoys sharing heirloom tomatoes and good conversation with friends and family. She attends music and theatre venues as often as possible and volunteers with community groups at food pantries and reading programs.

Website: https://www.EvelynAnnCasey.com

www.ingramcontent.com/pod-product-compliance
Lightning Source LLC
Chambersburg PA
CBHW051100030726
47504CB00006B/1710